PRAISE FOR THE NOVELS
OF LAUREN WILLIG

The Garden Intrigue

"Willig delights time and again with her clever, witty, intelligent, and thoughtful Pink Carnation series." —*Romantic Times*

"Eloise, of course, is amazing, but it's truly the plot of *The Garden Intrigue* that shines . . . wonderful!" —Romance Junkies

"[An] enchanting, exciting, and clever story." —Romance Reviews Today

"Enlightening and entertaining as always, and full of plenty of romance and intrigue, this is a strong choice for historical fiction readers." —*Library Journal*

"As fresh and charming as its floral theme . . . a reliable romp through Napoleon's court, filled with romance and yet another adorable and very active heroine." —*Kirkus Reviews*

"Humor, love, espionage—yet again there is absolutely *nothing* that this incredible author leaves out. . . . [These stories] just keep getting better and better every time!" —Once Upon a Romance

The Orchid Affair

"[A] supremely nerve-racking, sit-on-the-edge-of-your-seat, can't-sleep-until-everyone-is-safe read . . . successfully upholds the author's tradition of providing charming three-dimensional characters, lively action, [and] witty dialogue." —*Library Journal*

"Willig's sparkling series continues to elevate the Regency romance genre." —*Kirkus Reviews*

"Willig combines the atmosphere of the tempestuous era with the perfect touches of historical detail to round out the love story." —*Romantic Times*

The Betrayal of the Blood Lily

"Newcomers and loyal fans alike will love brash, flirtatious Penelope's exotic adventure in Hyderabad, India, told [with] Willig's signature mix of historical richness and whimsical humor." —*The Newark Star-Ledger*

continued . . .

"Reading [this book] is like getting a plate of warm-from-the-oven chocolate chip cookies: It's hard not to eat them all at once, but you also want to savor every bite." —*Library Journal*

"Willig hasn't lost her touch; this outing has all the charm of the previous books in the series." —*Publishers Weekly*

"Willig injects a new energy in her already thriving, thrilling series and presents the best entry to date." —*Booklist*

The Temptation of the Night Jasmine

"Jane Austen for the modern girl . . . sheer fun!"
—*New York Times* bestselling author Christina Dodd

"An engaging historical romance, delightfully funny and sweet . . . a thoroughly charming costume drama. . . . Romance's rosy glow tints even the spy adventure that unfolds . . . fine historical fiction . . . thrilling."
—*The Newark Star-Ledger*

"Another sultry spy tale. . . . The author's conflation of historical fact, quirky observations, and nicely rendered romances results in an elegant and grandly entertaining book." —*Publishers Weekly*

The Seduction of the Crimson Rose

"Willig's series gets better with each addition, and her latest is filled with swashbuckling fun, romance, and intrigue." —*Booklist*

"Handily fulfills its promise of intrigue and romance." —*Publishers Weekly*

"There are few authors capable of matching Lauren Willig's ability to merge historical accuracy, heart-pounding romance, and biting wit." —*BookPage*

The Deception of the Emerald Ring

"History textbook meets *Bridget Jones*." —*Marie Claire*

"A fun and zany time warp full of history, digestible violence, and plenty of romance." —*New York Daily News*

"Heaving bodices, embellished history, and witty dialogue: What more could you ask for?" —*Kirkus Reviews*

"Willig's latest is riveting." —*Booklist*

"Smart . . . [a] fast-paced narrative with mistaken identities, double agents, and high-stakes espionage. . . . The historic action is taut and twisting."

—*Publishers Weekly*

The Masque of the Black Tulip

"Clever [and] playful. . . . What's most delicious about Willig's novels is that the damsels of 1803 bravely put it all on the line for love and country."

—*Detroit Free Press*

"Studded with clever literary and historical nuggets, this charming historical-contemporary romance moves back and forth in time."   —*USA Today*

"Willig has great fun with the conventions of the genre, throwing obstacles between her lovers at every opportunity . . . a great escape."

—*The Boston Globe*

"Willig picks up where she left readers breathlessly hanging. . . . Many more will delight in this easy-to-read romp and line up for the next installment."

—*Publishers Weekly*

The Secret History of the Pink Carnation

"A deftly hilarious, sexy novel."

—*New York Times* bestselling author Eloisa James

"A merry romp with never a dull moment! A fun read."

—*New York Times* bestselling author Mary Balogh

"This genre-bending read—a dash of chick lit with a historical twist—has it all: romance, mystery, and adventure. Pure fun!"

—*New York Times* bestselling author Meg Cabot

"Swashbuckling. . . . Willig has an ear for quick wit and an eye for detail. Her fiction debut is chock-full of romance, sexual tension, espionage, adventure, and humor."   —*Library Journal*

"Willig's imaginative debut . . . is a decidedly delightful romp."   —*Booklist*

"Relentlessly effervescent prose . . . a sexy, smirking, determined-to-charm historical romance debut."   —*Kirkus Reviews*

"A delightful debut."

—Roundtable Reviews

The Passion of the Purple Plumeria

A PINK CARNATION NOVEL

LAUREN WILLIG

NEW AMERICAN LIBRARY

New American Library
Published by the Penguin Group
Penguin Group (USA) Inc., 375 Hudson Street,
New York, New York 10014, USA

USA | Canada | UK | Ireland | Australia | New Zealand | India | South Africa | China

Penguin Books Ltd., Registered Offices: 80 Strand, London WC2R 0RL, England
For more information about the Penguin Group visit penguin.com.

First published by New American Library,
a division of Penguin Group (USA) Inc.

First Printing, August 2013

 REGISTERED TRADEMARK—MARCA REGISTRADA

LIBRARY OF CONGRESS CATALOGING-IN-PUBLICATION DATA:
Willig, Lauren.
    The passion of the purple plumeria: a Pink Carnation novel/Lauren Willig.
      p. cm.
    ISBN 978-0-451-41472-4
    1. Spies—Fiction. I. Title.
    PS3623.I575P37 2013
    813'.6—dc23   2013001734

Printed in the United States of America
10 9 8 7 6 5 4

Set in Granjon
Designed by Alissa Amell

A Note on Timing

In the early nineteenth century, travel between London and Calcutta could take anywhere from four to six months, depending on weather. *The Betrayal of the Blood Lily*, in which we first met Colonel Reid, opened in the autumn of 1804. Colonel Reid left Calcutta in October of 1804 and arrived in England in March of 1805. Because of this, he has no knowledge of anything that occurred in India after he left.

That is why, although *Purple Plumeria* takes place several months after *Blood Lily*, the main actors are unaware of some information that the seasoned Pink Carnation reader already possesses.

The seasoned Pink Carnation reader and anyone who managed to get mail onto a faster ship . . .

The
Passion of the
Purple Plumeria

Prologue

Sussex, 2004

"I seriously doubt the lost jewels of Berar are under your bath mat," I said.

My boyfriend straightened, narrowly missing banging his head on the underside of the sink. He squinted at me, myopia rather than malevolence. "I dropped my contact lens."

"Yeah, yeah, that's what they all say." I spotted a glint of blue on the tiles near the mat. I don't know why, but even clear contacts always turn blue when they dry out. "Over there. No. Your other there."

"Thanks." Colin groped for the bit of plastic. "I was afraid I'd stepped on it."

"Ah," I said, slipping my arms around his waist. "Then you'd be entirely at my mercy."

He considered that. "Until I put my glasses on."

I gave him a peck on the back and let go of him. "Spoilsport."

We were being very touchy-feely these days. At least I was. I'm not usually much of one for PDA, even when the only public was the mold in the grouting, but at my back I could already hear time's winged chariot hurrying near. Or, in this case, time's winged 747. My flight back to the States was booked. It was one of those flexible STA Travel things, but even so. I had a time. I had a flight number. I had a ticket.

I had only two more months with Colin.

Time is a strangely malleable commodity. When I moved to London, last fall, the first two months had lasted for years, and not in a good way. I had come to London on a ten-month grant. Like a good little academic squirrel, I was meant to be gathering the nuts of primary sources, great armloads of them, and then scurrying back to Cambridge—the other Cambridge—to crack and dissect them in the calm of my basement office in the history department. At the time, I had yearned for the comfortable familiarity of the history department, the basement vending machine, the caked-on coffee in the bottom of the department coffee machine that no one ever remembered to clean.

Everything in England was just so . . . English. As an Anglophile, I'd thought I'd known what I was getting into, but years of *Masterpiece Theatre* hadn't prepared me for the realities of life in London: the miniature bottles of shampoo, the peanut butter that didn't look like peanut butter, the sun that set at three in winter. Of course, all that would have been bearable, war stories for later, if only the research were going well.

Scrap that: if the research were going anywhere at all.

I was on the trail of the most elusive element of the Napoleonic Wars, those shadowy men and women who had donned aliases rather than uniforms. Spying might have been considered more than a bit ungentlemanly at the time, but there was no denying either its utility or its glamour. With images of the Scarlet Pimpernel dancing in my head, I had envisioned myself making the scholarly coup of the century, unmasking the one spy who had never been unveiled, the spy who sent Napoleon's Ministry of Police into palpitations and launched a series of florally themed fashion crazes among England's aristocratic elite: the Pink Carnation.

Yes, admittedly, the name might be a little less than fearsome, but the roster of exploits attributed to the Carnation was impressive indeed. In addition to the usual mocking notes on Napoleon's pillow (there were times when it seemed that the little dictator's bedroom must have been busier than Grand Central on a summer Friday), the Carnation had thwarted a plot to kidnap George III, intercepted shipments of Dutch gold, spiked Bonaparte's plans for a naval invasion, and cured the common cold.

The accounts were all inconclusive and contradictory in the extreme. If you believed the contemporary newsletters, the Carnation was reputed to have been simultaneously in India, Portugal, France, and Shropshire, and possibly somewhere in the Americas, as well. He kept popping up like Elvis, minus the shiny suit. The French Ministry of Police were constantly finding him under their pillows; the British press attributed every French disappointment to his good agency.

In short, it was a mess. After months in the archives, I had been no closer to sorting it out. I was on the verge of sourly ascribing to the popular academic theory that the Pink Carnation had been a deliberate fictional construct, invented by the English government to throw fear into the hearts of their French foes, with the role of the Carnation being played, successively, by a variety of English heroes ranging from Sir Sidney Smith to Lord Nelson's first cousin twice removed. In other words, the Dread Pirate Roberts, Napoleonic edition.

In one last, desperate attempt, I'd played my final card. I'd sent out letters to the holders of private family archives, hoping against hope that something, some tiny clue to the Carnation's identity (or identities), might have survived, something that would give me something to put into my dissertation other than the theoretical mumbo jumbo that is the scholar's best smoke screen for the complete dearth of any actual sources. I'd sent those letters out on the off chance.

Those letters led me to the Pink Carnation. And Colin.

Life works in weird ways, doesn't it? Romance had been the last thing on my mind in October—I was more concerned with ABD than MRS—but those letters, mailed in desperation, had netted me more than a crack at some private sources. They had plunged me right into the heart not just of historical drama but of a modern one, too. Colin and I had been together, officially, for just a little more than six months now. Just enough time to put down roots, not enough time for declarations. We were betwixt and between and the clock was rapidly running down.

Just because I was going back to the States didn't mean it was over.

Why did that sound less and less convincing the closer we got to August?

Colin squirted multipurpose solution on his contact, regarded it philosophically, and maneuvered it back into his eye.

"Jeremy rang this morning," he said thickly. Like mascara application, contact lens insertion requires a partially open mouth.

I could see my own face in the mirror, lips pinched, eyes narrowed. "Oh, did he?"

I mentioned modern drama, didn't I? That drama had a first name, spelled *J-E-R-E-M-Y*. Jeremy was both Colin's cousin and his stepfather. If it sounds complicated, it's because it is. There was some debate as to whether Colin's father had been cold in his grave yet when Jeremy took up with his cousin's widow. There had been a suspicious interval of overlap while Colin's father was in the hospital—or, as they say over here, in hospital—struggling through the final stages of pancreatic cancer, and Colin's mother had been, shall we say, being comforted by Jeremy, said comforting involving lots of long walks on a beach in the Grenadines.

Don't think that I was jumping to conclusions or basing my opinion of Jeremy entirely on rumor and hearsay. After some rather intensive observation, I had come to my own conclusions about Jeremy: He was a loathsome cad.

Yes, I know it sounds all Barbara Cartland, but trust me, the phrase had never been more apt. Like a Cartland cad, Jeremy was the sort of man who would gamble away his daughter at cards and never think twice about it. Human beings were just another form of coin to him. I'd seen him play fast and loose with Colin's family. Colin and his sister were still barely speaking, thanks to one of Jeremy's lovely machinations. Of one thing I was sure: Jeremy was pure poison.

Colin blinked experimentally and then, once he was sure the contact was firmly in place, raised a brow at me. He was so cute when he tried to be all supercilious. I didn't say that, of course.

"You know he rang," he said drily. "You were on the other extension."

"I hung up," I protested. "As soon as I heard who it was."

Okay, maybe there might have been a few seconds of lag time. No one's halo is quite that shiny.

"You could have stayed on the line," Colin said gently. His eyes met mine in the bathroom mirror. "I wouldn't have minded."

I shrugged, poking at a patch of peeling paper on the wall. "I didn't want to pry."

It wasn't true, of course. I was dying to pry. But now that I knew that I was leaving, I was feeling particularly scrupulous about our respective realms, what was his and what was mine. I might be living in his world, but my stay was only temporary.

I could feel Colin looking at me, but all he said was, "When it comes to Jeremy, I'd rather have witnesses."

Fair enough. I pushed my hair back behind my ears and perched on the edge of the bathtub. "So what did he want?"

Colin squirted toothpaste onto a blue plastic toothbrush. "He says he called to apologize."

"Huh," I said. The only place I could see Jeremy voluntarily burying the hatchet would be in Colin's skull. He'd probably keep the scalp, too, and call it installation art. Jeremy is something to do with art sales. That's his career; his vocation is bedeviling Colin. "What did he *really* want?"

Colin's lips quirked. "You don't pull your punches."

"That's why you like me," I said cheerfully.

Toothbrush suspended in space, Colin looked back over his shoulder at me. "It's not the only reason."

It hurt to look at him looking at me like that. It hurt when I knew that the clock was ticking, marking the moments until I climbed on that plane, back to the other Cambridge, the American one.

It would have been easier if I could have blamed someone else for it, but the decision to go back had been mine. It had seemed like a good idea at the time. Now . . . Well, there was no changing my mind, was there? The teaching contract for next year was already signed, sealed, and delivered, or the e-mail equivalent thereof. What didn't break us up would make us stronger. Or something like that.

I lifted the shampoo bottle in mock toast. "Cheers."

Through a mouthful of foam, Colin said, "You also make a decent toasted cheese."

I set down the shampoo and scrubbed my hand off on the knee of my jeans. "Only decent? Thanks. Thanks a lot."

Colin rinsed and spat. "Superlatively brilliant toasted cheese?"

"Too little, too late." I tossed him a hand towel. "Jeremy?"

"Wants to come over for lunch. To make his amends."

I leaned back, bracing my hands against the enamel sides of the bath. "You'd think if he really wanted to make amends, he could at least take us out."

"But then," said Colin, "he wouldn't have an excuse to come to the house."

We exchanged a look in the mirror. We both knew why Jeremy wanted to come to Selwick Hall.

He was looking for the lost jewels of Berar.

Berar was in India. Selwick Hall was in Sussex. Slight anomaly there, no? The jewels had disappeared during Wellington's wars in India, back in the early nineteenth century. It was the usual sort of hoard: ropes of pearls, piles of rubies, emeralds bigger than pigeons' eggs (having never seen a pigeon's egg, that descriptor wasn't quite as useful for me as it could be), and, the pièce de résistance, the one jewel to rule them all, a legendary something or other called the Moon of Berar. I say "something or other" because the contemporary commentators differed as to what exactly made up the Moon. Opals? Sapphires? Diamonds from the mines of Golconda? No one knew for sure. What they did agree on was that the jewel was credited with all manner of mystical powers, ranging from omniscience to invulnerability to minty-fresh breath.

Okay, maybe not the minty-fresh breath, but everything else and then some.

But here was the kicker: Somehow, somewhere, the legend had started that the jewels were hidden in Selwick Hall.

It sounds ridiculous, doesn't it? A treasure in Indian jewels hidden in an English gentleman's residence. We're not even talking a grand estate, just a pleasant, reasonably unpretentious gentleman's house of the sort that spring up like mushrooms in Jane Austen novels, closer to the Bennet house than to Pemberley. Ridiculous, yes, but Jeremy believed it—believed it enough to rifle through my notes in search of clues. Jeremy believed, and Colin . . . Well, let's just say he didn't entirely disbelieve it.

It had become something of a running joke between us over the past two weeks. Stay too long in the bathroom? "What were you doing in there, looking for the lost jewels of Berar?" Lose an earring? "Perhaps it's gone to find its friends." You get the idea.

We hadn't, however, actually done anything constructive about looking for them. With the threat of a full teaching load staring me in the face, I'd been knuckling down on my dissertation. I had enough experience of ungrateful undergrads (genus *Harvardensius undergradius annoyingus*) to know that I would be spending the fall term fully employed fielding e-mails proffering inventive excuses for missed classes and late papers. Colin, meanwhile, was hard at work on the novel he was convinced would make him the next Ian Fleming. In the evenings, once our respective papers had been put away, neither of us was particularly inclined to hunt around the house with flashlights like a pair of attenuated Nancy Drews. With only two months left, we had far better things to do.

Like quiz night at the local pub. If only either of us knew

anything about science, we would have been undefeated. As it was, the vicar trumped us every time.

One of these days . . .

Only we didn't have that many days left. I hated thinking that way. I couldn't stop thinking that way. I needed an off switch for my internal monologue.

"It makes no sense," said Colin for the fiftieth time. "What would a rajah's ransom in jewels be doing in a house in Sussex?"

"Things turn up in strange places all the time," I said. For example, library books, which possess a disconcerting ability to move from place to place, seemingly of their own volition.

"We're not talking about a stray pair of socks," said Colin.

"That would be great. Can't you just see it? 'King's Ransom in Jewels Found in Sussex Sock Drawer.'" Why not? Colin had an odd habit of sticking odds and ends in his sock drawer, from cuff links to credit card receipts. I'd learned, when in doubt, to check the sock drawer. Occasionally, there was even a pair of socks. "Hey, everything else seems to be in there."

Colin didn't seem to share my amusement.

I fished out a loofah that had got knocked over into the bath. It still had the Body Shop tag attached and smelled faintly of raspberry body wash. "Seriously, though. How did the rumor get started? There must have been some origin to it all."

"No smoke without fire?" Colin rinsed his toothbrush and shook it out in the sink. "I don't know. I remember my father telling me about it when I was little—not in a serious way, mind you. Just as another family story."

"What did he say?" Colin didn't talk about his father much.

I knew that he had been a great deal older than Colin's mother and that he had been involved in some branch of the secret services, but that was about it. It was after he died that Colin had thrown over his old career in finance and moved back to Selwick Hall.

Sometimes I wondered what that other, earlier Colin had been like—not that I was going to trade in the one I'd got.

"These were children's stories," Colin emphasized. "Once upon a time and all that."

I nodded vehemently to show I understood. "All warranties and disclaimers acknowledged. Go on."

Colin stuck his toothbrush in a chipped old mug and leaned back against the sink, resting his elbows against the marble countertop. "It's complete rubbish," he said warningly, "but . . ."

"Yes?" The suspense was killing me. So was the edge of the tub, which was distinctly uncomfortable. I shifted forward a bit.

Colin held out a hand to help me up. "According to my father, the story was that the jewels were brought by the Carnation from India to Selwick Hall."

I felt absurdly disappointed. "But we know that the Carnation wasn't *in* India."

My research had turned up the true story of the Carnation's supposed Indian exploits. Yes, a French plot to rouse the country against the British had been routed, but it had been accomplished by a junior political officer named Alex Reid, not by the Carnation herself. The Carnation had been busy in France at the time, watching Bonaparte crown himself emperor.

"Exactly," said Colin. "It's just a story. There was even a bit of doggerel verse—something something Plumeria's tower."

I wrinkled my nose. "That sounds like a Whittlesby poem."

Colin waved that aside. "No," he said slowly, "it wasn't. It was just the three lines, and it went something like this: *Hard by Plumeria's bower / Underneath the brooding tower / The Moon awaits its hard-won hour.*"

"Tower?" My ears pricked up like a spaniel's. "As in your tower?"

Behind the house loomed the original Norman keep, or the remains thereof, built by Fulke de Selwick to keep those pesky Saxons down. Now semiruined, it was the perfect location for a lost treasure—at least, in theory. In practice, it would be like putting up a neon sign that said, "Get Your Treasures Here!" The place was like a beacon for treasure seekers.

"Is that why you keep it locked?" I asked, tagging along after Colin into the bedroom.

"No. It really is just because of the farm equipment," he said apologetically. As I had discovered on an earlier, unauthorized foray, the most exciting thing that the tower appeared to be housing was rusty farm equipment. "But we can take a look around if you like."

"You've searched it already, haven't you?" I said accusingly.

"And my father, and his father before him. Everyone and his mother's had a go."

"All his sisters and his cousins whom he reckons by the dozens," I murmured. "But Jeremy still thinks it's here."

Colin spread his hands in silent acknowledgment.

"He'll go on pestering you until you find it," I said seriously. "You do realize that."

"You can't find what isn't there to be found," said Colin.

"Hmm." I wasn't ready to admit defeat that easily. "Who was Plumeria?"

Colin's eyes crinkled. "You know my family tree better than I do."

"Only the early-nineteenth-century bits of it." I sank down on the edge of the bed, which made a faint creaking noise in protest. Okay, fine, I had done a bit of poking around into the more recent bits of Colin's family tree, purely recreationally, but I didn't want him to know that. It was like admitting you had Googled someone before a first date. "The name does sound oddly familiar, though. . . ."

"Yes?" There was no mistaking the eagerness in Colin's voice.

Where had I heard that name before? For a moment, I thought I had it, but the wisp of memory drifted away like smoke, nothing to hold on to. Plumeria . . .

"No. It's gone." I looked up at Colin, who had busied himself buckling his watch. "Why not ask your aunt Arabella?"

He shook his head. "She won't give us a straight answer. She doesn't believe such things are meant to be found."

"Direct quote?"

"Pretty much."

"Let's go anyway." I liked Colin's great-aunt, not least because she was the one responsible for setting us up. All right, "set up" might be too strong a term, but she had certainly contrived to throw us in each other's way. "It'll be a field trip. Fun!"

Colin came to stand in front of me. "You mean you don't want to work on your dissertation."

"Pretty much." It wasn't just summer slump. I'd hit a snag in the material and I didn't know how to deal with it.

Thanks to Colin's truly excellent archives, I could plot the movements of the Pink Carnation with a fair degree of accuracy between 1803 and 1805. I knew who the Pink Carnation was (Miss Jane Wooliston), where she was living (the Hotel de Balcourt, her cousin's home in Paris), and exactly what she was doing to thwart Napoleon. Between 1803 and 1805, the Pink Carnation lived in Paris with her chaperone, Miss Gwendolyn Meadows. She kept up a regular coded correspondence with her cousin by marriage, Lady Henrietta Dorrington. And then, in the late spring of 1805 . . .

The paper trail stopped. Cold. No more letters to Lady Henrietta. No more letters to her cousin Amy Selwick. Nothing. Nada.

There were several options, none of them good.

The least awful option was the most obvious: The letters hadn't survived. As my adviser was fond of saying, just because something wasn't there didn't mean it hadn't existed. It was a miracle that any of these documents survived.

But why meticulously maintain the correspondence up to that point and then burn the rest? It didn't make sense.

Option two: The Pink Carnation had changed aliases or contacts. If the French had caught on to her coded correspondence with Lady Henrietta, she might have changed her modus operandi, started writing under a different name to a different contact. Clearly, if she had done so, she had not been thinking about the convenience of future historians. On the other hand, at least it meant she was still alive and kicking.

Then there was the final and deadliest option: Something had happened to the Pink Carnation.

It wasn't impossible. The Carnation was living in constant risk of discovery, her sole protection the French Ministry of Police's inability to ascribe that kind of cunning to a woman, and a beautiful one at that. All it took was one slip, and it would all be over. The life of a spy wasn't exactly without danger. The Carnation's old nemesis, the Black Tulip, had gone up in smoke, quite literally, in the middle of a botched assassination attempt, but a new French spymaster had risen to take the Tulip's place, a shadowy figure known only as "the Gardener."

Talk about nerve. It was one thing to pick a flower alias like everyone else, quite another to proclaim yourself master of the whole garden, with the power to cultivate—and to cull.

True, legend ascribed years more of deeds to the Pink Carnation, but by 1805, the Carnation's reputation had been firmly established. It would have made sense for the English government to continue the use of the alias.

Even in the warmth of the un-air-conditioned room, the thought made me shiver. I'd spent months living in the Pink Carnation's head. The idea of anything happening to her was anathema to me.

I know, I know. Even if she'd lived to a ripe old age, she'd be long dead now. In the grand scheme of things, it didn't matter. But it mattered to me.

Of all of them, option two was the most likely. It made sense for the Pink Carnation to change up her routine from time to time to keep the Ministry of Police off her tail. Complacency led to discovery. Wasn't Hotmail constantly reminding me to change my password?

But. That was always the problem, that word "but." Miss Jane Wooliston and her chaperone, Miss Gwendolyn Meadows— known to the young men of Paris as something that roughly translated to "the Purple Parasol–Wielding Dragon"—were both fixtures on the Paris social scene until spring of 1805. In April 1805, there was a brief mention in the Paris gossip sheets of Miss Wooliston returning to England for a short trip home to deal with what the paper referred to only as a family matter.

After that, nothing. I'd paged through the archives of *Le Moniteur*, *Le Monde Parisien*, and even that notorious scandal rag *Bonjour, Paris!*, sheer up through 1807. True, the microfilm was blurry, but I didn't think I'd missed anything. There were no further references to Miss Jane Wooliston and Miss Gwendolyn Meadows in Paris after April 1805.

Why had they gone back to England? And what had happened to them there? I was as far from the answer as I was from tracking down the Moon of Berar.

"Anything I can help with?" asked Colin gently.

I bit down on my lower lip. I'd been trying not to yank Colin into my work—I didn't want him to think I was with him just for his archives. Not that he would think that, hopefully, but love is paranoid. Or at least I was paranoid.

"I don't think so," I said slowly. "But I wouldn't mind a trip to London."

"Wednesday?" suggested Colin.

I'd have preferred to hop on the next train, but that might have fallen under the heading of running away.

Why had Jane and Miss Gwen left Paris so precipitously? What had driven them back to England? Discovery? Or something else?

"Wednesday," I agreed, and went off to look up anything I could find about the elusive Plumeria.

Chapter 1

Plumeria redoubled her speed as the footfalls of her pursuer pounded ever closer, reverberating through the close confines of the subterranean passage. Her breath rasped in her throat as she spied a faint gleam of light in the distance. At last! But could she reach it before it was too late?
    —From *The Convent of Orsino* by A Lady

(and if you were any kind of gentleman, you would stop trying to inquire into her identity!)

The spy wore purple.

Only amateurs wore black. Miss Gwendolyn Meadows knew that the true color of a Paris night wasn't a flat black, but a deep purple, composed of a hundred shades of shadow. Coal smoke masked the moon, diffusing the light of the lampposts, dirtying clothes and shading faces. Tonight she had left off her gown, her gloves, her elaborately curled plumes. She had even, with some reluctance, left behind her trusty parasol and taken up a cane instead. A sword cane, of course.

Paris was a dangerous city, even for those engaged in innocent pursuits.

Gwen's pursuits were anything but innocent.

No one of her acquaintance would recognize her as she was tonight. For tonight's romp, she had dressed as a dandy in breeches that hugged her legs and an elaborate frock coat of deep purple brocade. The stiffness of the fabric disguised any unseemly curvature of the chest, the tapered silhouette the same as that of any other fop in Paris. Her Hessian boots had been made to her own specifications, supple enough to allow for easy movement, the soles muffled with a thin layer of soft leather.

Her face was masked by a set of elaborately curling sideburns and matching mustache. Not that any of the young bucks who regularly shied away from her in the drawing rooms of the Tuileries would recognize her face. They were usually too busy sidling past in the hopes of saving their shins. Tall for a woman, she was comfortably average height for a man. Long and lean, her body might have been made for breeches roles. In this getup, she looked no different from any of the other gallants who thronged the cafés on the Rue de Richelieu.

There was one major difference. None of them were crouched on the corner of a balcony.

She had followed Bonaparte's foreign minister from the Théâtre des Arts, marking his limping progress. Talleyrand had gone masked too, but his uneven gait made him easy to follow. They hadn't far to go. She had tracked him three houses down, to this ramshackle inn. Talleyrand had taken the stairs;

Gwen had taken the trellis. Whomever he was meeting, it must be important for Bonaparte's foreign minister to come himself, and in this much haste.

A light guttered in the room. "Not so bright!"

The voice was the barest whisper, yet still recognizably female. Recognizably female and almost recognizable. Gwen knew that voice from somewhere—she was sure of it. She slouched closer, pressing her ear to the side of the shutters. The overhang of the balcony above shrouded her in shadow, the railing shielding her from the gaze of curious passersby below.

"No one followed me," said Talleyrand soothingly.

Ha. That's what he thought. Gwen nobly forbore to preen. There was no point in gloating until she knew what there was to gloat about. He might be meeting a mistress. But if so, why such subterfuge? Talleyrand's many affairs were fair game; he made no move to hide them.

She would give him one thing: The man recognized his bastards. Not every man could say as much.

"You're back sooner than I would have thought," he said. There was an edge of censure in his voice. Gwen heard the shuffle-thump of his passage across the room, the sound of a drink being poured.

"Not from dereliction of duty." The female's voice was stronger now, her French lightly accented with a hint of the south. Italian. Not the coarse Corsican of Bonaparte's cronies, but pure Tuscan, the accent of Dante and the Medicis. And of the opera.

Gwen crept closer. Through the shutters, she saw the lady ease back her hood, revealing a rich mass of auburn hair, elaborately arranged. "I have not forgot our bargain."

Talleyrand's voice was dry. "I should be very surprised if you had. Have you secured our prize so swiftly?"

"His Supreme Majesty was not so easily wooed."

The lady turned, giving Gwen a clear view of her profile, a profile that appeared on countless prints and snuffboxes throughout London, the handsome features of the famed Italian soprano Aurelia Fiorila.

There was just one problem. Fiorila was meant to be in England, recuperating from a nasty bout of something or other.

Yet here she was, as large as life, meeting with Talleyrand in the back room of a none-too-prosperous inn. "The Sultan was much put off by Brune's clumsy handling."

Brune. The man had recently returned from a stint as envoy to the Sultan of the Ottoman Empire. A sultan with a noted taste for opera. And opera singers.

It was an open secret that Bonaparte sought to seduce Selim III away from his alliance with Britain. Bonaparte had bullied the Pope into crowning him emperor not four months past, but the Sultan, entwined in old alliances with England and with Russia, balked at recognizing the imperial title. It was a thorn in Bonaparte's increasingly rotund flesh. His choice of ambassador, however, had only widened the breach. Brune had been sent back with a flea in his ear.

It shouldn't have surprised Gwen that Talleyrand had taken matters into his own hands; Talleyrand was a wily old fox.

What did surprise her was that Aurelia Fiorila was the means of doing so.

Gwen heard the snap of a snuffbox lid. "Sending Brune," said Talleyrand, "was not my decision. I trust you were able to sing the Sultan into sweeter temper?"

Fiorila's voice, the voice that had seduced audience after audience at Covent Garden, was ruefully amused. "Even my voice, sir, has not such power as that." Talleyrand must have made some move, because she added hastily, "I did gain audience with the Sultan. He told me what he will require to meet your desire. He says he will consider no treaties without a token of France's good intentions."

"I should have thought," said Talleyrand, a courtier to his bones, "that the presence of a beautiful lady would have been token enough."

Fiorila's voice was pensive. "The Sultan has beautiful women enough in his harem, sir. He requires no more."

"Not even one with a voice such as yours?"

Fiorila's voice sharpened. "I have no desire to sing from a cage. That was never in our bargain."

That was rather sweetly naïve of her, thought Gwen. She suspected that the terms of Talleyrand's bargains shifted with his needs. For all his courtly aspect, the man was as slippery as an eel.

"Certainly," said Talleyrand smoothly. "You know I would never ask that of you."

Gwen stifled a snort. Talleyrand would ask what he pleased, and they all knew it.

Talleyrand sniffed delicately at a pinch of snuff, coughing neatly into a lace-edged handkerchief of the very finest lawn. "What does the Sultan desire, if not your own fair form?"

Fiorila twisted her hands together. Her face was still youthful, but her hands were beginning to show the signs of age. "He had a more specific token in mind."

"Which was?" Beneath the charm, Talleyrand was all business.

The singer looked him in the eye. "The Moon of Berar."

For once, Talleyrand, Talleyrand the unflappable, was genuinely unsettled. "Good God," he said. "Would the Sultan rather have feathers from the tail of the phoenix, or a ruby made of the final drop of dragon's blood? They would be as easily obtained. The Moon is a myth."

"I sang of it in an opera once," said Fiorila. "Not a very good opera, but the story did catch the imagination. A jewel that makes the wearer impervious to harm, bright enough to blind the most determined assassin, a shield for the body and a mirror for the soul."

"Stuff and legends," said Talleyrand. "Not that one might not try to manufacture one . . ."

"But the effects would hardly be what the recipient would expect," said Fiorila practically. She began to turn up the fabric of her hood. "I have brought you what you required. My part is done. If you would . . ."

Talleyrand moved to block her egress, surprisingly quickly. But then, he had been limping his way in and out of bedchambers for years, thought Gwen cynically.

His voice was gently sorrowing. "Is this the way you requite my generosity, my dear? Feeding me fairy stories? If you think so little of our arrangement—"

"No!" There was no mistaking the alarm in Fiorila's voice. "I swear, I have relayed it to you as he did to me. The Sultan believes it to be real. He claims it was in the royal treasury of Berar."

"The Rajah of Berar kept a legendary treasure with the ordinary run of pearls and rubies." Bonaparte's foreign minister was politely skeptical.

"According to the Sultan, there was nothing ordinary about any of the treasure of Berar." Fiorila held out both hands in supplication. "If you bring him the Moon of Berar, he will break with England. But only for that."

"And how are we to set our hands on it?" There was no mistaking the implication of that "we." Whatever hold he had on the singer, he wasn't prepared to relinquish it.

Fiorila's voice was quiet. "He claims you have it already. He says it fell into the hands of one of your agents at the sack of Berar."

"One of mine . . ." The tone of Talleyrand's voice changed.

He knew who it was. Gwen would be willing to wager her favorite parasol on it. She leaned forward to hear better, but she misjudged. The shutters, inexpertly attached at best, rattled against the frame.

"What was that?" demanded Talleyrand.

Gwen didn't wait for him to find out.

She swung lightly off the edge of the balcony, landing with

knee-jarring force in the alleyway below. Something squished under her feet, almost sending her skidding, but she had landed squarely; she had the sense to catch her balance before feinting sideways, around the back of the building.

Talleyrand must have set guards to watch the inn. She could hear their heavy feet, their loud voices. So clumsy! She ducked neatly into a cul-de-sac, pressed against the slimed stones of the wall, waiting as the sound of pursuit pounded past. Her blood raced in her veins, filling her with a high, pure exhilaration. She never felt more alive than when evading pursuit. The dash of danger only made it more interesting.

Botheration. One of them, more cunning than his fellows, was waiting at the entrance to the alley. Moving with painstaking care, Gwen scooped up a loose piece of cobble from the ground. A bit slimy, but it would serve. Choosing her course carefully, she lobbed it to the far left, out of the mouth of the alley. It made a very satisfying clattering sound, well away from her hiding place. As the guard turned to look, she made her move, smashing him hard in the back of his legs with her cane. Leaping over his fallen form, she ran like a rabbit, her heart singing in her breast, the wind whistling in her ears, every sense on fire.

She waited until she was across the bridge before she stopped, just another disheveled dandy among the taverns of St. Michel. She had done it. She had shaken her pursuers. And even if they had seen her, what of it? No one would associate the bravo crouching by the window with the Dragon of the Drawing Room, Miss Gwendolyn Meadows, prim of the prim, scourge of importunate swains.

Merciful heavens, she loved her work.

Absurd to think that just two years ago—had it been only two years?—she had been entombed in the English countryside, a reluctant pensioner in her brother's household, "Aunt Gwen" to her brother's whining brats, "Oh, Gwendolyn . . ." to her brother's featherbrain of a wife. Twenty years she had wasted there, growing a little more seamed and a little more sour every day, dependent on the goodwill of her relations for every bite that crossed her lips. In return, she was meant to sit docilely and wind wool, to manage the household for her dolt of a sister-in-law, to pretend gratitude—gratitude!—for the condescension shown her in offering her a home in her own home. The fall from mistress to dependent had been bad enough; the servings of humble pie she had been expected to eat with it were too much.

But what else had there been for her to do? She had no dowry, not anymore. She had no funds of her own. She had been considered handsome once, and not entirely for the size of her vanished dowry. There were some men who appreciated a long, lean form, who preferred black hair to fair, and gray eyes to blue. Her tongue was accounted too sharp by some, but there were men, or at least so she had been told, who prized wit as well as wealth. She might escape through marriage— but to whom? Escape on those terms was no more than another cage. At least under her brother's roof she preserved the privacy of her own bedchamber, with lock and key when necessary.

Gritting her teeth, she had resigned herself to another

twenty years of the same, of watching her idiot nephews marry and procreate, producing offspring as imbecilic as themselves.

It filled her with a savage delight to have escaped that net. When her chance had come, she had seized it with both hands. She had never imagined that her impulsive offer to chaperone a neighbor's daughter and niece to Paris would provide more than a few months' reprieve, that it would lead her to emperors and sultans and intrigue beyond imagining. She had gone from counting sheep—her brother was constantly losing track of his herds—to meddling in the affairs of nations.

The League of the Pink Carnation had begun out of pique, an attempt to better the arrogant Englishman who had styled himself the Purple Gentian. But that first mission had led to another, and another after that. In the end, it was the League of the Pink Carnation who had rescued the Purple Gentian from various fates worse than death in the extra-special interrogation chamber of Gaston Delaroche. The Purple Gentian had gone home. The Pink Carnation had stayed on, making Bonaparte fume and his henchmen squirm.

Officially, Gwen's charge, Jane, was the Pink Carnation. Officially. As far as Gwen was concerned, the whole was a composite performance: Jane's cunning, Gwen's daring. They balanced each other, Gwen's inventiveness supplementing Jane's cool common sense. It was a pairing that worked ideally.

At least, it had been working ideally.

Over the past few months, Gwen had marked a change in her charge. Ever since Bonaparte's coronation, the Pink Carnation had embarked upon a policy of "watch and see," compiling dossiers of information through slow and painstaking effort rather than acts of derring-do. She didn't seem to be deriving the same relish from their activities that she once had. Admittedly, the game had become more dangerous. Fouché, Bonaparte's minister of police, had consolidated his hold, wiping out many of the networks of couriers on which they relied. They had also lost their long-term War Office contact, Augustus Whittlesby.

If Jane were another sort of woman, Gwen might have wondered if Whittlesby's departure had something to do with her malaise. The poet had made no secret of his admiration for Jane. She had sworn her heart wasn't touched, but— Jane was twenty-three now, an age when other women would be thinking of home and hearth.

Other women, Gwen reassured herself, tamping down a frisson of alarm. Not the Pink Carnation. They had work to do still; Jane knew that. She wasn't the sort to abandon her post for so unremarkable a creature as a man. Heaven only knew, she'd seen enough prime specimens over the years. A waste of good linen, most of them.

No. It was the lack of a challenge that had been plaguing the Pink Carnation; that was all. Gwen rubbed her gloved hands together. She'd tell Jane about this evening's gleaning. That should catch the Pink Carnation's fancy.

What person was proof to the allure of a missing mythical jewel?

Gwen let herself in through the servants' entrance of the Hotel de Balcourt, the home of Jane's cousin Edouard, a prime example of the failings of the male sex. Balcourt housed them reluctantly, turning a blind eye to their activities, less out of cousinly feeling than out of fear that if he were to turn them in, they would share with the authorities certain rather interesting documents in Jane's possession regarding Edouard's cross-Channel trade in muslin and brandy. It was an arrangement that suited them all quite well. They ignored the barrels of brandy in the cellar and Edouard ignored their odd comings and goings.

In her room, Gwen pressed the button that opened the secret back of her armoire. Here, hidden behind the respectable ranks of day dresses and evening gowns, she kept her real wardrobe: the breeches, the waistcoats, the serving maids' dresses, the floppy hat of a coastal fisherman, a wide array of wigs, and a small arsenal of firearms. She folded her purple frock coat back among its fellows, right above a footman's livery and the uniform of a minor officer in the imperial guard. With the ease of long practice, she sponged off her false whiskers, setting them aside to dry.

There was a light knock on the door. Gwen rapidly shut the secret panel, although there was reasonably only one person who would be knocking on her bedchamber door at this time of night.

"Yes?" she called.

The Pink Carnation slipped neatly into the room, shutting the door behind her.

"Miss Gwen?" Through all they had experienced together, Jane still employed the conventional honorific. Old habits died hard. Partners they might be, but Gwen was still Jane's chaperone.

"I'm glad you're still awake," said Gwen briskly, shaking her hair free of the tight queue in which she had bound it. "I have news."

"So have I," said Jane. She was in her nightdress, her long light brown hair streaming down her back, like Ophelia about to hand out weeds. Her face was pale and worried in the uncertain light of the candles. "Agnes has gone missing."

Agnes? Gwen's head was stuffed with sultans and emperors; it took an effort to bring it back to the quiet of the English countryside. Frowning, she managed to dredge up the image of a quiet girl with a long face and light brown hair, a pale copy of Jane. Agnes was the youngest of the Wooliston sisters and, in Miss Gwen's opinion, too docile to be memorable.

Jane held up a piece of paper, ill written and marred by blots. "I've had a letter from my father." That in itself was news enough. Bertrand Wooliston could write? Who knew? "Agnes has disappeared from Miss Climpson's seminary."

"Are you sure they haven't just misplaced her? She's not very noticeable." Allowed to join the adults, Agnes had blended into the background at the Christmas festivities at Uppington Hall that past year, noticeable only for taking up an extra seat at the table.

Jane shook her head. "She's been missing for well over a week now. They notified my parents first. They haven't been able to find her."

Gwen doubted they had looked very far. Bertrand Wooliston had eyes only for his ewes, and his wife was decidedly myopic.

She put a comforting hand on Jane's shoulder. "She's probably just run off with some scrounging half-pay officer," she said reassuringly.

Jane gave a choked laugh. "I wish I could believe that were all it might be."

"Why shouldn't it be?" Gwen picked up Betrand Wooliston's note from the table. The seal had been lost somewhere along the way. Not surprising. The postal routes between England and France were dodgy at best. Technically, commerce and correspondence between England and France were still strictly forbidden. In practice, a thriving postal service went on across the Channel, often with a side of muslin and brandy. "All young girls are flighty."

Jane looked at her askance. "Were you?"

"Flighty" wasn't the word she would have used. Headstrong, yes. Defiant and proud and infinitely foolish.

There were times when Jane reminded her uncannily of herself at a similar age. Oh, not in comportment. She had never had Jane's Olympian calm; she had always preferred to express herself directly. But Jane's self-containment was its own form of stubbornness. In that, they were alike.

"Your sister is probably halfway to Gretna Green by now," said Gwen heartily. "Let's just hope she picked a handsome one."

Jane shook her head. With her hair down, she looked very young and very vulnerable, hardly the mistress of the spy operation that had terrorized Bonaparte for the past two years. "She's not alone. Another girl has gone missing too."

"Even better," said Gwen. "They've run off together. They've probably gone to London to see Kemble perform, or some such fool thing."

Jane laced her fingers together. Aristocratic, Gwen's father would have called her hands, with his merchant's instinct for divining the details of his betters. "If that were the case," she said quietly, "they would have been back by now."

Gwen looked at the controlled face of her charge. "Are you suggesting foul play?"

"You think I'm overwrought."

Gwen gave a harsh bark of laughter. "You don't know what overwrought is." Her sister-in-law did a fine line in overwrought. A delay in dinner could bring out a performance worthy of Mrs. Siddons. "But foul play? It hardly seems likely. The girl is sixteen—"

"Seventeen," corrected Jane.

"A distinction without a difference. She's practically a babe in arms. How many enemies can she have?"

"She might not," said Jane. "But I have."

The words polluted the air between them, stinking like the Seine. Gwen looked at Jane's pale, anxious face. She wanted to argue her into comfort, to smash her theory into harmless little bits. But she couldn't.

"It's unlikely," she offered instead, knowing just how weak it sounded.

Jane's face was set in a way none of her suitors would have recognized. "But not impossible," she said.

No, not impossible. No matter how careful they were, leaks

occurred. Too many people knew Jane's double identity: former agents, former contacts, her loathsome toad of a cousin.
And those were only the ones they knew about. Various
French agents had sworn to unmask the Pink Carnation or die
trying.

The Black Tulip actually had died in the attempt—or so
they had been led to believe. The Tulip had an inconvenient
habit of resurrection. If the Tulip, or someone like him, had
Agnes . . . Not that she believed that Agnes had been kidnapped. The very idea was ridiculous.

But it wasn't impossible.

Jane read her conclusion in her face. "You see? We have to
find her."

Gwen rubbed at her cheek where her false whiskers had ir-
ritated her skin. "Not so fast, young lady. Have you considered
you might be walking into a trap? If someone has discovered
your identity—not that I'm saying that they have—but if they
have . . ." The Black Tulip hadn't been known for mercy.

"How could I leave Agnes to suffer on my behalf?" Jane's
indignation made Gwen feel small, small and selfish. "If I put
her into danger, it's my duty to get her out again."

Gwen's eyes met Jane's. "Have you considered that if you
leave, you might not be able to come back?"

Travel across the Channel was still technically forbidden.
If it were known that they traveled back and forth to England, it would arouse suspicion. For brief and necessary clan-
destine visits, Jane usually pretended an illness, "taking to her
bed" at the Hotel de Balcourt, with Gwen at her side to nurse

her. It only added to her mystique of fragile delicacy. In public, they went disguised, under other personae: the forbidding Ernestine Grimwold and her dithery niece Miss Gilly Fairly, or the widowed Mrs. Fustian and her daughter. They were themselves only within the safety of the family circle, and that sparingly.

"Miss Fustian," suggested Jane with unaccustomed hesitation, "might seek employment in Miss Climpson's school."

Gwen shook her head. "No. You look too much like Agnes. The students will suss it out in ten minutes, maybe less. Unless . . ."

She had an idea, an idea insane enough that it just might work. Part of her, the craven, selfish part, wanted to shake it away, to pretend helplessness. After all, wouldn't it make more sense to stay in Paris and delegate the task to one of their agents in England? The former Purple Gentian would leap at the assignment. If he were out of commission, there were half a dozen others who would take on the task with a great deal of enthusiasm and varying levels of skill.

And Jane would never forgive herself.

Reluctantly, Gwen said, "There might be a way."

Jane regarded her warily. "Does this have to do with wearing your false whiskers?"

"No," said Gwen. "We disguise ourselves by having no disguises at all. We go as ourselves."

Jane gave her a frustrated look. "I know you don't approve of the venture, but there's no need to speak nonsense."

"It's not nonsense. It's our best chance," said Gwen rapidly.

"We evade suspicion by being entirely aboveboard. What is there to hide, after all?"

Jane cocked an eyebrow. It was an effective trick, one the chit had picked up from her early mentor, the Purple Gentian. Gwen had practiced it herself, but it required one attribute she had never mastered: the gift of sustained silence.

"No, not like that." Gwen waved Jane's silent protest aside. "You apply to the Emperor for permission to travel. You tell him your sister has eloped and your family needs you. He, of all people, should understand the concerns of wayward sisters. Look at his! A scandal, all of them."

Jane sat down on the edge of Gwen's bed, a slender figure in a white nightdress. "You might be right," she said slowly.

Gwen harrumphed. "Of course I'm right. Aren't I always?"

What was she doing? The last thing in the world that she wanted was to go back to England. Here in Paris, she had presence, she had standing, she had fear, if not respect. Back in England, she was just Miss Meadows, spinster. The very idea made her stomach cramp.

She looked down at Jane's bowed head, the color of old whiskey in the candlelight, and felt something like pity twist in her gut, pity and a bit of envy. Her family had never given her cause to love them as Jane loved hers. They had abandoned her when she had most needed them and ground salt in her wounds when she was most vulnerable.

All for the best, of course. It had toughened her up, made her what she was. But there was no need for Jane to be toughened so. The girl had enough on her head already.

No need to repine, Gwen promised herself. It needn't take more than a week or so. They would find Agnes, give her a good ticking off, and come right back to their life in France.

"Get your things together," Gwen said regally. "We're going to England."

Chapter 2

The building sat on a low rise, shaded by a stand of trees. In spring, it might have been a happy place, but not now. A bolt of lightning forked through the sky as Sir Magnifico clattered into the courtyard, his senses rent with misgiving. Where were the joyful carols of the cloistered ladies? The voices of the virgins were hushed and anxious, as muted as the rain that dripped down the cold, gray stone.

Was it an ancient curse that lay over the building? Or some more recent evil?

—From *The Convent of Orsino* by A Lady

England wasn't at all what Colonel William Reid had expected it to be.

Back in the mess in Madras, his fellow officers were always nattering on about the lush green of the fields, the cerulean blue of the sky, the delicate touch of a spring breeze, as soft and sweet as a lover's kiss. They hadn't mentioned the driving rain that got beneath a man's collar, or the mud of the roads that sucked at cart wheels and caked the bottom of a man's boots. If the wind was the touch of a lover, this was less a kiss and more a hearty slap across the face.

Shivering in his newly purchased, many-caped coat, William felt like a piece of wet washing, damp down to the skin, and then some besides. Winter, yes. He'd expected winter to be cold. But this was spring, for the love of all that was holy. Birds should be on the wing and buds on the thorn, or wherever it was that buds went.

So much for April in England, of which the poets sang so sweetly and so falsely. William would have traded it in a moment for May in Madras. Faith, he'd even take July in Jaipur, sweating in his regimentals in the blazing sun, hotter than hell and ready to wilt.

Not that he had that choice. It was England for him now, will he nill he, a classic case of blithely making one's bed, only to discover, when the time came to lie on it, that it was full of lumps. He was good at that.

And didn't I warn you? He could hear his mother's outraged Highland brogue in his head, exaggerated by time and distance.

His mother would be turning in her tartan grave if she knew that he'd chosen to take up residence in England in his old age. They'd been committed adherents to the King over the Water, his parents; fled from Inverness in '45 in the wake of the disaster at Culloden. Committed from a distance, that was. In the safety of the Carolinas, their commitment had extended mostly to derisory epithets about the English and toasting the

Pretender's health, such as it was. They'd had some lovely glasses made up, crystal, with thistles, and some Jacobite motto or other scrolled about the bowl. Latin, it was, but what the words had been, he couldn't say.

Memory blurred. Or perhaps it was the drizzle driving into his eyes, that maddening, peculiarly English form of precipitation, not quite mist, not quite rain, but something in between, all but impossible to keep off. Give him a proper thunderstorm any day, like the sort they'd had in his youth in the Carolinas, winds howling, thunder crashing, not like this, insidious, invidious, and damnably damp.

For choice, he would have stayed in India. He'd had nearly forty good years there, posted all around the country, from Calcutta to Bombay. He'd served in the East India Company's army. Not as lucrative, perhaps, as the royal army, apt to be sneered at by snobs, but he couldn't see himself taking the King's shilling, not then, not now. Old prejudices died hard. It had been a polyglot group with whom he'd fought in the Madras cavalry, most of them wanderers like himself, all out to make their fortune in the fabled land of jewels and spices.

He missed India, missed it with a visceral longing he'd never felt for Charleston. He had come of age in India; he had learned his trade there, made his friends, fallen in love. It was in India he'd married and buried his Maria; in India he'd raised his children, three boys and two girls, only two of them what you might call legitimate. What did it matter? Legitimate, illegitimate, British, half-caste, what have you, they were all his children and he loved them all alike: conscientious Alex, prickly Jack, sunny-natured George, stubborn Kat, and his youngest, his sweet Lizzy. If the circumstances of his family life were sometimes a little . . . irregular, well, it was India, and such things were common there.

Common, yes, but not always easy. He'd learned that the hard way. Of his three sons, two were barred employment in the very regiment to which he'd given so many years' service, simply by virtue of having a native woman for a mother. William had got George settled, finding him a place in the retinue of a local ruler, the Begum Sumroo. As for Jack . . . It didn't matter that Jack's mother had been a lady of quality in her own land; he'd been barred all the same, barred as though his mother were the lowest bazaar strumpet.

The boy had taken it hard. Jack had ridden away, offering his sword to whomever would employ him against the men who had denied him his place. They hadn't spoken since. Jack's absence was a wound in William's heart that wouldn't heal.

The worst of it, though, had been sending his daughters away. It had been nearly a decade ago now, Kat seventeen, Lizzy an imp of seven, all curls and dimples. For their education, he'd bluffed, but the truth was it wasn't safe for them, not for Lizzy, who was a half-caste, child of a native mother. There were some young bucks who thought a half-caste girl fair game. He'd seen it happen, to his horror, to the daughter of a friend, raped and tossed aside. She'd died of the pox—and the shame, some said. Her father had aged ten years in as many months. And William had packed his girls onto a ship bound for England, bundling them off in the face of all their protests.

Just a few years, he'd told his girls as he handed them onto the launch in Calcutta harbor, Kat glowering, Lizzy clinging to his neck. Then he would come to England and join them and what grand times they would have then! But then had come Tippoo Sultan's rising in the south and unrest in the north and what with one thing and another a few years had stretched to another and another, until here he was, ten years later, standing on the stoop of a young ladies' seminary in Bath, a bouquet of wilted flowers in one hand, prepared to surprise a daughter he wasn't sure he would recognize. When he'd last seen her, she'd had two missing teeth and a scrape on her left knee. He could picture that scab as he could picture his own hand, every moment of their parting branded on his memory.

Would she be happy to see him, his Lizzy? He hoped so. He felt like a nervous suitor, about to call on a young lady for the first time. William straightened his collar and cleared his throat.

"It's Miss Elizabeth Reid I'm here to see," he said to the woman standing at the door, a young woman with soft dark hair, in a modest gray dress that matched the weather. She was a small woman, with the mushroom-like complexion of someone who had never encountered a tropical sun. She had identified herself as the French mistress, Mlle. de Fayette.

She also looked distinctly wary. William supposed he couldn't blame her, faced with a strange man holding a bouquet of battered flowers, standing at the doorstep. One couldn't be too careful with a house full of impressionable young ladies.

"I have the fear—," she began, taking a step back. "That is, I am most desolate, but—"

"It's her father, I am," William said quickly. He swept a quick half bow, smiling to show her that he wasn't a rake, rogue, or seducer, but just a parent come to call. "Colonel William Reid. Lizzy might have mentioned me?" He tipped the French mistress a wink. "Not that a mere father is much in the mind of a young girl."

If anything, Mlle. de Fayette looked even more distressed.

Was he losing his touch in his old age?

"Colonel Reid," she said, rolling out the syllables of the title in the Continental fashion. She twisted her hands together, pale against the dark material of her dress. "I am of the most sorry. Miss Reid, she is—it is of the most unfortunate!"

"What's she done now?" William asked resignedly. "In disgrace, is she?"

That sounded like his Lizzy. He could hear the lamentations of his housekeeper back in Madras, ten years past, in different accents, but the same general tone. Lizzy had a way of wreaking havoc, but with a smile so sweet it was hard to take against her.

"Miss Reid, she—" Mlle. de Fayette bit her lip, hard enough to leave a mark. "We would have sent the letter, but we did not know where—"

The hairs on William's neck prickled. This wasn't just a case of Lizzy eating the jam out of the biscuits or trying to climb the trellis on a dare.

"A letter?" he said, as casually as he could. "And what would that be about, then? She's not got herself sent down, has she?"

"No, no. That is—" The woman in the doorway made a notable effort to compose herself. She pressed a hand to her lips.

"There, there. I'm sure it's not so bad as all that," said William reassuringly. "Whatever she's done, I'll see it put right. Now, what's the minx done now?"

"Minx indeed!"

William's head snapped up as a voice rang imperiously through the hall.

A woman strode forward, wafting Mlle. de Fayette out of the way. The glass prisms on the wall sconces quivered with the force of her movement. Next to the diminutive French mistress, the newcomer looked like an Amazon, although a great part of her height were the tall plumes that curled from her elaborate purple turban.

She moved with rangy grace, her skirts moving briskly against her long legs. Paris tailoring, unless William missed his guess, the material fine and cut narrow. An expensive rig for the proprietress of a young ladies' academy.

"Are you the parent of Miss Reid?" she asked in ringing tones.

It felt like an accusation.

William retaliated with the full arsenal of his charm. "I have that honor," he said easily. "But I fear I haven't yet the pleasure of your acquaintance, Madame—"

The woman sniffed. It was a most effective sniff, conveying the full range of her displeasure. "Don't call it a pleasure until you've had a chance to judge." Using the point of her parasol, she neatly prodded the younger woman out of the way. "In or out? Make up your mind. You're letting in the most appalling draft."

William chose in. The door snapped shut behind him. Mlle. de Fayette stepped prudently out of the way.

William smiled determinedly at the woman in purple, whose commanding air seemed to imply that she must be the preceptress of this academy. Either that or the ruler of a small but warlike kingdom. William had met rajahs with less of an air of command.

He sketched a bow. "And is it Miss Climpson I have the honor of addressing?"

The woman drew back as though struck. "What an appalling notion," she said. "Most certainly not. *I* am Miss Gwendolyn Meadows." She said it much as one might say, *I am Cleopatra*.

Was he meant to know who she was?

"A pleasure," William said again. He deliberately included both women in his smile. He had one objective: finding his Lizzy. "Now, if you'd be so kind as to enlighten me, it's my daughter I'm after looking for, Miss Elizabeth—"

"Hmph," said Miss Meadows, smacking the ground with her parasol hard enough to strike sparks. "You won't find her here."

William dodged out of the way, shocked into brevity. "Why not?"

Miss Meadows looked down her nose at him, a rather impressive trick given that he would have wagered on her being some few inches shorter than he. "Your Elizabeth has run off with our Agnes."

"She's—what?" Who in the blazes was Agnes?

"Run off," said Miss Meadows succinctly. "Run. Off. Do pay attention, Colonel Reid. Really, it's quite simple. Your Elizabeth has run off with our Agnes."

William was stung into retort. "How do you know your Agnes didn't run off with my Lizzy?"

Miss Meadows looked superior. "Really, Colonel Reid. Do be sensible. Agnes isn't the running kind."

Whereas his Lizzy—what did he know of his Lizzy? He'd had a letter a month for ten years, just that. Twelve letters a year times ten, with an extra on his birthday . . .

William pressed two fingers to the bridge of his nose. "Forgive me, ladies. I've just come six months by ship, five days by coach, and the rest of the way uphill by foot. My wits are not my own. Are you telling me that my daughter has gone missing?"

Mlle. de Fayette opened her mouth, but Miss Meadows got in first. "That is precisely what we have been telling you. Elizabeth and Agnes have both gone missing. Presumably with each other. Theoretically of their own volition. Does that answer your question?"

Hardly. William's head was reeling with questions. He settled for the most pressing. "What's been done to find them?"

Miss Meadow's lips pursed. "Precious little. Come with me." She jerked her head down the hall. "You'll want to speak to Miss Climpson—for what good it will do you."

She set off down the hall, her skirts swishing around her legs, heels tapping briskly against the wood floor.

William hurried after her, his wet boots squelching. "Are you employed at the school, then?" he asked dubiously. Somehow, he'd got the idea that schoolmistresses were meant to be quiet, downtrodden creatures.

"Quiet" and "downtrodden" were not terms one could apply to Miss Meadows.

"Merciful heavens, no! You couldn't pay me to be a teacher." The idea was horrifying enough to stop Miss Meadows in her tracks. Drawing herself up, she regarded him with great dignity. "I am Agnes's older sister's chaperone."

It sounded like a French exercise. "I see," said William, although he didn't see at all. "And that makes you . . ."

"The only one with any common sense in this debacle." Miss Meadows stopped in front of the open door of a drawing room decorated in shades of blue. It was adorned with an alarming variety of porcelain knickknacks, mostly of the cherub variety. Porcelain cherubs simpered from the mantel, more cherubs lurked at the corners of the windows, and a truly appalling assembly of them smirked from a large oil painting in the center of the ceiling.

Of the non-cherub population, William counted four. A woman in late middle age, with a cap like an overgrown cabbage, sat in a chair before a tea table, flanked on either side by a man and a woman dressed in clothes of equally outmoded vintage. The man wore a frock coat and a slightly moth-eaten periwig, the woman a wide-skirted gown of heavy brocade. A slim girl in a blue gown stood by the windows, blending neatly with the draperies.

"Mr. Wooliston, Mrs. Wooliston, and Miss Wooliston." Miss Meadows fired off the names like pistol shots. She nodded at the woman in the immense cap. "And that's Miss Climpson, the prime preceptress of this academy, such as it is." She grinned at him, rather grimly. "Let's see if *you* can get any sense out of her."

It felt like a challenge. "I'll do my best."

His companion indulged in a smile that looked alarmingly like a smirk. "Do," she said. "Do."

It was not entirely encouraging.

Advancing into the room, William approached the woman in the massive cap. "Miss Climpson? I'm William Reid. Elizabeth's father," he added when Miss Climpson looked at him rather blankly.

Miss Meadows gave him an "I told you so" look.

William turned his back on her and concentrated the force of his charm on Miss Climpson. "What's this about my Lizzy going missing?"

The ribbons on Miss Climpson's enormous cap bobbed dizzyingly. "It is most inconvenient," she said spiritedly. "How is one to teach a girl when she is not on the premises? It presents a distinct pedagogical problem."

William would have thought their problems were more than pedagogical. "How long have the girls been missing?"

"Missing," said Miss Climpson, "is such a strong word. I prefer to think of them as having misplaced themselves. Most inconsiderately."

"Are you sure she's gone? She was always such a quiet child." The woman in the old-fashioned gown peered at a chair as though expecting to find her daughter lurking between the threads of the upholstery.

"Can't be trusted not to wander off. Temperamental things, ewes," said the man in the periwig expansively, rising from his chair to greet the new arrival. "But they tend to find their way back to pasture, don't they—er?"

William dodged a genial whack on the shoulder. "Reid. Colonel Reid. It seems we're in the same boat—er, pasture. My ewe appears to have wandered from the fold as well."

The man stuck out a hand. "Bertrand Wooliston." He nodded to the woman in the brocade gown. "My wife, Prudence. And I see you've already met our Miss Meadows."

"Yes," said William guardedly. "You might say that. Now, about the girls . . ."

"Never a bit of trouble," said Mrs. Woolison, squinting at him through a pair of pince-nez pinched far too low on her nose. "Agnes wound wool so beautifully."

"There, there, my love." Mr. Wooliston pounded her soundly on the shoulder, setting his periwig askew. "Leave them alone and they'll come home; that's how it goes."

"Wagging their tails behind them?" Miss Meadows snorted, an emission of air that rather adequately summed up William's feelings. "I sincerely doubt it."

William was beginning to experience grave doubts about Miss Climpson's academy. "Do the girls here misplace themselves frequently?"

"Fencing," said Bertrand Wooliston firmly. "That's what's needed. Good, strong fencing. None of these doors and windows." He nodded scornfully at the long sash windows that looked out into a scrubby sort of garden.

"Be that as it may"—William had always prided himself on his ability to adapt to the local idiom—"the, er, ewes have already left the pasture. I'd suggest we put our efforts to finding them, wouldn't you? How long have they been missing?"

Miss Meadows cut into a confusion of garbled explanations and deliberations from the others. "Two weeks," she said bluntly.

William's eyebrows soared towards his hairline. "Two *weeks?*"

He'd sent Lizzy to England to keep her safe, by God. She'd lived those first few years with his wife's mother, in Bristol, but when the letter had come suggesting Lizzy be sent to a young lady's academy for a bit of polish—well, it seemed a good solution to an awkward situation. Mrs. Davies was Kat's grandmother, not Lizzy's. It was a golden opportunity for Lizzy, Kat had assured him. The school catered to the children of the upper gentry, the daughters of landed ladies and gentlemen. The reflected luster would smooth Lizzy's way in the world, wiping out the taint of her birth. It was an opportunity William could never have afforded for her, and he had responded enthusiastically.

He had never imagined this. Didn't the affluent of England keep closer watch on their offspring than that?

Mlle. de Fayette stepped forward. "It is not entirely as it

sounds," she said hesitantly. "In the beginning, you see, it was thought that Miss Reid and Miss Wooliston followed one of their schoolmates to her home. Miss Reid was of the most unhappy when Miss Fitzhugh left the school."

"You've sent to this Miss Fitzhugh?" said William brusquely. He hadn't much of a temper, as a rule, but the idea of harm to his Lizzy . . . Lizzy, whom he hadn't seen in ten years. He could see her as she'd been when he put her on that ship, seven and without guile.

"We sent to Miss Fitzhugh at once!" Mlle. de Fayette hastened to assure him. Her face fell. "Miss Fitzhugh expressed the confusion entire."

William grasped at straws. "It's sure you are that she was telling the truth?"

Mlle. de Fayette lowered her eyes. "Miss Fitzhugh was of the most indignant at being, as she said, 'left out of the fun.' Her brother, Monsieur Fitzhugh, was of the most accommodating. He searched through all the wardrobes and under the beds, and even under the vegetable beds in the gardens. The girls, they were nowhere to be found."

"All right, then," said William grimly. "Where else?"

Mlle. de Fayette and her employer exchanged a long look.

"In other words," said Miss Meadows, before William could, "you haven't the slightest idea where they are."

"We know where they aren't," provided Miss Climpson brightly, and it was only with the greatest effort that William kept his hands from closing around her shoulders and giving her a hearty shake. There were no words for the nightmare images that assaulted him. They were too terrible to be given a name. "By the process of elimination . . ."

"There are only several million places the girls might be," said Miss Meadows crisply. William looked at her with gratitude. "This is useless. We need clues." She paced across the room, drawing all eyes as she whipped back and forth, back and forth, tossing out directives as she went. "The Fitzhugh girl will need to be questioned, as will the staff. Is there a porter in this establishment? No. Then we'll need to interview someone who can tell us of their comings and goings."

"Really, Miss Meadows," protested Miss Climpson. "I don't see why that should be necessary. The girls are most strictly chaperoned. . . ."

"Then why aren't they here?" said Miss Meadows with withering sarcasm. "Right. Let's to business."

Young Miss Wooliston untangled herself from the curtains and stepped forward, her voice pleasant and level, a soothing patch of calm in the whirlwind that was Miss Meadows. "Were there any letters before they left? Any"—she cast a glance over her shoulder at the older Woolistons—"billets-doux?"

"She means love letters," said Miss Meadows baldly.

Love letters? William's mouth opened indignantly. He could picture his daughter, all tousled curls and sun-browned hands, a little imp of mischief. Why, his Lizzy was too young for that sort of thing, practically a baby yet. She was all of—

Seventeen.

The realization of it hit him like a stone. Seventeen. His Maria had been fifteen when he'd met her, sixteen when they'd married. When he remembered what they'd got up to behind her parents' backs—well, it was a distinctly sobering thought. William's mouth snapped shut again.

"They've not been"—William had trouble getting the words out—"consorting with men?"

The French mistress hastened to correct him. "Oh no. They were not the sort. I have seen"—with a guilty look at the head-mistress, she quickly caught herself—"that is, one comes to recognize the signs of an affair of the heart. These girls, they were still girls."

Oh, one did, did one? "You've had girls run off with men before?" William asked faintly.

"'Run off' is such a harsh term," said the headmistress. "It was really more of a precipitate departure."

"It was only the once," put in the French mistress. "The gardener who passed the notes, he was—how do you say?—let go."

William failed to find that entirely reassuring.

"I think," said Miss Meadows crisply, "that we ought to see their rooms."

"Yes," William agreed hastily. "Yes, we ought."

Miss Meadows regarded him imperiously. "Come along, then. Mademoiselle de Fayette, you'll show us the way? No, no, Prudence, no need to come with us. We'll see ourselves back, won't we, Jane? Bertrand, see your wife home; there's nothing more for you to do here."

William watched with amazement and admiration as Miss Meadows neatly sent everyone packing. The elder Woolistons departed for their lodgings. Miss Climpson, routed, made excuses about seeing to the girls. Miss Wooliston watched the proceedings with a faint smile of amusement.

"Well?" Miss Meadows turned to William with a raised eyebrow. "What are you standing around for? Are you coming to their room or going home?"

William saluted. "I am yours to command. At least so far as the second landing."

Miss Wooliston covered a smile.

Miss Meadows regarded him haughtily. "Hmph," she said. "Come along, then."

Without waiting to see whether they followed, she stalked towards the stairs.

Chapter 3

"I seek my daughter," quoth bold Sir Magnifico.

"Seek her not here," warned the Mother Superior, "for she is not within these walls."

She spoke him fair, but Sir Magnifico's misgivings misgave him. "Show me to her cell," he commanded, "and then we shall see what is to be seen."

The Mother Superior regarded him with a weary eye. "Bold sir," she said, "it is not what is seen but what is unseen that we needs must see."

"Madame," quoth the knight, "your speech be passing strange."
                              —From *The Convent of Orsino* by A Lady

G wen didn't like any of this. She didn't like it one bit.

All her instincts, well honed over years of midnight raids, were shouting "trouble." How much of the trouble was coming from the situation and how much from a certain sun-bronzed colonel was a matter for debate. Bad enough that Agnes had gone missing; worse yet to have to deal with the parent of the other girl, poking his nose in—however attractive a nose it might be—and posing questions that might prove inconvenient for everyone.

And by everyone, she meant the Pink Carnation.

The last thing they needed was someone else taking an interest in the matter. Not that she thought there was a matter, of course. Until proven otherwise, she was firmly of the opinion that those empty-headed chits had simply jaunted off on some expedition of their own, never thinking whom they might worry in the process.

Even so, just on the off chance, on the very, very off chance, there were anything more nefarious about it, anything that came in a tricolor package with a faint whiff of frog, much the better to keep it all as under wraps as possible.

Behind her, Gwen could hear Colonel Reid gently quizzing that insipid gudgeon of a French mistress, drawing her out about the number of pupils in the school, their routines, their habits. His accent was a lilting drawl, distinctly un-English without being recognizably anything else. There was a pleasant burr to it, deep and musical. And quite, quite deliberate, Gwen reminded herself. She knew a born rogue when she saw one. There might be threads of silver among the red of Colonel Reid's hair, but that crooked smile was pure danger.

No matter. Gwen was proof against that sort of thing. He wasn't going to get anything out of *her*. She had learned her lesson the hard way—unlike the weak-willed Mlle. de Fayette, who appeared to be lapping it up, relaxing in the Colonel's company, taking the arm he offered to help her up the stairs as she told him everything and anything he wanted to know.

Catching her eye, the Colonel had the effrontery to wink at her.

To wink! As if they were in some sort of conspiracy together. Admittedly, they were the only ones with any wits in the room, but he was a fool if he thought she was going to let herself be drawn in that way.

Stiff backed, Gwen marched up the stairs. The use of charm as a tool made her hackles rise. She respected a more direct approach. A battering ram approach. At least one knew where one stood with the battering ram, none of this butter-wouldn't-melt nonsense that could mean yes, no, or maybe.

Not that Colonel Reid didn't get results that way, she admitted grudgingly. He was doing far better eliciting answers from the French mistress than she had. The woman had simply stared pop-eyed at her. No spine, no spine at all.

"The room, it is this way," said Mlle. de Fayette, gesturing diffidently down the landing. "If you would be so good?"

"Good" wasn't quite the word Gwen would have used. She turned to the French teacher. "How many students on the hall?"

The hallway was far longer than the frontage of an average townhouse. Miss Climpson must have knocked two or three houses together to make up her school. The doors were neatly labeled with the names of the pupils who inhabited them, two or three to a room. The large rooms at the corners appeared to be reserved for those lucky pupils whose parents had secured for them a suite of their own.

"Twenty-two on this floor, twenty-three on the floor above.

The mistresses live on the floor with the students," added Mlle. de Fayette quickly. "I and the games mistress on this floor and two other mistresses on the floor above. That way, there is always someone near."

Twenty-odd students to two teachers? The faculty didn't stand a chance. It was a bit high for the students to try the trellis—not that she'd put it past them—but there were plenty of other ways for an enterprising young lady to effect an inconspicuous exit.

"How many staircases are there?" asked Gwen.

"There are three." Mlle. de Fayette looked mildly surprised at the query. "The front stair and two back stairs."

Gwen exchanged a look with Jane. "Where do the back stairs let out?"

Mlle. de Fayette was beginning to look distinctly nervous. "One by the garden and the other by the alley."

In other words, two potential means of escape. Having seen the standards prevailing in the rest of the school, Gwen would be surprised if the doors were bolted. The main stair was in the middle and the back stairs at either end of the long hallway, presumably the stairs belonging to each of the original houses. It would be ridiculously easy for the girls to wait until the mistresses were distracted at one end to make their escape down the other.

Presuming, of course, they had left of their own volition.

"This is the room," said Mlle. de Fayette, opening the door onto a square chamber the size of one of the small anterooms at the Hotel de Balcourt.

It wasn't an unpleasant room. Two long windows looked out over the scraggle of the back garden, letting in the pale gray light of a rainy day. Water seeped mistily along the window-panes. There was a narrow cot on each side of the room, neatly made with a plain blue blanket, standard issue from the look of it, although Agnes's was embellished by two elaborately embroidered pillows. Fashion papers torn from magazines had been pinned to the whitewashed walls. Two desks gave testament to their owners' personalities, the Reid girl's cluttered with books and papers all jumbled together, Agnes's neatly arranged.

Jane began unobtrusively sorting through the material on Agnes's desk while Gwen, without waiting for leave, opened the wardrobe. Matching white muslin dresses hung from pegs, seemingly all the same. It made it very difficult to ascertain whether any were missing—although, presumably, if the girls had run away, they would have had the sense not to do so wearing the uniform of the school.

One thing, however, was missing. There was no sign of a portmanteau.

Her curiosity whetted, Gwen stood on tiptoe to inspect the top of the wardrobe. Nothing there either. She felt a burst of euphoria. If the girls had taken bags with them, it made it more likely that they had planned their own departure. Kidnappers seldom afforded one time to pack.

"What I don't understand," said Colonel Reid, looking to Mlle. de Fayette with an expression of appeal that Gwen was sure worked beautifully with most women, "is why my Lizzy would choose to run away. Was there any reason she might want to go?"

Mlle. de Fayette shook her head. "Miss Reid seemed of the most happy. She was to play a shepherdess in the spring theatricals. She took the interest most keen in her costume."

"And the other girl?"

"Agnes," Gwen snapped, although the pronouncement lost some force when delivered with her head stuck under the bed. She had found the missing portmanteaux.

Blast and botheration.

"Agnes," repeated Colonel Reid, with an apologetic smile. "Was she happy?"

"Of all the students, Miss Wooliston was the most accomplished in her studies," said Mlle. de Fayette. "The studies were a thing of great interest for her."

Jane had drifted from Agnes's desk to Lizzy's, leafing with seeming nonchalance through the blizzard of debris that coated the surface, not just papers, but bits of ribbons, a broken bit of jewelry, the cheap sort of bracelet one purchased at country fairs, and even a half-eaten biscuit.

"Did the girls receive any letters?" she asked quietly. "Or packages?"

"Miss Wooliston had very little correspondence." Mlle. de Fayette took a deep breath. "Miss Reid had many packages from her brother—in India, sometimes as many as two in a month. There was one just before she left."

"That would be my Alex," said the Colonel, and there was

no mistaking the pride in his voice. "My oldest. He's always taken an interest in the little ones."

Mlle. de Fayette looked up in confusion. "I had not thought— It was not an Alex of which Miss Reid made mention. It was another brother."

"George, then," said the Colonel, nodding knowingly. "He's the closest to Lizzy in age. A good lad."

Gwen squirmed up from under the bed, putting an end to the Reid family reminiscences. She thumped the portmanteaux down on Agnes's bed. "Well, we know one thing. If they left, they didn't take any luggage with them. Their bags are still here."

"If I were running away," said Colonel Reid, a certain reminiscent gleam in his eye, "I shouldn't want to be weighing myself down with baggage. That's a sure way to catch someone's eye. No, I'd be rolling a few things up in a bundle, as small as possible."

As much as Gwen hated the notion of agreeing with Colonel Reid, the idea had merit. "Street clothes beneath their school dresses," she guessed. "They could discard the school dresses later on, in an inconspicuous alleyway. They might even have gone dressed as boys."

Colonel Reid nodded thoughtfully. "Not a bad notion, that. I don't know your Agnes, but our Lizzy could pass as a lad right enough. She'd probably think it a lark."

"Hmm." Gwen pursed her lips. "Well enough for a short period of time, but hardly for two weeks. Unless you're in a

Shakespeare play, breeches roles are difficult to maintain for any length of time."

She must have spoken with a little too much authority, because the Colonel gave her a curious look. Fortunately, she was saved by Jane, who was frowning over a crumpled piece of paper on Lizzy Reid's desk.

"Mademoiselle de Fayette? What was the name of the girls' friend? The one who disclaimed their appearance."

"Fitzhugh," Mlle. de Fayette said promptly, hurrying across the room. "Miss Sally Fitzhugh."

"There's a fragment of a letter, rather blotted"—from what Gwen could see, that was a kind assessment; the letter appeared to be mostly blots—"expressing an intention to shortly pay the recipient a visit. The name on the top isn't Sally, though. It appears to be Kit." Jane turned the letter this way, then that. "Or Kat."

"Kat? That will be my older—" The Colonel broke off, his face lighting up like the royal fireworks on the King's birthday. "That's it! By Gad, I don't know why I didn't think of it before! That's where they'll be." He looked eagerly from Gwen to Jane and back again. "Don't you see? Lizzy will have gone to Kat."

He was all but dancing a jig in the middle of the room.

"To whom?" said Gwen with great attention to diction.

A great smile broke out across Colonel Reid's face. "My older daughter, Katherine. She lives with her grandmother in Bristol. It's as simple as that. She's been all but a mother to Lizzy. Lizzy will have run to her, you mark my words."

"Bristol isn't so very far from here," said Jane slowly. "It's an easy trip by stage."

"That's what it is," said Colonel Reid with great certainty. He let out a gusty waft of air. "She'll have gone to Kat, the minx."

Before Gwen's eyes, Colonel Reid performed a remarkable feat of reverse aging. He seemed to drop ten years in as many minutes, the lines on his face clearing, his back straightening, his eyes glowing. Even his hair seemed springier. He slapped one leg with a resounding smack.

"And after all the bother they've caused! They'll be safe as safe can be with Kat's grandmother. Nothing to worry about at all. Mother Davies is a minister's widow. She'll have them reciting psalms until they're begging to be allowed back."

It was certainly an attractive image, but Gwen wasn't entirely convinced. "If so, why haven't they sent word? Why hasn't Mrs.—"

"Davies," supplied Colonel Reid. His smile lit up his face like a candle. It was a most remarkable effect. His happiness was dizzying. "Mrs. Davies. She's my Kat's grandmother."

"Whatever her name may be," said Gwen crushingly, "you would think she would have written."

"Not if the girls haven't told her they're away without leave," said Colonel Reid cheerfully. "If I know my Lizzy, she'll have told her it's half term, or whatever it is they call it here. She can spin a tale, that one."

His Lizzy wasn't the only one. "Arriving by themselves without luggage?" Gwen said witheringly.

"My Lizzy will have found a way to make it sound entirely plausible," he said. "Trust me."

"After that," said Gwen tartly, "I don't see why I should."

For a moment, the Colonel was taken aback. Then he let out a hearty bark of laughter. "Fair enough! I'll not deny the gift of the gab runs in the family. Come with me, then, and see for yourself." He turned to Jane. "You said it's not far to Bristol?"

"Only two hours by stage," said Jane, who knew the routes of every major method of transportation and the relative travel times involved.

"Well, then," said Colonel Reid, his blue eyes sparkling. "We can be there and back in no time. Shall we go retrieve those erring ewe lambs?"

The full force of Colonel's Reid's smile was a dangerous thing indeed. "The stage will have already gone," said Gwen.

"Tomorrow, then," he said heartily. "I shall call for you in the morning."

"No need," said Gwen coldly. "I can just as easily meet you at the White Hart. The stage leaves from there at—"

"Nine twenty-three," Jane supplied.

"As you like," said Colonel Reid easily. "Then we can collect our wayward lassies and give them the dressing-down of their lives, eh, Miss Meadows? Unless"—he had caught something of the look that had passed between the ladies—"is it not the thing for the chaperone to go unchaperoned? I'm new to these conventions. I can just as easily go myself, and faster, too."

"Nonsense," said Gwen, stung by the implication that she

couldn't go anywhere she chose. "I'm far past the age of scandal."

The Colonel was too happy to be wise. "Hardly that far, Miss Meadows," he said gallantly.

Gwen looked at him loftily. "Flattery will get you nowhere, Colonel Reid."

"Not even to Bristol?"

Was he flirting with her? If so, it was time to put a quick stop to that. "You can try your charm on the stage master," retorted Gwen, "but I suspect he'd prefer hard coin to empty words."

"Sure and that's preferable to hard words and empty coin," the Colonel concurred blandly.

"It's a soft wit that turns hard coin to hard words," said Gwen scornfully.

Colonel Reid waggled his brows. "But a sure wit that turns empty words to hard coin."

Jane and Mlle. de Fayette turned one way and then another, like spectators at a tennis match.

"In that case," said Gwen triumphantly, "you can book our passage for tomorrow, and there are my empty words for your hard coin."

"As they say, touché." Colonel Reid assayed a bow. "Madame, I bow to your powers of persuasion. One passage to Bristol, at your disposal."

"And back," Gwen reminded him.

Colonel Reid caught her eye and grinned. His eyes were blue, pale in his sun-browned face. The lines around them crinkled when he smiled. "And back," he agreed. "It will be my honor and my privilege."

Gwen let out a crack of laughter. "That's doing it a bit too brown, Colonel Reid. It will be your honor, certainly, but many would question the privilege."

"Then," he said, with a courtly tilt of his head, "they are both foolish *and* rude."

Jane cleared her throat slightly. Nobody paid her any mind.

"I look forward to our journey tomorrow," said Colonel Reid cheerfully. "And to retrieving my wayward Lizzy."

"And my wayward Agnes," Gwen reminded him.

Jane cleared her throat again, more loudly.

"We'll herd them safely home," agreed Colonel Reid.

"*If* I might be so bold?"

The Pink Carnation's voice came dangerously close to a shout.

"Forgive me for interrupting." Jane waited until she had their full attention before saying, mildly, "It might be simpler to send a message to Mrs. Davies to make certain the girls are with her. If a note were sent by the mail tonight, you might have a reply by noon tomorrow."

"No," said Gwen decidedly. There was no way she was backing down from this trip now, and the more she thought about it, the more she was certain that the Colonel was right. Where else could the girls have been for two whole weeks without exciting comment? No, they must be with this grandmother in Bristol. "Messages go astray. Let's put an end to this now. Colonel Reid and I will go in the morning and bring the girls back—if they're there," she added, just to put the Colonel in his place.

"Oh, they will be," said the Colonel cheerfully. "They will be. I can't imagine where else they could be."

"You seem rather keen to go to Bristol," commented Jane as they made their way back to the Woolistons' hired house in Laura Place.

She didn't say "with the Colonel," and for that, Gwen was grateful. Jane did show odd inclinations towards matchmaking from time to time.

The rain had stopped and the women had furled their umbrellas. Gwen used hers to poke at a wayward cobble. "I'm keen to get those troublesome chits back. The sooner they're home, the sooner we can get back to doing what we need to do."

"Assuming they're in Bristol," said Jane.

"Why would we assume otherwise? There were no signs of a struggle." Gwen began ticking points off on her gloved fingers. "The schoolmistress said that they were annoyed at the departure of their friend. This Lizzy girl sounds like the sort who would egg Agnes on to run off. And it's ridiculously easy to sneak out of that so-called young ladies' academy. I saw three ways within five minutes."

"I know," said Jane, tucking her chin into her collar. "I know." Then, "Mademoiselle de Fayette seemed quite nervous, didn't she?"

"You would be too, if you had to tell a parent his child had gone missing," retorted Gwen. The change in the Colonel, once he had solved the mystery of his missing child, had been remarkable. He had looked like a sinner who had been assured the hope of salvation.

"I suppose," said Jane.

Gwen looked at her charge with mingled affection and frustration. There were times when Jane's reserve sorely tried her patience. Not that she'd ever pretended to have much of that particular commodity. "What is it, then? Out with it!"

"It's not anything I can put my finger on," said Jane hopelessly. "Just a feeling. I know, I know. I sound like the heroine from one of your novels."

"Not my novel," said Gwen, offended. She had begun working on her novel several years before, and the project was dearer to her than she liked to admit. "My heroine would never indulge in such foolishness."

"I know," said Jane with a slight smile. "She would go charging forward, parasol at the ready."

Once, they had both gone charging forward. This new reluctance on Jane's part . . . Gwen didn't like it.

Gwen rapidly changed the subject. "I'm surprised you were able to find anything on Miss Reid's desk. It looked as though Bonaparte had dropped a shell on it."

"Yes, it was rather mussed, wasn't it?" said Jane. "Whereas Agnes's was . . . almost a little too tidy."

Gwen looked at her shrewdly. "What are you saying?"

Jane picked her way carefully across the rain-slick cobbles. "If you were to search someone's desk, you wouldn't leave it looking as though a shell had exploded. You would put everything back in what you believed to be its place. Wouldn't you?"

Gwen didn't like where this was going. "It seems a trifle extreme to abduct two girls simply to rifle through one desk. And if so, why not the other girl's as well?"

There were dark purple circles beneath Jane's gray eyes. "You know why."

Her silence spoke louder than words. She didn't need words. They had worked together long enough for that. Lizzy Reid's desk would be of no interest to someone looking for anything that might incriminate the Pink Carnation. Agnes's, however, would be.

If someone wanted a bargaining chip, they could have found no surer one than the Pink Carnation's youngest sister.

"It's one thing to put oneself at risk," Jane said in a small, tight voice. "But one's family . . ."

"You're starting at shadows," said Gwen firmly. "It's nothing of the kind, you'll see."

She could tell Jane wasn't convinced. She could tell in the way she pressed her lips together, in the way she stared unseeingly at the street ahead. But all she said was, "I hope you're right."

"Aren't I always?" said Gwen. "I'll even bear with the company of that Colonel tomorrow to give you peace of mind."

"Bear?" Jane raised an expressive brow. "You seemed to be enjoying him, rather."

"The man's a born rogue," said Gwen repressively. "All stuff and no substance. I know the kind. And so ought you, young lady. A rogue's a rogue."

Jane considered that. "A shrewd one, though. I shouldn't think that Colonel Reid is anyone's fool."

Gwen remembered the way he had sparred with her, turning her words in on themselves. No, he was no one's fool, even if he played one for sport. She wasn't sure that was entirely reassuring.

"If there's anything worse than a rogue, it's a shrewd rogue," said Gwen with authority. "Give me your common garden rogue any day, all ego and bluster. But it's just Bristol and back, and then you and I will be back to Paris."

"Hmm," said Jane. "All the same, while you're in Bristol, I might take another look at Agnes's room. Just to be sure."

Chapter 4

London, 2004

We took the train up to London two days later.

They had been relatively peaceful days. Jeremy must have been regrouping for an alternate line of attack, because we didn't find him lurking in the shrubbery, hiding behind the shower curtain, or inviting random film crews onto the grounds. Colin managed to get his characters into two high-speed chases and one Russian mafia kidnapping. And I learned many interesting and entirely useless facts about the plumeria.

Did you know that the flower was named after a seventeenth-century French botanist, Charles Plumier? Neither did I. Given that he had been dead for a good century by the time the jewels of Berar disappeared in the siege of Gawilghur, the bearing of that information on our quest remained dubious. It turned out that there were more than three hundred varieties of the plant, indigenous to all sorts of different places. Wherever it went, though, there appeared to be rather ominous associations: vampires in Malaysia, funerals in Bangladesh.

Was the Plumeria poem meant as a metaphorical way of telling us that the quest for the doomed jewels brought only death and despair?

"I don't think anyone thought it out quite that much," said my boyfriend, with his head buried inside the pages of the London *Times*. "They might have just liked the sound of the word."

I wouldn't necessarily claim that he was avoiding me, but I had the feeling that Colin was getting a little bit burned-out on fun facts about flowers.

Well, *one* of us had to do something to find the lost jewels of Berar.

Not that this had anything to do with my avoiding working on my dissertation. Or the fact that my research had come to an abrupt and uncompromising halt somewhere in the spring of 1805.

No matter where and how I looked, I couldn't find any reference to Miss Jane Wooliston or Miss Gwendolyn Meadows in my sources post-1805. Edouard de Balcourt went on merrily living in the Hotel de Balcourt, toadying up to the Emperor (until the Restoration, at which point he abruptly remembered that his father had been decapitated during the Revolution and he'd never liked that upstart Corsican dictator anyway), but his cousin and her chaperone had left the building. Jane's coded correspondence with Lady Henrietta Dorrington stopped cold in April 1805. Let me rephrase: All of Jane's correspondence stopped cold in April 1805.

Something had happened, something big, and I had no idea what it was. I didn't even know where to begin to look.

I'd found only two leads, both of them tenuous. The first was in Jane's final (coded) letter to Henrietta, in which she made a lighthearted comment about Miss Gwen enjoying a performance by the noted opera singer Aurelia Fiorila in the company of the foreign minister, Talleyrand, on an Oriental topic. Roughly translated, it meant Miss Gwen had eavesdropped on Talleyrand talking to Aurelia Fiorila and it was most likely something to do with the Ottoman Sultan. The timing fit—in the spring of 1805, Napoleon was doing his darnedest to get the Sultan to abandon his old alliance with England and team up with France.

What Aurelia Fiorila had to do with this, though, I had very little idea. Although I did vaguely recall reading something about Selim III having a thing for opera. Or opera singers.

I sincerely hoped this didn't mean the Pink Carnation had upped and swooshed off to the Ottoman court. Istanbul was a very long way from Selwick Hall.

The second, and more useful, tidbit came from the memoirs of Mme. de Treville, one of the Empress Josephine's ladies-in-waiting, almost all of whom had written their memoirs after the Restoration, largely because everyone else was and none of them wanted to be left out. Mme. de Remusat and Mme. Junot had nothing to say about the disappearance of Miss Jane

Wooliston, but Mme. de Treville remarked that the lovely Mlle. Voolston was gone from court with the gracious permission of the Emperor, who had urged her to admonish her parents to keep a closer rein on their daughters. Mme. de Treville, whose literary style was of the "oh and by the way, I forgot to mention" variety, thought it might have something to do with Mlle. Voolston's sister eloping with someone unsuitable, but she wasn't quite sure, and weren't the fashions this season lovely?

Well, that was something, at least. Mme. de Treville wasn't the most reliable of sources, but Napoleon proffering unsolicited parental advice rang true.

Okay, so they'd gone back to England—*if* they were telling Napoleon the truth and not using that as an excuse to hide other, more interesting activities (like Istanbul). I'd done some poking around, and Aurelia Fiorila had been performing in Bath in the spring of 1805. Had Miss Gwen been following Fiorila? Was there really something amiss with Jane's sister? And why, in either case, had they disappeared so entirely off the record after 1805?

There were other avenues I could pursue. Miss Gwen had made use of a plethora of aliases in the past: Ernestine Grimstone, Mrs. Fustian, Lieutenant Triptrap (like Shakespeare, Miss Gwen enjoyed her breeches roles). I could run all of those through the database in the British Library and see what came up; I'd followed that route before, with a certain measure of success.

But it would all take time.

At this point, time was the one thing I didn't have. And instead of using the limited time I had to good purpose, I had been frittering it away, reading up on the blooming habits of genus *Plumeria*. One of Colin's ancestors had obviously been into horticulture; I'd found everything from reprints of Elizabethan herbals to nineteenth-century botanical treatises.

I poked the paper barrier that separated me from Colin. "The only hopeful bit is that 'plumeria' seems to be another name for frangipani."

"Why is that hopeful?" came my boyfriend's muffled voice from between the pages of the *Times*.

"Have you read no M. M. Kaye novels?"

"M. M. who?"

Apparently, he hadn't.

"Frangipani always seems to be blooming profusely around the bungalows of minor British military officers in novels set in colonial India," I explained importantly. "Indian flower . . . missing Indian jewels . . ."

Colin's nose poked up over the top of the newspaper. "Isn't that a bit tenuous?"

I settled back against the nubby back of the seat. "Hey, at this point, I'll take what I can get."

Colin set down the paper, looking at me just a little too thoughtfully. "There's no need to go on with this," he said quietly. "We've known from the start that it's a hopeless project."

I really hoped it was just the hunt for the jewels he was talking about.

"No," I said. "I want to. Now that we've started, it would be a shame to cop out."

Colin raised one brow. "Even if it's a lost cause?"

"Especially if it's a lost cause!" I said, a little too enthusiastically. "Aren't those always the most glamorous kind? Wouldn't you rather be a Cavalier than a Roundhead?"

Colin folded the paper back in on itself. "You're just saying that because you like the hats."

Maybe. "Either way, there's something noble and grand about lost causes."

"Except when they lead to heartbreak and frustration," Colin pointed out sensibly. "After a while, a lost cause ceases to be romantic and just becomes futile."

There was no point in pretending that this was just about the jewels. "Frustration, maybe," I said awkwardly. "But I hope not heartbreak."

"Eloise—"

"*Victoria Station,*" squawked the PA system. "*London, Victoria Station.*"

"Looks like we're here," I said. "Come on."

We were both very quiet the rest of the way to Mrs. Selwick-Alderly's flat in South Kensington.

Colin had to poke me to remind me to get out at South Kensington. Out of sheer force of habit, I'd been ready to stay on until Bayswater. That had been my route to and from Colin's back in the winter when we'd first started dating and I was spending only the odd weekend out at Selwick Hall: Hove to Victoria Station to the Circle Line to Bayswater, where I had my flat.

Only, I no longer had a flat, at least not one here in England.

There was someone else living there now, in the tiny basement studio down the flight of blue-carpeted stairs where the bulb never seemed to be working properly. Someone else would be picking up their mail on the old radiator in the hall and inserting pound coins into the funny little meter at the back of the closet that made the lights go on. I'd given up the flat when my fellowship ran out at the end of May, moving in with Colin at Selwick Hall instead.

This was the first time I'd been back to London since then. It hadn't kicked in until now that it wasn't just an extended long weekend at Colin's, that my flat wasn't still there, waiting for me.

This, I reminded myself, was why I had made the decision to go back to the States—or part of it, at any rate. I wasn't ready to depend so fully on Colin, to subsume my life into his. It was bad enough that I was dependent on his ancestors for my academic credentials.

All the same, I wasn't ready to declare it all over. I hoped Colin wasn't either.

I looked at his profile as we surged through the mob of museum-going tourists, but I couldn't read what he was thinking. I never could. Not an altogether surprising attribute in the descendant of generations of spies, but frustrating all the same.

What did I expect? Lifelong guarantees? Those only came in cereal boxes.

Colin's aunt's flat was just around the corner from the tube stop, on Onslow Square. She was waiting for us at the top of the landing, the door slightly ajar. Behind her, someone was singing in Italian of love and loss—at least, I assumed it was of love and loss. My Italian is limited to "Cappuccino? Grazie!"

"You don't have a soprano hidden away in there, do you?" said Colin.

"Radio 3," said Mrs. Selwick-Alderly, pressing her cheek against mine, then Colin's. "I'll shut it off, shall I?"

"Please," said Colin. It was one of the surprising things I'd discovered about him. The boy was functionally tone-deaf. Any musical performance bored him stiff.

"Philistine," I said. "*I* like it. We brought you these."

I held out the slightly squashed bucket of raspberries that was our offering from the country. I'd like to claim we'd picked them, but we'd bought them from the local farm stand instead.

"Thank you," said Mrs. Selwick-Alderly, taking the container from me with a polite disregard for the effect of raspberry stains on her elegant pale blue pants suit. She glanced over her shoulder. "We can have them with our tea."

Her usual poise was frayed around the edges. In the sitting room, the music abruptly cut off. There was the sound of footsteps against carpeting.

Colin and I exchanged a quick glance.

"Do you have—," began Colin, but he broke off as the source of the steps appeared in the hall.

"Hullo," said Jeremy. "Hot today, isn't it?"

It might be hot, but the atmosphere in the hallway was suddenly distinctly frosty.

"I'll just put these in the kitchen," said Mrs. Selwick-Alderly, and beat a retreat with the raspberries.

It was summer, so Jeremy wasn't wearing his signature black cashmere turtleneck. Instead, he was garbed in a caricature of summer wear, an impeccably tailored white linen suit that looked like a novelist's idea of what gentlemen might wear to go boating. Which, of course, no one would ever actually wear to go boating, since it would get all streaked and muddy within five minutes, but, hey, why let reality interfere? All he needed was a straw boater and an ivory-headed cane.

"Eloise," he said, and pressed crocodile kisses to my cheeks, first right, then left.

Oh, we were on first-name terms now, were we?

"Jeremy," I said, and gave him my most polite social smile, the one you give to people about five minutes before you rush off to the ladies' room to spread vicious calumnies about them behind their backs. "How's business?"

He winced slightly at my crassness. Business. So American. "Don't let's stand here," he said, with false bonhomie. "Come. Sit down."

He led the way into the sitting room as though it was his by right. Although, I supposed, in a way it was. Mrs. Selwick-Alderly was Jeremy's grandmother. A grandson trumped a great-nephew in the familial pecking order. I was used to thinking of Mrs. Selwick-Alderly's flat as Colin's London pied-à-terre. I had never stopped to think that there might be someone with a greater right.

There was no fire lit in the sitting room at this time of year. The windows had been left slightly ajar to catch whatever breeze might be ruffling the leaves of the trees in the square.

No air conditioners marred the woodwork of the window frames. Otherwise, the room was much as I remembered it, high ceilinged and airy, glossy coffee table books scattered across the cocktail table. The twin portraits of Amy Balcourt and Lord Richard Selwick smirked down from their places on the wall.

Mrs. Selwick-Alderly returned, sans raspberries. If she had been anyone else, I would have suspected her of just having a quick nip in the kitchen. I would have. "I just put the kettle on," she said, seating herself in a straight-backed chair at a right angle to the sofa. "I trust you're having a pleasant summer?"

"Yes, it's been lovely," I said guardedly.

"Sussex *is* beautiful this time of year," said Jeremy blandly. "I do hope you're enjoying it."

I cast a quick sideways glance at Mrs. Selwick-Alderly. I didn't know if she knew that I'd given up my basement flat to live with her great-nephew—or what she would think if she did. I knew she liked me, but there was a great difference between liking someone as a historical protégée and liking someone as a potential great-niece.

If she knew, it didn't show on her face. There was only polite interest.

"How much longer are you in England?" she asked.

I perched uncomfortably on the edge of my seat. "Two months," I said, before Jeremy could say anything. "I head back to the States in August. I'm teaching a full course load this semester."

"Head teaching fellow," said Colin proudly. The fondness in his voice made my heart swell, like the Grinch's growing too many sizes all at once.

"They couldn't find anyone else to do it," I said. "It's the horrible Modern Europe survey course, the one they stick all the non-history majors in and a bunch of cranky medievalists who need to make up their modern credits."

"Does that mean you've found everything you needed to find in our little archive?" asked Jeremy smoothly.

What was this "our"? They were Colin's documents, Colin's archives. Jeremy might be married to Colin's mother, but that didn't make the house his. More than that, I didn't like this attempt to make me into the outsider—even if I was.

"It would take a lifetime to go through it all," I said, addressing myself to Mrs. Selwick-Alderly. I had, I realized, gone into schoolgirl mode. My hands were clasped in my lap, my legs were crossed at the ankle, I was sitting on the very edge of my seat, and my voice had gone up half an octave. Five more minutes of this and I would start apologizing for having snuck out of gym class. "But if I don't start writing it up soon, I'll never get my degree."

"You've found everything you need, and now it's time to go," said Jeremy understandingly. The implication was unmistakable.

My hands clenched into fists in my lap. "I wouldn't exactly put it that way." He wanted to play dirty? Fine. I looked Colin's cousin straight in the eye. "I'd say there's still plenty to be found at Selwick Hall. Wouldn't you?"

I had the satisfaction of seeing Jeremy's eyes slide away. Ha. Take that.

"That's the kettle," said Mrs. Selwick-Alderly, with some relief. Her hearing had to be keener than mine; I hadn't heard anything at all. "Will you help me, Eloise?"

I wasn't sure about the wisdom of leaving Colin alone with Jeremy, but I knew a command when I heard one.

"Certainly!" I said, and wiggled up off my chair. With all the sitting on the train, the skirt of my sundress was irreparably rumpled. I made one abortive effort to smooth it and gave up, too aware of Jeremy's smirk.

Mrs. Selwick-Alderly rose with less than her usual ease. She moved stiffly, as though her hip pained her. I wondered, for the first time, if her request for help had less to do with leaving the cousins together to sort things out and more to do with actually needing help. For all her energy, she had to be in her mideighties, at least. She was Colin's grandfather's younger sister, and Colin had been a fairly late-life baby. His father had been a good generation older than my parents.

"Shall I help?' asked Colin, watching his aunt with concern.

"No, no," said Mrs. Selwick-Alderly. "We won't be long, will we, Eloise?"

Especially not if one of them started screaming. The second either of them yelled bloody murder, I'd be back down that hall like a shot, tea or no tea.

"Do you think they'll be all right in there?" I murmured as we made our way down the hall, past the dining room and the guest bedroom I had stayed in back in October, the night I'd met Colin.

Just to be clear, I wasn't staying in it with Colin. That was before he had been brought to an acute awareness of my manifold charms.

"I don't think either is going to go after the other with the letter opener." Mrs. Selwick-Alderly preceded me into the kitchen. "At least, I hope not."

The door swung shut behind me, noiseless on its well-oiled hinges. We were too far down the hall to hear anything that went on in the sitting room. By the same token, they were too far away to hear us.

I took advantage of that to ask, "Why do they hate each other so much?"

What I really wanted to know, of course, was why Jeremy hated Colin. As far as I could tell, the feud might be two-sided now, but only because Jeremy had started it.

But I couldn't very well say that to Jeremy's grandmother.

Mrs. Selwick-Alderly slowed in the act of setting cups and saucers out on a tray, the same lacquered tray she had used the first time I had been to tea in her flat. But all she said was, "Would you mind pouring the water? There should be leaves in the pot."

There were, a generous scoop of them, some variety of orange pekoe, at a guess. A gypsy fortune-teller might have used them to divine the future. I squinted down at them, but they told me nothing, so I poured the boiling water over them instead, trapping the aromatic steam with the china lid.

I looked over my shoulder at Mrs. Selwick-Alderly, who was

setting biscuits out on a tray: ginger biscuits and Colin's favorites, the dark-chocolate-covered McVities. I wondered if the others, the ginger biscuits, were for Jeremy.

"It hasn't been easy for Jeremy," she said, so abruptly that I nearly dropped the lid of the teapot. "Growing up in the shadow of Selwick Hall."

I didn't know what to say. So I didn't say anything at all. I just stood there, holding the teapot like an idiot.

"It's my fault, really." She turned and took the teapot from me, setting it on the tray with a muted clink. "Filling him full of stories about his ancestors. He would have done better without them. He might have been . . . more free."

"He seems to be pretty successful," I said. It was the most neutral thing I could think of to say. None of the other possibilities were complimentary.

Mrs. Selwick-Alderly was lost in her own thoughts. "His father died so young. He was army," she added, belatedly remembering my presence. "Jamie—he was Jamie then; he only changed his name to Jeremy later, when he started dabbling in the art world—was shuttled around from place to place and person to person. It was no life for a child."

I wasn't sure that excused the adult, but I held my tongue.

"He always wanted what Colin had," she said, and set the sugar bowl down on the tray.

"Selwick Hall?"

"No," said Mrs. Selwick-Alderly with a wry half-smile. "Well, yes, but not just the Hall. The poor boy wanted to belong. He wants so very badly to belong."

"He's making Colin's life miserable," I blurted out. "Did you know about—"

"Yes. I know." Mrs. Selwick-Alderly's lips thinned into a determined line. "And I intend to put a stop to it. Would you be so good as to take the tray?"

She had never let me carry the tray before. I hoped she was okay. I was also confused. I hefted the tray.

"How?" I asked.

But she didn't answer. Fairy godmothers never do.

I trailed after her to the sitting room, awkwardly clutching the heavy tray. I'd overfilled the teapot; the spout showed a dangerous inclination to leak on the biscuits.

Personally, I didn't see how anyone was going to stop Jeremy, short of a restraining order. Or a mallet.

I favored the mallet.

I set the tray down with a thump on a cleared patch on the table. After months of lifting nothing heavier than a folio volume, my arm muscles were protesting the weight of the tray. Mrs. Selwick-Alderly sat down serenely in her usual chair.

"I know why you're both here," she said, conversationally. "Biscuit?"

Colin took a biscuit. It was one of the ones that had got tea sogged. I made an apologetic face.

"To see you, of course," said Jeremy smoothly.

His grandmother gave him a look I wouldn't exactly call doting. "You're treasure hunting, both of you." She made them sound like little boys in a sandbox. "And you want me to help you."

"I wouldn't call it treasure hunting—," Jeremy began.

"Eloise wanted—," trotted out my loyal boyfriend.

"Don't look at me!" I hastily put in.

Mrs. Selwick-Alderly overrode us all without raising her voice. It was an impressive trick, that. "Did you really think I would help one of you against the other?" she said.

From their faces, it was very clear that each had.

"I am your grandson—," began Jeremy, just as Colin started with, "Selwick Hall—"

"I don't know where the jewels are," Mrs. Selwick-Alderly said, effectively squelching them both. I cowered quietly by the teapot. "I don't even know if they exist. But I will tell you what I know—on one condition."

The room was so quiet, you could have heard a biscuit drop on the carpet.

The biscuit was mine, and it was one of the ginger ones. I hastily scooped it up again.

"What's the condition?" asked Colin. He had a smudge of chocolate on his upper lip, which made him look endearingly like Charlie Chaplin, if Charlie Chaplin were large, blond, and distinctly wary.

Mrs. Selwick-Alderly looked from her grandson to her great-nephew before dropping her bombshell.

"That you work together."

Chapter 5

"Come!" cried Plumeria. "We must away! There is some old treachery within these walls—far darker and deeper than even the vaults beneath the Convent itself, a secret so dark and deep that the very walls must quake to hear of it."

"But my daughter," protested Magnifico. "What of she? I cannot leave without—"

"Sir," quoth wise Plumeria. "If your child you would save, you must first save yourself. But haste! A carriage waits, even as we speak! I shall tell you more, ere this!"

—From *The Convent of Orsino* by A Lady

G wen arrived early at the White Hart the following morning.

She preferred to be first. It gave one such a sense of moral superiority, not to mention forcing the other party into unnecessary and demeaning apologies.

It was always good to set the proper tone from the beginning.

It was busy at the White Hart, ostlers running to and fro, men shouting for their parcels, farmwives bustling in with baskets of produce. A small cluster of people by the door of the inn looked as though they might also be waiting for the stage, a schoolboy and his tutor, from the look of it, and a rather greasy man with more chins than the good Lord usually thought to provide.

There was a commotion at the entrance to the inn as a man stormed out, demanding that his carriage be made ready *at once*, at once, did they hear?

Gwen would have been surprised if they hadn't heard him in Bristol.

"Yes, Lord Henry, at once, Lord Henry," murmured the landlord, with more forelock tugging than was strictly necessary.

Gwen didn't know the man, but she knew the type: the cloak with too many capes, the hat with the too-curly brim, the jangle of far too many watch fobs. He wore a very flashy ring with a large red stone on one hand. In short, overbred and underoccupied. Gwen gave him a wide berth as she strolled across the courtyard, using her trusty parasol to ward off an inquisitive fowl who had the audacity to peck at her petticoat.

If Colonel Reid were right, Agnes and her friend would most likely have caught the coach for Bristol in this very yard. Yes, decided Gwen, it would be easy enough for a pair of girls disguised as lads to lose themselves in a place such as this, among the bustle and din. All they would need would be a story about traveling home from school or on their way to school and no one would give them a second glance. There were several such in the inn yard at the moment, including two gawky lads of roughly thirteen who were taking turns eating an apple and ogling a poster on the wall, featuring a woman wearing a variety of veils in what Gwen could only assume was meant to be the Oriental fashion—Oriental, that is, as imagined by the proprietors of the Theatre Royal.

The woman's hair was a very vivid and familiar auburn.

Gwen shooed the boys off with her parasol, clearing them out of the way so that she could see. The poster had been slapped haphazardly over another, creating an odd effect of shadow images, half-seen through the cheap layers of paper and paste, so that the veiled lady appeared to be shadowed by a dark creature standing just behind. Despite the relative warmth of the morning, Gwen felt a cold sense of foreboding as she read the bold print below the picture.

"Artaxerxes!" the poster proclaimed. A new production at the Theatre Royal in Sawclose. The title role was to be played by Nicolas Peretti. As for the role of Semira . . .

The role of Semira was to be played by Aurelia Fiorila.

That same Aurelia Fiorila whose famed voice Gwen had last heard not raised in song, but lowered in supplication as she pleaded with Bonaparte's foreign minister.

It wasn't entirely surprising to find her back in England. As far as most were concerned, she had never left it. Fiorila had, officially, been sick with the influenza and then "resting" for the past several months. This particular performance might have been prepared months or even years before. Bath was busy right before the start of the Season; it was a logical place for a singer to gravitate. Many did.

But not Fiorila. Her contract was with the Opera House in the Haymarket. She had sung for the Prince of Wales in Brighton at a command performance, but never before in Bath.

Gwen didn't believe in coincidences, not as a rule. What was there in Bath—in Bath, of all places!—to draw Talleyrand's agent? Somehow, she doubted Fiorila was here to take the waters.

"Miss Meadows?"

"Hmm?" She was so engrossed in the playbill that she only vaguely registered someone saying her name.

"Miss Meadows?"

She started, bumping into the man standing behind her. "Colonel Reid!" She covered her confusion with a stern, "You're late."

"I'm just on time," the Colonel countered with easy good humor. "You're early."

Since it was true, there was very little Gwen could say to that, so she contented herself with a quelling, "Hmph. Let us hope the coach will be equally timely."

She subjected the Colonel to a sweeping scrutiny. He bore little resemblance to the rumpled, travel-stained man of yesterday. His breeches and jacket, while still too comfortably cut for fashion, were impeccably clean, his exuberant red hair brushed to sleekness. The sun glinted silver off the white streaks in his hair, but his smile was brighter by far.

"I've cleaned beneath my nails, too," he said teasingly. "And brought a clean pocket handkerchief."

Gwen gave him a look. "I am not your governess, Colonel Reid."

She had never been a governess. She had contemplated it once, briefly, in the miserable period after her father's death, but the idea of being dependent on a strange family, neither guest nor servant, was even more unpalatable than being dependent on the family she knew. Better to be Aunt Gwen, with a room on the floor with the rest of the family, than Miss Meadows, relegated to the attics and sent a tray in her room for supper.

Colonel Reid gave a shout of laughter. "I should think not," he said. "You'd have been in the nursery while I was in the schoolroom. I've a decade on you, I'm sure."

Gwen frowned. "I'm older than you think."

She'd spent so much time working on appearing older than she was, making herself properly fearsome to the young. Age was the only leverage the penniless spinster had. Age and illness, but she refused to be one of those carping maiden aunts, taking to her bed of pain with hartshorn in order to gain the simulation of affection. She had chosen to be fearsome instead.

The Colonel, however, did not seem properly intimidated.

The Colonel's lips quirked in a smile. "In spirit, perhaps, Miss Meadows—that I'll grant you—but not in years." He nodded to the poster in front of them. "Are you a devotee of the opera, Miss Meadows?"

"Of the—oh." Blast the man, he had thoroughly discommoded her, treating her like a sprig of a green girl. She shrugged a shoulder, glad that she was wearing her best traveling dress, tailored in Paris, and designed to put upstart Anglo-Indian army officers in their place. "I take an interest." Especially when the star soprano happened to be employed by Bonaparte's slippery foreign minister. "It depends on the production."

"I've always been one for Mozart myself," said Colonel Reid. "There's a nice bounce to his music, and it always all comes out right in the end."

"Hardly realistic," Gwen shot back.

"Neither is singing out one's woes at the top of one's lungs," countered Colonel Reid. He grinned. "When was the last time you've done that? With an orchestra to follow one about, no less."

"Most of the orchestras I've encountered," said Gwen, "are remarkably stationary."

The lines at the corners of Colonel Reid's eyes crinkled. "Do you ever allow anyone else the last word, Miss Meadows?"

"Not if they haven't wit enough to seize it," said Gwen.

"That," said Colonel Reid, "sounds remarkably like a challenge."

Oh, he wanted a challenge, did he? Gwen was about to put him quite soundly in his place—she wasn't quite sure how, but she was certain she could have come up with something—when the same arrogant young lordling she had seen before shoved past them, making for a curricle that was just being drawn up in the courtyard.

"What took you so bloody long?"

"Apologies, my lord. The horses were spavined, the tack was frayed, and the replacements delayed—"

"I don't care if they were stayed, flayed, and spayed," said the young man arrogantly, climbing up onto the high perch. He reached out impatiently for the reins. "Well, give me that!"

The landlord handed over the reins, murmuring apologies.

"For your troubles," said the lordling, and tossed a coin in the air. It glinted dully, copper rather than gold, before landing in the churned mud. The landlord jumped out of the way as the curricle shot forward, the horses' hooves kicking up clods of dirt as they went. The horses, fresh and restive, pulled at the bit, yanking the carriage sideways, straight at Gwen.

Before she could even get a grip on her trusty parasol, she found herself flung back against the wall, the Colonel pressed against her, shielding her with his body.

Flecks of mud spattered the wall next to them. There was the sound of men cursing and horses whinnying and geese squawking.

"Are you all right?" the Colonel asked, looking down at her with concern.

"I would be"—they were pressed together, front to front, the buttons of the Colonel's coat biting into her chest, his hands braced against the wall on either side of her arms—"if I could breathe."

He looked at her quizzically. They were close enough that she could make out the faint hint of a scar beside his lip, close enough to kiss.

Where had that ridiculous thought come from?

Gwen mustered the breath to say, "Your buttons, Colonel. I

am sure they are most attractive, but they are also rather poking."

"What? Oh! My apologies!" The Colonel gallantly removed himself from her person, looking her over with a concerned eye. "You are unharmed? That idiot in the curricle . . ."

"Perfectly," said Gwen crisply. She bent to retrieve her parasol, noting, as she stood, that there was a gash across the poster of Fiorila. The carriage lamp must have ripped right across.

She had been standing directly in front of that poster, her nose on a level with Fiorila's bisected bust.

The Colonel had noticed as well. "Young buck," he said with heat, frowning after the rapidly disappearing curricle. "He'll get himself or someone else killed if he goes on like that."

"More likely someone else," remarked Gwen with some asperity. She could still feel the impression of Colonel Reid's buttons pressing against her chest. If he hadn't thrown her to the side . . . She'd give him one thing, no matter his ridiculous banter—his reflexes were good. She shook out her skirt with more force than necessary. "That type has more lives than a cat."

"And the morals of one, too," agreed Colonel Reid. "We get a fair number of that kind in India, sent off by their families or out for adventure. They cause more trouble than they're worth."

There was a note of authority in his voice that hadn't been there before. Despite herself, Gwen found herself taking notice of her companion. "How long were you in India, Colonel Reid?"

"Most of my life," he said, his bright blue eyes looking out across the courtyard at lands far, far away. "I came there as a lad of sixteen and never thought to go anywhere else. It's a grand place, Miss Meadows, a grand place."

He held out his arm to her and she took it, picking her way across the courtyard with him towards the newly arrived stage. "And yet you chose to come back here."

"It's not back for me," he said. "I was born in the Carolinas. In America," he clarified, and seemed amused by the expression of horror on his companion's face. "It's not so wild as that, Miss Meadows. I spent my youth in Charleston, which is as fine a city as you'll find."

Gwen deeply doubted that. It was in the Americas, after all. Any colony that wantonly rebelled against its rightfully ordained monarch didn't know what was good for it. "Why leave it, then?"

"Why does any youth do what he does? A longing for adventure, a thirst for new worlds—and, of course, the desire to thumb one's nose at one's parents." He gallantly gave her a boost up into the carriage, his hand sturdy on the small of her back. "Not that you'd know anything about that, Miss Meadows, a paragon of virtue such as you are."

For some reason, this irked her. "I was young once too," she said sharply.

So painfully, painfully young. She had been such a fool back then, so convinced of her own innate wisdom and superiority.

She was still convinced of those things, but with a difference; now she'd earned it, through hard experience and grinding humiliation.

"You're still young," said Colonel Reid, settling himself into the seat behind her.

"I'd have you know that I count four decades to my credit— and a half!" Take that. One couldn't quibble with forty-five. "I'm well on the way to my half century."

"As I said," said Colonel Reid, his lips twitching in a most unfair way, "a mere sprig of a girl. Now, I've my half century and a few years plus that."

"And burnt brown for most of them," said Gwen acidly.

"The sun in India will do that to a man," said the Colonel amiably. "But I don't see you as the sort to bundle under a bonnet and hide away from the sun."

The man was too perceptive by half. A shrewd rogue, Jane had called him, and she was right. Not that it mattered. They would collect the girls and Colonel Reid would be well away out of her life again.

"The situation has never arisen," said Gwen crushingly. "The climate of Shropshire is far from tropical."

The tutor and his charge took their seats in the stage across from them, the schoolboy showing a lamentable tendency to squirm. The man with many chins considered the schoolboy and then made an ill-advised attempt to squeeze in next to Gwen instead, squashing her against the side of the Colonel.

"Impossible!" she fumed. "Sir, there is no room for you on this bench."

"Na, there's room right enough," said the man, the lower sort of clerk by his accent, wiggling his ample backside in the space on the seat that ought by right to have been hers.

"You might try the other side," suggested the Colonel politely.

Squashed up against him, Gwen couldn't see his face, but she didn't like the hint of amusement in his voice.

"And sit next to that young scamp!" The clerk nodded at the schoolboy, who had taken out a small cage with what looked like crickets in it and was engaged in poking at them with a stick. "Can't believe the sort they let on the stage these days, can you?"

"No," said Gwen coldly.

Behind her, she felt the rumble of the Colonel's chest as he chuckled.

Hmph. If he thought it was amusing to have her all but sitting on his lap, so be it. Gwen made her spine as straight as it would go, a rather difficult feat given that she was tucked up against the Colonel's side.

"Comfortable, Miss Meadows?" he asked heartily.

Gwen didn't dignify that with a response.

The coach rocked, none too steadily, into motion. Ignoring her companions, Gwen pointedly opened her reticule and took out her notebook and a small black lead pencil. She had got lamentably behind on her writing recently.

Plumeria had just joined forces with Sir Magnifico to find the missing Amarantha—who, in Gwen's opinion, could just as well stay lost. She had penned her as a parody of the common Gothic heroine, always cringing and whinging. When it came down to Amarantha and the villain, Gwen's sympathies, such as they were, were with the villain. He had no idea what he had kidnapped, but the poor man was rapidly finding out.

Plumeria, on the other hand . . . Now, there was a heroine.

Forced by dire circumstance into the role of companion and chaperone to the insipid Amarantha, Plumeria was a lady of good family (Gwen had toyed with making her a dethroned princess but decided it was trite; besides, she disapproved of excessive alliteration) with an extensive classical education, as well as knowledge of indigenous plants and swordplay. So far, she had already thwarted a poisoning attempt, bested the villain in a fencing contest, and cracked a riddle couched in the thorniest sort of classical Greek. The only reason the villain had managed to get away with Amarantha—aside from it being a necessary part of the plot—was because the Mother Superior of the cursed Convent of Orsino was secretly Amarantha's mother's sister's former bosom friend turned sworn enemy, who had vowed revenge on Lilibelle and all of her seed. Or her sister's seed, as the case might be. "Seed" was a very broad term.

Amarantha should satisfy the critics who wanted to see their heroines young and nubile—Gwen had plans to marry her off eventually to an especially insipid young princeling—but the chaperone was the real heroine of the piece.

Currently, Plumeria and Sir Magnifico were being set upon by a band of Gypsies unleashed upon them by the Mother Superior. The Gypsies were attacking Plumeria tooth, nail, and with flying monkeys. Fortunately, Plumeria had practiced on flying squirrels, so the monkeys proved little challenge. Back to back, she and Sir Magnifico, wielding his mammoth broadsword, were beating back the Gypsies, when, suddenly, from the caravan leapt—

"No, no," said Colonel Reid over her shoulder. "If you deploy them like that, the Gypsies will cut off their left flank."

"Colonel Reid!" Gwen slammed her notebook shut.

"So you're writing a novel, are you?"

On her other side, the clerk had descended into slack-lipped snoring. The tutor and his charge were scrabbling on the ground, attempting to find the presumably escaped crickets. Gwen pulled her feet in closer. She'd forgotten how much she hated the stage. "Has anyone ever told you that it's rude to read over other people's shoulders?"

"I can't help it," said Colonel Reid. "I'm taller than you are."

"That," said Gwen severely, "is a poor excuse of an excuse."

"You know," he said, ignoring her censure entirely, "that scene wouldn't be half bad if you'd drop that bit where the wizened old Gypsy crone curses them for all eternity and skip straight to the flying monkeys instead. I liked the flying monkeys."

Everyone was a critic. "I'll have you know that Gypsy curses are very popular this season," said Gwen loftily.

"'May you be doomed to roam the night like a creature of the night'?" The Colonel's mobile face wrinkled. "It just lacks a certain something. As curses go."

Gwen tucked her notebook firmly back into her bag. "Do you have your daughter's direction in Bristol?" she asked pointedly. This wasn't, after all, a pleasure jaunt.

Insufficient malediction indeed!

"Yes," he said. "I've never been, but the girls have described it to me so often I feel as though I've been through every room. It's Kat's grandmother's house," he added, by way of explanation. "My wife's mother."

"Yes, I know. The minister's wife," said Gwen, before the curious construction of his phrasing struck her. Kat's grandmother; not the girls' grandmother, not Lizzy's grandmother, just Kat's.

The house was in a quiet neighborhood a brisk walk from the posting inn. It wasn't a fashionable or an overly affluent area, but the houses were tidy and well maintained, with curtains at the windows and boot scrapers by the doors. The house to which the innkeeper at the posting inn had directed them had a corner plot, set back enough to allow room for a patch of yard and a stone path leading up to the door. Gwen saw the curtains twitch and drop again as they walked down the path.

"It looks just as my Kat described it," said the Colonel with deep satisfaction. "Lavender bushes and an apple tree in the yard. Many's the letter I've had from her written from that bench, just there. Hello," he said to the maid who opened the door. "Is Miss Katherine in?"

"Miss who?" The maid was doing a very creditable village idiot impression.

"Miss Reid," interjected Gwen. "We are looking for Miss Reid."

"Begging your pardon, ma'am," said the maid, "but there's no one of that name here."

She started to close the door.

The Colonel stepped forward, blocking her. "Will you tell Mrs. Davies we're here, then?"

"Mrs. Davies?" The maid had to think for a moment. "Oh, you mean the old minister's wife. She doesn't live here anymore."

"But—" The Colonel's face was a study in confusion. He looked at the lavender, at the apple tree, at the bench in the yard. "That can't be—"

The maid, having remembered, went right on remembering. "It's been—oh, three years now. No, four, since it was the winter my mistress had the pleurisy and the bottom burnt out of the kettle."

"Where does she live now?" Gwen asked crisply, before the domestic catalogue could go on. "Mrs. Davies."

"I don't rightly—yes, I do know!" The lappets on the maid's cap bobbed.

"Would you care to *tell* us?" Gwen prompted.

"If you'd be so good," the Colonel put in. His ingratiating smile had gone rather frayed around the edges. He fished in his threadbare purse and pressed a coin into the maid's hand. "With this for your troubles."

The coin unleashed a complicated spate of directions. The maid's directions led them down towards the docks, to a neighborhood that made Gwen take a firmer grip on her trusty parasol. The houses could be called ramshackle at best, paint peeling scabrously off the sides, betraying the crumbling brickwork below. To say that the gutters were inadequate was to do them a disservice; they were barely functional, which didn't seem to deter the wretch who sat splay legged in one, holding a gin bottle clutched in his or her arms. The gender was indeterminate. The smell of gin was strong. Even that, however, was preferable to the other smells that pervaded the area.

"This can't be right," said the Colonel, looking around him with furrowed brow.

"We've followed the maid's directions exactly." Gwen hated to admit it, but her feet were starting to pinch. She wasn't sure what had possessed her to wear her new boots. Other than the fact that they were dyed a delightful purple that exactly matched her traveling costume. After walking a few yards down this particular road, they were no longer quite so delightfully purple. "It has to be here."

"She might have been making it up," the Colonel argued. "Or got muddled."

"She sounded quite certain to me," said Gwen, treading delicately around a patch of something she'd sooner not examine closely. "Fifth house on the left, she said. There it is."

Like all the others on the street, the house was tall and narrow, clinging to its fellows on either side, with a peaked roof and uneven shutters. It looked a bit like an emaciated and inebriated man attempting to maintain his balance.

The house had been broken up into lodgings by floor. Following the maid's direction, they went, not to the front steps, but to the side. A very narrow alley led into a dispirited yard. There was a large wash pot on the boil over a makeshift stove. Laundry in various stages of drying hung from ropes strung across the yard.

"No," said the Colonel. "This can't be right."

"We'll never know until we try," said Gwen, and rapped smartly on the door with the handle of her parasol. There was, unsurprisingly, no knocker.

"Yes?" The door opened with gratifying promptness, and a woman stepped out into the yard, blinking in the light. Her accent didn't go at all with the redness of her hands, or the laundry tub propped against one hip. Her dark red hair had been pulled sternly back from her face, knotted at the base of her neck, partly covered with a white kerchief. "If you've come about—"

Catching sight of the Colonel, she broke off midsentence.

Her eyes weren't blue like the Colonel's; they were a dark brown, almost black. But there was no mistaking the family resemblance. She had the same broad cheekbones, the same generous lips, even if hers were tucked into a firm, straight line.

Since the Colonel appeared incapable of speech, Gwen took it upon herself. "Miss Katherine Reid, I presume?" she said.

Chapter 6

The trees crowded close overhead, blotting out the feeble rays of the setting sun. Above their caravan, a raven cawed. It was a forsaken place, more desolate by far than the cursed convent they had fled.

"My mind mislikes this forest much," quoth Sir Magnifico.

Plumeria could not find it in herself to disagree.

—From *The Convent of Orsino* by A Lady

"Kat?"

William pushed past Miss Meadows, his eyes fixed on his daughter.

He felt like a man caught in a dream—or a nightmare. It was Kat, but not Kat. Older, thinner, harder than the seventeen-year-old he had put, protesting, on that launch in Calcutta. But it was Kat's voice, Kat's voice and her eyes, so like those of her twin brother, Alex. Maria's eyes.

For a moment, her eyes lit like they used to when she was a little girl, when he would come home and she would run to him and fling her arms around his neck as he hugged her close, swinging her round and round in circles until she squealed in delight.

"Father?" she said, and the wariness in her voice broke his heart. His daughter looked at him in confusion. "What are you doing here?"

Miss Meadows looked around at the spare yard, at the laundry hanging on the line. Her nose wrinkled against the smell of wet washing and boiled cabbage. "We were going to ask the same of you."

Kat's face hardened. "I don't believe we've been introduced," she said in a tone of dangerous politeness.

Miss Meadows was unfazed. "I," she said, "am Miss Gwendolyn Meadows."

Kat looked from Miss Meadows to her father. "Are felicitations in order?" said his daughter in a brittle voice.

She thought he was here because—

"What? No!" said William. He'd met the woman yesterday! Even he didn't work that fast.

"You needn't sound like *that* about it," said Miss Meadows. "Are you going to embrace your daughter, or shall we continue to stand on this somewhat insalubrious doorstep while you make your belated amends to your neglected offspring?"

Miss Meadows's ringing tones resonated throughout the little yard.

By a miracle, Kat actually smiled. She set down the washtub on a wooden block and gestured to the door. "Please do come in. I'm afraid it's not any more salubrious inside, Miss Meadows."

Miss Meadows subjected his daughter to a long, assessing look. "You may call me Miss Gwen."

She made it sound like a mark of royal favor.

William had to duck his head to keep from hitting it on the low doorframe as he went in.

He followed numbly after the two women into a sitting room that looked as though it were kitchen and dining room and everything else besides. A large hearth, with a bench beside it, provided cooking and sitting area all in one. The rough collection of cooking instruments stood in harsh contrast to the delicate marquetry card table on one side of the room and the blue-and-white porcelain in the corner cabinet.

William recognized the paired portraits that hung on the roughly whitewashed walls in oval gilded frames: Maria's grandparents on her mother's side, prosperous merchants from Cardiff. It was their money that had been set aside, that was supposedly supporting Maria's mother in her old age.

What had happened to that money? Why were they living here, like this? If he'd known . . . When he'd written to Maria's mother, eleven years past, to tell her about his dilemma with the girls, she'd written back that she had a pleasant house in a good part of town, with a bit of a garden where her flowers grew. He'd imagined the girls, sitting winding wool for their grandmother in that bit of a garden, flowers blooming around them, so different from the punishing seasons of India, the heat, the dust, the bugs, the monsoon.

Instead, he had found his older daughter in a basement,

cooking on an open hearth, boiling her laundry on a scrap of dirt where no flowers could ever hope to bloom.

"Tea?" said Kat, going to the kettle that hung on a hook over the fire. She seemed determined to preserve the amenities, whatever the circumstances.

Would she have behaved otherwise if he had shown up alone? He didn't know. He couldn't tell whether that reserve was directed at his companion or at him.

"Kat . . . ," William said, scrounging for his wits. "What are you doing here?"

Kat's lips pressed into a thin line. "I live here," she said.

"But, surely . . ." William didn't know what to say. He'd known people in England didn't live as they did in India, that lodgings and servants were more expensive, but this wasn't even genteel retrenchment; this was poverty, pure and simple. "What about your grandmother? Is she—"

"She's here," said Kat quickly. "She's in her room."

Her room. There were two doors opening off the far wall, one on either side. Bedrooms, presumably. William's incredulous eyes took in the peeling paint, the crooked portraits. "What happened to the house with the yard, with the lavender? Why didn't you tell me?"

Kat's face set. "There was nothing to tell." She had always been stubborn, his Kat, as stubborn as a mule. "We get by."

From the other room rose a piteous cry. "Maria?"

William felt the hairs prickle on the back of his neck. It was his mother-in-law's voice, but as he had never heard it before, thin and weak and querulous. The Mrs. Davies he had known had been a brisk, bustling little brown berry of a woman, with a sense of humor that offset her husband's more sanctimonious excesses.

"Maria? Who's there?"

"Excuse me," said Kat with dignity. "She forgets sometimes. I'll be back in a moment."

William sat heavily on one of the chairs by the card table. The legs wobbled but held. The room swam in front of his eyes. He felt as though he had been punched, hard, in the gut. This was so far from his imaginings of the way his daughters had lived, the way they had allowed him to imagine they lived.

Miss Meadows raised her brows at him.

"I had no idea," he said heavily. "No idea."

"That," said Miss Meadows succinctly, "is very clear. Unless I'm much mistaken, your daughter has been taking in other people's washing. There were male unmentionables on that line. In a variety of sizes."

William barely felt the sting of it. He was too numb from the rest. "To pay for . . . this." He looked around the damp, barren little room. There were no windows. It would be dark in winter, dark and cold and choked with smoke. "If I'd known . . ."

"You'd have done what?" said Kat, wiping her hands on her apron. She closed the door of the bedroom carefully behind her. Her eyes were tired, but she held herself defiantly straight. "There was nothing to do."

William took stock of his daughter. She'd changed, his Kat.

When he'd sent her off, she'd been seventeen, as strong-willed as they came, but with the round cheeks and the blush of youth on her still, for all her air of assurance. The intervening ten years had hardened her. Her face had lost the softness of youth, all lines and planes, and her spine was uncompromisingly stiff. Her hands, clenched at her sides, were reddened and work hardened, as he'd never thought any daughter's of his should be.

He leaned forward and grasped one of her work-reddened hands, squeezing it hard.

"I've come to stay, Kat. For good. We'll be together at last, you and I and Lizzy—I am only sorry that it's taken this long." Remembering, belatedly, the source of his mission, he leaned back in his chair, looking over Kat's shoulder at the other door. "Is Lizzy here with you?"

Kat drew her hand away. "No. Why would she be? She's at school." Her eyes narrowed. "She should be at school."

"She's not," said Miss Meadows succinctly. Mrs. Meadows hadn't taken the other seat. She was standing by the card table, watching the scene with cool detachment. William couldn't begin to imagine what she must be thinking. "She and another girl—my ward's sister—ran off from the school. We thought they might have come to you."

Kat's face betrayed none of her surprise. She must, thought William, have grown accustomed these past years to dealing with the unpalatable.

All she said was, "Won't you sit down, Miss Meadows?"

"You haven't heard from her?" William felt as though the bottom were dropping out of his world. It felt like years since he had stood on Miss Climpson's doorstep, a withered posy in his hands, full of plans for his grown daughters, both of whom would be overjoyed to see him, prosperous and blooming. They had never given him any reason to suspect otherwise. If they had hidden this, what else? "She said nothing to you?"

"No," said Kat, "not since last month. Are you sure she's not visiting a friend? She usually spends her holidays with the Fitzhughs. This"—Kat's gesture encompassed the dreary basement apartment, the courtyard with the washing in it—"hardly provides a festive environment."

"Is there no other friend she might have gone to?" asked Miss Meadows, since William was largely incapable of speech. "No one other than the Fitzhugh girl?"

Kat gave the matter due consideration. "Something ovine. Wooliston. That was it. Agnes Wooliston."

"She's the other girl that's gone missing," said William dully. "They've been gone two weeks now. There must be someone else—another girl, another friend. . . ."

Miss Meadows took charge. "Did your sister say anything to you? Anything about a romantic attachment?"

Kat shook her head. "No. Lizzy might have been a bit . . . impulsive at times, but not in that way. It would never have occurred to her. She is," she said, choosing her words carefully, "very young for her age."

William wondered what his older daughter had seen to make her sound quite so world-weary at twenty-seven.

"No male visitors at the school?" Miss Meadows persisted. "No mention of strange goings-on?"

William roused himself from his stupor. "What sort of strange goings-on?"

Miss Meadows waved a hand. "Anything out of the usual routine, that's all. Unexpected excursions, changes among the staff?"

"There was a girl who ran off with the music master," said Kat, "but that was over a year ago. Lizzy was very scornful about his mustachios."

Miss Meadows was looking distinctly frustrated. "What about letters? Packages?"

"I know that Alex—my brother—sent her regular packages from home." She still thought of India as home. She looked up. "As did Jack."

That was news. William hadn't been aware that his estranged middle son had been in touch with either of his sisters. "Jack sent presents to Lizzy?"

Kat nodded. "Trinkets and baubles and little things he thought might amuse her. She showed me some bangles he had sent her and a necklace of glass beads." Her lip curled. "He sent me a parcel too, just last month."

"Beads and baubles?" said Miss Meadows.

"Nothing half so useful," said Kat scornfully. "It was quite typical of Jack. Here. See for yourself."

She fished a piece of paper off the table, the cheap brown paper of the bazaars. The ink had smudged in places, but the hand was unmistakably Jack's, uncompromising and angular. His very writing was an assertion of will.

"Let me." Miss Meadows plucked the paper neatly from her hand. "If I may?"

His daughter nodded. "There's nothing there that can't be seen."

Miss Meadows lifted the paper so that it caught the few rays of reluctant light that managed to squirm through the grimed window. *"Darling Kitty-Kat—"*

"I hate it when he calls me that," said Kat.

"I can see why," said Miss Meadows.

"That's why he does it," said Kat grimly.

Miss Meadows perched her pince-nez on her nose and resumed reading. *"Things have got a bit hot for me in Hyderabad. I'd tell you where I'm going, but then you'd only send me more Christmas packages, and I've enough embroidered slippers to wear until Doomsday."*

"You sent him slippers?" Knowing his oldest daughter's feelings towards her half-brother, William was deeply moved.

Kat shrugged uncomfortably. "I had to send him something. I couldn't very well send packages to Alex and George and not include anything for Jack, could I? Of course, had I known that he would reward me with this, I would have spared myself."

William's brows drew together. "With what?"

Kat nodded to the letter. "Read on, Miss Meadows."

"I've sent a few odds and ends into your keeping. Hold on to them for me, won't you? I'll be back to collect them by and by. Your loving brother, J."

Kat gestured towards a large crate sitting by the wall. "That's it, over there. Bazaar trash, most of it. Used cooking pots and old crockery. I can't think why he went to the trouble of shipping it here, other than to inconvenience his relations," she added bitterly. "We've already had someone calling here, claiming Jack had promised him something. I let him have a look through the rubbish and he soon went away again."

William sat up straighter. He had sent his daughter home from India to get her away from men like that. "Was he— importunate?"

"Oh no," said Kat. "He was most gentlemanly, all kitted out in the latest rig. I'm sure he wouldn't have done anything to bloody his tailoring."

Miss Meadows regarded his daughter with appreciation. "I like you."

The corners of Kat's lips turned up, fleetingly. "Thank you. But there was really no danger. He just wanted his box, whatever it was."

William had an idea what it might be.

"Jack had a sideline in opium trading—selling it to young bucks with more money than sense." William turned to Miss Meadows, adding hastily, "He wouldn't touch the stuff himself, not Jack, but he'd no compunction fleecing those he thought deserved it. I'd thought he'd given it up."

"Have you ever known Jack to turn his back on anything which might profit him?" said Kat tartly.

Yes. His family.

"He'd not have sent any here, though," William said quickly. "He wouldn't endanger you that way."

Kat gave him a look.

"He wouldn't," William repeated, and wished he were more

sure of it. "That's not to say there wasn't another parcel that went astray."

Miss Meadows frowned. "Is it your theory that an opium fiend might have attacked the younger Miss Reid in the hopes of discovering a trove of opiates beneath her bed? Or, perhaps, made off with her in the hopes of blackmailing your son into compliance?"

Put that way, it sounded rather ridiculous.

"Jack wouldn't do anything that might hurt Lizzy," said William. "He's that fond of her."

As much as Jack was fond of anyone.

"Yes," said Kat flatly. "Everyone is fond of Lizzy."

Miss Meadows rose, drawing her gloves up over her wrists. "We'll have to go back to Bath. There's nothing else for it."

"The other family might have heard something from their daughter," said Kat. She turned to her father. "If there's any word from Lizzy, I'll send to you immediately."

William looked with concern at his daughter, his firstborn, and said, "Would you like to come back to Bath with us, lass? I can take another room at the inn."

"But there's Gammy," said Kat. "I can't leave her."

"We could take her with us."

"No," said Kat. "She gets so easily confused. She's comfortable here."

Comfortable? How could anyone be comfortable like this?

"How long has she been like this?" William asked. He had thought it had been bad when Maria had died, but this—this was what it felt like to know one's heart was breaking.

"Four years now," said Kat dispassionately. "My grandfather's death did something to her wits. Losing the house finished it off. Sometimes she thinks I'm my mother. Sometimes she thinks I'm *her* mother." She smiled a smile that didn't quite reach her eyes. "It's all right. It's easier for her this way, I think. Half the time, she thinks she's in India and you and Mother are just courting."

William's eyes stung. From the smoke of the hearth; that was all.

"Once I find Lizzy, I'm coming back for you," said William. "We'll take your gammy with us."

Kat smiled. "Of course," she said.

He felt like a monster.

It was a good thing Miss Meadows knew the way, because William was largely oblivious to his surroundings, walking in a daze down the narrow, odiferous alleys. The light was already beginning to fade behind the tops of the ramshackle houses. This was what he'd sent Kat to, the underbelly of Bristol, gin and mud and other people's washing.

If he'd known . . . But would he have kept them at home with him? Could he have kept them at home? At the time, it had seemed like a recipe for disaster. There had been a cholera epidemic; little Annie Lennox had been raped by a bunch of arrogant junior officers; his regimental duties were taking him farther and farther afield.

And there was that house, with a garden . . .

"I had no idea."

"Yes, you've said that," said Miss Meadows, picking her way along with her parasol for a walking stick.

"I couldn't leave my regiment." He had to remind himself of that. "I'd have come sooner, but there was no help for it. I'd no way to earn a living here. My only fortune is my sword."

"In other words"—Miss Meadows's voice cut into his reverie—"you like playing soldier."

William rounded on his companion. What did she know of it? "I wouldn't call it playing. Those weren't toy swords on the other side."

Miss Meadows sniffed. "I should think not. What would be the amusement in that?"

"It wasn't *amusing*—," William began, and broke off.

Only, it had been. He'd loved his regiment. He'd loved the camaraderie, the politics, the rush of it all. It was the only employment he'd had and the only one he'd ever wanted. He was a soldier already when he'd met and married Maria. He'd never stopped to consider what it might mean for a family. By the time he had a family, willy-nilly and higgledy-piggledy, there was no going back.

"I sent them money back." William hated how defensive he sounded, how mewling.

It had been precious little he'd sent back, at that, little bits and pieces, scrounged here and there, hardly enough to pay for his girls' room and board. It didn't matter, Mrs. Davies had said; she'd more than enough. It was a comfort to have her Maria's daughter with her, and she liked that scamp of a Lizzy.

William had accepted with gratitude and a minimum of questions. Money had never been thick in his pocket. Mess fees kept rising every year. There was the boys' schooling to pay for, their kit, a commission for Alex, a substantial bribe to the Begum Sumroo to take George into her retinue. His horse had gone lame; the price of feed had gone up. There was always something, something that made the coins drain out through the hole in his pocket as fast as it came in. The salary of a colonel in the East India Company's army was far from munificent. It was enough to keep a man in comfort in India, not enough to spread towards multiple households on two continents.

Even so, if he had known, he would have found a way, skimped somehow, borrowed, begged. "Why didn't they tell me?"

"The school fees at Miss Climpson's select menagerie can't come cheap," said Miss Meadows.

William cleared his throat painfully. "It's not that." They'd told him that Lizzy had won a free place at the school. The details were hazy, but it was a scholarship of some sort. He'd never known his Lizzy to have the slightest academic inclination, but he wasn't inclined to look a gift horse in the mouth. "The fees were forgiven. She's a charity girl."

The words galled him, evidence, if he needed further, that he'd done a miserable job taking care of his family.

Miss Meadows gave him a sharp look. "I didn't think Miss Climpson took charity girls. Her academy is a strictly for-profit institution."

"Well, she did this time," said William shortly.

Instead of pressing the argument, Miss Meadows regarded him quizzically. "How many children do you have, Colonel Reid?"

"Not enough to render any of them expendable."

Miss Meadows looked at him, both brows raised.

"Five," he said heavily. There was no call to behave like an ass, as much as it helped to relieve his feelings. "Three sons and two daughters. Kat's the oldest, Kat and her twin brother, Alex. George and Lizzy are the youngest. Then there's Jack in the middle."

"Jack and his opium trade," said Miss Meadows musingly.

"It was only the once," said William hastily. "As far as I know."

Jack kept himself private. It was only by chance that William had learned that it was Jack who had been funneling opium to that group of idiots who were running a Hellfire Club in Poona—and overcharging them for it, too. Given that those were the men responsible for Annie Lennox, it was hard to hold Jack to account for either.

But that was the least of it. His son had hired out his sword to the Maratha leader, Scindia, in his uprising against the British, and, when that had failed, he'd turned mercenary, fighting for this petty princeling, then that. As long, of course, as they were fighting against his father's people.

What was Jack about now? He'd like to think that the parcels to Lizzy and Kat were by way of conciliation. The baubles for Lizzy—that sounded like a peace offering, right enough. As for Kat and the bundle of bazaar rubbish—well, Jack had never been able to resist riling his older sister. The two were chalk and cheese and always had been.

"Ouch!" William rubbed his arm where Miss Meadows had poked him with the tip of her parasol.

She gripped his forearm, hard. "Did you hear something?

No, no, don't stop walking! Keep going on as before. Do you hear that?"

William shook the cobwebs from his brain. "Yes," he said. Footfalls. Behind them. More than one person, unless he missed his guess. His hand went automatically to where his sword should have been.

"They've been following us since we left your daughter's," said Miss Meadows in an undertone. "I had thought at first that it was coincidence, but they've been coming steadily closer."

"Footpads?" he said.

"Most likely." Miss Meadows was remarkably composed.

William took a swift appraisal of their surroundings. The alley through which they were walking was far from inviting. Many of the houses had blocked or broken windows. There'd be no help from those who lived inside.

"We're five minutes yet from the posting inn," he said. "Possibly more."

Miss Meadows looked at him from under the truncated brim of her bonnet. "Too far to make a run for it."

"Too far for both of us to make a run for it." The footsteps were definitely getting closer, speeding up. William swallowed a hearty oath. There was no way but to fight it out. "If I hold them off, can you go for help?"

"And let you have all the fun?" Miss Meadows said.

He realized, with amazement, that she meant it. Her color was high and her eyes were bright with anticipation. She pressed a button on her parasol and eased the casing forward, revealing a glimpse of a long, slim blade.

"Your brawn, my sword. What do you say?"

There was no time to say anything. There was the pounding of feet on the pavement and a hoarse cry. The brigands were upon them.

As one, they whirled to face their assailants.

There were three of them, all clad in tattered, dirty garments, kerchiefs covering their faces. But there was one thing they hadn't reckoned with. They hadn't expected their prey to fight back.

William saw Miss Meadows fling the casing of her parasol aside and heard the snick of her thin, wicked blade.

"To me!" she cried, and lunged forward.

Chapter 7

"Hark!" said Plumeria. "Do you hear? Those footfalls portend some fell pursuit!"

Sir Magnifico drew forth his sword. "'Tis they who shall fall! Fell shall be their fall, my lady, never fear."

"Do you think me so faint of heart as that?" Plumeria whipped back her cloak, revealing the slim, silver blade strapped to her side. "I fear only that there shall not be sport enough for us both. To me!"

—From *The Convent of Orsino* by A Lady

"They never said they'd be armed!" complained one of the ruffians.

"Stop whining and get on with it," hissed one of his fellows, pushing him back into the fray. It was hard to tell through the kerchief, but his voice seemed less rough than that of the others.

Two of them made a rush at Colonel Reid, who sent one flying back with what Gwen believed was popularly termed "a leveler." It certainly sent the man reeling to the ground, spitting blood and a loose tooth.

Gwen pinked the second man in the backside, just enough to make him release his grip on the Colonel. That left the third ruffian, who was so importunate as to make a grab at her while her sword arm was otherwise engaged. She was made aware of this by a low bellow from the Colonel, who elbowed his own assailant out of the way and swept the feet out from under the man who was attempting to draw her out of the fray. The miscreant landed with a most satisfactory thump and a curse, but there was no time to gloat. The second man was back, his temper hardly improved by her sally against his posterior. A fist narrowly missed Gwen's nose.

She resented that. She rather liked her nose. It was excellent for looking down at people.

She retaliated with a lunge that clipped a button off the man's loose jacket. She wasn't aiming to kill, just to deter. Unfortunately, it appeared to have the opposite effect. The man leapt back and came up with a knife in his hand. It was a rather nasty-looking piece of work.

"Don't even think of it," said Gwen sharply.

In front of them, the man the Colonel had leveled was rising, blood dripping down his chin. He was missing two teeth and he looked angry. Very angry. His knife looked even larger and nastier than the other.

"Back to back!" commanded the Colonel in a low voice.

Gwen had never stopped to consider what his title indicated; for the first time, it was borne in on her that this was a man who knew his way around a battlefield. She found herself obeying as the ruffians circled nearer, knives in their hands.

"You have no sword."

"It could be worse," said the Colonel philosophically.

Gwen tilted her head towards him, while keeping an eye on the men circling around them. "There could be four of them?"

"No." She could hear the laughter in the Colonel's voice. "They could be Gypsies."

If he thought writing a novel was easy, he should try it.

There was no time, however, to give him the set down he so richly deserved.

Launching blood and spittle through the new gap in his teeth, the man in the middle uttered those immortal fighting words: "Let's get 'im!"

The brigands were upon them. They all converged on the Colonel, leaving Gwen waving her épée in the empty air.

That wasn't sporting.

Gwen flung herself on the brigands from behind, rapping one smartly on the head with the butt of her parasol, pinking another in the calf, and then, when he jumped back, jabbing him neatly in the toe. That should keep him sneaking up on anyone for some time.

Near her, a knife clattered to the ground as the Colonel twisted the arm holding it. Gwen kicked it out of the way before the brigand could dive for it, and then kicked the brigand for good measure. She aimed her kick even better than she had intended. The man doubled over, clutching himself and howling in a high-pitched note that would have elicited envy from a professional countertenor. It was a very impressive high C, especially given the tears streaming down the man's face.

"Enough," he gasped. "Away!"

"I'm going as fast as I can!" protested his companion, hopping on one foot, while lopsidedly cradling his right arm with his left. It made for a rather erratic progress.

They lurched away, followed by their toothless companion, who gave Gwen a look over his shoulder that could best be described as malevolent.

Gwen brandished her sword parasol at him. "Let that teach you to set upon innocent citizens!"

Retrieving the parasol portion, she rammed the casing back down over her épée. It slid back into place with a professional click. Really. Villains never stopped to consider these things.

Turning to the Colonel, she said with satisfaction, "Well! We certainly sent them— What's wrong?"

Colonel Reid staggered as he tried to walk. His hand was pressed to his left side, but even against the dark fabric of his coat, Gwen could see the blood beginning to seep between his fingers.

"Nothing," he grunted. "Nothing. Just a scratch."

"That's not a scratch." Gwen moved to shore him up as he stumbled again, sliding an arm around his waist to brace him. "Scratches don't bleed like that."

It must have happened when all three had converged on him, knives in hand. A man could fight off only so many at once. It was a move she hadn't anticipated.

"At least it wasn't"—Colonel Reid lurched slightly as he tried to move forward—"a Gypsy curse."

"Stop talking and save your breath for dripping blood down

my dress," said Gwen sternly. She didn't like the way he looked. His skin was sickly white beneath his tan and his breathing was labored.

"Sorry," he said, managing a smile that looked more like a grimace. "I'll try—drip—on the ground."

"I'd prefer you not drip so much at all," muttered Gwen. The wound was bleeding freely. She supposed that was a good thing, in terms of cleaning it out. On the other hand, he might need some of that blood.

Colonel Reid must have caught the expression on her face, because he said in a labored voice, "Don't—fret. I'm an old campaigner. I've had worse. 'S just a—flesh wound."

But he winced as he said it.

"Hold your peace," said Gwen. "I know it pains you not to hear your own voice, but I'd rather get you somewhere where I can take a good look at that *flesh wound*. Once I've got you properly bandaged up, you can expound to your heart's content."

"Coaching inn—," he managed, and caught himself on a wince.

"Yes, yes," she said. "One more word out of you and I'll stab you myself."

The ridiculous man smiled at her. It wasn't much of a smile, but it was a valiant attempt. "Thank you," he said, and subsided against her shoulder.

After that, the Colonel saved his breath for walking, if walking it could be called. It was more of a sluggish stumble, more and more of his weight resting on Gwen's shoulder. She was a tall woman, but the Colonel was taller and broader. She knew it was bad when he accepted her assistance. She knew it was even worse when she felt the hand clutching her shoulder start to go slack.

The Colonel slipped and Gwen gripped his waist harder, eliciting a sharp intake of breath. Gwen looked at him with concern. His face had gone a curious greenish color beneath his tan.

"Not far now," he gasped, giving her what was meant to be a reassuring smile.

Gwen wasn't reassured.

Five minutes to the coaching inn hadn't seemed far before, but now, with the Colonel stumbling beside her, it might have been as far as Bath.

"There," she said with authority. There was a public house in front of them. They would have a few rooms to let, she had no doubt. It wasn't exactly York House, but it looked reputable enough, as public houses went, and, more important, it was there.

"The coaching—," began the Colonel.

"The coaching inn is too public," Gwen said brusquely.

It was better than telling him that she didn't think he was going to make it another ten yards, much less another ten minutes. If he thought they were getting back on that mail coach tonight, he was crazier than she'd given him credit for. She just hoped those ruffians hadn't hit him in any sort of vital spot.

No. If they had, he would be on the ground, five streets

back, not swaying next to her, trying to redirect her towards the coaching inn.

She took resort in an out-and-out lie. "What if we were seen together in a private parlor at a busy inn? My reputation would be in tatters."

"Oh," said the Colonel, brow furrowing. Then, "Sorry to be—bother."

"Yes," said Gwen rallyingly, hauling him over the threshold of the Happy Hare. "A great bother. It was the rankest effrontery on your part to get yourself stabbed."

From the public room, she could hear the sounds of a very loud debate about keelhauling. She grabbed the arm of a woman who was bustling past her from the public room to the parlor on the other side. From her no longer quite so white apron and the tray of comestibles she was holding, Gwen deduced that she was employed by the establishment.

"My husband has suffered a mishap on the road," Gwen said imperiously. "Do you have a room where I might attend to him?"

She had blood on her gown and no ring on her finger, but her hauteur spoke for her. The maid set down her tray on a table and bobbed a quick curtsy.

"Will you be wanting a room for the night, or just the now?"

"For the night." Next to her, the Colonel stirred. Gwen squeezed his hand, hard. "Do you have one?"

Someone in the other room was bellowing for his meal. The maid glanced nervously over her shoulder.

"Ye-es," she said slowly. She was clearly not the brightest flower in the garden.

"Good," said Gwen. "Take us there at once. We will also be needing a cold collation, hot water, and some brandy. Some clean cloths, as well. Oh, and a pot of honey, if you have it. Well, what are you waiting for?"

The maid looked anxiously from the taproom to Gwen and back again. Gwen glowered. The maid bowed to a force beyond her control. "Yes, Mistress—"

"Fustian," she said promptly, using a name she had employed as an alias before. "Colonel and Mrs. Fustian."

"I'll bring your . . ." The maid looked around, confused. "Baggage?"

"We don't have any," said Gwen crisply. "We were set upon by ruffians in the road. They made off with our curricle and all of our baggage. We were lucky to escape with our lives. It was," she added, "most impertinent of them."

From beside her, she heard something that might have been a faint chuckle from the Colonel. Just maybe.

"Upstairs with you," she said briskly. "Now."

The room into which the maid led them was less than luxurious, but it was private, it was reasonably clean, and it had a bed.

One bed.

The Colonel took one look at the single bed and sagged heavily against the wall. "This," he said faintly, "is worse than a private parlor. Your reputation—"

"Stuff and nonsense," said Gwen, chivying him forcibly

towards the bed. "My reputation isn't such a fragile thing as all that. Do you really think anyone would believe you intended me a mischief? In such a state as you are? You don't have the strength to seduce a flea."

Even in a state of severe blood loss, the Colonel found the energy to quip, "I've never—found anything—the least bit—attractive—about the insect population."

He sat down heavily on the bed. The ancient cording screeched in protest, but it held.

"Am I meant to be relieved by that? Or is that meant to be a crushing set down for the fleas?" Gwen eased him back against the pillow. He had lost his hat somewhere along the road, and his tousled hair, worn longer than the current fashion, was springy against her fingers. It looked very red against his pale face. "With any luck, you won't be sharing your bed with any."

The Colonel breathed in deeply through his nose, mustering his strength. "I've bedded down in worse places."

He opened his eyes and looked up at Gwen, his expression stripped of its usual levity. Catching her hand, he squeezed it. His grip was weaker than it should be, but she could feel the press of each finger as though it were branded on her. She made to pull away, but he held tight, his blue eyes fixed on hers.

Without raillery, he said, "Thank you."

For a moment, she let her hand linger in his, strangely touched by the simple profession, stripped so bare of his usual foolery.

"I suppose if you can flirt, it means you aren't quite at death's door just yet," said Gwen tartly. She slipped her hand out of his weak grasp, wrapping it in the folds of her skirt as she made a show of bustling across the room to the door. "Where is that dratted girl with the hot water? She's had time enough to heat an entire Roman bath by now!"

The word "bath" had been a mistake. She heard Colonel Reid's voice behind her. "Once you patch me up—we can go." She looked back to find him struggling into a sitting position. "Catch the stage—to Bath."

Gwen hurried back before he could do himself further injury. "Lie down, you ridiculous man!" She pressed down firmly on his good side, forcibly settling him back down among the pillows. He went down with barely a murmur of protest. Gwen leaned over him, pinning him in place. "Do you want to make me tie you to the bed?"

"—can only hope," the Colonel mumbled.

Gwen gave him an eagle-eyed stare. "What was that?"

"Nothing," the Colonel said meekly.

"Hmph." With one last quelling glance over her shoulder, Gwen retrieved her reticule. She removed a pair of tiny scissors. "I'm afraid I'm going to have to cut your shirt away. Trying to take it up over your head will only hurt you."

And she wasn't sure she wanted to grapple with him quite that intimately. She could still feel the press of his fingers against hers.

"Never liked it anyway," said the Colonel gallantly.

The cloth over the wound itself was deeply crusted and clotted; that would have to wait until she had hot water to soak the cloth away. She feared doing him more injury otherwise. Either way, it was going to hurt like the very devil. She knew. She was nimble, but not always nimble enough.

"I do hope you're not missish," she said, mostly to distract him from the sound of the scissors. She began snipping away, the small scissors snagging on the dense fabric. "I'm going to be seeing a good deal of you before this is done."

"Oughtn't I be saying that to you?" said the Colonel weakly, trying to lift his head to see what she was doing. He gave up and let it fall back against the pillows again.

"Most certainly not! You'll see of me exactly what you've seen." Gwen set aside the scissors. "No more, no less."

The Colonel gave a weak chuckle. "I meant about the missishness."

"I passed the age of missishness a good ten years since." Gwen carefully peeled the lacerated shirt away from a torso that was as sun-browned as the rest of him. He was in remarkably good shape for a man his age, his stomach still flat and firm.

The Colonel drew in his breath between his teeth as Gwen eased the cloth away from around the wound. It was still oozing blood. Blood was good. Blood wasn't pus.

The Colonel's head popped up again. "Are you sure you know what you're doing?"

Gwen ignored him and examined the wound. "It's not so bad as it could be. It's shallow, at least."

Shallow but jagged, with flecks of cloth, driven in by the knife, still clinging to the opening. She suspected that ruffian's knife had been none too clean. The blow itself wouldn't kill him, but wound fever might.

It was impossible to imagine the vital man who had teased and bedeviled her all the way from Bath to Bristol laid permanently low by one sneaky back-alley footpad's knife.

Well, that wasn't going to happen. Not if she had anything to say about it.

"Mrs. Fustian?" The door squeaked open a careful few inches.

It was a different maid this time, no more than seventeen at a guess, awkwardly balancing a tray laden with assorted plates, bowls, and jugs, all covered with roughly woven cloths. She goggled over Gwen's shoulder at the Colonel sprawled half-naked on the bed.

"That will be all," said Gwen firmly. Hadn't the chit seen a half-clad man before? If she hadn't, this wasn't the time for her to start. She relieved the maid of the tray and smacked the door firmly shut behind her.

Taking the tray, she headed back for the bed. The Colonel did look unfairly debonair, shirt gone to the waist, clad only in a pair of tight breeches and scuffed black boots to the knee. She should probably see about getting those boots off, but she didn't think the leather would succumb to her sewing scissors.

The Colonel made a weak attempt to lift himself up on his elbows. His bare arms were very brown against the white of the sheets. "Can we still make the stage?"

"Perhaps," said Gwen noncommittally. "Let's see how you're feeling once I've bandaged you up, shall we?"

She lifted the covering from the largest bowl. Steam rose satisfactorily from the surface. Good. They had boiled the water, not just warmed it and called it hot enough. There was a jug of brandy on the tray, too, just as she had asked. Not surprising. A fair amount of smuggled French goods came through Bristol. It wasn't the best vintage, but it would serve.

Making sure her back was between the tray and the Colonel, Gwen released the tiny catch that opened a hidden compartment in her onyx ring. White powder sifted into the pewter mug. Gwen poured the brandy over it, swirling it to make it mix.

"We'll need to let them know at the school," said the Colonel, struggling to a sitting position. His face was seamed with worry. "That we didn't find them."

"Stop that!" She'd never before met anyone more stubborn than herself. She whirled around, the doctored brandy in hand. "You're only making it bleed again. You can't do anything for either of them if you exsanguinate."

"Nice—word."

"Hardly," said Gwen. She handed him the doctored brandy. "Drink this."

"Precise, I meant." His hand wouldn't quite close around the cup.

Gwen took it from him, holding it to his lips. "Yes," she said, "and it's precisely what will happen to you if you don't behave."

She saw the ghost of a smile. "Touché," he said, and swallowed the brandy from the cup she held to his lips.

Gwen set the cup back down on the tray, fetching the bowl of water and a pile of linen cloths. She dipped the corner of a cloth in the water. Beneath the gash left by their assailant's knife, the Colonel's chest was a map of old wounds, white scars pale on bronzed skin. Apparently, military command in the East India Company's army was less of a sinecure than she had thought. There was the puckered scar of an old gunshot wound on his side, and a long, thin line that curved from just below his left nipple straight down below the waistband of his breeches.

Gwen resisted the urge to follow it to its logical conclusion. Instead, she wrung out the cloth with a little more force than necessary, saying, "This isn't the first wound you've taken, is it?"

"Told you." The Colonel bared his teeth in what was meant to be a smile. "Old campaigner."

He drew in his breath between his lips as Gwen dabbed the damp cloth against the crusted blood on his chest, swabbing away the clots of blood, the caked-on dirt, the tiny—but deadly—flecks of fabric. It all had to go, every last speck of it.

"This is going to hurt," she warned him, rather belatedly.

"It already does," quipped the Colonel.

Gwen gave him a look as she dipped her cloth back in the rapidly reddening water. It was almost clean enough, although hard to tell with the fresh blood oozing out. She'd clean it with brandy next.

She did her best to keep the Colonel distracted. "You'd quibble with Satan himself, wouldn't you?"

"Only"—the Colonel's voice was barely audible, but he

made the attempt all the same—"if he had—half so quick a wit—as you."

His voice was weak and cracked, but something about the gallantry of the gesture touched Gwen, despite herself. "Flattery won't make this hurt any less, Colonel."

She could tell the opiate was beginning to take effect. The keen blue eyes were starting to glaze, his lids to tremble.

"William," he mumbled.

Gwen paused with the brandy bottle poised over the Colonel's bared chest. "What was that?"

"If you're—to see me—in this little—you'd best—call me—William," said the Colonel, and then his eyes rolled back in his head and he subsided into merciful oblivion.

Chapter 8

Ride though they might, there was no escaping the dreadful force of the curse of the Gypsy queen. His armor discarded beside him, Sir Magnifico fell fitfully into fevered sleep in the forest glade. Plumeria employed all her arts of healing, but none of her soothing draughts, none of her cooling potions, was of the least avail. He twisted and writhed, crying out in a language strange to her ears, his glazed eyes fixed on sights beyond her mortal comprehension.

~~"I am cursed!" cried~~

~~"Oh, what curse is this!"~~

~~"Curse this blasted curse!"~~

"The curse has come upon me!" cried bold Sir Magnifico.

—From *The Convent of Orsino* by A Lady

He had lost his regiment.

William fought his way through the jungle. There was a fire burning somewhere; he could see the light of it, orange against the sky, against the blackening trees. Sweat beaded on his brow, dripped down his face as he battled his way through the brush. His shirt clung to him, sopping wet, but his mouth was dry, drier than he had imagined possible. Why hadn't he brought water with him? He didn't know.

Somewhere in there, one of his children was calling to him. He wasn't sure if it was Lizzy or Kat; all he heard was the high, childlike cry: "Papa! Papa!"

She was just ahead, just a little ways in front of him. If he could just make his way through the vines, the clawing, clinging vines that held him fast, pulling at his arms, looping around his legs. The more he fought against them, the tighter the foliage bound him. His collar was too tight, that blasted high gold-frogged collar. He ripped at it with his fingers, fighting for breath. There was a burning pain in his side; it hurt when he moved.

A tiger moved in the underbrush, its sleek orange pelt the same color as the fire in the distance, banded in black. William froze, but it was moving, moving on, sliding back into the brush, seeking other prey. He looked where it had gone, but the sun was too bright; it hurt to look into, and the sweat was dripping into his eyes, blinding him.

"I live here," said Kat, looking at him with such scorn that it hurt like a blow.

He tried to follow her, but the vines were in his way, the blasted vines, yanking and tearing at him, and just ahead, he could hear laughter, Lizzy's laughter, the high, clear laughter of the six-year-old she had been.

"I broked the vase," she said, looking up at him, all wide-eyed innocence with mischief lurking behind, and he hugged her as hard and tight as he could, trying to keep her safe, until he opened his arms to realize that there was nothing in them, nothing in them at all.

The scene shifted, and he was at a party, in the tedious social round of Calcutta. He couldn't stand these things, for the most part, but it was necessary, necessary if he wanted to get Alex a good appointment. A district of his own to govern— that was what Alex needed, and he would do it well and fairly, not like some of those oafs just out from England who couldn't even speak the language. Alex was a good lad, but without guile. He didn't know how to play the game, which was why William needed to do it for him, his last gift to his son before he went away across the seas, to that alien and icy island his parents had held in such contempt.

A government official's wife was tugging at his arm; he could hear her overbred accents: "Colonel? Colonel?"

He tried to smile back at her, but there was a weight against his lids, and suddenly it wasn't an English lady; it was Maria calling him, his Maria, her voice shrill with concern, "William? William!"

"I'm here," he tried to say. "It's all right."

But it came out all slurred, as though he had been drinking. Drinking. He had drunk a great deal after Maria had died, running up the bills in the mess, port, claret, rum punch, whatever would temporarily dull the ache of her absence, his best girl, his better half.

"William? You're dreaming," she said.

She always had been a practical woman, his Maria, even when she was imaginary. It had been a very long time since he'd dreamed of her, those dreams in which he was always following, following, reaching for her, his hand brushing nothing but empty air.

This time, his hand caught the end of a sleeve, made of a fabric that was fine and smooth between his fingers.

"This isn't good," he heard the woman say.

William fought with his heavy lids, struggling to open them. He blinked, dazzled by brightness.

Whatever apparition stood before him, it wasn't Maria. Surrounded by an orange halo, she wore only a long white shift that had slipped from one shoulder. She held a candle in one hand, throwing the light across her face, creating strange planes and shadows. She was terrible in her beauty, the sort of goddess at whose feet one laid offerings of grain and flowers. Her long hair streamed unbound around her shoulders, black and silver, the silver over the black glowing like mother-of-pearl in the moonlight. There were candles lit behind her, a semicircle of them, shining through the thin lawn of her gown, outlining the shape of her long, slim legs, the curve of her waist.

"You have a fever," said the apparition. She leaned over him, and her long black hair brushed his bare chest, sending chills straight through him. "William, do you hear me?"

He nodded to show he understood, although he didn't understand at all. He was bound in whatever strange spell this might be. She glittered black and silver, light and shadow. He reached up a hand to touch her hair. It slid through his fingers like silk, not the cheap, adulterated stuff of the back-alley bazaars, but a courtier's best finery, heavy and rich, chased in silver.

"Beautiful," he said, and his voice sounded strange and slow to his ears. "Beautiful."

He wasn't sure if he spoke in English or in Hindi. It didn't matter. Goddesses were above such minor matters as translation.

She twitched her hair away, bundling it back behind her. The movement made her white robe slip from her shoulder, revealing a collarbone as carefully wrought as any ivory carving by a Moghul emperor's master sculptor.

"Bother," the goddess muttered, and laid a hand against his forehead. It was blissfully cool, her hand. He tilted his face up towards it, towards her. "You're burning up."

He couldn't argue with that. There were flecks of flame on either side of his eyes. She seemed to glow and shimmer as she turned to the table, mixing something in a glass.

She held out a chalice to him, cupped in two hands. "Drink this," she said.

It smelled strongly of spirits and something more, something musty, like incense. Obediently, William lifted his head and drank. The metal of the cup was cool beneath his hands, but the liquid scourged his throat going down. He coughed, weakly, and she held a cloth to his lips, her dark hair swinging down between them, tickling his bare shoulder.

She set down the cup and tested his forehead with her hand. "With any luck, this should bring the fever down."

Her hand cooled wherever it touched. He felt her fingers like balm against his brow, his cheek. He caught them in his hand, brought them to his lips, pressing a kiss against her open palm.

"Delirious," she said. "Distinctly delirious."

The words ran like water against his ears, a gentle burbling, musical and meaningless. He was in a pleasure garden, a pleasure garden such as the Moghuls made. There was a fountain in the center, a fountain tiled in shades of palest blue and green. The water sang sweetly, water glistening in the sun like diamonds, as brightly plumed birds whirled above, diving in and out of the spray. The air was heavy with the scent of flowers, of frangipani, jasmine, and lotus blossoms. William felt drunk on the scent of them, the scent of the flowers and the sound of the water and the beauty of the woman lolling on the divan beside him.

She made to pull her hand away, but William kissed the inside of her wrist, where her pulse beat blue against her ivory skin. He could feel her shiver, even in the blazing heat of the day.

"Lakshmi," he appealed to her in Hindi, "goddess of beauty and fortune—"

"What—," she began, but he twined his hands in the black silk of her hair and drew down her mouth to his, stopping her words with a kiss.

She tasted like flowers and brandy—or maybe she tasted like flowers and he tasted like brandy. He was floating with the sensation of it, swirling round and round like the birds around the fountain. Her lips weren't cool anymore; they were warm on his, warm and sweet. He had wronged her if he thought her coy. She kissed him back, kiss for kiss, matching her ardor with his, no ivory goddess but warm and vital in his arms, her hair falling like a screen around them both.

They parted, panting. He could feel his own chest moving up and down with the exertion of it, and a pain he didn't care to heed, not now, not here in the garden.

He bracketed her face with his hands. Her eyes were wide and startled, dark against her pale face, her hair wild around her shoulders.

"This is a dream." He didn't know why the woman in the pavilion was speaking English, but it didn't matter. It didn't matter if nothing made sense when everything felt exactly right. "A fever dream."

He followed a strand of silver through the darkness of her hair, like moonlight on water. He traced it past the curve of her throat, smoothing the hair back, away from the place where her linen shift fell away from the hollow of her shoulder.

"In that case"—William pressed a kiss to the sweet spot between her neck and her shoulder, letting his lips trail along the length of the throat that arched so obligingly for him—"I don't want to wake. . . ."

He tightened his arms around her, but she was already slipping from his grasp, leaving him to fall into a deep, dream-ridden sleep, in which a moon-tinged goddess danced tauntingly through a garden maze just past his reach.

*　　*　　*

Gwen stumbled back, catching herself on the edge of the table. Her hair fell about her in wild disorder; her shift was halfway off her shoulder. There was no need to catch her own reflection in the panes of the window to know that she looked thoroughly ravished.

In front of her, the Colonel had slipped into sleep. Into pleasant dreams, it seemed. There was a smile on his lips as he slept.

Gwen's hand lifted to her own lips. The fact that her hand was shaking did nothing to improve her mood.

What in the blazes had just happened? One moment she had been checking the Colonel's head for fever, the next—the next she had been all but rolling on the mattress with him!

A fever dream; that was all. A fever dream.

Gwen rubbed her hands up and down her bare arms beneath the loose sleeves of her shift. Perhaps she oughtn't have disrobed, oughtn't have let down her hair, but the Colonel had been fast in drugged sleep, and even if he hadn't been, she was she, the epitome of respectability, everyone's maiden aunt, steeled and girded against human desires.

These sorts of things didn't happen to Miss Gwendolyn Meadows, spinster. That word was her shield and her armor. Well, the word and her sword parasol. But she hadn't had to beat anyone off—at least, not in that way—for quite some time. A beady glower and a sharp retort had been all the deterrent she needed, until she had arrived at the point where there really wasn't anything to deter anymore. Not that she minded, of course. She'd done with all that long ago.

In the uncertain light of the guttering candles, the mirror

cast back her own image to her, dark hair around a pale face, lips swollen, eyes wide and uncertain. For a moment, it was like looking back in time, a reflection of her younger self, twenty-two, proud and foolish. So very, very foolish.

A trick of the light; that was all.

With hands that weren't entirely steady, Gwen twisted her hair back away from her face, plaiting it into a braid, pulling it back so firmly that it made the skin at her temples ache. She glowered at the man in the bed, sleeping heavily now, one sun-browned arm flung out above his head, the sheets pulling down over his bare torso.

He didn't look the least bit like Tim.

Tim's hair had been dark, nearly as dark as hers; the Colonel's was flame red against the pillow, sun-bleached nearly to blond in some places, threaded with silver in others. Tim had worn his hair long, clubbed back in a queue. She remembered running her fingers through it as he slept, watching him, so convinced of the life they were going to have together on his great-uncle's horse farm in Ireland. He'd made no secret of the fact that he had no money, but that didn't matter; she'd had money enough for them both. She was the greatest heiress in two counties, with a tongue as sharp as a razor and an inflated sense of her own consequence.

She'd had no doubt her father would agree to the match. Why wouldn't he? He had never denied her anything before. He had encouraged her in her outrageous rudeness, cosseted and praised her. He was proud of her sharp tongue, her quick wit, her hard head.

"You show them, girl," he would say.

And so she had. But not as he'd intended.

Tucking her hands into her sleeves, Gwen cautiously approached the bed, but the Colonel was out cold now. She reached down to retrieve the sheet, where he had kicked it down by his feet. She'd managed to get his boots off, but she'd left his breeches on. They covered him from waist to knee. The rest was bare.

She paused with the sheet, shamelessly examining the man in front of her. And why not? It wasn't as if she'd have the opportunity again anytime soon. It was research, she told herself. Research for *The Perils of Plumeria*. The last man she had seen so bare was Tim, half a lifetime past.

No, he didn't look like Tim. Tim had been a boy, with a boy's slimness, slight and wiry. The Colonel was a man grown, broad in the shoulder and chest, his arms and thighs heavily muscled from a lifetime spent on horseback. A cavalry man. Tim's hands had been long and slim; the Colonel's were wide and broad knuckled, with calluses on the palms and scrapes on the knuckles, from their skirmish this afternoon.

He had sent those ruffians reeling quite handily, but those same hands had been gentle, even tender, when he had touched her hair, her cheek, her—

Gwen gave the sheet a yank. That was quite enough research for the moment.

She looked at his face, the little pucker of pain between his brows. Instinctively, she reached out to touch his cheek, to sooth the hurt away. He moved in his sleep, and Gwen snatched her hand away like a thief caught rifling through someone else's larder in the night. This was no time to go sentimental, she told herself sternly. He wouldn't remember a bit of it in the morning. The man was out of his mind with fever. He didn't know who she was. He'd thought she was someone else; that much was clear.

Who was she, this Lakshmi? Wife? Mistress? Whoever she was, those caresses had been intended for her, not for Gwen.

Enough. They were comrades; that was all. Comrades of war. Gwen seated herself at the little table, taking up her notebook and her pencil. Tearing a sheet from the back, she spread it flat against the scarred surface of the table. Next to her, on the bed, the Colonel was talking in his sleep again, arguing with someone only he could see. There was a fine sheen of sweat on his forehead, although the room was chill, chill enough to make her skin prickle beneath the fine lawn of her nightdress.

They weren't going to be making the stage tomorrow.

Gwen grimaced. It was the worst possible timing. If they had the girls neatly in tow, they might have stayed at this miserable inn a week or more while the Colonel recovered, the mystery solved, Jane's misgivings disproved. But Lizzy and Agnes were still missing, Fiorila was inexplicably in Bath, and she was immured here, guardian of the Colonel's sickbed. She might, she supposed, call on the Colonel's daughter, the older one, but it seemed a poor trick to play. The girl had her hands full with her grandmother. She didn't need a delirious father, as well. And however unsatisfactory their room at the inn, it was better than the floor of Mrs. Davies's basement apartment.

No. There was no escaping it. She had her own honor. She wouldn't leave a comrade in arms. Those unfortunate ruffians had rendered her neatly hors de combat until the Colonel's fever abated.

She wished she'd pinked them harder.

A memory teased the edge of her consciousness. One of them, complaining to the other: *They said they wouldn't be armed.* At the time, she hadn't paid it much attention; she had been too busy keeping the ruffians at bay, caught up in the battle lust. But now . . . Gwen frowned over her piece of paper.

It hadn't been a chance attack.

The footpads had followed them from Mrs. Davies's house. They might have been lying in wait there already, waiting for whatever mysterious package the Colonel's son was meant to have sent his sister. But then, if they'd been looking for opium, why not simply ransack the house? The bolt on the garden door was scarcely sophisticated. Two women alone, one of them bedridden, would have been easy prey for three large men.

No. More likely that the ruffians had followed them to Mrs. Davies's before following them from it.

It was not a reassuring thought.

Unless the Colonel had some enemy he hadn't seen fit to mention, it meant the one they were following was she. (Emotional agitation, Gwen had always contended, was no excuse for sloppy grammar.) True, the footpads had all converged upon the Colonel, but it wasn't an entirely unreasonable strategy for a group of men, tasked with a kidnapping, to immobilize the man first and grab the woman second. Of course, that worked only with a lesser sort of woman, but since few had her dexterity with a sword parasol, Gwen was willing to allow the ruffians that.

If—and it was a very broad "if"—someone had discovered the identity of the Pink Carnation, what better way to get to the Carnation than to lure her back to England by kidnapping her sister and then rendering her unprotected by nabbing her chaperone?

Actually, Gwen could think of several better ways, involving fewer intermediate steps, but the French villains she had met over the last few years seemed to have a convenient weakness for convoluted plots. There had been Gaston Delaroche, with his extra-special interrogation chamber, complete with rack, thumbscrews, and the latest in designer iron maidens. Then there was the Black Tulip, who had been so entirely over the bend that he made Delaroche, a raving lunatic by anyone's standards, seem sane by comparison.

Delaroche was safely in government custody, but the Black Tulip had never been caught.

Gwen caught herself biting a nail and made herself stop. The Black Tulip, so far as anyone knew, had accidentally incinerated himself nearly two years ago in the midst of a less-than-cunning plan to assassinate King George. But that didn't mean there wasn't someone else out there on the trail of the Carnation. These French spymasters sprung up like weeds, each more tenacious than the last. There had been rumors of another, called only the Gardener. Gwen had been able to discover next to nothing of him, which wasn't entirely reassuring. It meant either that he didn't exist, which would be good, or that he was clever enough to cover his tracks, which was quite the opposite of good.

The more she thought about it, the less insane it sounded, the possibility that those men had been after her, not the Colonel, not some imaginary shipment of opium. Whoever wanted the Pink Carnation wouldn't be out purely for a quick kill. The Pink Carnation had access to all sorts of information: underground networks of French and British agents, locations, code names. A knife to the gut would only ensure that that information went with the Carnation to the grave. On the other hand, if someone were to kidnap those nearest and dearest to the Carnation and threaten them with harm unless the Carnation revealed her secrets . . .

The Colonel cried out in his sleep.

Gwen rose from her chair, grateful for the distraction. No matter what she might have seen over these past few years, no matter how deep her thirst for adventure, some things were still too unpleasant to contemplate. She had never come to terms with torture. She particularly despised the cooptation of noncombatants.

Noncombatants like Agnes. Like Lizzy Reid.

Like the Colonel.

Gwen smoothed the hair back from his brow. It was dark with sweat, clinging to his damp skin. His fever was rising again, despite the opium she had given him. Taking up the candle, she delicately peeled back a corner of the poultice she had bound over his wound. She didn't see any of the telltale red streaks that would signal a truly dangerous infection, but the light was poor and the night was still young.

For the first time, the true magnitude of what Jane had said back in Paris was borne in upon her. If this attack had been directed at her, then his wound, his fever, his missing daughter, were all on her conscience. She remembered the laughing man who had accompanied her in the coach that morning, swinging her out of the way of that out-of-control carriage, teasing her about her novel. To see him brought low, like this . . .

They might merely have been footpads.

Gwen bathed the Colonel's forehead as best she could with the water in the ewer by the bed. She had already used the last of her opium on him, and too much opium probably wasn't the best idea in any event. If his fever hadn't broken by morning, she would have the maidservant call a doctor. Not that a doctor was likely to do much she couldn't do, other than take away perfectly useful blood and prescribe foul-smelling nostrums. She'd do better to tend him herself.

But first she needed to alert Jane.

Licking the tip of her pencil, Gwen wrote, "A and L not here. Misfortune encountered on the road. Unalterably delayed. Pursue inquiries in Bath." After some thought, she added, "Eager to see opera. Please acquire tickets."

That should be suitably oblique to confuse anyone who intercepted the communication but specific enough to alert Jane to the presence of Aurelia Fiorila.

She signed the letter "Mrs. A. Fustian." Jane would understand without needing to be told. They had used the alias together often enough.

The League of the Pink Carnation had formed only a little over two years ago, but Gwen had known Jane far longer than that. She had known her from the time she was born, from a small tot with downy blond curls to a quiet child with pale brown hair and a book in her hand. All of the other children in the neighborhood—Jane's siblings, her own nieces and nephew—had been afraid of her, but never Jane. From the beginning, they had had their own quiet rapport.

If she were to dip into maudlin sentimentality, she might even go so far as to say that she loved Jane like a daughter.

It was a good thing she didn't go in for such sentiments. But all the same, she couldn't shake a slight sense of foreboding.

In small, cramped letters on the bottom of the page, she added, "Be careful."

Chapter 9

London, 2004

"You must be joking," said Colin flatly.

"See?" said Jeremy, all injured innocence. "Every time I try . . ."

"Enough," said Mrs. Selwick-Alderly, and even though she didn't raise her voice, it silenced them both.

It was an excellent trick. I wondered if she could teach it to me. I could use it on my undergrads next year.

"I've had enough of this," she said. "From both of you. How badly do you want the treasure? Or are you more interested in hurting each other?"

I could have answered that for her. Hurting each other. Definitely hurting each other. At least on Jeremy's part. Colin just wanted to be left alone.

Not like I was biased or anything.

"This isn't my fight," Jeremy said suavely.

"Don't try to lie to me, Jamie Alderly," said Mrs. Selwick-Alderly majestically. The use of his childhood name pulled him up short, like a dog on a leash. Jamie Alderly sounded like a very different person from Jeremy Selwick-Alderly, transatlantic man of douche baggery. "I know the trick you pulled with that production company—and a nasty trick it was, too."

Jeremy's thin veneer of charm was beginning to show wear around the sides. He set his chin pugnaciously. "Caroline has a one-third right to the Hall."

Caroline was Colin's mother, Jeremy's wife, bubbly and oblivious. She went through life with a champagne glass in one hand, completely unaware of anyone's needs but her own. She was charming but, as Mrs. Selwick-Alderly had once told me, entirely irresponsible. I'd seen the truth of that for myself. She hadn't batted an eyelash when her husband threw her son under the bus. Scratch that—she hadn't even noticed. It was all "kiss, kiss, isn't it lovely!"

"My mother wouldn't care if Selwick Hall burned to the ground," said my boyfriend, driven to the end of his rope. "In fact, she'd probably prefer it. She'd be able to collect the insurance money without a white elephant dragging her down."

Then Jeremy uttered the truly unforgivable. "And Serena agreed."

Serena was Colin's sister. Jeremy had bought her for thirty pieces of silver, or, in more modern parlance, a part ownership of the gallery at which she'd been working for several years.

"Yes," said Mrs. Selwick-Alderly, "I heard about that, too."

There was something in her voice that quelled even Jeremy.

"Do you want to live there, Jamie?" Mrs. Selwick-Alderly had clearly had it. There was no mistaking the edge of exasperation in her voice. "Do you want to get the home farm back in order? I didn't think so." She turned to her nephew. "As for you, Colin—"

If Colin's jaw got any tighter, it was going to shatter.

"Putting the Hall back together isn't going to bring your father back." For a moment, I thought Colin meant to get up and leave. His hands tightened on the arms of his chair. Mrs. Selwick-Alderly's expression as she looked at her great-nephew was ineffably sad. "The Hall isn't a shrine."

"No," said Colin shortly. "It's my home."

He used to have a flat somewhere in London, but that was before I'd met him, before his father had died and he had become the Selwick of Selwick.

For the first time, I wondered, uneasily, if his aunt might not have something there, if Colin might not be happier in a sleek modern flat in one of the newly reclaimed areas down by the water, with a view of the river and hot and cold running tourists. After years of dates with men who thought the Scarlet Pimpernel was a form of pumpernickel, I'd been delighted by Colin's interest in his own family's history. He spoke my language. But for me, it was my career, my path to a PhD, a book, and, with any luck, a permanent teaching job on some pleasant campus with a good coffee shop and students who were marginally more literate than their peers.

For Colin, it had become an idée fixe.

Even this book he was working on, the spy novel that was meant to bring him fame and fortune, was an homage to his father, who had read him Ian Fleming novels and told him contraband stories of his days in MI6.

The life we were leading—it wasn't really a normal twenty-something life, was it? Puttering about in the garden, trivia night with the vicar at the pub on Tuesdays, maybe a day trip into London to visit an aging relative if we were feeling really daring. I knew Colin had friends from his university days, I'd even met a couple of them, but they were living their own lives, here in London. We hadn't seen them since I'd moved into Selwick Hall. Colin kept talking about getting together with Nigel and Martin, but we'd sunk into our lives in Selwick Hall, like feet slid into a pair of woolly socks, too comfortable to kick out of them and put on proper shoes.

I felt a little bit sick all of a sudden. Here I'd thought I'd been so good for him, coaxing him to open up about his mother and sister (with minimal success, but still), and instead I was only reinforcing his neuroses.

I loved him, but I was beginning to realize that underneath that charming BBC accent, he really was more than a little messed up.

"You mean," said Jeremy, "one-third of it is your home."

"Would you like me to draw a neat line down through the kitchen?" said Colin tightly. "Would you prefer I confined myself to the bit with the sink or the refrigerator?"

I couldn't take it anymore. "Fine," I said. "Do you want Colin to buy you out?"

I knew it was an empty threat. I know Colin couldn't afford it. But I was curious to see how Jeremy would react.

"You wouldn't understand," he said patronizingly, before adding, "Rather a nice deal, living there rent-free, isn't it?"

"I make up for it in labor," said Colin. "Or would you rather muck out the stables yourself?"

Mrs. Selwick-Alderly's voice rose over their bickering. "Eloise, dear, will you pour?"

I would have loved to have poured the boiling liquid straight into Jeremy's lap, but that would have been a waste of good caffeine. Tight-lipped, I followed instructions, lifting the heavy teapot and tipping it carefully over the silver strainer balanced on one of the delicate Spode cups.

"This," said Mrs. Selwick-Alderly, while I had my hands full with a pot of scalding liquid, "is exactly what I'm talking about. You can't go on like this. Regardless of what may have happened in the past—"

If I hadn't been holding the teapot, I would have been tempted to say a few choice words. "Regardless" just didn't cover a man marrying his cousin's mother.

"—you are family and you have to live with each other." She lifted her silver head, looking first at one, then at the other, impeccably aristocratic in her blue wool pants suit. "I have a proposition to put to you both."

"You don't have an interest in Selwick Hall," pointed out Jeremy.

Did the man think only in dollars and cents? I meant, in pounds and pence?

Mrs. Selwick-Alderly stared down her grandson. "No, but I have an interest in you. In both of you." Then she played her trump card. "And I do know rather a bit about those jewels you both want. Are you agreed, or no?"

"All right," said Jeremy reluctantly. "I'm game."

It took Colin longer. "Why?" he asked.

For the first time, Mrs. Selwick-Alderly's regal gaze faltered. "I am—not well." She busied herself with her teacup. "It would give me peace of mind to see the two of you come to terms."

If it had been my family, this would have been followed by a noisy inquiry about her health. But Colin's family didn't work that way.

Colin nodded curtly. "I'm in."

Which I knew really translated to, *I love you and I'm worried about you.* In Colin-speak.

Fortunately, Mrs. Selwick-Alderly knew that too. She reached out and pressed his hand with her papery, blue-veined one. "Thank you," she said.

Rising from her seat on the sofa, she went to one of the many white-painted shelves that lined either side of the fireplace. The books were an eclectic mix, modern hardcovers jostling spines with the faded leather covers of lengthy matched sets. Unlike the collections of books designers bought by the yard at the Strand, these had all been purchased by some long-ago Selwick for content rather than aesthetics, read and battered and read again. On many, the titles had been all but rubbed from the spine.

This book was covered in faded red leather, the first in a series of identical volumes. Mrs. Selwick-Alderly set it down on the tea tray, next to the biscuits.

I craned my neck to read the title, which was inscribed with the maximum number of curlicues. "*The Convent of Orsino?*"

"The original title," said Mrs. Selwick-Alderly smugly, "was *The Perils of Plumeria.*"

I gave a little hop in my chair.

Colin groaned.

Jeremy looked blank.

"So that's Plumeria!" I turned to Colin, nearly knocking my tea over with one knee. "After all the hours I spent poking around in horticultural manuals . . . Does she have a tower?"

"Not that I remember," said Mrs. Selwick-Alderly, "but it's been a rather long time since I read it."

"What does this have to do with the jewels?" asked Jeremy.

"It's that old rhyme," said Colin reluctantly. "Hard by Plumeria's bower, or whatever it was."

Mrs. Selwick-Alderly looked at him sharply. She knew as well as I did that he knew exactly how the rhyme went. So much for immediate entente.

Jeremy, however, didn't. He leaned back in his chair, propping one immaculately clad ankle against the opposite knee. "Of course. I remember now. We used to run around reciting it when we were little."

"Yeah," said Colin, and I wondered just what he was remembering, whether there had been a halcyon time when they had played together as boys.

Jeremy was only six years older than Colin. Had they played Robin Hood together in the woods outside Selwick Hall with Serena as Maid Marian? It put a rather different complexion on things.

I picked up the book, red tooled leather on the outside, a heavily engraved frontispiece on the inside. "By a Lady?"

"Not just any lady," said Mrs. Selwick-Alderly. "It was written by Miss Gwendolyn Meadows."

"Are you sure?" There had been mention, from time to time, in Jane's letters to Henrietta of Miss Gwen's Gothic novel, but they had made it sound like a big joke.

Mrs. Selwick-Alderly pointed to the flyleaf. Underneath the title, in a sprawling hand, was written, "To Amy: I trust you shall benefit from Plumeria's example. G.M."

That sounded like Miss Gwen all right. "Got it," I said.

"Plumeria is the heroine of the novel," said Mrs. Selwick-Alderly helpfully. "Rather an unusual heroine too."

"If Miss Gwen wrote her, she must be," I murmured. "But what does this have to do with the lost jewels of Berar?"

"I don't know," said Mrs. Selwick-Alderly, "but I gather that it was the runaway bestseller of 1806. It wasn't eclipsed until Byron came out with *Childe Harold* in 1812. That," she added, "is a first edition."

Jeremy, who had been surreptitiously checking his phone, looked up with sudden interest.

I hastily put it down again, well away from the tea.

Mrs. Selwick-Alderly smiled. "Don't worry, it's not that valuable. Literary scholars haven't been kind to our Miss Meadows."

"No, I can't imagine they would be," I said, turning over the small morocco volume in my hands. Its spine proclaimed that it was Volume I of V.

"There's a much grander copy at the Hall," said Mrs. Selwick-Alderly, "or at least there was when I was young. It belonged to Colonel Reid's youngest daughter, who married Richard's son. It's the size of a dictionary, though, all five volumes in one. You'll do better with this one."

"Thank you?" I said. I still wasn't quite sure what I was meant to do with it.

"Many years ago," she said, "I was told that the clue was in the book. I wasn't able to figure it out, but perhaps the three of you together will. Three minds, after all, are better than one."

Not if two of them were occupied with plans for mutual destruction. But I didn't say that. Instead, I thanked her nicely and slid the book into my capacious shoulder bag.

Colin glanced at his watch. "We should be going if we want to catch the early train back."

I knew that really translated to *we should be going before I kill Jeremy*.

Mrs. Selwick-Alderly was always her most dangerous when she was her most serene. "No need," she said airily. If she hadn't been a dignified woman of over eighty years, I would have called her expression impish. "Jeremy will drive you up."

This was apparently news to Jeremy, too.

"Well, you can't all look for the jewels at the Hall if you aren't all up there together." As we all sat stunned, she lifted the teapot. "More tea?"

Ten months ago, she had pulled a similar move to get a reluctant Colin to take me up to the Hall with him. At the time, I had thought it was great. This time, I was on the other side of it. The teeth-gnashing side of it.

It didn't help that Jeremy's car was a convertible clearly designed for two. I offered to sit in the back, since my legs were shorter than Colin's. I was voted down. I spent the drive back down to Sussex with my hair blowing across my face like Cousin It, Colin in the backseat behind me, legs folded to his chin, sending off waves of annoyance so palpable that they probably counted as toxic waste.

It felt like a very long drive.

No one spoke. We couldn't think of anything neutral to say. Miss Gwen's book burned in my bag against my leg. I was itching to take it out and start flipping through it—maybe someone had hidden a note in there? Nancy Drew was always finding things under the lining of old books—but (a) Jeremy was right next to me, (b) Jeremy wasn't putting the damned top up and I didn't want to risk it blowing away, and (c) Jeremy was right next to me. Collaboration went only so far.

Windblown and sullen, we all fished up in the front hall of Selwick Hall, kicking our feet against the hall rug and not looking at one another. The Hall felt different with a houseguest, especially an unwanted one. For the past few months, this had been, as odd as it was, my home. Colin's home, of course, not mine, but this was where I wandered around in my pajamas with my hair unwashed and a toothbrush sticking out of my mouth. I knew how to navigate the kitchen with the light off to get to my favorite coffee mug, and I'd internalized the trick of not stepping on the squeaky step on the front stairs.

With the introduction of Jeremy, who had grown up in and out of this house, the one-third owner, I was suddenly a guest again.

I didn't like it.

Not that I had any right to complain. I was leaving in less than two months, after all. I picked unhappily at the corner of a nail. We still hadn't really talked about that, Colin and I, and I didn't think we were going to with Jeremy in the house. It was like having the Ghost of Christmas Future, the grim, funereal one, brooding over you—that is, if the Ghost of Christmas Future wore expensive linen suits.

Jeremy had an overnight case with him. His grandmother, he said, had invited him to stay for a few days. I believed him. It seemed like the sort of ploy Mrs. Selwick-Alderly would concoct. She had probably already cooked up her little plot to send him up to the Hall so the boys could play together and make up.

Colin obviously didn't believe him but wasn't going to say anything. So he didn't say anything at all.

The silence stretched on. And on. It was so quiet that I could hear the drone of bees in the overgrown roses in the garden and the tick of the grandfather clock on the landing.

Someone had to take charge. "You." I pointed at Colin. "Search the tower. I know you've done it before, but someone has to do it again."

"Why not me?" asked Jeremy.

"I wouldn't want you to break a nail," said Colin.

I intervened before it could get nasty. "We don't need both of you in the tower. Jeremy, you can handle nineteenth-century handwriting, right?"

Jeremy looked like a cat who had been offered the generic brand instead of Fancy Feast. His nose twitched with disdain. "Naturally."

"Good. There's a whole stack of Lady Henrietta's letters I haven't gone through yet. There might be something in there."

I hated having anyone but me going through those, but unlike some people, I knew Jeremy had zero interest in ripping off my dissertation research. He couldn't care less which spy had done what when unless it led him to the jewels. Besides, like the rest of the family, he already knew the identity of the Pink Carnation.

It gave me a rather icky feeling that he was family, but in this case, it came in handy.

Not that I wouldn't go through the letters myself to make sure that he wasn't hiding anything, but we could cover more ground if we all divvied up.

Jeremy gave me a look. "And what will you be doing?"

I'd saved the short straw for myself. "Me? I'll be reading through all five volumes of *The Convent of Orsino*. If either of you want to trade, just let me know."

My boyfriend dropped a kiss on the top of my head. "Have fun with that," he said.

"Better you than me," agreed Jeremy.

Lovely. They were getting along better already. And I wanted to kick both of them.

"Dinner at seven," I said. "And one of you had better be doing the cooking."

Chapter 10

Sir Magnifico woke under the gnarled branches of a squat and stunted oak tree. Where was the perfumed pavilion, the silken pillows? The only mattress beneath him was the moss, sere and scratchy. He lay in a barren and blasted heath, open to the elements, the only sign of habitation the stark shape of a dark tower in the distance.

The sky lowered, as if with impending rain—or impending doom.   —From *The Convent of Orsino* by A Lady

William woke in a room he didn't recognize.

It was nearly dawn outside, the sky that peculiar yellow-gray that precedes the sunrise, the trees outside blurry and dim through the uneven glass of the windows. A woman lay in the bed beside him, curled on one side. Her head was buried in the crook of one arm. He couldn't see her face, just the crook of her arm, the curve of her hip. Her hair had been tightly pulled back, braided and coiled around her head. Dark wisps curled like question marks against the nape of her neck.

Who in the blazes was she, and why were they in bed together? He didn't conduct casual affairs, not anymore. He especially didn't conduct casual affairs with women wearing all their clothes and lying on top of the covers.

William tried to move, to ease the covers off, but a sharp pain in his side made him subside against the pillows. His head ached like the very devil.

Memory flickered and wavered like a candle flame, brigands in the road, a white-robed houri in a Persian pleasure garden, Kat's reddened hands, the flash of a slim silver blade in a lady's hand.

He needed to get somewhere, to do something. One of his children was in trouble—Lizzy, little Lizzy. Lizzy had run away.

It came back to him in a rush, with a sick, sinking feeling at the pit of his stomach. Lizzy was in trouble and he was meant to be finding her. Only . . . only . . . what in the hell was he doing here?

Gasping against the pain, he struggled to sit, reaching for the candle on the nightstand. His groping hand knocked against the pewter base, sending it tumbling to the ground. It landed on the uncarpeted floor with a horrible, hollow clang.

The woman beside him lurched upright, instantly awake and on the alert. She reminded William of a tigress in the jungle, sniffing the air for danger, head turning this way, then that. The coronet of braids on top of her head, loosened by sleep, trembled with the movement.

"What's that?" she demanded.

That clipped voice was familiar. William had heard it before. He tried to sit, but the movement made him wince.

"Stop that!" she said. "You'll hurt yourself."

Meadows. Miss Gwendolyn Meadows. *You may call me Miss Gwen....*

"Gwen," he said slowly. It came out as a croak, like a frog. It didn't sound like him in the slightest.

Gwendolyn Meadows pulled her dress up around her shoulders. "Well, I suppose given that I've seen you with your clothes off, I shouldn't quibble at your use of my name." She must have loosened the lacings to sleep; the purple traveling costume gaped at the neck, revealing a glimpse of a surprisingly frivolous shift embroidered with purple flowers. She gave her dress a tug and the flowers disappeared. "At least you know me this time. A few hours ago you were still calling me Maria."

He blinked at her, more confused than he had ever been in his life. His mouth felt like someone had crammed it with cotton wool. As for his head—his head didn't bear thinking of. Had someone been pounding his forehead with a mallet?

As muddled as he was, it took a few moments for the impact of her words to kick in. *Given that I've seen you with your clothes off...*

He could see his calf poking out from under the sheet. His bare calf. His shoulders were bare too. He could feel every lump in the mattress against his bare back. Breeches? Was he wearing breeches? He seemed to be. Not that they covered much, and the lacings at the top were most definitely undone.

William looked at his companion with panic in his eyes. "I didn't—we didn't—"

Gwen made a face at him. "Calm yourself, Colonel. You were the perfect gentleman." She slid off the edge of the bed, the movement of her body tugging the covers with her. William made a feeble grab for them before the whole of his body could be exposed to the world. "You didn't have the energy to be anything else."

That he could believe. He had never felt so weak in his life, not even after a bout of dysentery his first summer in India, his body fever racked and convulsing, with a coolie ineffectually pulling a slow-moving punkah above.

But this wasn't India; this was England. He had come back to England. For Kat. And Lizzy.

"Bath," he said, wiggling back against the pillow. The sheet slipped, revealing a neat basket weave of bandages across his chest. "We have to get to Bath."

"Sit!" barked Gwen. "You're not getting anywhere by tearing your stitches open."

Stitches? He had had stitches?

He remembered none of this. William subsided against the pillow, baffled and infuriated by his own weakness, his own patchy memory. The dimness of the room didn't help. He hated not being able to see properly, unsure whether it was his eyes or the maddening half-light of dawn.

Gwen Meadows scooped up the candle he had knocked over, lighting it from the embers of the fire. A small flame appearcd, shielded by her hand. The room was small and close, with the musty smell of the sickroom.

"How long have I been like this?" It hurt to talk. His throat felt cracked and dry.

"Drink this," said Gwen Meadows, and poured something from the jug on the bedside table into a battered pewter goblet.

He tried to take it from her, but his hands betrayed him, shaking so that the liquid sloshed over the sides, wetting the sheet that covered him. He felt shamed, shamed many times over.

Brushing aside his ineffectual efforts, Gwen held the cup neatly to his lips, tipping it so he could drink. It was water, slightly stale from sitting in the jug, but liquid nonetheless. He drank thirstily, the liquid trickling down his chin.

"You needed that, didn't you?" said Gwen, with some satisfaction, blotting the damp from his chin. It was maddening being so helpless. "You wouldn't believe the time I've had getting anything into you."

Yes, he vaguely remembered that. He remembered someone spooning broth into his mouth, scolding and cajoling by turns. But he also remembered a goddess holding out a chalice in both hands, a goddess in an enchanted garden, her dark hair unbound, offering him mead and honey. Reality and dream warped and melded.

"I had the strangest dreams," he said slowly.

Gwen busied herself with the miscellany on the bedside table. "I shouldn't be surprised," she said. "You were raving like anything. Most of it in foreign tongues, although I believe there were one or two sea shanties in there."

William winced. "Not the one about——"

"Yes," said Gwen. "That one."

William didn't know what to say. "I'm sorry?"

"Don't be," she said serenely. "It was most instructive. Especially the bit about the sailor's rest, sa-ha, sa-ha."

William could feel his cheeks burning with something other than fever. The sailor's rest was upon his lady's breast. They were very buxom breasts, an attribute that was described in detail. The song became even more explicit from there. Sex-starved men on a long voyage were apt to become more than a little imaginative.

William tried very hard not to look at his companion's breasts, even though they were directly in his line of vision.

He raised his eyes back to her face. "I spent some time on a ship in my youth," he ventured, by way of apology. "Amazing the things that cling in one's head."

"Amazing," Gwen agreed drily. "Don't tell me you didn't have songs just as vulgar in your mess in Madras."

He might have tried to make the argument, but there were fairly good odds that she'd heard some of them while he was out cold.

He scratched the stubble on his chin. It was longer than it ought to be, the grizzled hair halfway to a beard and itchy to boot.

"How long was I out?" he asked again.

She seated herself on the edge of the bed, carefully, so that the mattress wouldn't sag and jar him. "Four days."

"Four *days*! I must——"

"Don't even think of it," she said. She loomed over him, pinning him neatly into place, one arm on either side of his shoulders. "I didn't patch you up just to let you make yourself ill again."

Again he felt himself falling into that odd gap between dream and memory. It was Gwen leaning over him, but not Gwen, a woman with long black hair that streamed around her shoulders, long black hair and full red lips, stroking hands and twisting bodies.

Even the memory had the power to arouse him. He was grateful for the protection of the dim light.

He blinked up at her, fighting his way back to reality. "It seems I owe you my thanks," he said slowly.

"Yes," she said, "you do. Although if I'd been faster on my feet, you might not have been skewered in the first place."

"We were waylaid." William's head ached abominably. He rubbed it with the heel of one hand.

She patted his hand. "Yes, by a trio of brigands with the temerity to draw knives on you."

"You beat them off." He was beginning to remember now, the men, the knives, Miss Meadows and her parasol that turned into a sword.

"You weren't doing too badly yourself," she said graciously. "You were at a disadvantage, bare hands against blades."

Her words echoed strangely, slurring together in his head. He could feel himself slipping again into sleep. He felt a cool hand against his forehead, his cheek, easing him down again against the pillows, and one word, "Rest."

This time, he slept without dreams.

When he woke, it was full dark again. He was alone in the bed. In the hearth, the fire had burned down, and the temperature in the room was noticeably colder than before, nipping at his nose and bare shoulders. Gwen sat at the table by the window, scribbling busily in a notebook, a shawl draped over the shoulders of her purple dress. There were four candles lit, all guttering merrily away, more than half burnt down, and the remains of a hunk of bread, cheese, and cold meats on a round platter beside her.

William blinked, as if he could will the sky outside the windows to change color. It had been dawn, not even dawn, the last time he'd woken. He couldn't have slept through the whole day!

Apparently, he had. Another day lost. Another day . . .

He heaved himself up. This time, his body obeyed. He still felt as though someone had gone after him with a mallet, but the wretched fuzziness was gone, and his limbs, although weak, obeyed his commands.

"You're awake!" said Gwen, closing her notebook over her pencil and hurrying over to him. She set the back of her hand against his forehead, paused a moment, and then nodded. "No fever."

"Did you put something in the water?" he asked accusingly.

"No," she said.

William raised his brows. They were one of the few parts of his body that didn't hurt.

"I would have," Gwen said frankly, "but I ran out. You needed the sleep; that's all. Since you're awake . . ."

She turned towards a basin on the nightstand, dunking a roll of cotton into the water.

"What are you doing?" William asked warily.

Gwen wrung out the towel with a snap. "Washing you." The next thing he knew, his face was enveloped in a damp, soapy cloth.

William came up sputtering. "What the—"

"Be quiet or you'll get soap in your mouth." The cloth descended again, with particular attention to his ears.

"You don't have to do this," he said, trying to inch away as she dunked the cloth back in the water. "In fact, I'd rather you didn't."

She ruthlessly peeled back the covers, baring him straight down to his breeches. William was very grateful that he was still wearing breeches, such as they were. It was a pity he had never invested in pantaloons. Those would have covered far more. As it was, he tried to sneak his hairy lower shanks under the blanket, only to find himself being swatted on the leg by Gwen's towel.

"Would you rather I let you stink?" As she began efficiently sponging his torso, he heard her mutter, "This was a great deal easier when you were unconscious."

She had done this before? If he had been capable of blushing, William would have. The idea of lying here, helpless, next to naked . . . He felt like an adolescent again, caught in an embarrassing position.

Scrunching his neck, he looked down at the top of her dark head. From this angle, it looked as if she were—

William cleared his throat. Hard. He'd lost enough blood without it going to inconvenient places.

Gwen took advantage of his momentary confusion to poke him in his good shoulder. "Raise your arm."

He raised his arm. He had, at this point, no personal dignity left. This woman had seen him at his worst, in every possible way, physical and spiritual.

She had even seen Kat.

As if she were reading his thoughts, she said, "Your daughter stopped by. Not the missing one," she added, before he could get his hopes up. "The other one."

"Kat?" Perfect. All he needed was for his daughter to also see him lying low. He would have liked her to retain some of her illusions. When she was little, he had been her hero, her knight errant, carrying her on his shoulders, soothing her childish hurts and bruises.

When had it all got so much harder?

"Kat," Gwen confirmed, dabbing carefully around his bandages. "I like her."

"So you've said." He grabbed at the sheet as she started pulling it down below his waist. "Um, I think I'm clean enough."

Gwen shrugged. "Suit yourself," she said, retrieving her washcloth. With deliberate bravado, she added, "No need to be ashamed. Nothing there I haven't seen anyway."

This time, he definitely was blushing.

"What did Kat say?" he asked in a strangled voice.

"She told me to tell you not to worry, that she and her

grandmother will be staying with friends for the rest of the month."

A wave of sadness swamped him. He had never felt so weak, so useless. "She's lying."

"She's lying," Gwen agreed, wringing out the cloth in the basin. "But it was a noble lie. She has character, that girl."

"She's not a girl anymore," said William. She had been a girl when he put her on the boat in Calcutta, a girl of seventeen. She was twenty-seven, and deserved better than he'd given her.

"Whatever she is," said Gwen, "she's strong. You should be proud of her."

He would have been more proud if he'd kept her closer, safer. And then there was Lizzy, missing.

"When do we leave?" he asked.

Gwen eyed him assessingly. "Your fever only broke this morning."

"When do we leave?" he repeated.

"Has anyone ever told you you're as stubborn as a mule?"

In fact, they hadn't. He usually got his way with charm rather than brute force. But he didn't have the energy to be charming. And he didn't think she'd fall for it, anyway.

"It takes one to know one," he said instead.

Gwen grinned at him. "As long as we understand each other," she said. "You're not going anywhere tonight—no, don't argue with me! We'll never make the stage and I'm not letting you near the reins of a curricle like that. You'd overturn us both, and then where would your daughters be?"

He had to acknowledge the logic of that, but he didn't like it. "I don't like it," he grumbled.

"And I don't like tripe," she said. "We all have to deal with things we don't like in this world."

Tripe? How did tripe get into it? "They're hardly on the same order."

"Distracted you, though, didn't I?" Sobering, she said, "Think it through. The girls have been missing for nearly three weeks now. One night will hardly make a difference."

William folded his arms across his chest, ignoring the pinch in his side. "You're not making me feel any better."

"I wasn't trying to," she said. "But I would prefer to keep you alive. I've invested too much effort to see you collapsing somewhere between Bristol and Bath."

She said it matter-of-factly, but there was something in her voice that hadn't been there before. For the first time, he noticed that there were purple circles under her eyes to match the color of her dress. Her face seemed thinner than before, thinner and more drawn. She had pulled her hair back ruthlessly from her face, but the severe hairstyle only emphasized the hollows below her cheeks, the fragility of her long neck.

William reached out and caught her hand before she could turn away. "Have you had any sleep these past four nights?"

She twitched her hand away. "Some," she said. "Enough." But she didn't quite meet his eyes.

William's memories of the last few days might be fragmented, but what he did remember was Gwen leaning over him, tending him, feeding him, her hands as gentle as her tone was rough. "I'd rather you not kill yourself in tending me."

She put her nose in the air. "I'm not such a weakling as that."

"No," he said, the first smile in days beginning to curl across his lips. "You're not. Has anyone ever told you you're a dab hand with a sword?"

She made an airy gesture with one hand. She wore several rings, heavy things in twisted gold and enamel, but not a wedding ring among them. "I had a reasonably competent fencing master."

"Is it the thing in England for ladies to have fencing masters?"

She shrugged, avoiding his eyes. "I get easily bored. And, as you see, my little toy can be rather useful. The roads aren't as lawless as they were twenty years past, but one still encounters the odd highwayman with delusions of competence."

"Delusions of competence," William repeated. There was no denying that the woman had a way with words.

She mistook his slow headshake as something else. "You mustn't overtire yourself." Frowning, she leaned over him, testing his temperature. "The fever seems to be gone, but you'd best rest still. If you make it through the night without it rising, we can take the stage back to Bath tomorrow."

She stood over his bed like an avenging angel, ready to chivy him to sleep with a flaming sword.

"Only if you get some rest too," said William stubbornly.

"I shall," she said, and weak or not, William still knew enough to know when someone was lying. She sat herself down in the chair by the bed with a flounce of her crumpled skirts. "Presently."

If he believed that, he'd also believe she had a commission to sell him in a regiment of her own making.

William looked around the room. It ought to have been evident to him before, but his mind hadn't been all that it could be. "There's only the one bed."

"Yes," she said. She absently rubbed her shoulder with one hand. "I am aware of that."

"You've not been sleeping in that chair?" Even as he said it, he remembered waking to find her next to him, curled up in sleep.

Gwen's cheeks darkened. "I took a little rest now and again on the bed—on top of the covers," she added hastily. "You were too far gone to notice. Besides, it would have looked odd if anyone had come in and I wasn't in the bed with you. We're meant to be married, remember? No, of course you don't. You were tottering with blood loss. I had to tell the innkeeper that we were married. Don't worry, it's not binding."

There was something rather endearing about her obvious discomfort. "I'm not worried."

If anything, that seemed to annoy her. "Well, you should be. If it were Scotland, we would be married by now whether we liked it or not. All it takes is a pronouncement in front of strangers for a marriage to be legally binding."

"I'll remember that," William said, "the next time I find

myself in Scotland. In the meantime, there's a broad bed, and room for you in it."

He patted the covers next to him.

He watched as she surreptitiously flexed her shoulders, eyeing the lumpy mattress like a tiger sighting an unattended goat. With an effort, she straightened her back. "No matter," she said. "I'll just read for a bit."

William hoisted himself onto one elbow. "You said you'd slept here before."

"Yes," she said, frowning at him. "But you were asleep. And delusional."

"I intend to be asleep very shortly," he said. "And it's safe to say that I'm still delusional."

"Not like before," said Gwen with authority, but she rose, stiffly, from the chair, stretching.

William was reminded of a cat, having scorned a dish of meat, waiting until the humans' backs were turned before inching towards it.

"That reminds me," she said brusquely. "Who is Lakshmi?"

Puzzled but game, William said, "She's the Hindu goddess of fortune." As Gwen seated herself on the other side of the bed, leaning over to unlace her leather boots, he added, "She's a bit like the Roman Venus, in that she's meant to be the embodiment of beauty, but with other aspects beside. Not quite so dim as poor old Venus."

Lakshmi, goddess of beauty and fortune . . .

He could hear the faint echo of his own voice, fever hoarse. Confused images, brightly colored birds, a fountain, and always, always, that fall of dark hair, brushing his bare arms, caressing his face, as he feasted on her lips, his hands around a lithe waist that slipped away, just out of his grasp.

William shook himself back to the present. "Why do you ask?"

Gwen had tucked her bare feet up under her skirt. She curled up on the far side of the bed, on top of the covers, her shawl spread over her.

"Nothing," she said quickly, and if his eyes didn't ache quite so much, William might have thought she had turned slightly pink. "Just something you said in your sleep."

Their faces were on a level now, pillow to pillow. William eyed her with interest. "Did I say anything else interesting in my sleep?"

"Just those sea shanties," Gwen shot back. She twitched her shawl, trying to get it to cover more of her. It was a flimsy thing, a lady's shawl, intended for ornament rather than real use.

"You're shivering," said William, sitting bolt upright. The covers fell away from his chest. He yanked at the blanket on top of which she was lying. "Come under the covers."

Gwen rolled away. "I am quite all right, thank you," said her muffled voice from the other side of the bed. She still had the blanket trapped beneath her.

William tapped her on the shoulder. "There's no one here to know. I won't have you take a fever now, not after all the effort you've put in to save my sorry hide." She stayed curled up just where she was. Cajolingly, he added, "You can put a sword between us, if that would make you feel better."

That got her attention. She rolled her neck to look over at

him. She ought to have been vulnerable in her prone position, but she managed to pack her voice with a full measure of disdain. "I prefer to keep my sword where I can reach it, thank you very much."

She patted the handle of her parasol, which was propped beside the bed.

"And don't think that I don't appreciate that," said William, "but I'll not have you freezing, and that's my final word."

"*Your* final word— Stop that!"

William gave the covers a sharp yank, enough to unbalance her, trying to pull them out from under her so that he could put them over her. Gwen rolled over to stop him, and somehow, he wasn't quite sure how, after a bit of scuffling and tussling, and a "mind your bandages, you fool!" she was lying beneath him, her hair tousled from its pins, both of them breathing hard.

They stared at each other for a moment, both slightly dazed.

At least she wasn't blue anymore. There was flush on her cheeks and her lips were red and slightly parted.

"All right!" she said, squirming away from him. "All right! You win!" She pushed at his chest—making sure to avoid his bandage—with both hands. "Move, you great lug. I can't get under the covers with you on top of me."

For some reason, William couldn't stop grinning, despite the dull ache in his side. He obligingly rolled over, swinging his legs over the side of the bed, hitching up his breeches to preserve his decency. It was the first time he'd been out of bed in days, and his legs felt wobbly, but he'd be damned if he'd let her see it.

With a courtly gesture, he held up the sheets so that she could climb under.

"Can I have that in writing?" he said. "About the winning?"

"We tell no one of this," Gwen said fiercely, staring him down for all she was worth. "Do you understand? No one."

"Agreed," he said, and slid back in on his side of the bed.

Gwen scrunched herself in the smallest possible space at the edge of the bed, pointedly turned her back on him, and yanked the covers up over her shoulders, her hand resting on the handle of her sword parasol.

She'd left the candles burning on the nightstand. One by one, William lifted them and blew them out, plunging the room into darkness.

He waited before the last candle was out before saying, "Gwen?"

She wriggled deeper into her side of the bed, pointedly ignoring him. "I'm not talking to you," she muttered.

Despite all the worries crowding around him—or perhaps because of them—William smiled.

"Sleep well," he said. "And may all your dreams be sweet."

"Hmph," said Gwen. But he noticed that she didn't push the covers away.

Chapter 11

Plumeria resolved never to tell Sir Magnifico of the liberties he had taken, ever so unwittingly, in the secluded environs of the ~~olive~~ oak grove. What happened in the oak grove stayed in the oak grove. Thus she resolved, but as they made their unsteady way towards the dark tower, she could not help but notice a strange change in the formerly voluble knight. Was it the Gypsy's curse at work? Or some greater, even more mysterious power?

—From *The Convent of Orsino* by A Lady

G wen was warm, truly warm, for the first time in days. She hadn't realized just how exhausted she had been, sleeping in fits and starts, waking to minister to William, waking because she couldn't stop shivering, until she had grudgingly accepted a place in the bed, under the covers. The clergy could go on all they liked about angels with harps, but as far as she was concerned, heaven was a large bed and a warm blanket.

Then the blanket moved. One might even say it wriggled.

She was, she realized, snuggled up against William Reid, his front pressed against her back, the position of his body mirroring the shape of hers. There was a knee tucked up behind hers and a heavy arm draped over her waist. She could feel a chin bumping up against her shoulder blade and a nose tucked up against the nape of her neck.

Gwen's first, sleepy thought was that this would be very useful for her book, for the scene where Plumeria and Sir Magnifico fell into an enchanted sleep in the olive grove. Or perhaps an oak grove. Somehow, olives just didn't spell out romance and enchantment. Yes, Magnifico's arm around Plumeria's waist, just so. Only, she wasn't sure that Magnifico's arm should be quite so, well, bare.

Her brain went back to that "bare" and stuck there. Bare. Arm. Bare.

Good Lord, she was in bed with a naked man. Not that that was a surprise—she'd known that when she went to bed, seduced by the siren song of warm bedcovers—but he was ill, and on the other side of the bed. His attire or lack thereof had hardly seemed to count. Obviously, that was before some point in the night they had got stuck together like— Her brain lurched at simile and came up short. He was just so . . . unclothed.

She was being embraced by a naked man. Well, a man in breeches. A largely naked man. Not as if the percentage of his nudity made any difference, as if only being half-nude was somehow more respectable than being two-thirds nude. No, the key factor was the embrace. They were tucked up together like peas in a pod, if peas had a habit of tucking their partners around the waist and pulling them back against them.

Deep breaths. There was nothing to panic about. It was purely an accident of sleep. She would just remove herself from his embrace and he would never know she had been there. She'd wager that he embraced any woman in his bed the same way. For all she knew, he might think she was a pillow. Yes, a pillow.

Doing her best to impersonate a pillow, if pillows had the power of independent motion, Gwen began inching out from under William's arm.

William stirred in his sleep. He mumbled something completely unintelligible. His arm tightened around her waist, clamping her firmly back in place. Then he threw a leg over her for good measure. Her skirts must have got hitched up while she was sleeping. She could feel his bare calf against her leg in the most shockingly intimate way.

Murmuring something in his sleep, William burrowed against her neck, his nose rubbing against the sensitive skin at her nape.

Was he . . . *nuzzling* her? Yes, that was quite definitely a nuzzle. The motion sent little tingles along the back of her neck, straight down her spine. She felt a most unaccountable desire to purr.

Gwen reminded herself that the man behind her knew not what he nuzzled, and with any luck, he wouldn't remember any of this by the time he woke up. Rather like that kiss the other night, the one where he'd got her confused with some goddess or other.

If one was going to be confused for anyone, it wasn't at all unpleasant to be mistaken for a major deity. One wouldn't at all like to be confused for the lesser sort of deity.

But a deity known for beauty and good fortune? That was . . . gratifying. Yes, gratifying. What with the nuzzling, Gwen was having trouble keeping her train of thought straight. She knew she should remove herself, but the bed was so cozy, so warm.

It was a long time since anyone had compared her to anything that didn't breathe fire and sport sharp claws.

Tim had written poetry to her once. Sonnets, odes, sestinas. She hadn't been particular about the form. It had been enough that he was writing poetry to her, about her. She had taken it as her due, believing every exaggerated simile, believing that her skin was like pearl, her hair black silk, her eyes daggers in Cupid's own arsenal. Aphrodite, he had called her, the first time he persuaded her out of her clothes—not that she'd taken all that much persuading.

It was all a sham, of course, like the rest of Tim's avowals. She was sure he'd presented the exact same verses to the heiress he'd married two months later, changing jetty locks for curls of gold and ebony eyes for azure, or some such rot.

If one thing was constant, it was the inconstancy of the male sex. A man could nuzzle and nuzzle and still be untrue.

With that salutary reminder, Gwen plunked the Colonel's arm off her waist and neatly extracted herself from his sleepy embrace. It was very cold outside the nest of blankets. Bracing— that was what it was. Bracing. Her neck still tingled from the nuzzling. Gwen ruthlessly rubbed it with the heel of her hand, scrubbing the memory away. She flung herself down on the chair by the bed, yanking on her stockings, then her half boots, all the armor of her daily garb.

There were mumblings and rustlings from the bed. The Colonel burrowed deeper into the pillow, one brown arm flung over his head, before emerging, tousled and sleepy. His cheeks were flushed, his eyes heavy with sleep, his hair any which way.

"Good morning," he said, smiling at her.

If this had been another set of circumstances, she might have smoothed the tousled hair from his brow. She might have leaned forwards and pressed her lips against that smile, might have let herself be lured back into the sleep-warmed nest of the sheets.

But that was all a world ago. The girl who might have done such things was gone, long ago.

Gwen hardened her heart and applied herself to lacing up her boots. "Is it?" she said disagreeably. "It looks like rain."

"Bother the rain," said the Colonel expansively. "I feel like I could conquer the world."

He stretched his arms out over his head, sending the sheets tumbling down to his waist, revealing the broad expanse of his chest, grizzled with red-white hair and seamed with old scars.

He winced as the movement made his stitches pull. "Or at least a very small province."

"Try getting out of bed first," said Gwen tartly, but she held out a hand to help him.

To her surprise, he took it, his large, calloused hand closing tightly around hers. He swung his legs over the side of the bed. His breeches dipped before he caught them with his other hand. He wobbled a bit, his legs unused to the job of holding him, and Gwen quickly moved to brace him, one hand against the side of his chest, the side without the bandages. His skin was warm beneath her fingers, not fever hot, but the normal temperature of a healthy male. She could feel his chest rise and fall with his breathing.

"It's all right," he said, half laughing, his breath ruffling her hair. For a moment, he rested his cheek on the top of her head. "I shan't topple over on you."

"It's not me I'm worried about," she said, but she stepped back anyway, near enough to catch him if he fell. "I don't want you bashing your head and keeping us here another five days."

His lips quirked. "You've a gallant soul, Gwen Meadows."

She knew it was absurd, but she'd liked it better when he was comparing her to Indian goddesses. Of course, he hadn't known that she was she, which was entirely beside the point, if she had any idea what the point was meant to be.

"Gallant is as gallant does," she said in her best chaperone voice, as starched as a dandy's collar and as sharp as the point of her sword parasol. "Let's find you some clothing, shall we?"

He looked down, seeming to realize his nakedness for the first time. He smiled sheepishly at her. "Er, might you have any idea as to the location of the rest of my clothes? I appear to have lost them while I was sleeping."

She shouldn't be blushing, really she shouldn't. They were pretend married, after all. And she was a spinster and beyond such things. No matter that those arguments were mutually contradictory. A little bit of illogic in the service of a good cause had never bothered her before.

"I had to cut your shirt off you," she said. She busied herself searching through a pile of clothes on the chair, coming up with a plain cambric shirt. "I've bought a replacement from the landlord. I'm afraid it's not very elegant, but it will have to do."

"So long as it covers me, I'm not particular."

"Yes, I can tell," said Gwen, holding up his jacket by two fingers.

William wasn't offended. "I'm not used to being out of a uniform," he said. "I've no idea what the fashions are."

She held out the shirt to him, helping him to guide it over his head. "You won't get far among society, then."

"I've no interest in society." His voice was muffled by the fabric. His rumpled head emerged through the neck hole. "I just mean to collect my girls and—"

"And?" Gwen held out his jacket to him.

William just stared at it. "I almost forgot," he said, in a dazed voice. "I was so happy to be out of that thrice-damned bed, I almost forgot."

His voice cracked on the last word and he turned away, making a show of shaking out his jacket.

Gwen's heart gave an unexpected spasm of pity. She crushed the urge to reach out to him, to comfort him. Instead, she said, her voice deliberately matter-of-fact, "Is there anyplace else your Lizzy might have gone? Does she have any other family here?"

"There might be some still in Scotland," he said, "but I doubt it. They mostly scattered to America."

Gwen began efficiently packing her bits and pieces back into her reticule. "What about her mother's family?"

William glanced at her sideways, his normally open face guarded. "Lizzy's mother was from Bengal," he said.

"So she won't have any other relations here, then," said Gwen briskly. And then, because there were times when plain speaking was one of the benefits of age, "Illegitimate?"

"Legally," said William. "Her mother and I never went through any semblance of marriage. But as far as I'm concerned, she's as true a daughter of mine as Katherine—and that was a marriage presided over by more than one parson!"

Gwen held up her hands. "Hold your artillery, Colonel! I'm not casting aspersions on your daughter. Or her birth. The world would be a better place if every man stood by his leavings." She had spoken a bit too vehemently. She said hastily, "What about her other siblings?"

The Colonel still looked ready to do battle. "Are they illegitimate, too, do you mean?"

"No. What does that have to do with anything? Other than your conscience." Having scored her point, she went on, "Would your Lizzy have contacted any of them?"

William shook his head. "The boys are all in India. There's Alex, Kat's twin, who's assistant to the Resident of Hyderabad, and George, Lizzy's full brother, who's in the service of the Begum Sumroo—she's a sort of queen, you might say."

"You left out the opium trader."

"I don't know that he's still trading opium," said William. "As far as I know, he's in India still."

"As far as you know?"

"We're estranged," he said briefly. "Last I heard, he was in the service of one of the Maratha chieftains—you won't have heard the name."

"Won't I?" Gwen couldn't resist showing off. "Holkar, perhaps? Or Scindia?"

William raised his sandy brows. "You're very well informed."

"Just because I wear a skirt doesn't mean I can't read a paper," she said.

"My apologies. I should know better than to underestimate you."

"Yes, you should."

He didn't know the half of it. For a mad moment, Gwen wondered if she were doing him a disservice by not telling him about the other powers that might be in play.

He didn't need to know about the League of the Pink Carnation, but she could tell him, surely, that there had once been a flap involving French spies at Miss Climpson's seminary, a flap in which Lizzy had been peripherally involved. It made a reasonable explanation for why a schoolgirl might be the target of French spies, leaving aside the fact that it was more likely Agnes who was the target than his Lizzy.

The moment the idea occurred to her, so did half a dozen arguments against it. It had been one of the other schoolgirls and her fiancé who had been selling information to the French, information the girl had gleaned from her father, a man high in the government. As far as Gwen knew, the girl and her fiancé were still in custody.

Besides, once opened, the topic of spies might raise uncomfortable questions. Such as why she carried a sword in her parasol.

Just because she had tended him for five endless days, attuned to every rasping breath, every fevered utterance, didn't mean that he was worthy of her trust. What did she know of him, really? She knew every inch of his body—well, almost every inch—she knew his smell, his favorite ribald song, the mumbling noises he made as he slept, but other than that, he might be anything or anyone. He might not even be Colonel William Reid. She had only his own and his supposed older daughter's word for it. If she was his daughter.

No. The family resemblance had been too strong to be denied. Kat Reid was William's daughter. That much was true. It didn't mean that any of the rest of it was.

She had come too far to be incautious now.

"Do you have everything?" she said instead.

William ran a hand along his chin. "I should like to shave before we go," he said apologetically. "Lest someone mistake me for a pirate."

"You'd need a parrot for that," said Gwen, "or at least an eye patch." But she called for the maid all the same.

The maid bobbed a curtsy as she departed. "Thank you for your custom, Mrs. Fustian. Colonel Fustian."

William slanted Gwen a glance from under his brows. "Fustian?"

Gwen certainly wasn't going to tell him that it was her usual alias. She gave him a superior look. "It seemed appropriate for someone who speaks so much nonsense as you."

William laughed, a great rolling laugh that came from deep in his chest. "I've never met anyone who manages to call me to account as you do."

Gwen wasn't sure if that was intended as a compliment. "That," she said, "is because you bamboozle them all with your flummery."

He looked down at her, his eyes a clear, bright blue. "It's not all flummery."

Gwen's treacherous stomach fluttered. "That is exactly the sort of thing I mean," she said sternly. "Don't think you can get around me that way."

"I would never be so foolish," he said solemnly. "Particularly not while you're holding a blade."

They cleared their meager possessions from the room. The tumbled sheets on the bed told a false tale. Gwen took one last look out the window from which she had seen so many sunrises and sunsets. For five days, she had left the room only to summon the maid, to procure food, to demand hot water or cold ale. For five days she had kept vigil over the man beside her, sitting in that chair, lighting and snuffing those candles, cursing the blasted recalcitrant chimney. It felt as though it had been a year, not a mere week, less than a week.

It had been one thing to nurse him, but now that he was clothed again, now that he was on his feet, she didn't quite know what to do with him. His clean-shaven face seemed unfamiliar, bare and shiny.

Once on the stage, it was too crowded to speak privately, or to speak at all, so they sat silently, wedged into a corner of the backwards-facing seat. With every jolt and jostle, the Colonel turned a little bit more gray in the face, his smile a little more strained. He was the Colonel again, Gwen realized. Not William anymore. This clean-faced stranger was the man she had met at Miss Climpson's, not the man she had nursed through a grueling bout of wound fever.

And she was Miss Meadows again, armored in respectability. There would be no more fever-stricken kisses, no waking to an arm around her waist.

She ought to be glad of that. That had been a detour, an aberration. They would return to Bath, find the girls, and she could return to her life in France, a life—she reminded herself—that she had chosen for herself, a life of infinite possibility and power.

A life of being Miss Wooliston's fearsome chaperone.

Despite his obvious weakness, the Colonel insisted on walking her to the Woolistons' hired house in Laura Place.

They stood before the front steps, the Colonel's hat in his hand, Gwen's parasol dangling from her wrist, neither of them at all sure what to say to the other.

What did one say to a man to whom one had been pretend married not six hours before?

Gwen could see the drapes twitch, the butler waiting for her to mount the steps so he could open the door and take her rather battered hat and parasol. There had been a butler who had come with the house. He had been in residence when they arrived. The following day, he had received an unexpected bequest from an unknown cousin and gone off to take a holiday of his own at the spa at Tunbridge Wells.

Jane took no chances. The new butler was one of their own. He would give her all the time she needed.

What, exactly, she needed that time for was another question entirely.

"Well," said Gwen. "That was certainly an enlivening episode." When in doubt, resort to sarcasm.

The Colonel's wide smile lit his face. Fifty-four and the man still had freckles. They lent him an entirely deceptive air of boyishness.

"From where I was lying, I'm not sure 'enlivening' is the word I would choose." To Gwen's surprise, he possessed himself of both her hands, the laughter gone from his blue eyes. "I don't know how to thank you. You might have left me at that inn, but you didn't. For that, I shall always be grateful."

Gratitude was a weak substitute for any form of true emotion. She would rather have scorn than gratitude. "Reserve your gratitude, sir. It was no more than anyone might have done."

"Perhaps. But there aren't many I would trust to guard my back. May I"—William paused, clasping and unclasping his hands—"call on you tomorrow?"

There was no reason for her to feel like a girl at a country assembly being asked for her first dance. He had made himself clear. His interest in her was purely that of a comrade at arms.

"I had assumed you would. We still have two young ladies to find, after all." Gwen turned and stalked up the stairs, pausing on the top step to add, "Don't get yourself skewered again in the meantime."

"I wouldn't think of it," he said, and then ruined all her composure by adding, with a smile, "Mrs. Fustian."

Didn't he know that she always got the last word?

"Colonel," she said grandly. The butler obligingly opened the door and she sailed through. Her grand exit was only somewhat marred by tripping over someone's walking stick just inside the door.

"I do beg your pardon," said the gentleman—Gwen used the term broadly—in a voice that carried the faintest hint of a French accent.

He looked her up and down, from her bedraggled purple traveling costume to the maltreated hat she had crammed on her dirty hair. "The missing chaperone, I presume?"

Chapter 12

When they approached, they saw that the tower was not black at all, but silver, a silver so bright that it hurt their eyes and caused them to shy back. From within the tower there was the ringing of a bell, and a drawbridge came clanging down before them. A man stood on it, caparisoned in silver armor, darkly chased in mysterious designs of gold and ebony. "I am the Knight of the Silver Tower," quoth he. "What business have you with me?"

Plumeria liked him not. . . .

—From *The Convent of Orsino* by A Lady

Jane made the introductions. "Miss Gwen, may I present to you the Chevalier de la Tour d'Argent. Chevalier, Miss Gwendolyn Meadows."

The Chevalier bowed over her hand, which was considerably the worse for travel. If he noticed the stains on her gloves, he made no sign. "Enchanted, Madame."

He might be, but she wasn't. Gwen thumped her parasol on the ground, dangerously close to the Chevalier's too-shiny boot. "The Knight of the Silver Tower? What sort of name is that?"

The Chevalier pressed a hand to his heart. A heavy gold signet ring showed bright against the dark superfine of his jacket. "The name with which my birth burdened me, no less and no more."

"There could hardly be more," contributed Jane, "unless one wished to add a few adjectives to it for ballast."

A hint of a dimple appeared in the Chevalier's cheek as he glanced at Gwen's charge. "The Knight of the Exceedingly High and Rather Unwieldy Silver Tower? My acquaintances should expire of boredom before the introduction was complete."

"If one were to choose a tower," said Gwen grumpily, "why not gold?"

"I believe," said the Chevalier gravely, "that the appellation was originally awarded to a great-great-great-grandparent during the Crusades."

Jane raised a brow. "For deeds of great valor?"

"No," said the Chevalier sadly, but there was a glint in his eyes. "For cupidity beyond imagining. It was, I fear, the ill-famed Fourth Crusade, and this most unprincipled knight returned from the sack of Byzantium with so much purloined silver plate that his peers enviously dubbed him the Knight of the Silver Tower. I assure you, it was no honor, but those of his line have stubbornly held to it ever since."

"Most families have equally ignominious origins when one comes down to it," said Jane.

The Chevalier's smile was only for Jane. "Does yours?"

"We're quite dull, really. A great-grandparent too many greats back to remember took a fancy to a particular patch of soil in Shropshire and we've been there ever since."

"Bucolic, perhaps," said the Chevalier gallantly, "but never dull."

That was quite enough of that. Gwen glowered at the upstart Frenchman taking up valuable space and even more valuable time. "How do you come to be in our front hall?"

Jane cast her a quelling glance. "The Chevalier has been kindly assisting us in our inquiries."

"Oh, have you, then?"

The Chevalier affected a half bow. "There are places that a man might go that I fear are barred to you ladies. As I have told Miss Wooliston, my curricle and escort are at her disposal."

"How very . . . helpful of you. To what do we owe this solicitude? You're not related to the Reid girl, are you?" She was reasonably sure the Colonel would have mentioned a Frenchman running amuck on his family tree. On the other hand, given his amorphous gaggle of offspring, one couldn't be sure. She doubted he was a Reid pretending to be a Frenchman, but one never knew. "You don't happen to be named Jack, do you?"

"Er, no." The Chevalier was all that was apologetic. "Forgive me for that oversight. My elder brother was a Jean-Marie, but we have no Jacques of which I know. My family calls me Nicolas. Or occasionally that limb of Satan. The two appear to be largely interchangeable."

He was making eyes at Jane again. Gwen rapped her parasol on the ground, calling them both to attention. "What's your interest in the girls, then?"

"The Chevalier's cousin is a teacher at the school," said Jane calmly. "You met her last week. Mademoiselle de Fayette. The girls were on her hall."

"She takes this matter very much to heart," said the Chevalier with seeming sincerity. The emphasis on "seeming." Earnestness did not become him. That face of his was made for mischief and deviltry, from his too-exuberantly curling locks to his laughing eyes.

"Hmph," said Gwen. "So you've taken it upon yourself to clear her good name, have you?"

"Something of that nature." The Chevalier indulged in one of those indeterminate Gallic gestures somewhere between a wave and a shrug. "Delphine is the only family I have. I take my responsibility to her quite seriously indeed."

Gwen vaguely remembered the French mistress, small and sweet faced, meek in the gray gown of a schoolmistress. She certainly bore no resemblance to the imp of a dandy in their front hall, rigged out in the height of fashion down to the cameo fobs on his watch chain.

She folded her arms across her chest. "Your cousin, you say?"

"Yes." He winked at Jane before turning back to her chaperone, as innocent as a choirboy. "My mother was the Comtesse de Brillac."

"An old and honorable line," Jane said diplomatically.

The Chevalier shrugged. "Once. Perhaps. Of all my family,

Delphine and I were the only ones to escape the bite of the guillotine."

There was one problem with his story. "Why are you then not the Comte de Brillac rather than the knight of the so lengthy silver tower?" asked Gwen accusingly.

The merriment fled from the Chevalier's face. He looked, for a moment, considerably older than his presumed age, harsh lines marring the skin around his mouth. "I would not take his title."

The words echoed harshly through the hall, at odds with the delicacy of the too-fussy mirror that hung on the wall, the mincing tile squares on the floor.

The Chevalier shook himself back to the present. He raised his eyebrows at Jane with a wry expression, the charm firmly back in place. "How could I take his title, knowing the end he met? I had a brother, too, my older brother, Jean-Marie. That title would one day have been his. I will not profit from his death."

"Your feelings do you credit," said Jane gently.

Gwen refrained from a snort.

What was Jane thinking, letting this French coxcomb accompany her on her inquiries? The man himself might be nothing to do with the school, but his cousin—his presumed cousin, Gwen corrected herself darkly—was the mistress in charge of Agnes's hall. She would have been a prime suspect even without the accent.

The Chevalier spread his hands. "A wound is a wound only so long as it remains open. That life was a lifetime ago—and I find nothing to complain of in my existence here. It is Delphine who has suffered most, and if I can make her easier in any way, I shall."

"Charming," said Gwen combatively. "Nicely said. Why, then, is she teaching at that ridiculous school?"

The Chevalier's coat alone cost more than a teacher's salary for a year. It certainly cost more than Gwen had to her name. For a moment, she thought of the Colonel's coat, the cheap fabric stiff with blood. She had wrung it out over the basin in that little inn room, doing her best to rehabilitate it. He had donned the stained and crumpled garment without a murmur.

But this wasn't about the Colonel; it was about the Chevalier. There was something about the situation that didn't add up, and Gwen was determined to winkle it out.

The Chevalier spread out his hands, not one whit abashed. "You mean when I have every worldly good, all of which I am prepared to shower upon her?"

"If you wish to put it that way, yes." It was exactly what she'd meant, yet somehow he'd managed to turn it to his credit.

"She refuses to accept my aid." The Chevalier turned mournful eyes on Jane. "She escaped only with the clothes on her back, through the good offices of your—how was it again?—your Purple Gentian."

There was a charged silence in the hall.

"I believe I have heard the name," said Jane demurely. "His exploits were much in the papers in my youth."

"Nonsense, all of it," said Gwen brusquely. "Spies flying through windows, leaving notes on pillows—pure palaver."

The Chevalier turned his attention back to her. "You, then, are not an admirer of these men?"

"I might be if I believed the half of it," grumbled Gwen. "Pure puffery, puffery and nonsense."

The Chevalier gave her a crooked smile. "Yet that nonsense, as you call it, saved the life of my cousin. I find I cannot bring myself to dismiss these men so entirely as you do, however absurd their noms de guerre." He held out a hand to Jane. "I fear I overstay my welcome. I will call for you tomorrow?"

To Gwen's annoyance, Jane allowed the bounder to possess himself of her hand, to bow over it, dusting a kiss over the back of it. It wasn't the sort of kiss of which a chaperone might justly complain. He didn't hold her hand too long or essay a rogue's trick like turning her hand to press a kiss into the palm.

But there was something undeniably intimate about it nonetheless. It might have been the way his eyes held Jane's as he raised his head, or the way Jane looked back at him, as though she were equal parts apprehension and fascination.

Gwen had seen Jane flirt with many admirers, but she had never seen her look like that.

"Yes, tomorrow." Jane walked with her admirer to the door, Gwen trailing along behind, fuming helplessly. "We shall see you at the opera?"

The Chevalier retrieved his hat and gloves from the butler, pressing the entire mess of belongings to his heart as he said, "I shall count the minutes."

He clapped the hat upon his head and departed.

"I hope all that counting doesn't overtax his mathematical

skills," muttered Gwen. Through the window, she could see the Chevalier climbing into a flashy high-perch phaeton, painted an impractical pale blue.

"Welcome back," said Jane drily. "I trust you had a pleasant journey?"

Gwen followed her into the morning room, which, like all the other rooms in the Woolistons' rented house, had been relentlessly decorated by someone who had lurched at good taste and missed by the length of several yards of bric-a-brac. Portraits of someone's idealized ancestors leered at them from above the fireplace, interspersed with Watteau shepherdesses, Fragonard fetes, and miscellaneous simpering putti.

"I see you've been busy in my absence," said Gwen pugnaciously, flinging her reticule down on the settee. "Entertaining dubious gentlemen callers."

"Would you like some tea?" suggested Jane, entirely unperturbed. "Some cakes perhaps?"

Gwen wasn't going to let herself be distracted by cakes, not even the little iced ones that the Woolistons' cook made so well.

"Your Chevalier was lying," she said, thumping down on the settee next to her reticule. The impractical edifice buckled but held.

"Yes, I know," said Jane calmly. She seated herself on a silk-upholstered chair by the fire. "I'm not so green as that. I did have him investigated."

"And?"

"His father is the Comte de Brillac; his mother, father, and sister all died in the Terror."

"But?" Gwen prompted. Jane had an aggravating habit of dragging out her revelations. It drove Gwen absolutely mad, which was probably why Jane did it.

"The tender filial picture he presented might not have been entirely the case. Brillac publicly disowned him at birth, refusing to acknowledge him as his son. The Comtesse de Brillac tried several times to flee her husband but was every time brought back."

"So Brillac was a brute and your Chevalier was a by-blow."

"Or his father believed him so. According to my sources, the Comte's favorite epithet for his second born was 'you bastard son of an Englishman.' It is unclear," added Jane delicately, "whether the national identification was meant descriptively or pejoratively."

"Yes, but what is the man about now?" Gwen brushed aside the question of the Chevalier's parentage. That sort of tittle-tattle was all very well for the readers of scandal sheets, but they had more pressing business in hand. "You say he has been assisting you?"

"Oh, yes, most assiduously," said Jane blandly.

Gwen gave her a look. "That man is after something."

"And it's probably not my person," said Jane cheerfully. "That's why I accepted his offer. I'd rather have him under my eye."

Was that the only reason?

She had seen Jane flirt for England many times. She did it very well, with wide, admiring eyes, a coy glance here, a demure smile there. It bore very little resemblance to what she had seen with the Chevalier in that hallway.

But no matter how Gwen tried, she couldn't find the words to ask her. They had no vocabulary for navigating the shoals of sentiment. After two years of their common enterprise, they were expert at dissecting facts. Feelings they gave a wide berth, unless they were other people's feelings and might somehow have a bearing on the great game of nations that they played. Sentiment, personal sentiment, had no place in their work. It was nothing more than a snare and a distraction.

Gwen only hoped that Jane would remember that.

Since she could say none of that, she said, gruffly, "What have you discovered thus far?"

Jane folded her hands neatly in her lap. To all outward appearances, she was the very image of a well-bred young lady, a picture in white muslin in a prettily appointed morning room. It was only her voice that was at odds with her appearance, brisk and businesslike, her voice and the calculating glint in her eye. Gwen found herself reassured. This was the Jane she knew, detached and analytical.

"The school is hopeless," she said. "There are half a dozen ways in and out, including a convenient trellis that could easily be scaled by a determined man or a fleeing girl."

"Harder to carry someone out that way," Gwen pointed out. "A kidnapper might get in, but he'd have a hard time getting out again."

"True," said Jane. "Especially with two."

She had that look in her eye. There was something she wasn't telling. "You know something," said Gwen sternly. "Out with it."

"There is," said Jane, "a small hut on the grounds, not far from the main house. It was previously the abode of the gardener, before the last gardener was let go. I found this beneath the dresser."

She drew something out of her pocket and laid it on the table. It was a trumpery thing, a bracelet of gilt and pale pink enamel, with tiny seed pearls embedded in a pattern in the plaques. Gwen recognized it instantly.

"That is part of the set you gave Agnes for Christmas."

"Yes, and look." Jane turned the bracelet over. "The clasp isn't broken."

Gwen took the bracelet from her, examining it. The silver gilt was worn off in places, but it was the wear that would come with regular use, not anything that betokened foul play. "Which means it is unlikely that it was torn from her wrist. Were there any other signs of a struggle in the cottage?"

"No," said Jane. "Of course, it's been three weeks, so someone might have tidied the place since. But there were ashes in the fireplace. They did not look over a year old."

Gwen looked hard at Jane, trying to winkle out what she was surmising. "You think the girls stayed there. Of their own volition."

Jane nodded. "Possibly. Or someone made every attempt to make it look as though they did. There was also," she added, as though it were a matter of minor import, "a schedule for the London stage on the table."

Two young ladies, fleeing their select seminary for adventures in town, leaving their timetable behind . . .

"No," said Gwen. "It's too easy."

"That was my thought too." Jane rose, her skirt drifting gently around her as she wandered towards the mantelpiece, ticking off theories on her fingers. "One possibility: The girls were lured out into the garden, abducted, and held overnight in the gardener's cottage. The kidnapper left the stage schedule as a false trail."

"I don't like it," said Gwen. "Why would the kidnapper keep them on the school grounds overnight? There would be too much chance of being discovered. Someone might have heard them struggling—and, again, you say there was no sign of a struggle— or seen the smoke from that fire. No. I don't believe it. Next?"

"Possibility the second." Jane took a deep breath. "The girls planted their own false trail, deliberately leaving the bracelet to let us know they had been there."

Gwen pulled at a loose thread on the silk upholstery. That made somewhat more sense. The girls, unused to being on their own, would have wanted someplace familiar to shelter. "Yes, but it still doesn't tell us where they went. Or why they went," she added as an afterthought.

Jane leaned an elbow against the mantelpiece, regarding her chaperone seriously. "Do you incline towards the kidnapping theory?"

"I don't believe they were taken from the school, but there is some sort of foul play afoot." Gwen left off tugging at the upholstery. "Colonel Reid and I were attacked in Bristol."

"I gathered as much from your note," said Jane.

Gwen shrugged. "I deemed it better to be oblique. They

might merely have been footpads, but one complained to his fellows that he hadn't been warned that we would be armed."

"Which suggests a planned attack," said Jane. "On you or on the Colonel?"

"I don't know. All three rushed the Colonel, although that might have been an attempt to immobilize him and make off with me."

Jane was quiet, thinking. She looked like a statue, entirely still, her muslin dress falling in the required classical folds by her feet. The only jarring note was the locket she wore on a ribbon around her neck. On the other side lay her signet, the sign of the Pink Carnation.

"They might just have been footpads," said Gwen.

Jane smiled wryly, her expression too old, too world-weary for someone so young. "I thought you didn't believe in coincidence." She stepped lightly away from the mantel, her usual mask back in place. "Speaking of coincidence, I have secured us the tickets to the opera that you required. Aurelia Fiorila sings the part of Semira in *Artaxerxes*." She raised a brow. "I hear it is *much* anticipated."

Gwen rose too, lifting her reticule by the strings. Her dirty dress made her skin itch. She was yearning for a bath and some clean linen, but she had to ask, "Will the Chevalier be attending this much-anticipated event as well?"

"He will be most honored and delighted to escort us."

Gwen looked back over her shoulder at her charge. "Are you sure you know what you're doing, missy?" she demanded. "Love—"

"Has no place in grand schemes, I know," said Jane patiently. "Who said anything about love? You yourself once told me to keep one's enemies close enough to poke with a parasol."

"Yes," said Gwen crossly. "Arm's length."

"Shall I ring for water for a bath for you?" said Jane, crossing the foyer ahead of her.

Gwen scowled at the back of her charge's head, which was, as always, impeccably coiffed, no hair out of place. Her dress was spotless, her back straight, everything was entirely in order, and, yet, Gwen had a slight sense of impending doom.

"I have a slight sense of impending doom," she declared. The words resonated rather nicely in the marble hallway.

Jane turned, one brow lifted. "A *slight* sense of impending doom? Isn't that rather like saying that one has a mild case of bubonic plague?"

"That," said Gwen, stalking towards the stairs and the promised bath, "isn't the least bit funny."

"Plague seldom is," Jane agreed.

Gwen paused on the landing, glowering down at her charge. "Nor is allowing oneself to be distracted from one's mission."

For a moment, Jane seemed flummoxed. But only for a moment.

"Shall we invite Colonel Reid to the opera as well?" she asked.

Gwen was tempted to point out that Colonel Reid wasn't a rogue of a Frenchman with dubious antecedents. No. He was a rogue of an American with dubious offspring. Since that argument wasn't going to go very far, she stuck her nose in the air and said, "Do what you like. It's no concern of mine."

"We do have room in the box . . . ," said Jane.

At some point, she would have to sneak away to investigate Fiorila's dressing room. At least with the Colonel in the box, she would know that someone was keeping an eye on Jane. She would give him instructions. Explicit instructions. He was the father of daughters. He would understand.

"Fine," said Gwen loftily. "Invite the Colonel. But it is entirely your decision, not mine."

Chapter 13

Plumeria waited until the others were occupied at the feast before slipping quietly away. From the Hall, she could hear the sounds of mirth and revelry, but in the rest of the Tower, all was silence. Somewhere, somewhere in those house of dark enchantment lay her charge, she was sure of it, no matter the many protestations of its master. It was but a matter of finding her. . . .

—From *The Convent of Orsino* by A Lady

The Colonel was waiting for them in the lobby when they arrived at the theatre the next night.

He had spruced himself up for the occasion, his shirt points starched and his red hair brushed to sleekness. He had traded the tattered and bloodstained jacket of their Bristol expedition for another of equally mediocre tailoring.

The elder Woolistons greeted him with pleasure and a marked lack of recollection. Upon discovering that what he knew of sheep could fit inside a bowl of porridge, Mr. Wooliston rapidly lost interest and went back into his pre-theatre sulk.

Jane walked ahead with her parents while the Colonel fell into step with Gwen behind.

"I missed you last night," he said. "It was rather odd not having you sniping at me to drink my broth."

"Shhh," said Gwen automatically. Not that anyone was listening. No one would ever think to impugn her morals. She was, in the eyes of the world, not only unassailable, but hardly worth assailing. "Did you drink your broth?"

The Colonel looked like a small boy caught with his hand in the cookie jar. "I decided a leg of mutton would do just as well."

"They're hardly the same thing."

"No," said the Colonel. "The mutton was tastier."

The box the Woolistons had rented was off to the side, all the way to the right. It might well have been that by the time they'd arrived in Bath, all the better boxes were taken. Given that Jane had chosen the box, Gwen suspected that the choice was quite deliberate. One might not have the best view of the stage from the box, but one could see everyone else in the theatre, and far into the wings on that one side.

Gwen noticed that the Colonel relied heavily on the banister as they climbed the stairs. "How is your wound?" she asked.

"Healing cleanly." A curtain blocked off the back of their box. The Colonel held it aside for Gwen to precede him. "Thanks to you."

"Stop being grateful." Gwen thumped down into the chair he held out for her. It was little, and gilded, and rocked slightly as she sat. "That much gratitude is excessively trying."

"Would you rather I be ungrateful?" The Colonel pulled up a chair beside hers, adding, with an impish hint of mischief, "Mrs. Fustian."

For a moment, she could imagine them back in that tiny room in the inn, waking beside him, his arm around her, his nose nuzzled into the back of her neck, the Colonel and his lady.

All pretense, she reminded herself. Pretense and expediency.

"I would rather," said Gwen pointedly, "that we put the whole episode behind us."

"You were the one who asked after my wound," said the Colonel innocently.

Gwen drew herself up in her seat, her purple feathered headdress bobbing. "I was being polite."

"You, polite?" The Colonel grinned at her. "Pull the other one."

Blast the man. It was impossible not to smile back. Gwen did her best to convert the expression into a grimace. She was aided in that by the addition of the final member of their party, who came breezing into the box on a wave of expensive cologne.

"Forgive me," said the Chevalier, executing an elaborate bow. "I did not mean to be late."

"You're hardly late," said Jane. "It's only the tumblers."

On the stage, a bunch of dispirited acrobats turned somersaults, aided by projectiles from the pit. A handstand devolved abruptly into a roll as a tomato found its target.

The Chevalier appropriated a chair beside Jane. "What is tonight's entertainment?"

"Other than the limber gentlemen on the stage?" Jane made a show of consulting her program. "The main performance is Arne's *Artaxerxes*. Have you seen it before?"

"I have not had that pleasure." The man managed to make even a simple sentence sound like an innuendo.

Jane, thank goodness, seemed largely unaffected. "I would reserve the praise until you've seen the play. It's a rather dark piece." She consulted her program again and then looked up at the Chevalier. "The son of Xerxes revenges himself on his father's murderers."

"Not a comedy, then," said the Chevalier. He looked up under his lashes at Jane. "I would ask you to translate for me, but that it's in English."

"I could translate it into Italian for you if you like."

"Not into French?"

"My French," said Jane demurely, "is hardly that polished. I should hate to embarrass myself before you."

"Nonsense!" said Bertrand Wooliston, rousing himself from his pre-theatre sulk. "Croaks like a Frog, that one! Can't think where she got it. Although there was that sister of yours, Prudence . . ."

Prudence Wooliston beamed mistily. "Dear Elinor. Did you know her, Chevalier? She married the Vicomte de Balcourt. He had," she added, "the loveliest tapestries."

"I had not the honor of her acquaintance, but I would have to have been the veriest bumpkin not to have heard of her beauty and wit." He indicated Jane with a courtly gesture. "All of which I see live again in her niece."

"A compliment as prettily tailored as his coat," groused Gwen to the Colonel.

"I take it you don't like the lad?"

Pointedly ignoring the Colonel, Gwen leaned forward and rapped the Chevalier's shoulder with her folded fan. The fact that there was a slim knife embedded in the ivory shaft gave the ornament a pleasing added heft.

"Now that you're here, you might as well make yourself useful. Lemonade. And some of those little iced cakes."

"But of course," said the Chevalier, rising gracefully from a chair. "Lemonade it shall be. In the company of such inebriating beauty, champagne would be a tasteless excess."

"Just the lemonade," said Gwen tartly. "None of your commentary."

"I shall return with your lemonade." A dimple appeared at the side of the Chevalier's mouth. "And iced cakes."

The Colonel hitched his chair closer to Gwen's. His knee, respectably garbed in buff breeches, brushed the folds of her skirt. "Did you really want the lemonade, or was that just an excuse to remove the man from the box? You look like you've had the lemons without the sugar."

"The man's all stuff and puffery." Gwen glowered at him. "Would you like a libertine like that sniffing around your daughters?"

The humor fled from the Colonel's face. He swallowed,

painfully. "Right now," he said. "I'd like them here with me, sniffing or no."

Gwen looked at him shrewdly. "When is Katherine arriving?"

The Colonel drummed his fingers against one knee. "She says she won't move her grandmother. I'm to go out there again tomorrow. If I can't persuade her to come back with me, I want to see what I can do to make her more comfortable."

Gwen remembered him in the alley, blanched and bleeding. "Be careful," she said roughly, and then, before she could be accused of undue sentiment: "Is there any word of your younger daughter?"

The Colonel's face was grim. "No. I went back to the school today. They let me look through her room again, but—" He shook his head, the picture of hopelessness. "You've not heard from your Agnes?"

"Not a word," said Gwen.

The Colonel drew in a deep breath. "I had hoped, when you invited me tonight . . . Never mind that." So that was why he had responded to her invitation with such alacrity. Gwen swallowed a sour smile. She should have known better than that. "I've placed advertisements in twenty papers, all across the country, and one in Scotland. If anyone sees a girl of her description, or perhaps a lad of her size, they're to contact me care of the White Hart."

"That describes a good many people," said Gwen.

The Colonel lifted an anguished face to hers. "I know. But

what else am I to do? If I were at home, in India, there are favors I could call in, friends I might ask for help, but here—I've no idea where to begin. They've told me," he added, diffidently, "that there are men who search out the missing for a fee. Runners, they called them."

"You mean the Bow Street Runners?" The last thing they needed was the Bow Street Runners involved, bumbling about, poking into things that didn't involve them. "There's no need to be hasty."

"Hasty? It's been near on a month, now!"

"Yes," said Gwen, improvising quickly. "But they're not a good sort of people, those runners."

There was steel behind the Colonel's jovial facade. "I don't care what sort of people they are as long as they bring my daughter back."

Before Gwen could think of anything to say, the curtain at the back of the box breezed open.

"Your lemonade, Madame." The Chevalier snapped his fingers, producing, like a magician, a parade of footmen bearing carafes of lemonade, a platter of cakes, and a small three-legged table, which the gaggle of servitors hastened to set beside her.

He had brought a truly alarming quantity of lemonade. Gwen suspected she was being mocked, but as it played rather neatly into her own plans, she let it go. For now. She and the Chevalier would have their reckoning later.

The Colonel poured her a glass of lemonade. "Forgive me," he said, with an attempt at a smile. "I shouldn't take out my ill humor on you."

"No," said Gwen, draining her glass. It was very sweet, sweet and sticky. Had they used any lemon at all, or pure sugar? "You should take it out on the coxcomb in front of us. I'll cheer you on if you do."

Grimly, she drank another glass, and then another. The beverage was disgusting, but it was all part of her plan. By the time the opera was under way, she had consumed the better part of the pitcher of lemonade, making sure everyone saw her refilling her glass again and again. When Arbaces and Mandane launched into "Fair Aurora, prythee stay," partway through the first act, she was squirming quite convincingly.

Gwen stood, abruptly. "I shan't be long," she said.

Jane glanced back over her shoulder. "Oh," she said, and glanced at the nearly empty carafe. As a dumb show, it was certainly more effective than anything the actors were accomplishing on the stage. They had played these roles before, she and Jane.

Hardened by many years of female companionship, the Colonel made as if to rise. "Shall I accompany—"

"Most certainly not!" snapped Gwen. "I shall hardly be accosted between here and the retiring room!"

It made a good note on which to stamp off. It also made clear to everyone in her box and the two boxes on either side that she was going to the retiring room, and not by any means sneaking off into the wings to search a prima donna's dressing room.

Gwen ducked behind a convenient pile of sandbags as Fiorila's dresser bustled out of the dressing room, in search of a prop that had gone missing. The prop had been inconveniently stashed on the far side of the wings, behind two stacked stage sets. Gwen should know. She'd put it there herself. It was a jeweled hairpiece that Semira, aka Fiorila, wore in Act II. She had banked on the fact that the dresser wouldn't notice it was missing until partway through Act I.

And had she been right or not? She would have preened, but there wasn't room behind the sandbags.

Gwen waited until the dresser was around the bend of the hall before slipping into the dressing room, shutting the door softly behind her. If caught, she could always claim to be a great aficionado of opera, hoping to reach her idol before the rest of Fiorila's adoring fans. People would believe anything if only one said it authoritatively enough.

The dressing room was larger than Gwen had hoped, large and cluttered, with two wardrobes spilling forth costumes, trunks of props, dressing tables stacked with paints and paste jewels, and flowers in various stages of decomposition attesting to the attentions of Fiorila's many admirers. The room was obviously also being used partly as a storeroom. There were pieces of set and scenery stacked against the far wall.

The theatre had been new built that past year, with this *Artaxerxes* their first performance. They had contrived to finish the ornate public areas, but the backstage lagged behind; there were open beams still overhead, part of the elaborate superstructure of the warren of backstage areas.

Gwen moved to Fiorila's dressing table, set in an area of relative privacy in a small nook around the corner of the room.

Here were her pots of paints and powders, her dressing gown tossed casually over the back of the chair, where she might slip into it between acts as her dresser refreshed her paint. There was nothing in the little boxes of paint except paint.

Scrubbing her hands clean on the underside of her shift, Gwen slid her hands into Fiorila's dressing gown pockets. There was a comb in one, with a broken tine. It must have fallen and been shoved in the pocket and forgotten.

In the other pocket, paper crinkled.

Gwen drew it out. It had been folded, again and again, folded into a tiny square. A love letter, no doubt. Gwen opened the first fold, then the second. The ink was smudged, as though with tears. Gwen wasn't interested in Fiorila's lovers, but the opening salutation caught her eye.

Chère Maman, it began.

Maman? Gwen shook out the sheet of paper and a very small sketch fell out, a watercolor, inexpertly painted, of a young girl of perhaps eight or nine in a white muslin frock. Despite the shortcomings of the watercolorist, there was no mistaking the color of the girl's hair, a deep and familiar auburn.

Gwen quickly scanned the letter, blotched and blotted though it was. Her mother shouldn't worry, she was being treated very well, everyone was all kindness at the château, and when was she to be allowed to go back to school? It wasn't that she was ungrateful, and the country was very nice, but she felt awful about not saying good-bye, and could Maman please send her a new pair of slippers since she had quite worn through her old ones? Her affectionate daughter, Adele.

Fiorila had a child. Not surprising. The woman was roughly Gwen's age, a year or two younger perhaps. If the child were eight or nine, that would put Fiorila in her midthirties when the child had been born. Audiences would have come to see her anyway, but the powerful men who protected her, who championed her against rival singers, might not have been so eager had there been a child in tow.

Yes, a child, tucked away somewhere, being educated at a young ladies' academy, wasn't at all a surprise.

It made some things Gwen had overheard in that conversation in Paris quite, quite clear. Talleyrand—or more accurately, one of his minions—must have discovered the child and taken her into custody in exchange for Fiorila's compliance. Talleyrand had needed an opera singer to sway the Sultan. Fiorila had provided him the perfect pawn.

Gwen had a fairly good idea what the quid pro quo would be: Fiorila got her daughter back when Talleyrand got the jewels.

No one was more dangerous than a woman whose child was in danger.

Carefully putting back the letter and the watercolor just where she'd found them, Gwen resumed her search. Most of the surfaces in the main part of the room were laid out with various costumes, the role of Semira obviously occasioning a good many changes from one diaphanous robe into another, many of them sewn with fake jewels that glittered in the light.

Fake? Or simply designed to look so?

It would be a rather cunning way to smuggle out the jewels of Berar. Who would look too closely at an actress's costume?

She could return to France with a king's ransom hidden on her body, in plain sight.

Gwen poked at a ruby. No. That was quite definitely paste. She could tell from the way it crumbled.

Maybe no one would notice?

She was just about to replace the gown in the wardrobe when she heard voices outside, voices and footsteps, coming towards the door. There would be no way out that way. Gwen glanced at the wardrobes. She refused to be that kind of cliché. Not to mention that hiding in an actress's wardrobe bore with it a very high chance of discovery.

There was only one way out.

Dropping the gown, she clambered onto the settee. It was a bit of a reach, but with a desperate leap she managed to lock her arms around one of the wooden slats in the unfinished ceiling, using the momentum to swing her legs up, locking her ankles around the beam. She wished she were wearing her breeches; her purple evening gown had been designed to hide the wear and tear of espionage, but the skirts still got in the way.

With a desperate wrench, she managed to swing herself around, on top of the beam. She was inching down the beam on her hands and knees when the door to the dressing room opened. Gwen froze, inches away from safety. One more foot and she would be over what looked like an empty storage room next door.

"—can't think how it got there," the dresser was saying.

"No matter." Even off the stage, Fiorila's voice was musical and pitched to carry. "You have it now."

She sounded tired, tired and ineffably weary. It was not the voice of a woman who had just received multiple encores.

"How did this get here?" The dresser was shaking out the gown Gwen had dropped. "I could have sworn . . ."

Fiorila swung around sharply. "Has someone been in here?"

"I was looking for the crown," began the dresser, flustered. "I did not see . . ."

Fiorila sat down heavily at her dressing table. Gwen saw her hand go to the pocket of her dressing gown, assuring herself that her letter was still there. Her hand fell away again. Gwen could see her face, darkly, in the mirror, her auburn hair piled on top of her head in an elaborate cascade of curls, her white robe, crusted with make-believe diamonds, falling off her shoulders. Next to all that glitter, her face was pale and strained.

"I do not like this," said the dresser darkly.

"I know, Justine." Fiorila pressed the heels of her hands to her temples as though her head hurt. Given the volume of the chorus, it probably did. There were a few rather overenthusiastic baritones out there. "I don't like it either, but there's nothing else to be done."

"What about the father of the child?" From the tone of her voice, the dresser had been with Fiorila for some time, long enough, at least, to know her secrets. "Surely, he would—"

Fiorila cut her off. "I cannot ask him for aid." Her voice softening, she said, "He is only recently married. I hear it is a love match, at that. He has been too good a friend these many years for me to play him such a trick as that."

"But if he knew—"

"He will not know." Fiorila's voice was final. "I'll get us out of this coil myself. I have before."

Gwen felt a reluctant sense of kinship with her, with the straight set of her spine, the determination in her voice. They were both women who knew what it was to stand alone.

A woman would risk much for her child.

"Not like this," said the dresser darkly. "Not with—"

"Hush," said Fiorila. "And bring me the gold-spangled gown for Act II."

"Foreign places, intrigues . . . I liked it better when we were in London," grumbled the dresser.

"I, too," said Fiorila. She was stripping the paint from her face with a damp sponge. She dabbed a tiny brush into a pot of rouge, prepared to start again. "We're so close, Justine, so close. It will all be over soon, I promise."

"But at what cost?" The dresser took the brush from her mistress's hand and began applying the rouge for her.

Fiorila's voice was wry and more than a little bit sad. "There is always a cost, Justine. It is simply a matter of the price. Yes?" Her voice rose in response to a knock on the door.

It opened to reveal one of the chorus girls bearing a large bouquet. "A gentleman sent this for you," she said, and giggled.

Gwen took advantage of their distraction to scuttle away, as quickly as she dared, along the beam, past the partition that separated the rooms. Outside, a boy was calling principals for the second act. Gwen lowered herself as carefully as she could, dropping lightly to her feet in the storeroom. Quickly, she brushed her dress clear of the dirt and grime from the beam. The dark purple satin absorbed the stains admirably. According to the watch she wore pinned to her breast, she had been gone just over ten minutes. It felt like longer.

It was surprisingly easy to thread her way back through the side of the stage to the boxes. Everyone was bustling about their own business, carrying props, shifting sets, gossiping about so-and-so's gaffe in the opening ballet. No one noticed a woman in purple making her way quietly through the corridors. There were the usual loiterers in the corridor, ladies engaging in flirtations, dandies making wagers.

Gwen sailed haughtily past them, back in her role of disapproving chaperone, her feathers firmly in place.

Below, the second act had begun. The audience, waiting for the signature arias of the third act, were doing as they usually did and paying very little attention. There was a lively game of cards going on in one box, loud laughter and boisterous voices from another. The orchestra scraped vainly on.

There were voices coming from her own box, but pitched less loudly. Gwen paused, one hand on the curtain, struck by the unpleasant tableau of Jane tête-à-tête with the Chevalier. On her other side, Jane's father was fast asleep, head resting on the balustrade and periwig tilted over one eye. Mrs. Wooliston nodded over her embroidery frame.

The Colonel was nowhere to be seen.

Where was the blasted man? Gwen felt a surge of entirely unjustified indignation. He should have known better than to leave Jane alone with that cad—even if Jane weren't technically alone. But any fool could see that her parents were hardly the most diligent of duennas. One might as well leave a pair of sheep as chaperone.

Her temper wasn't the least bit improved by the Chevalier's tone, low and intimate, as he said, his lips dangerously close to Jane's ear, "I should like to lure you off your pedestal."

Jane leaned back in her chair, regarding him coolly. But was that a glint of amusement Gwen saw beneath her vaunted calm? "You are certainly at leave to try, sir, but I warn you, I enjoy the view too much to be easily swayed."

"What are challenges for, but to be conquered?"

Jane settled her skirts demurely around her ankles. "Sometimes, the best lessons are learned in defeat."

The Chevalier leaned forward. As if sharing a secret, a delicious, scandalous secret, he murmured, "But success is so much more pleasant."

Jane cocked a brow, a queen who deigned to be entertained. "You are very sure of yourself, sir."

"Am I?" The Chevalier sat back in his chair. Gwen could happily have slapped the smug look from his face. "A man must be adamant if he seeks to move marble."

"You mix your metaphors—or at least your masonry."

He pressed a hand to his heart. "So long as I build a small home in your heart."

"I doubt you should be content with anything less than a palace."

"You wrong me, Mademoiselle." The Chevalier's voice was warm. To Gwen's horror, he took possession of Jane's hand.

Even worse, Jane made no move to stop him. "I should dwell in a willow cabin so long as it were at your gate."

No. No, no, no. Gwen stood frozen at the back of the box, unable to believe the evidence of her eyes. This wasn't her Jane. Yes, certainly, she had seen Jane flirt before. In fact, she had done everything she could to aid her in it. Her chaperonage waxed and waned depending on its utility to the mission. She had, without qualm, left Jane alone in gardens and on balconies for as much as half an hour at a time, ready to burst in if needed, but just as happy to leave Jane to work her magic on the ignorant mark of the moment.

The idea that Jane might actually fall in love wasn't to be thought of.

Not now, in any event. Eventually. Somewhere down the road. Then she would see Jane happily wed to some worthy soul who held her in the proper sort of esteem. She might even condescend to stay on to bully their children. But not now, not this. She wasn't ready for it all to be over yet, for Jane to throw it all away for such a petty specimen of a man, all superficial charm and glib compliments.

She had been just Jane's age, exactly Jane's age, when she had done just that.

"There you are."

It was the Colonel, all cheerful bonhomie, as though there weren't a dark farce taking place in front of them. Jane gently drew back her hand, but too late; she had let it lie there too long, long enough for liking.

The Colonel regarded Jane and the Chevalier. "They make a handsome pair," he said.

A handsome pair? They weren't any kind of pair.

Gwen turned on the Colonel. "Where have you been?" she snapped. "What were you thinking, leaving them alone?"

"Looking for you," he said. "And they're hardly alone. Her parents—"

"Haven't the sense God gave a sheep!" Gwen burst out.

The Colonel possessed himself of her arm, making the sort of soothing noises one might to a fractious child. "Why are you taking on so? What harm can the young ones come to in an open box? Surely, even the greatest sticklers couldn't find fault with that."

The fact that he was right only made Gwen angrier. She yanked her arm away. "You oughtn't have left them! Just because you leave your own children to roam the earth without supervision doesn't mean that some of us don't take our responsibilities seriously."

The Colonel dropped his hand as though he had been stung. His face went white, whiter than it had in the alley, with his blood draining out along the seams of his coat.

"What did you say?" he said, his voice low and dangerous.

She had never seen him like this before, never imagined that he could look this way. If a human could breathe fire, there would have been flames shooting from his nostrils. Every inch of his body quivered with tension. His blue eyes were as cold as the Thames in winter, hard and frozen.

She wasn't going to back down. She was Miss Gwendolyn Meadows and she bowed to no one.

She raised her head, matching him stare for stare.

Or tried to. Something in his gaze shamed her. Her eyes shifted sideways. "I said that some of us take our responsibilities seriously."

It came out wrong, somehow, low and sulky.

"Right," said the Colonel. His nostrils flared. His hands clenched in fists at his sides. But he held his temper. She could practically see the effort, the tight leash on which he held himself.

"You'd best see to them, then, hadn't you?" he said, and turned and walked away.

Gwen watched him march away, his back straight, his hands balled at his sides, the silver in his hair shining in the candlelight, and felt shame such as she had never known descend on her like a fog, miserable and choking.

She felt like an earthworm.

It was a concept so foreign as to be almost unimaginable, but she had been . . . wrong. She wasn't used to being in the wrong. It was a distinctly uncomfortable feeling.

In the box, Jane and the Chevalier were still engaged in close conversation. Gwen glanced at them and then back at the Colonel.

Dropping the curtain, Gwen set off after the Colonel, the slap of her slippers against the marble floor echoing in her ears.

Chapter 14

"Wherefore do you follow me?" protested Plumeria. "Go back to the feast. The danger there is far less than the perils that face us below the earth, where this cursed crew hold their deadly revels."

"Think you I would allow you to face this danger alone?" quoth Sir Magnifico, and drew her forth into his embrace. "I go with you, or we go not at all."

Plumeria lifted her torch high. "Come, then. For the hour grows late. And the hour of reckoning draws nigh."

Down, down, down they went, through a maze of stairs, deep into the heart of the Tower. Only the torches flickering along the walls illuminated their way, for there was no light of moon or star to penetrate this cursed place. As they descended, the sound of a rhythmic drumming grew ever louder. . . .

—From *The Convent of Orsino* by A Lady

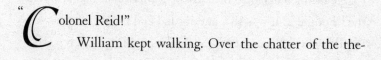"Colonel Reid!"

William kept walking. Over the chatter of the theatregoers, over the flat sound of his own footfalls, he could hear a clear soprano voice singing of the soldier tired of war's alarms.

War's alarms hadn't broken him. War, he understood. It was peace that was confounding him, a thousand times more complex than anything he had been forced to confront in any of his varied commands. He had fought through deserts, jungles, and the narrow and twisting streets of hostile cities. He hadn't always won the day; he had experienced his share of retreats, of rearguard actions, of desperate last-minute maneuvers.

But never before had he felt so entirely defeated as this.

The footsteps behind him quickened. "Colonel Reid! *William*." The sound of his name on her lips brought back a powerful memory of Bristol, of Gwen Meadows bullying and cosseting him back to health. She hadn't called him that since they'd left Bristol. "Wait."

Slowly, William turned.

"It's about time!" Gwen skidded to a stop on the slick marble floor. Her color was high, her breathing rapid. She paused just long enough to catch her breath before saying, in the hectoring tone of one who knew the value of a strong offense, "There's no need to go off in a huff."

William faced her without expression. "Don't you have a duty to discharge? I wouldn't want you to be remiss."

Just because you leave your own children to roam the earth without supervision . . .

He inclined his torso in a bow. It wasn't a polished bow, like the Chevalier's. It was stiff and formal and it hurt like the very devil. His wound might have scabbed over, but it still burned.

"Don't let me keep you," he said.

Gwen folded her arms across her chest. "I didn't mean it. Not that way."

Some of us take our responsibilities seriously. . . .

"You needn't sugarcoat it," he said, feeling, for the first time, every one of his fifty-four years and then some. Where had they gone, those sunny, laughing years? How had they come to this? "It is what it is."

Kat with her reddened hands and defiant eyes. And Lizzy. Where was Lizzy? Every one of those words scored his conscience like a cat-o'-nine-tails on raw flesh.

"Oh, all right, I— You touched me on the raw," Gwen said gruffly. She fiddled with her fan, making a fold of painted silk appear and disappear. "I oughtn't to have said it. I was out of line."

His lack of response seemed to madden her. In and out the fold of silk went, in and out.

"I was angry at myself, not you. Well, at myself and at that coxcomb of a Chevalier. I should have gone after him, not you."

William nodded at her fan. "If you keep doing that you'll break it."

"It's sturdier than you think." Gwen snapped the fan together. She looked up at him, a deep furrow between her eyes. "It was ill done of me. Unsporting. Say something!"

Somewhere, William managed to find words. "You were protecting your charge," he said flatly. "That was all."

"No," said Gwen. "It's not all. Stop standing there looking like a corpse! I'm telling you I was wrong. And I don't say that often."

He didn't imagine that she did.

She paced a few steps, her purple skirts whirling around her legs. "You were right. Her parents were with her." She couldn't restrain herself from muttering, "Even if they are without a stick of sense between them."

There was more than an apology at issue here. The formidable woman he had seen facing off armed men with a glint in her eye was rattled, and William would wager it had something to do with two handsome young people in an opera box.

It wasn't easy to lose a child, even if a surrogate one. Perhaps particularly if a surrogate one. No matter where they went, or whom they married, he had a claim on all his children, the most basic claim, the claim of blood. What call on a child's heart did a chaperone have once the chaperonage was done?

Looking at Gwen with compassion and a new understanding, William said, "You love her, don't you? Miss Wooliston."

Gwen stiffened. "I am very fond of Jane," she said guardedly. "Proud, even. I owe her a duty. Her parents entrusted me with her care."

He'd never known a woman who knew so many ways to hedge around the concept of affection.

"All that, too," he said.

Gwen glowered at him. "Love," she said succinctly, cutting off every word with a snap, "is a word too often used and too little meant. What does it matter to say you love someone if the word inspires no action?"

It reminded William of something he had heard once in a

play. *"My words fly up, my thoughts remain below. Words without deeds do not to heaven go."*

Gwen tapped her fan against her palm. "Don't try to distract me with doggerel verse. The Lord knows, poetry has done enough harm in its time, all sweet professions that last only until the ink has dried."

"Not all sweet professions are lies," protested William, "verse or no. Sure and it's no crime to put one's love into words."

"It is when those words are nothing more than empty air." Gwen regarded him militantly. "One can love volubly and publicly, with all the trappings of sentiment, and still fail someone entirely when it comes to the point."

Love his girls? Of course he did. He would have said so to anyone who asked. Volubly and publicly. But in the end, all his fine sentiments had led him here.

"Yes," William said slowly. "Sure and that's a fair assessment of my own situation, whichever way you turn it."

Gwen's head snapped up, purple feathers bobbing. "That's not what I—"

"Meant, I know." William's lips twisted wryly. "But you were right, all the same. I'm a poor excuse for a father. I've let my children go to wrack and ruin and I didn't even know it was happening. I'd brag of them to anyone who would listen. I waxed sentimental over their miniatures in the mess. But I hadn't the devil of an idea that they were out running about England entirely without resources or supervision."

He remembered his idealized image of them, all pastels and

frills, like someone off a piece of French porcelain, Kat in a muslin gown, sitting beneath the spreading branches of an oak tree, watching Lizzy, sprawled on a blanket on the grass, eating cherries and laughing, their rosy-cheeked grandmother calling them in for dinner.

His throat felt tight. The images were choking him. "I thought Kat was sitting prettily in a garden under a tree. A tree . . ."

"Stop that!" Gwen said harshly. Her fan swung down from its string as she grabbed his arm, her fingers biting into his sleeve. "I won't have it. You were thousands of miles away. How were you to know?"

"I ought to have made it my business to know."

"How often did you write them?"

William bristled. "As often as there was a ship to carry the letter."

They had both written back, regularly. He might have been suspicious otherwise. He hadn't realized it was all lies.

Gwen looked at him from under beetled brows. "Was there any way to have kept them with you?" She leveled her fan at him, poking him in the ribs, well below his bandages. "Don't fib! I'll know if you're lying. Did you send them away for your own convenience?"

William shook off her hand, stepping back. "Don't be absurd!" His voice echoed uncomfortably loudly off the marble and gilding. He swallowed hard, modulating his tone. "I hated to send them away. They were . . ."

Little Lizzy, all childlike exuberance, yanking him by the

hand, creating elaborate and imaginative excuses as to why eating all the jam out of the pot was really a favor to him; Kat, the oldest, protective of her status as the lady of the house, bullying him with all the confidence of seventeen.

"They were the best part of me."

"Well, then." That was all she said, but William felt as though he had somehow gone through a tribunal and been exonerated. She fixed him with a look of staggering smugness. "Hadn't you better stop flagellating yourself and get on with it?"

The smugness of her expression startled him into a laugh, hoarse and raw, but a laugh all the same.

He took her hand in his, looking down at the gloved fingers. "You are a remarkable woman, Gwen Meadows."

Gwen emitted a delicate sniff. "There's hardly much in the way of competition here. I shine by comparison. Besides, I can't have you wasting time in moping. I didn't patch you up just to have you go jump off a balcony."

"For all of that," William said gently, squeezing her hand before letting it go, "I thank you."

Gwen shrugged, not quite meeting his eyes. "As you say, it is what it is. One does what one must."

She did like to hide affection behind the guise of duty. He remembered her hands, gentle, washing the grime of the sickroom off his face in the inn room, the infinite patience with which she had spooned soup between his slack lips. There was a tender heart beneath that prickly shell, however hard she tried to hide it. On an impulse, William slid a finger beneath her chin, lifting her face towards his. "You seem to be making a practice of patching me up."

Her eyes were gray, a gray so deep that they looked almost purple against the frame of her headdress. He wondered if the swains of her youth had compared them to violets, or her skin to cream. It wasn't cream now, but ivory, strong and vibrant. With her hair pulled back away from her face under her absurd purple turban, he could see the strength in her face, the clean, bold bones, but the weaknesses, too, the faint purple shadows beneath her eyes, the sensitive dent below her lips.

She stuck her chin into the air. "You'll just have to stop blundering into trouble, then, won't you?"

She did a good job of looking stern, but her lips hadn't been made for sternness; they were full and generous, less a rosebud and more a Cupid's bow. She might pull back her hair and button her bodice up to the chin, but she couldn't hide those lips.

"I think I already have," he said honestly.

"There you are!" The sound of Miss Wooliston's voice broke the spell.

They jerked away from each other like marionettes at the hands of an inexpert puppeteer.

Miss Wooliston looked from one to the other with an expression of mild inquiry. "We were wondering where you'd got to."

It wouldn't have been quite so bad but for the carefully suppressed amusement in her tone. The Chevalier, standing just beside Miss Wooliston, winked at him. William pretended not to notice.

Bad enough to be behaving like a moonstruck calf, and worse still to be caught at it by the younger generation.

"The caterwauling on the stage was too much for me," said Gwen, stepping quickly away. Her skirts brushed William's legs as she walked past him. "It sounded like a bunch of cats being swung by their tails."

"That is most unkind, and untrue, as well." Miss Wooliston linked arms with her chaperone. "I thought it was an excellent production." She frowned. "Except for the third violin, which was sorely out of tune."

"I didn't think Fiorila was in her usual voice," offered the Chevalier.

Gwen eyed the Chevalier narrowly. "Know her, then, do you?"

She managed to imply that he was a rake, a rogue, a seducer, and a despoiler of opera singers. It was beautifully done.

"Not personally, no," said the Chevalier, unruffled. "But I have had the pleasure of hearing her sing many times in London."

"There's no music like the sound of the wind through the wool," contributed Mr. Wooliston poetically. He jammed his periwig back on his head. "I don't hold with this foreign entertainment."

Gwen looked at him with imperfectly concealed scorn. "*Artaxerxes* is an English opera, sirrah."

"No. Can't be." Wooliston shook his head, the tail of his periwig swaying mournfully. "What kind of name is Xerxes? No, the man's not an Englishman."

"Would you prefer that the opera be called *George*?" demanded Gwen.

"I prefer Harry, myself," contributed William blandly.

"I believe, sir," said the Chevalier smoothly, "that Xerxes was a Persian potentate."

"They make such lovely carpets," said Mrs. Wooliston.

"I rather think Xerxes was too busy conquering the world to weave," said Miss Wooliston peaceably.

"Only webs of intrigue," said the Chevalier, and bowed over Miss Wooliston's hand. "Many thanks for a most lovely—and edifying—evening."

Throughout the extended and elaborate leave-taking, Gwen was quiet. Too quiet.

William joggled her arm lightly with his elbow. "All right, there?"

Ignoring William, Gwen turned to her charge and said, "Go on without me. I've remembered something I have to see to."

A look passed between her and Miss Wooliston. "We'll send the carriage back for you," Miss Wooliston said, and, without seeming to do so, neatly turned her parents towards the exit.

"Not so fast," said William, grabbing Gwen's arm before she could slip away into the crowd. "What is it?"

For a moment, she looked as though she meant to argue. Arriving at her decision, she said, in a rapid, low tone, "I just saw one of the men who ambushed us in the alley. He went that way. If you'd unhand me, I might be able to follow him."

William followed her. "Not without me, you're not."

She didn't waste time fighting with him. "If you must come, keep quiet and try to keep up."

He still wasn't feeling entirely robust, but he would have keeled over rather than admit it. "I'll do my best not to swoon on you."

She cast him a long look over her shoulder. He could see the concern in her eyes, but they both knew there wasn't time to argue. "If you must swoon, do so quietly. Now, hush!"

She moved rapidly through the crowd, William following a pace behind. Their erratic route took them out a side door, away from the crowd waiting for their carriages, and around the back of the theatre, just in time to see a door slam shut.

Holding her finger to her lips, Gwen took hold of the door handle, waited ten seconds, and then pulled it open. In front of them was a long flight of stairs leading down, perilously steep. There was a red glow of light at the bottom. Gwen beckoned to William. He eased the door carefully shut behind him and followed her down into the darkness.

The landing let out in a cellar. To one side, he could see the storerooms of the theatre, boxes, crates, and barrels. But that wasn't where the light led. A lantern had been hung from a rough iron hook beside an aperture in one of the walls. Without hesitating, Gwen dropped down on her knees and crawled through.

Trying not to put too much weight on his bad side, William did the same, following the waggle of his companion's backside down a short tunnel. It let out into an edifice of stone that looked like an advertisement for a stonemason's junk shop, bits of statuary and fallen masonry littering the ground. A ramp of sorts curved off to the side, lined with the remnants of columns. Staying close to the wall, they started down.

"You're sure he went this way?" William murmured.

"Someone placed those torches to be followed," was all Gwen said.

Where in the devil were they? William felt as though he'd stumbled into the more fantastical sort of novel. Flaring torches marked their path, spaced at uneven intervals. In the patches of light, William caught sight of more fallen masonry and other tunnels leading out in other directions, an entire complex beneath the opera house.

"What is this place?" William whispered.

Gwen turned her head just enough to answer. "Roman ruins. The city of Bath is built on them. They must have unearthed them when they were building the new—"

She broke off abruptly, bumping into William as she backed up. His arms automatically went around her, keeping them both steady.

"Down!" she hissed, and pulled him back, behind an outcropping of stone.

They had come out onto a clear space, the remains of what had once been a form of balcony, looking out over a sunken area below. There was a stair that led down to their left, the steps cracked and treacherous.

From their vantage point, William could see that theirs wasn't the only open archway. There was a regular pattern of them, semicircular openings overlooking a great rectangular area below. There must once have been ornamental stonework creating a balustrade, but most of it had crumbled away, leaving uneven piles of rubble, some carved with what looked to be some sort of frieze.

There was a piece lying on the ground next to him, featuring the torso and part of the leg of a woman as she lolled in a position of considerable abandon. The carving was still clear and sharp, showing the sensuous curve of breast and hip.

"An old bath," Gwen murmured, without moving her lips. "The place is riddled with them."

There was no water now in the giant sunken area. Above them, the ceiling rose in a grand arch, so high that the top was lost in the shadows. There were darker spots among the shadows, and a sound, as of wings. William's lips set in a grim line. Bats, he'd be willing to wager. He wasn't afraid of the wee beasties, but that didn't mean he had to like them, either.

Around them, a series of arches, in various states of disrepair, overlooked the old bath. There was a tiered descent into the pool, ten steps down. What must once have been a fountain dominated one end, a satyr tugging at the legs of a fleeing water nymph, all floating draperies and bare limbs. Around the base of the fountain milled men, if men they might be called. They were all garbed in robes of a shiny black material that caught and reflected the torchlight.

Underneath the black hoods, their faces shone an eerie white in the uncertain light, their lips an unnatural red.

William shook his head. "What in the devil—"

"White lead and lip rouge," whispered Gwen.

"I'd gathered that," William whispered back. "But who are they?"

Gwen held up a hand to silence him. "Something is about to happen."

Smoke was belching from the old water pipe, billowing into the sunken pool, twining around the legs of the hapless water nymph. As the smoke rose, William caught a whiff of a familiar scent: opium, and a lot of it, mixed with some sort of incense, unless he missed his guess, sickly sweet and undeniably narcotic.

Down in the pit, the ghoulish revelers fell silent, turning away from the fountain, towards an arch at the other end.

Through the mist strode a man in a black cloak wider, larger, shinier, than the others. Where the others wore hoods, his was thrown back, revealing a face painted a dead white, his lips crimson. He must have been wearing lifts of some kind, for he seemed to tower over the others, taller than a normal man. As he passed, the other robed figures sank to their knees, touching their heads to the ground in obeisance.

Accepting the homage as his due, he strode through the ranks of his followers, jumping up onto a platform formed by a stone placed over the remains of two pillars. As he turned, William finally saw what it was that he carried before him.

In his hands, he held a human skull.

Slowly, the leader raised the skull over his head. Somewhere in the back of the room, William could hear the faint beat of a drum, only barely audible in the expectant silence.

"Brethren!" the leader called in a voice rich and dark. "Lords of the night!"

"Merciful heavens," murmured Gwen. "We've stumbled into a meeting of the Hellfire Club."

William had heard tell of a similar organization in Poona. "Orgies, debauchery, and general idiocy, all in fancy dress costume?"

"Precisely," said Gwen. Her eyes were shining with excitement. "What luck! I've always wanted to see one of these."

William wasn't so sure he would have called it luck. The atmosphere in the subterranean chamber was decidedly eerie. And there had been stories about that society in Poona, stories that had shocked him, world-weary old campaigner that he was. He had taxed Jack with them, Jack who had sold the young idiots the opium.

"What do I care as long as they pay on time?" Jack had said.

But William had cared. He had cared when they had raped the daughter of a friend, a half-caste, like Lizzy, in one of their debauched pseudo-ceremonies.

But by then, Jack had been gone.

Downstairs, the minions were getting restless. William could practically feel their intensity, like the crackle in the air before a storm.

"Rise, brothers!" the celebrant called. "Rise and greet your sacrifice!"

The men in the bath clambered to their feet. Slowly, then faster, they began clapping, clapping in time with the drums. The frenzied drumming pounded faster and faster, hands clapping, feet stamping in time to the beat, the hollow echo of booted feet against the old stone floor echoing through the hollow vault, bringing the pounding to a fever pitch, thrumming in and around them.

With a burst of flame and a whiff of sulfur, two women appeared, clad only in wisps of red gauze, their nipples rouged, red ribbons around their necks, their ankles, spiraling up their arms. They bore between them a litter, draped in black gauze, heaped with white flowers whose sickly scent warred with that of the drugged smoke.

Pale against the black cloth lay a young woman. She lay on her side, as though in sleep, her gown falling aside to display her leg as far as the knee. She was all that was innocent in her white night rail, the thin muslin edged with white lace and satin ribbon.

Over the side of the litter trailed her long, unbound hair, the red-brown curls bouncing with the movement of the litter.

William found himself leaning forward, his heart in his throat, his hands clutching the masonry, knuckles white, hunting for a glimpse of her face, praying and fearing, all at the same time.

The drumbeat rose to a frenzy pitch as the bearers slowly tilted the bier forward.

Chapter 15

"What ghouls be these?" marveled Sir Magnifico.

"No ghouls, sir, but members of a society so secret that even those with secrets know not what this society is. Tonight, they practice their ancient rites, with skull, tome, and torch. Hark! Silence! Their leader comes. . . ."

—From *The Convent of Orsino* by A Lady

"It's not Lizzy." William let out a deep, shuddering breath. "Thank God."

Gwen's hand briefly touched his arm before dropping again to her side. "God has little to do with this place." She looked critically down at the revelers. "Although if I were the devil, I'm not sure I would want to lay claim to it either. It looks to be a highly ramshackle operation."

William wasn't diverted. He edged forward, trying to get a better look at the bier. "Is it the other girl? Miss Wooliston?"

"No." Agnes was a paler copy of Jane. Her hair didn't have even the hint of a curl, and she still had all the gawkiness of youth. Even underneath that virginal white gown, one could tell that the woman on the litter sported the curves of a woman grown.

"It's someone's daughter." William started forward.

Gwen's hand closed over his arm. "Stop. Look."

As the bier tilted forward, she could see that the woman on the elaborate litter was older than she had originally supposed, and that what she had imagined as a drugged stupor was a pose of carefully staged languor. Gwen recognized her from her perambulations backstage.

"She's one of the ballet girls. She works here at the theatre."

William paused, his muscles tense beneath her fingers. "Hired?"

Gwen nodded. "Undoubtedly." Prima donnas might command rich protectors; the members of the chorus were forced to find alternative ways to supplement their incomes. "As are the other two. They wouldn't thank you for interfering."

William wasn't convinced. "She looks drugged."

"They're all drugged, every man jack of them." That was all she needed, for William to go charging in, half-healed wound and all. They would tear him to shreds and leave his body among the ruins.

The thought roused Gwen to real alarm. This might be playacting, but she had no doubt that the men below would turn violent if someone tried to balk them of their promised pleasures. They were panting like dogs down there.

"Does she really look unwilling? Besides, if we were to go charging down there, how would we fight them all off? I don't have my parasol with me." Only her fan, but he didn't need to know about the dagger in the ivory casing. "It's twenty to two, and those two unarmed."

William looked at her fiercely. "I shouldn't have thought that would stop you."

"It wouldn't," said Gwen, stung, "if I thought they needed rescuing."

As if in illustration of her point, the woman on the bier curled her legs beneath her and rose to her knees, stretching sinuously. Every man in the place—including, Gwen noticed, her companion—held his breath as she took hold of the fabric at the neck of her modest gown and, with one fluid motion, ripped it straight down the front, from breast to knee.

She wore nothing underneath.

"Point taken," said William, staring like the rest of them.

The woman on the bier was extremely well endowed. Gwen resisted the urge to glance down at her own neatly covered and far less protuberant chest. With every eye in the place on her, the girl shrugged out of the remains of her gown, shaking her long hair down around her shoulders, the twining brown curls highlighting rather than hiding her most obvious attributes.

"Showy." Gwen sniffed.

"Mmm," said William.

Gwen glowered at him. "You're not here to admire the view."

William lifted innocent blue eyes to hers. "If it's there . . . sure and I wouldn't want to let it go to waste."

"Hmph," said Gwen. It was all staging, anyway. She could look equally sultry lying on a bier. Not that she wanted to lie on a bier for the delectation of a gang of hardened roués. But it was the principle of the thing.

The celebrant went through a mockery of a blessing. Dipping his fingers in the wine, he anointed first the woman's closed eyelids, then her lips, tracing the shape of her lips with his finger. She sucked his finger into her mouth with every sign of pleasure.

Next to her, Gwen could hear William swallow. Hard.

Men.

Raising the skull in his hands, the celebrant upended it over the lounging figure of the woman. Red liquid trickled down around her breasts, down her belly, along her thighs, staining the crumpled material of her gown on the litter beneath her.

From a distance, it looked like blood.

"Wine," murmured Gwen. When she used the scene in her novel, she decided, it would be blood. Much more dramatic.

"Do you think the skull is plaster?" whispered William.

"One can only hope."

The wine traced elaborate trails along the woman's naked body, the reddish lines glowing in the torchlight against her pale skin like ancient runes. Or, thought Gwen sourly, like a treasure map leading to *X* marking the spot, with very little doubt what that spot might be.

The celebrant spread his arms wide. The broad black folds of his cape fell back to reveal a line of rich, crimson silk.

"Come!" he commanded. "Drink!"

His congregation didn't need to be asked twice.

From the front of the room, a man stumbled forward,

clumsy in his eagerness. The others were chanting something, low, rhythmic. It took Gwen a moment to realize that it was nothing more than "drink, drink, drink." In that tone, in that place, the words had a far more menacing sound. And above it all, the drugged smoke swirled.

For a moment, she thought he meant to bite the woman's neck. He hovered like one of the dark predators of fiction, his black cape flowing behind him.

Instead, he swooped down, his tongue licking up a long swath of wine, from her neck to her breastbone. Gwen knew it was all nonsense, but she couldn't look away, as the man followed the crazy, zigzagging trail of wine, over and around the woman's breasts, circling around her nipple as she writhed with every appearance of enjoyment.

The room was eerily silent. Gwen licked her dry lips. It was decidedly airless in the subterranean chamber. The neckline that had been modest and appropriate upstairs felt quite uncomfortably close down here; the lace frill around her neck was choking her.

As the first man continued his amorous ministrations, another man fell to his knees before the bier, taking possession of a foot, licking at a trail of wine that had dripped all the way down to her toes. He followed it up the inside of her calf, past her knee. The woman let her legs fall wide as he made his way up, farther and farther still.

Gwen had thought herself unshockable, after all these years, but there were some circumstances that took one by surprise.

The celebrant clapped his hands, twice, and the litter bearers stepped forward, flinging off their scraps of gauze. Reaching into the ranks of hooded men, they chose their lovers seemingly at random, pulling men to them in a heady, confused dance. The skull cup must have been refilled with wine; Gwen could see it making the rounds, being passed from hand to hand. One of the hooded men lifted it, laughingly trickling it over one of the dancing girls, who tipped back her head to drink, then, moving the cup aside, transferred her mouth to another object.

There was no chanting anymore, just the unmistakable sounds of murmurs, laughter, and heavy breathing.

Gwen was having trouble breathing at all. She forced the air through her throat. It came out as a sort of wheeze.

Good heavens, was that woman really—yes, yes, she was.

"So. This is what an orgy looks like." Wiping the sweat off his brow, William cleared his throat. "Warm in here, isn't it?"

Warm? She was boiling. Her dress felt painfully tight, the fabric of her bodice rasping against her nipples. The fichu at her neck was smothering her; she wanted to rip it free, to yank the turban off her hair and shake it free, to reach out . . .

Well.

"Suetonius suddenly makes so much more sense," she said shakily.

It made it easier to think about Roman emperors, something far removed, dull and dry and long past, as if the writhing, twining bodies in front of them were something out of the illustrations in one of those forbidden books on the top shelf of the library.

"They're certainly"—William tugged at his collar, loosening his cravat—"inventive."

His throat looked very brown against the white of his shirt. There was a little hollow right in the middle, where the pulse was pounding. She could see the sweat beading there, just as it was beading down her own throat and between her breasts. It would be so easy to lean forward, to lick away that drop of saltwater as the man below had tasted the wine, to pull open jacket, waistcoat, shirt, and follow the paths of the scars she had seen there before, curving and winding, down, down, down.

"Indeed," Gwen said hoarsely. "Although I imagine it's nothing that hasn't been done before."

William looked at her. "No," he said, and there was a curious intensity in his gaze, in the light in his eyes as he looked at her, the way his eyes traveled over her. "It's as old as time, it is."

Good heavens, was there no air in here?

Gwen tore her gaze away from William's, drawing in deep breaths of the dense, drugged air, trying to make sense of her muddled thinking. Gwen dug her nails into her palms, forcing herself to concentrate, to think. The man who had ambushed them—that was what they were after. He was down there somewhere. But where? Below, hoods had been thrown back, and more than hoods, but it was impossible to identify a face.

There were, however, two men who weren't participating, either as actors or as voyeurs. They had removed themselves to the side, to the relative privacy of a niche between two pillars. One was still hooded, in the same anonymous black cape and hood as all the others. The other was the celebrant.

Gwen poked William in the arm, leaning just close enough to whisper, "Look over there. Those two. They're not participating."

She could feel the warmth of his body beside her, the heat coming off his skin in waves. Blinking, with an obvious effort, he directed his gaze where she pointed.

"So they are." He nodded towards the crumbling staircase to their left. "There might be a way down. Are you game?"

She would sooner bite off her own hand than admit otherwise. "Of course."

After all, if they caught her, it wasn't as though she was the sort of woman from whom they would strip every last scrap of clothing and whom they would tie to a bier and . . .

"Gwen?"

She could feel her face going a deep, betraying red. "Be careful on those stairs," she said curtly. "They don't look stable."

"A pity we don't have the cloaks," he murmured as they picked their way carefully down, keeping to the shadows. "We could slip right in."

In more ways than one. "See something you like down there?" muttered Gwen.

William's blue gaze lit on her.

"No," was all he said, but she found herself shivering at what he left unsaid, her skin all goose bumps. She had drawn off her long gloves, and her arms felt naked and bare.

"Keep to the shadows," she shot back, "or it's all over for us."

"Hush," he said, and reached for her hand. To her surprise,

she let him take it. His thumb pressed intimately into her palm, silencing her. "I've done reconnaissance before. Stay close."

She would have told him what she thought of his giving her orders, but he was right. This once. She followed softly behind him, picking her way carefully down the crumbling stair, which must once have been a path from the galleries to the side of the bath. It led out into the shadowed arcade.

On the ground, the smoke was chokingly strong. The shimmering of the torchlight through the smoke made Gwen's eyes ache, turning the smoke into a living, shifting, treacherous thing. It formed shapes, like clouds, dragons and dancing girls and menacing satyrs, and through it all, intensified by the smog, she could hear the pants and grunts, the cries of pleasure, as the orgy throbbed around them.

William tugged on her hand, pulling her into a narrow aperture. Yanking his cravat from his throat, he tied it around his own nose and mouth, creating a screen. His eyes, tearing from the smoke, narrowed at her over the cloth. It took her a moment to realize what he meant. Then, fumbling, she tugged the fichu from the neck of her gown.

Without it, the gown felt dangerously décolleté, the satin of her gown slippery against her damp skin.

With fingers that wouldn't quite obey, she tried to fold the fabric into a triangle, to tie it at the back of her head as her companion had done, but her hairpins kept getting in the way. William took the cloth from her, draping it carefully over her nose and mouth.

She could feel his knuckles brushing against the nape of her neck as he tied the lacy fabric into a clumsy but effective knot. His touch tingled. She looked up at him and found his eyes on hers. It must have been the smoke that made breathing so difficult, the smoke and the lace-trimmed muslin brushing her lips.

His fingers stroked her neck in a caress before his hand dropped to his side.

Gwen bit down hard on her lip, using the pain to recall herself to their purpose. Her eyes stung and her head spun, but she forced herself to attention, turning on her heel, using the rough wall to guide her through the smoke, towards the alcove where the two men were still in conference. She could see the crimson lining of the celebrant's cape through the smoke.

There must have been a form of colonnade at some time, a place for people to lounge and eat by the side of the bath in the privacy of their own niches. A corridor ran behind, a service corridor, at a guess. There were openings in the walls, by which food might once have been passed. Gwen shamelessly put her ear to the opening. A few feet down, she could see William doing the same.

"This is the last of the old lot." It was the celebrant speaking. She could see only the back of his head, his hair close cropped in the fashionable style. "We were supposed to have a shipment a month ago."

The man next to him still wore his hood, the fabric draping down on either side of his face, muffling his words. "I've arranged for an alternate means of supply."

"We've never had delays before."

The hooded head turned. "There have been . . . unforeseen circumstances."

The celebrant leaned his back against the wall of the niche, his relaxed pose at odds with the tinge of excitement in his voice. "So it's true. The Moonflower has defected."

"No names," said the other man shortly. "That was part of the bargain. Wasn't it . . . Sir Francis? Or would you rather seek your supplies elsewhere?"

Sir Francis inclined his head, acknowledging the point. "A nom de guerre is hardly the same as one's proper name. But let us not quibble about details. Far be it from me to violate the terms of our agreement." His lips curved, the motion exaggerated by the red paint he wore. "I take it our mutual friend is no longer a friend?"

"My associate"—the hooded man stressed the distinction—"will no longer be associating with us. But you needn't worry. There are other channels. Your people shan't be balked of their entertainments."

Sir Francis raised a brow. "I understand that the Moonflower bilked you of more than my pretty poppies when he decided to change allegiances. The price of his redemption, was it?"

"Allow me to worry about my own affairs." The other man's voice was too faint to hear properly. Something in the inflection put her in mind of the Chevalier—but his voice was muffled by that blasted hood, by the hood and the acoustics of the alcove. Gwen strained to hear more but found her cheek scraping against rough stone. "You have your toys. Enjoy them."

"One can never have too many toys." Sir Francis was clearly

enjoying himself. "Especially those that glitter. Such attractive things, mythical jewels . . . if one can hold on to them."

Pressed against the stone, Gwen froze, desperately scrabbling to remember what she had just heard, to piece it all together.

The Moonflower. Redemption. Mythical jewels. They were talking of the jewels of Berar; she had no doubt of it. Somehow, this hooded man in front of her was linked to the jewels of Berar, stolen by an agent called the Moonflower.

The hooded man spoke quietly, but even through the stone, Gwen could hear the note of menace in his voice. "You dabble in matters that do not concern you."

"Poisonous waters, I know," said Sir Francis languidly. "Don't worry. I have no desire to wake with a dagger in my back, however prettily jeweled. I simply wished to ascertain the—how shall I say this?—stability of your organization. My people are used to their diversions. They should grow restless if they went too long without."

The hooded man had moved. Gwen couldn't see him through her narrow window, but she could hear the swish of his robe against stone. "Your supplies will arrive as promised."

"I thank you," said Sir Francis blandly. "That was all I needed to know."

The hooded man was moving, leaving. Gwen couldn't see him through the smoke. She dodged to the next aperture, the window onto the next niche, but all she could see was the swirling smoke, the glare of the torches lighting the slow-moving forms of the writhing, rutting naked bodies in the pit.

William tugged at her hand. Stumbling a bit, Gwen followed him through a break in the masonry. There was a passageway leading up.

He put his lips close to her ear, over the edge of her kerchief. "Let's go—before they find us."

Gwen tugged away, back towards the bath. Somewhere in there, the hooded man was on the prowl, the man who might lead her to the jewels of Berar. The man who might be Jane's Chevalier. Or might not. Damn that hood! "But—"

William held fast. "We'll not hear anything else, not tonight."

She looked at him, and the truth of what he was saying sunk in. There was no way of following the hooded man through that mob below; they'd stand out too sorely. And even if they did follow him, what then? It was the Moonflower she had to look for, an agent named the Moonflower.

Her brain was too muddled to make sense of it all. Later. Later in the clear air, when the drums stopped throbbing and her skin stopped tingling; then she would parse it all out, with clear, uncluttered logic. But for now . . .

"This way," she said, pulling him towards the passageway.

Hand in hand, they lurched their way up the slope, alternately pulling each other, half walking, half running. Gwen couldn't have said with any certainty what they were running from, but an urgency had infected them both, as frantic as the beat of the drums and the pants and cries of the revelers below. The path twisted, bumping them up against a ladder that led to a trapdoor.

William gave Gwen a boost up, his hands lingering just a

bit too long on her bottom as she scrambled up, pushing the light wood trapdoor aside, breathing deep of the stale air, which felt, smoke-free, as clear and clean as that to be had on any mountaintop. William clambered up behind her, dropping the trapdoor back into place.

They were in a cluttered, dusty room, lit by the moonlight coming through the windows. A storage room, under the theatre.

They stood, their hands on their knees, panting with their exertions, looking at each other, chests moving in and out, dusty, sweaty, disheveled. Gwen could feel her bodice gaping open, the cool air on her damp breasts.

All of a sudden, William started laughing, a great bark of laughter, and Gwen was laughing too, only half-sure why, from the exhilaration of it all, from the adventure, from being safe here in this little room with the orgy going on below.

William kicked a box over the trapdoor to hold it in place.

"You look like a harem girl with that over your mouth, so," he said, his eyes tearing, his voice shaky with laughter.

"You look like a bandit," retorted Gwen.

She was flying high on something, exhilarated down to her bones. She reached behind to tear off the makeshift kerchief, but the knot held firm.

William tugged his own bandanna free, dropping it on the floor. "Let me," he said, and reached around her to untangle the knot. "Before you end up in some sultan's harem."

"I'd like to see one try," Gwen tried to say, but the fabric got tangled in her lips.

His own lips quivering with laughter, William plucked it free.

"There," he said, but he wasn't laughing anymore, his eyes fixed on her lips, the fichu forgotten in his hand.

Gwen reached up and pulled his head across to hers. His hair was thick beneath her fingers, thick and springy, with the hint of a curl. It rasped against her hands as she twined her fingers through his hair, yanking him closer.

His arms closed tight around her, tipping her back, as he kissed her with a ferocity that matched her own, both of them caught up in the madness, her head still whirling, swirling with the dark rhythms of the room below, and something else besides, two weeks' worth of frustrated desire, the memory of an accidental kiss in a moon-dark room in an inn in Bristol.

Only this time, she wasn't an Indian goddess. This time, it was she he was kissing, urgently, desperately. No illusions, no mistaken identities.

Just . . . folly. Pure folly.

They broke apart, panting. She couldn't see his face clearly in the moonlight, but she could tell his cheeks were flushed, his eyes glittering.

"This is absurd," rasped Gwen. "Absurd."

"I agree," said William, breathing hard.

It was hard to say who grabbed whom. They lurched together like boulders rolling downhill, propelled by a force as strong as gravity. There was no finesse to it, no art. She could feel him tugging at the bodice of her dress, yanking at the buttons, pulling it down over her shoulders while she nibbled at an ear, the side of his neck, his shoulder, any skin she could reach.

He tugged her bodice down over her shoulder, his lips at her neck, her breast. Her head fell back, like the woman on the bier. She could feel her hair coming free from its pins, teasing her shoulder blades, tickling the bared skin of her back as she arched towards his teasing, sucking mouth, her hands in his hair, urging him on.

"Gwen—," he groaned, bracing his hands on her waist, looking up at her with dazed blue eyes, as though he meant to say something more, something earnest and utterly, utterly wrong. "Gwen—"

No, no, no. A tiny bubble of panic rose and broke. He was going to spoil it all, spoil it with those sweet words that meant nothing at all. She didn't want that. She didn't want to have to think. She didn't want to have to resent him.

She put a hand over his mouth, silencing him. "No words," she said urgently.

No words, no lies. Just body moving against body. She'd had enough lying protestations of love to last a lifetime. This, on the other hand, this was honest. This was nothing more than what it was, desire raw and simple.

She had earned it, hadn't she? Years of being good, of being proper, of bodices buttoned up to her neck and caps over her hair. She'd had enough. This was for her, an atonement for all those years of atonement.

They didn't bother with such niceties as removing their clothes. That would have taken too much time. Gwen could feel William tugging at her skirts, pushing them up, past her knees, her thighs, the fabric bunching around her waist. She wiggled to help him, backing up against a crate, just the right height to serve as a makeshift seat. Her hands went to the buttons of his breeches, unsteady enough that one button popped, and another stuck, sideways, before finally giving way.

"Gently," he said, and there was laughter in his hoarse voice, laughter that worked on her like champagne, sending bubbles through her blood.

She tossed her hair back over her bare shoulders. She didn't know when it had come loose, and she didn't care. Her gown was hanging, half on, half off.

"Do you want it gentle?" she demanded.

It was a challenge, and they both knew it. He grinned, a reckless, piratical grin. Looking like that, he ought to have been marauding on the high seas, not a respectable former member of the East India Company's army.

"Never say I don't yield to a lady's wishes. . . ."

Gwen linked her arms around his neck, one sleeve slithering down along her arm. She felt sultry and daring, a world removed from the prim spinster chaperone she had left behind downstairs.

She put her lips close to his ear as she locked her legs around his waist. "No words. Remember?"

And that was the last that either of them said for quite some time.

Chapter 16

Through the drunken, dancing throng they ran, Sir Magnifico holding tight to his lady's hand. They tied scarves around their faces, but even so, the treacherous fumes of the poisoned smoke did their work, sending their senses swirling, as they battled the overwhelming urge to throw their morals to the winds and join the shouting revelers in the sensual movement of the dance.

—From *The Convent of Orsino* by A Lady

William came to his senses, if sense it could be called, sprawled on the floor of a storage room at the back of the Theatre Royal.

He rolled onto his back, blinking for a moment at the ceiling, as the remnants of what used to be his mind tried and failed to pull together what exactly had just happened. He hadn't felt so dazed since he'd wound up on the wrong side of a rocket fusillade. His horse had bolted with him, shying and rearing in the midst of the flashing lights, the colors bursting all around him.

Compared to this, that had been bland.

A box scraped against the floor as Gwen braced herself against it, hoisting herself to her feet. Her dress was off her shoulders, her hair tumbling down her back. Her headdress had got lost somewhere; her petticoat straggled down below her hem. She looked wonderful.

William could have gone on lying there on the floor indefinitely—it was surprisingly comfortable for a floor—but since his position put him rather at a disadvantage, he hauled himself up to a sitting position.

Gwen was pacing around the room, searching for a lost slipper. He didn't remember removing her slippers, but they must have been kicked off somewhere along the way. He did remember her stockings, the luxurious silk of them, and the even softer bare skin above.

"Ha!" said Gwen, and pounced on the slipper, jamming her foot into it with an air of triumph.

Shouldn't there be—well, some cuddling? Some postcoital discussion? "Come back to the floor" didn't have quite the same ring as "Come back to bed."

On the floor . . . and on that crate . . . and against that piece of scenery propped against the wall . . .

To be fair, it was a matter of dispute as to who had been ravishing whom, but William couldn't help but feel as though some sort of grand gesture or reparations were called for. He just couldn't figure out what. He'd little experience with affairs of any sort, much less the sort that resulted in lying on the floor of a theatre storeroom in a confused mess of scattered clothing. He had no idea what the protocol might be.

He spotted Gwen's other slipper lying on the floor and leaned over to snag it. "Here," he said, offering it up to her. "It's not made of glass, but it will fit you just the same."

She looked him up and down. "You might want to button up your breeches before we go."

The words felt like a slap in the face.

Doing up the offending buttons, William rose slowly to his feet with the aid of the crate. "I don't know what to say."

Gwen tugged at the shoulders of her dress, yanking the fabric back into place. "That must be a first." She looked at him fiercely. "If you say that you're sorry, I'll slap you."

"Is that what I'm meant to say? It would be a lie."

She took a step back, giving him a warning look. "Don't think you can hoodwink me with honeyed words." She twisted her arms behind her, trying to reach the buttons at the back of her dress. "It won't work."

"Do you think I would be such a fool as that?" he said, which in retrospect, wasn't the brightest question, given the way they had both been behaving. He went to help her with her buttons, gently moving her hands away and pulling the two sides of fabric together. "I know you better than that."

And, oh, how much better he now knew her. William pushed the thought away. It wasn't the time to think of that.

"Hmph," said Gwen, but she moved her hair out of his way, twisting it up so that the long strands wouldn't tangle in the fastenings. It had been a long time since he'd helped a lady do up a dress, an English dress, that was. He remembered helping to lace Maria into the ridiculous fashions to which English ladies clung, even in the tropical heat, the stomacher, the panniers.

There was no mistaking this for then, Gwen for Maria. Maria had been a good head shorter than he; he used to have to bend to reach the laces. Gwen, her back uncompromisingly straight, was only a few inches shy of his height. Soft tendrils of dark hair dusted the nape of her neck, smelling faintly floral.

There were only six buttons from the high waist of her dress to her nape. It was short work sliding them back into their place, not nearly enough time to settle his confused thoughts.

"There," he said, stepping back.

Gwen turned slowly, her hair tumbling back down her shoulders, black threaded with silver. Her hair reached nearly to her waist, thick and wild. A bit of a purple feather clung to one side.

William plucked it out for her, solemnly offering it to her.

"Thank you," she said regally, a patchwork empress in a disordered gown. "That was most diverting. But you needn't think it's going to happen again."

She looked different with her hair down, framing and softening her face. Different, and yet strangely familiar. Pieces of a fever dream floated through his drug-fuddled brain, the memory of a woman in a long white gown, her dark hair falling down over her shoulders.

William took a step forward, his eyes intent on her face. "That night in Bristol—it wasn't a dream, was it? I kissed you."

"What has that to do with anything?" Avoiding his eyes,

Gwen began bundling her hair back up, skewering it in place with pins. "You kissed the woman in your dream."

He could hear the tinkling water of the fountain, the flap of the bird's wings, the sound of a sitar. He had woken with the blurred image of a white gown and long black hair. For the first time, he saw the woman's face clearly. It was that of the woman standing in front of him, so assiduously pretending he didn't exist.

"You were the woman in my dream."

Shrugging, Gwen turned away. "Be that as it may."

What was that supposed to mean? William would make a fair bet that she didn't know either.

Gwen fished up her crumped fichu and shoved it, without grace, into the neckline of her dress. She was Miss Meadows again, buttoned and pinned, her back as straight as her stays. "I should be getting back."

William hastily shoved his shirt down into his breeches, buttoning his jacket over the wreckage of his evening attire. "I'll see you home."

"There's no need."

"There's every need." He wasn't letting her walk back alone, not at this time of night, and not looking as she looked now. For all her hasty repairs, she still had the look of a woman who had been quite thoroughly ravished. "It's been quite some time since we parted from the others. That carriage won't be there anymore."

"It's not a long walk," she said, with a fine show of indifference.

"No, but every walk feels shorter when there's another to share it."

She cast him a look of undiluted scorn. "Do you really think to sway me with platitudes?"

"Do you really think I'd leave you to make your own way back at this time of the night?" William countered. He tried to make a joke of it. "If you'd your parasol with you it would be a different matter, but since you haven't . . ."

"Don't you dare start feeling obliged to me." Gwen slapped the remains of her turban back on her head. "We had a satisfactory romp; that's all. Nothing more."

It shouldn't have hurt that much, but it did. "What about friendship, then? I'd thought we had that."

She looked at him with guarded, watchful eyes. Not for the first time, she reminded him of an animal at bay, ready to strike out for its own protection. "Does the one necessarily preclude the other?"

William spoke as honestly as he knew how. "It does if you won't allow me to show you the basic solicitude I would a friend."

Gwen stalked in front of him towards the door. "Fine words, Colonel."

William caught her hand, bringing her to a halt. "No," he said firmly. "You'll not shut me away like that. I've been William to you this past fortnight."

She breathed in deeply through her nose. "Those were—extraordinary circumstances."

"And this isn't?"

A glimmer of humor showed in her eyes. "Think highly of yourself, do you?"

William couldn't help but grin. "Those weren't moans of boredom I was hearing."

Her cheeks flushed a rosy pink. "One rule," she said forbiddingly, holding up a hand to silence him. "If I go with you, we don't discuss this—this—"

"Night of incredible pleasure?"

"Anomalous interlude," she finished crushingly. "We go on as we were."

"Sure, and that's a lot of syllables for something that never happened."

Gwen marched outside into the crisp night air. "Take it or leave it," she said.

He'd have been more likely to argue if he'd had any idea what he wanted to argue for. He was left grasping at a blank. On a rational level he knew that she'd the right of it, that this wasn't the time or the place to enter into a courtship, if courtship it could be called when one started with the bedding and went from there to the wooing. He'd come to England for his children, not for amorous intrigue, and a fine mess he'd made of it already.

And, yet, to close that door and pretend nothing had happened sat ill with him. It didn't matter that he hadn't been looking for it or that this wasn't the time; it had happened, and it was a cad's trick to pretend it away.

Which left him . . . nowhere.

"If that's what you want," he said, not liking it, but not knowing what else to say.

"It's what makes sense," she said, and her lips clamped down quite firmly on whatever else she might have said.

For several minutes, they walked in silence, taking the less traveled byways and side streets to avoid being seen. William snuck a glance at his companion. Her profile was uncompromising, her expression brooding. Having no desire to have a fan cracked over his pate, William kept his pace and held his tongue. What was there to say, even if he had the courage to say it? His tongue was tied by his own conflicting emotions.

In silence, they made their way towards the river, to the bridge that would take them back to the genteel environs of Laura Place, where he could deposit Gwen again with her friends and return to his own lonely cot at the White Hart Inn.

The river lay silent in the moonlight, but the torches from the bridge sparked mirrored bursts of flame from the water below, swaying and dancing in the current, like the undulating revelers in the cavern below the opera house.

"It was all that ridiculous drug, anyway," Gwen burst out. "We were under the influence."

Was that what she had been thinking about all this while? William opened his mouth to agree and then closed it again. Drugged they might have been, and by something more than opium, but he hadn't been under the influence of the drug an hour earlier, in the corridor of the theatre, nor yet in Bristol. It might be more comfortable to pretend otherwise, but it would be a lie, and his spirit rebelled at the thought of such subterfuge.

Gwen looked at him challengingly. "Weren't we?"

William picked his way across the cobbles, choosing his words carefully. "It's true, that is, and there's no denying it." He looked up from his careful perusal of his feet, into Gwen's turbulent eyes. "But I can't deny that I was wanting to have my way with you long before we went down into that cave."

He'd caught her off guard; he could see it in the way her mouth dropped open, in the confusion that chased across her face in the moonlight.

She hid it with a loud sniff. "Am I meant to be flattered by that? I doubt you've met a woman you haven't fancied."

William bristled. "What's that meant to mean?"

"Nothing." Not meeting his eyes, she made a broad gesture with her fan. "Just that you seem to have cut a broad swath through the female population."

He stopped her with his hands on her shoulders, out of the lights of the streetlamps, where no one could see them. "Do you really think me such a libertine as that?"

She shrugged, turning her face away. "What does it matter?"

It mattered because . . . well, just because. "Sure, in my youth I took advantage of what was offered me—and it wasn't as much as you might have thought!—but once I met my Maria, all that was over."

"Then why do you have children by how many other mothers?"

"Two," he said, and the words seemed to scald his tongue.

Old wrongs never really went away. "Only two. My Maria's been gone twenty-five years now. Would you have had me remain celibate all that time?"

Her eyes had a cold glitter in the moonlight. "A good thing for you, then, that I'm too old to present you with another bastard. I'd hate to ruin your numbers."

He felt as though he'd had a bayonet run straight through the gut—it burned that badly. "Do you really think I'd get you with child and walk away?"

Her voice was like ice. "It's been done before."

"Although I know you don't believe it, I'm not in the habit of ravishing and walking away." William could feel the anger churning in his gut, slow to ignite but quick to burn. "There have been three women in my life, and of them I've only regrets of the one, Jack's mother. After that, I swore I'd not take up with anyone lightly."

"We've hardly taken up—," Gwen began, but he rode right over her.

He spoke rapidly, his voice rising with his agitation. "I was faithful to my Maria while she lived and to Lizzy's mother, too. Eight years we were together, and never once would I have thought of dishonoring her by straying."

There had never been any grand passion between them, but it was a comfortable relationship for them both, a marriage in everything but name until Piyali had announced that she was leaving him for a Bengali merchant. He wouldn't have minded on his own account, but she'd cut all ties with Lizzy and George when she'd gone. Not without tears—there was that much at least—but it would have been uncomfortable with her new people to admit that she'd two children by a *feringhi*. She was starting new, and a half-British boy of seven and girl of six were no part of her plans.

It was another reason William had sent Lizzy to England when he had. In a new world, she'd feel the absence of her mother less than she would in the old.

"As for Jack's mother . . . I never meant to hurt her, and I did my best to make it right. I'll bear the guilt of it until the day I die."

Gwen made a swift gesture of negation. "You needn't—"

William wasn't done yet. "I've five children by three mothers, yes, but I've been that careful to make sure there'll be no others." Until tonight. He hadn't thought; he'd just acted. It was entirely contrary to everything he believed. The knowledge of his culpability made him even more vehement. "I'd not leave a child in the world to fend for itself. And I'd certainly not leave a woman alone to fend for my child!"

Gwen stared at him, as well she might. He felt a bit mad, ranting like that.

"There's no need to tell me any of this," she said, but her voice lacked its usual bite.

"There is if you think I would—use you"—William's voice broke with the force of his feeling—"and think nothing more of it."

Gwen lifted her chin. "Perhaps I was using you."

"No," he said, and the force of his own reaction surprised him. "No. I'll not believe that either."

"Why not? What do you know of me? I might"—only the slight hesitation gave her away—"I might bed half a dozen men a week."

"Only half a dozen?" he said. "Not the full set?"

"You're mocking me," she said flatly, and began walking rapidly.

William hurried to keep up. "You were talking nonsense," he protested in his own defense.

It wasn't, he realized, the wisest thing to have said.

Gwen's lips tightened. "You can't imagine a dozen men would have me?"

What was this? William caught up with her just outside the house on Laura Place. "I can't imagine a dozen men you would have." He dropped his voice so they wouldn't be heard by any of the respectable people in their respectable houses. "You've better taste than that. Tonight aside."

There was something very vulnerable about her, standing there in the moonlight, her fan hanging from her wrist.

"I don't know what happened tonight—well, I do, but that's not what I mean." Reaching out, William took both her hands in his. They felt strangely stiff in their leather gloves. "This is a damnable time for both of us. I feel like I've been dropped hard on my head. I don't know which end is up or what I'm meant to be doing or how to make things right. But I do know that I'd be the poorer if I'd never met you."

Gwen shook her head, as though trying to clear it. "You're not the only one addled." Her lips twisted wryly. "I say we blame it on the smoke."

"It's not the smoke." Whatever else he might not know, he was sure of that. "I don't know what this is, or what it can be, but whatever it is, I don't want this to be the end of it. I like you, Gwen Meadows. I don't want to lose you over a tumble in a back room."

"This was what it was. Nothing more." Her hands tightened briefly around his before drawing away. "We both have our own obligations—and I'm not the marrying kind."

He didn't know what to say; he only knew he didn't want her to go. "Would you rather I told you my intentions were dishonorable?"

She gave a short, quick bark of laughter. "Thank you for seeing me home," she said. "You're a decent man, William Reid."

Then, without giving him warning, she leaned forward and kissed him, full on the lips. For a moment, she was pressed against him, body to body, limb for limb. But only for a moment. When his arms would have closed around her, she twisted away, as lithe as a cat.

"Good night, Colonel Reid," she said, and disappeared down an alley, around the back of the house.

He stood there for a moment in front of the house, frowning into the darkness.

She might have said good night, but it had sounded like good-bye.

Gwen's hand was shaking as she lifted the latch on the French doors that led into the morning room.

It was what it was; that was all. Pure physical gratification. Whatever he said, she knew that. They both knew that. It was a pity that what one knew with one's mind didn't always go hand in hand with what one believed in one's gut.

But then, her gut had been wrong before, hadn't it? With Tim.

It was a moot point. She wasn't an impressionable twenty-four anymore. Whatever this was or might be, in a matter of days or weeks, she would be back to France, to do the work she was needed to do. And the Colonel would find someone else to charm with his ready wit.

It was easier to think of him as the Colonel. The title conjured up impersonal images, a uniform, a parade-ground bellow, not William, red hair rumpled, grin lopsided, his shirt sticking out of his breeches.

Damn the man. Bad enough that he'd got under her skirts, but did he need to get under her skin as well?

It was, as she had pointed out to him, a good thing that she was too old to fear any untoward consequences.

I'd not leave a woman alone to fend for my child.

The memory made her eyes sting—a very silly sort of weakness. It was probably just the remains of the smoke; that was all, or the grit from someone's coal fire. There was no point in engaging in sentimental weakness. She had had her little fling, and now it was time to return to the real world, to her duties and obligations.

There was no reason to feel quite so bereft.

Gwen lifted the latch, letting herself quietly into the morning room. The house was silent, the only sound the small porcelain clock ticking above the mantel.

Jane's voice came out of the darkness. "Did you have an interesting night?"

Gwen stumbled, nearly knocking over a Chinese vase. "Don't do that!" she snapped. "What in the blazes are you doing up at this hour?"

A tinder sparked. A candle glowed gently into flame. "I couldn't sleep."

As Gwen's eyes adjusted, the blur on the settee resolved itself into Jane, in a pale blue dressing gown, her hair in a long braid that fell down over one shoulder. Her legs were curled up beneath her.

"You couldn't sleep?" Gwen made no effort to hide her skepticism.

Before major missions, when she'd been pacing the halls, she'd seen Jane sleeping the sleep of the annoyingly well organized. The girl could sleep through anything, up to and including amateur musicales.

"I am . . . concerned about Agnes," she said, but there was just enough hesitation to make Gwen wonder. "What kept you so long? Was that the Colonel's voice outside?"

There were some things Jane just didn't need to know. "I was attending a meeting of the Hellfire Club," Gwen said quickly. "They've set up shop here in Bath."

"The Hellfire Club?" As she'd hoped, it caught Jane's attention, distracting her from more personal concerns. "I'd thought they met at Medmenham Abbey."

"Not anymore. They've found some convenient Roman ruins beneath the opera house." Gwen seated herself on a chair a safe distance from her charge, trusting to the shadows to hide the signs of ravishment. Ravishment. Who would have thought that would be a concern? "The celebrant calls himself Sir Francis."

"Sir Francis Medmenham." Jane uncurled her legs, swinging her feet to the floor. "There were rumors that he—and his club—were connected with that plot to kidnap the King last year. He was too close a friend of the Prince of Wales for anyone to persist in proving anything."

"Friend of the prince or not, he has some rather dubious associates." Gwen leaned forward in her chair. This was what it was about, she reminded herself. The thrill of the hunt. She was good at this, she and Jane. They made an excellent partnership. "He drugs his followers into ecstasy with opiates he purchases through channels that could only be termed irregular."

"That's hardly news," said Jane practically.

"No, but this is." Gwen drew off her gloves, dropping them on the arm of the chair. "He acquired his opium from the same man who stole the jewels of Berar."

Jane was all attention. "Did you get the name?"

"Oh, yes—and more." In memory, the smoke swirled around her as she crouched beside that tiny aperture, eavesdropping on Sir Francis and his companion. "The man's name is the Moonflower. And he's switched sides. He's gone from being one of theirs to being one of ours. And he's taken the jewels with him. Jane? Jane!"

The girl looked as though she'd been taken with some kind

of attack, silently staring. "That's what it is," she said softly, so softly Gwen had to strain to hear her.

"That's what what is?" Gwen waved her hand back and forth in front of Jane's face. "Jane!"

Jane looked at Gwen, but her eyes were still somewhere far, far away. "So that's why the girls ran from the school," she said. "He must have sent the jewels to Lizzy. Or someone thought he did. They were either taken, or they ran."

There was only so much flesh and blood could bear. "What in the blazes are you talking about?"

This time, Jane looked at her, really looked at her. Her gray eyes gleamed. "I hadn't known the Moonflower had switched sides. That is the missing piece, the piece that ties it all together. The jewels, Agnes, everything."

"Are you certain you're feeling quite well?" said Gwen sharply. Too much time with the Chevalier appeared to have unhinged her brain.

"More than well," said Jane gently. "It all follows quite logically once you know the connection. The Moonflower is the key."

"And what," demanded Gwen icily, "has the Moonflower to do with our girls?"

"Everything," said Jane. "You see, the Moonflower is Jack Reid. Colonel Reid's son."

Chapter 17

Found! Amarantha was found! But in what strange circumstances? There were no guards at her door, no chains to bind her wrists. "We have come to rescue you!" quoth Plumeria. "Make haste!"

Amarantha stretched her slender body on the silken settee. "But what if," sayeth she, "I have no wish to leave? Make no mistake—I jest not. I wish to stay here, in the Dark Tower."

"Do not do this thing," proud Plumeria pled. "For if you do, you shall break my heart."

—From *The Convent of Orsino* by A Lady

"He can't be," said Gwen flatly. "The Moonflower? Colonel Reid's son? Nonsense."

Even as she spoke, fragments of half-remembered conversations came back to jab at her. Colonel Reid's son, who traded in opium with unsavory elements. The brother who had sent his sister packages in school. The man who had come rummaging through Kat Reid's lodgings.

"Do you think Colonel Reid knows?" asked Jane.

"He said they're estranged," said Gwen automatically. Would he have kept from her such a thing as this? He had seemed genuinely surprised by his daughter's disappearance. No man was as good an actor as that, particularly not a man she had seen stripped bare, raving with fever. "How did you know?"

"As soon as I heard Agnes was missing, I gathered everything I could on Lizzy Reid and her family. One brother is in the East India Company's diplomatic service and another in the service of a local ruler. Then there was the third brother. He was rather harder to track down, but what did come back was . . . interesting. I did not know," Jane added in the interest of fairness, "that he had reconsidered his allegiances. Or that he had run off with the Berar hoard."

Gwen looked at Jane. The candle flickered in front of Gwen's eyes, creating a shifting, smoky haze. "You knew Colonel Reid's son was a spy."

All the while she was in Bristol, sponging his fevered body, at the opera, tonight. Jane knew and she had sent Gwen in blind. That it concerned Colonel Reid made it even worse. It felt like a double betrayal that Jane knew something about him that Gwen didn't.

Gwen couldn't quite wrap her mind around it, the idea that Jane would know something so important and yet keep it from her. "You knew this and you didn't tell me."

"We haven't had much time to talk since Paris," said Jane calmly.

"Whose fault is that?" Gwen pressed her palms flat against

the arms of the chair. All the anger and frustration and confusion of the long night surged to the fore. "If that coxcomb of a Frenchman weren't always sniffing around . . ."

Jane seemed to retreat into herself, her face as remote as a statue's. "I have my reasons for keeping him close."

"Yes, I imagine you do!" Gwen's blood boiled. A dozen things she might say burbled to her lips, jumbling and confusing themselves. Did Jane know her precious Chevalier might be prancing about in a hood, hawking opiates to the Hellfire Club?

She opened her mouth to say it, but the words wouldn't come. Because it would be worse, so much worse, if Jane did know and hadn't bothered to tell her. It hit her like a blow to the belly. That made far more sense than an amorous attachment, however Jane might look at the man. But why not tell her? Why not confide in her? Jane always told her everything.

But she hadn't told her about Jack Reid.

The horrible silence went on and on, a silence so total that it made Gwen's ears ache.

Into that dreadful silence, Jane spoke. "I didn't tell you about Jack Reid because I didn't want you to say anything to the Colonel."

Gwen felt like a gaping chasm was opening beneath her feet, the ground shaking and shifting. "You kept this from me deliberately?"

Jane shifted on the settee. "It seemed prudent."

Prudent? *Prudent?* Gwen groped at her meaning. "You can't think— However fond I might be of the Colonel, I would certainly never let that blind me to— That is—" Fond. She hadn't meant to say fond. She hadn't meant to admit—

She broke off, pressing her fingers to her cheeks. No need for Jane to see the color in her face. No need for Jane to know that her friendship with the Colonel had progressed to a rather more intimate level. It didn't matter. It didn't change anything. They had their own obligations; she had told him that. The League came first.

Sitting up very straight, Gwen said formally, "Whatever the circumstances"—on the floor, on the crate, against the scenery—"you know I would never do anything that might jeopardize our mission."

Jane was all that was apologetic and insincere. "I know that, but I couldn't risk your saying something that might reach the wrong ears."

As an apology, it wasn't much of an apology at all. It was more than a little bit offensive, really. Just because she happened to find the Colonel attractive didn't mean she had forgotten their purpose. Besides, wasn't Miss Jane conducting a little flirtation of her own?

Guilt made Gwen sharp. "Did you really think I would compromise our mission for a man?"

"Not for a man, no." Jane paused. "But you do sometimes speak without thinking. I couldn't take that risk."

The full force of the blow took a few moments to hit her, to sink through flesh and muscle, striking straight to the heart, all the more cutting for being delivered so casually, so matter-of-factly. *Not for a man.*

No, just in general.

Gwen struggled for calm. "Have I ever betrayed your trust? Led you astray?"

She had never done anything that would put the League in danger. Not without good and sufficient reason, at any rate, and if it had all turned out right in the end, wasn't that proof enough of her good judgment?

It took the Pink Carnation just a little too long to reply. "You do get a bit carried away sometimes," Jane said apologetically.

"In moments of action, perhaps—but only when it's necessary." Gwen shot up from her seat on the chair, her entire body trembling with hurt. "If you took issue with the way I conduct our affairs, you ought to have told me before! Not—" In a voice that she didn't recognize as hers, she demanded, "Just how much have you been keeping me in the dark?"

Jane's silence was answer enough.

Gwen felt sick. Her stomach churned; her hands were cold and clammy. She could feel the drops of sweat on her forehead. Even the smoke, that ridiculous, drugged smoke, hadn't made her feel so sick as this. The world seemed to shift and sway around her, as everything she'd thought she knew rearranged itself around her.

What else hadn't Jane told her? How many times had she been deliberately left ignorant? She had always assumed that she was indispensible to Jane, that the two of them were hand in hand and glove in glove. They were a partnership. It didn't matter that Jane bore the title; if Jane was queen, then Gwen was prime minister. Jane planned; Gwen executed. They might not always see entirely eye to eye, but they thrashed everything out together.

Or so she had believed.

Wrongly.

"It was for your own safety," Jane said, and there was a pleading note in her voice.

"I'd thought I was your chaperone," said Gwen belligerently. "Not the other way around."

"In our ordinary lives, yes. But when it comes to the League, I couldn't have any of my agents knowing everything. Not even you."

There was something terribly sad in the way she said those last words. Sad and more than a little bit forlorn.

But that wasn't the part that caught Gwen's attention.

"Any of your agents?" Gwen repeated flatly. Her voice rose. "*Any* of your agents?"

Jane had missed the warning signs. She twisted her hands together in her lap. "It's safest for everyone if I don't share too much."

As if Gwen were just another subagent! Just someone paid to deliver secrets. Gwen's pride stung, pride and something else.

You love her, said William's voice in her head.

Shut up, she told it.

It wasn't about love; it was about justice. It wasn't because she had known Jane since she was a tiny little girl, chasing butterflies. It was because she had helped Jane out of more tight corners than either of them could remember. She had helped her pick the blasted name of the League, for heaven's sake.

And Jane called her just another agent?

"Fine," said Gwen furiously. "Maybe that's the case with all your other agents, but I'm not just another agent. I'm your *chaperone*. We founded this League together! Or don't you remember that?"

"Yes," said Jane hesitantly, "yes, but that was a very long time ago, before we knew . . ."

"Before we knew *what*?" Gwen bit out.

"Before we knew the real dangers of what we were doing." Jane looked seriously at her chaperone, and Gwen was struck by how young she looked, how young and frail. "It's not a game anymore."

Gwen was immediately on the defensive. "I never said it was."

"All this swinging through windows and jumping off balconies—"

"Was necessary!" Just because she enjoyed it didn't mean it wasn't useful. "Would we have known about Talleyrand and Fiorila otherwise? No, I thought not."

"I'm not criticizing your methods." Jane took a deep breath. "I'm just saying that we need to be doubly careful. Triply careful. I've tried to take extra precautions. This affair with Agnes—"

"Isn't about Agnes at all! Isn't that what you've been telling me? It's Lizzy Reid and her ill-gotten brother." Even as she said it, Gwen felt a pang of guilt. Foolish. It was just an expression, ill-gotten. She wasn't betraying William's confidence.

Fortunately, Jane didn't seem to notice. "But it might have

been Agnes," she said earnestly. "It might have been Amy. It might have been any of my family. What happens next time?"

"Fine," said Gwen shortly. "We'll be more careful. It would be easier to be careful if you would condescend to tell me what I might need to know!"

This was the point where Jane was meant to make soothing noises. Not apologize, per se; Jane wasn't the apologizing kind. A terse "all right" would do. Then they could get back to work and everything could be just as it was.

Rising from the settee, Jane picked up the candle. "It's late," she said. "We should get some rest."

No. This wasn't right. Gwen followed Jane towards the stairs. "What else aren't you telling me?"

"It's late," Jane repeated.

She lifted her trailing hem to start up the stairs, leaving Gwen standing below, bewildered and frightened.

Late? Or too late?

She had been cut off and cut out, without even realizing it was happening.

Who needed Jane, anyway? If Jane didn't want her, she would form her own league. She could be the Invincible Orchid. She'd always thought that was the better name, but she'd let herself be voted down by Jane and her cousin, the one who'd run off with the Purple Gentian. The Invincible Orchid would rise from the ashes of the Pink Carnation like a floral phoenix.

Even as the thoughts swirled through her mind, she knew them to be an impossibility, nothing more than the phantasms of anger and indignation. Even if she had the skill, she hadn't the resources. It was the Wooliston fortune, husbanded over generations of innovative sheep breeding, that had funded their work in Paris. One needed money, not just to live, but to pay for those networks of informers who were an agent's bread and butter.

Gwen had assumed that she had known at least fifty percent of Jane's shadowy network: the stable boys, the seamstresses, the footmen. Now she wondered if it might not have been an even smaller fraction, if Jane might have kept more of her work from Gwen than she knew. There was no way she could assemble anything similar on her own, even if she were mad enough to try. The Pink Carnation's league had been two years and thousands of pounds in the making.

She didn't know where she was to go or what she was to do. The obvious solution was to go home to Shropshire, to the house in which she had been raised, that monument to too much money and too little taste, to her sister-in-law's carping, to her brother's thick-throated idiocy.

The thought wasn't to be borne. She might have slunk home with her tail between her legs once, but not this time. She wasn't twenty-four anymore, friendless and penniless.

No. She was forty-five, friendless and penniless.

Not entirely friendless. *I like you,* William had said. *I don't want to lose you.* But what did that mean? The man had enough troubles of his own; she could hardly heap her own on top of them. He had two daughters to support and a son who was a French spy gone rogue.

No, she couldn't turn to him for solace, no matter how tempting it might be.

There was no need to panic. Gwen forced the air back into her lungs. She was overthinking, overreacting. It was late, and she was tired and perhaps not altogether herself. She had overlooked one crucial point. Jane was young, unmarried. She couldn't go back to France without a chaperone. She needed Gwen for appearances, if nothing else.

Unless, of course, she married.

The thought cut through Gwen like a cold wind. As a married woman, Jane wouldn't need a chaperone. She could go anywhere she pleased. Gwen thought of those two handsome heads together in the box in the opera, with her parents drowsing nearby.

Madame de la Tour d'Argent, the Comtesse de Brissac, would have immediate entry into the highest and most intimate circles of Bonaparte's imperial court. She would be above suspicion.

Gwen stared at Jane's slender figure, so calmly ascending the stairs. While she was off clinging to an exposed beam above Fiorila's dressing room, while she had been nursing William in Bristol, what exactly had Jane been planning?

An hour ago, she wouldn't have even considered such a notion. An hour ago, she had been living in a fool's paradise.

"One last thing." Gwen's voice cut like a lash.

Jane stopped, halfway up the stairs. "Yes?"

The words stuck in Gwen's throat. She didn't want to know the answer. Or, even worse, receive no answer at all.

In a harsh, flat voice, Gwen said, "I never relayed tonight's report. You probably know this already too, but Fiorila has a daughter. An illegitimate daughter. Talleyrand is holding the child as assurance for her good behavior."

The wariness turned to speculation. "So that's why Fiorila switched—"

Gwen cut her off. "I saw the letter and the picture. A little girl. She is being held somewhere in the French countryside."

"Do you know where?"

"No, but it would be easy enough to find out." Easy enough for Jane, with her resources. Hers. Not theirs. Never theirs. Gwen lifted her chin. "Fiorila has never acted against us before. She does this only under coercion."

"Are you suggesting we rescue the child?"

"We?" Gwen couldn't hide the pain in her voice. "There is no we. You've made that quite clear. But if I were you, I would see to it."

Without waiting for Jane's reply, she turned and walked away, back to the darkened morning room.

"We'll talk in the morning," she heard Jane say behind her.

But by the morning, everything had changed.

Gwen woke on the settee in the morning room. She felt as though someone had gone over each of her limbs with a hammer.

She dragged herself painfully into her room, discarding last night's much-abused dress. It still smelled faintly of smoke. She dredged cold water over her face, trying to wash off the grime of the Hellfire caverns. Her eyes felt sore and crusted, her cheeks sticky with tears she didn't remember having shed. She must have been crying in her sleep.

She had dreamed herself back twenty years ago, dreamed herself on the doorstep of Tim's house, that moment when she had tripped and fallen, unable to catch herself, cartwheeling down, down, down . . .

She raked a brush through her tangled hair, welcoming the pain. It made a distraction from everything she didn't want to think about.

When Gwen came down, Jane was at the table in the dining room, sitting beside a china pot of chocolate, her glossy head bent over a letter.

She looked so normal in her sprigged muslin gown, with her pot of chocolate. It might have been any morning, on either side of the Channel. Gwen moved stiffly forward, not sure how to begin, whether to maintain an aggrieved silence or just go back to things as they were and hope that the world would follow suit.

Jane looked up, her eyes lighting on Gwen. "I've sent someone to deal with Fiorila," she said.

Gwen wasn't sure if that was meant to be a peace offering.

"And?" she said brusquely.

"If we can get her daughter out, Fiorila will break her ties with Talleyrand and abandon the search for the jewels," Jane said promptly, and then ruined it by adding contemplatively, "Not that that matters. Now."

"It matters to Fiorila," said Gwen tartly. She'd had enough of Jane's omniscience. She could feel her voice rising with her emotions. "These are not just chess pawns; they're people. *People.*"

Jane looked up at her over her chocolate, quizzically. "I know," she said. Before Gwen could say anything else, she said quickly, "The girls have been found."

"What?" Gwen's throat was dry. "Where?"

"I've had a letter from Amy." Jane tapped the piece of paper in front of her. "They're at Selwick Hall."

"They ran, then." Gwen's mind was moving very, very slowly. Outside, the sky threatened rain. "They weren't taken."

"Yet. If they have those jewels, they won't be safe, not even at Selwick Hall." Jane rose and rang a bell. "I'm having the chaise brought round immediately. We leave at noon."

"We?" Gwen didn't move from her place in the doorway. "Do I have the honor of being part of your plans?"

"You don't think I'd go without you?" said Jane.

Gwen didn't know what to think. "I didn't think you would keep information from me either," said Gwen, "but look what's become of that."

Jane looked as though she meant to say something more, but the butler entered and she looked at him with something like relief. "Oh, Gudgeon. We'll need the chaise brought around and our trunks brought down."

"You'd best send a note to the Colonel," said Gwen gruffly, following Jane out into the hall. "He'll want to know."

He would be overjoyed. He would be reunited with his

daughters, and Gwen—Gwen wasn't entirely sure what she would do. Last night's conversation with Jane had left her deeply shaken.

Jane looked back at her over her shoulder. "Don't you think he'd rather hear it from you?"

"I'll see to the trunks," said Gwen, and did.

She was just supervising their removal to the front hall when a knock sounded. It was William at the door, a rather wilted bouquet of purple flowers in one hand.

"Who may I say is calling?" Gudgeon asked grandly.

William thrust the bouquet at the butler and stepped around him, cutting between Gwen and a pile of trunks. "Are you going somewhere?"

Unlike her, he had managed to have a bath somewhere along the line. His hair was clean and well brushed and his cravat was neatly, if plainly, tied. Gwen was very aware of her own greasy hair and the circles under her eyes that came from a night sleeping in an unnatural position on the settee.

William's voice softened. "I'd come to ask you if you'd come to Bristol with me." He switched to wheedling. "If anyone can get Kat to see sense, you can. She'll not listen to me."

"I can't. I was just about to send you a note—"

"Colonel Reid!" Jane was on the stairs. She trailed down in the best hostess manner. "And Monsieur de la Tour d'Argent. What a happy surprise."

Gwen hadn't even noticed the Chevalier standing there. He must have snuck in behind William. Not that it required much sneaking. Her attention had been elsewhere.

The Chevalier proffered his own floral offering, an alarmingly large bouquet of pink roses. "I hope you shall take this small offering—"

Gwen sniffed.

Next to her, William swallowed a grin. "Not much of an idea of scale, has he?" he whispered.

The Chevalier was still talking, the rolling phrases rolling on. "—token of my esteem and regret. I have come to take my leave. The Prince of Wales bids me to Brighton, undoubtedly on so pressing a matter as a new pattern of wall hanging." He pressed a hand to his heart. "But believe me when I say that I shall never have regretted a leave-taking so much as this one."

"What an odd coincidence," said Jane brightly, dropping the bouquet onto the top of a pile of trunks. "We leave for Sussex as well."

"You do?" It was absurd to feel quite so pleased by the distress in William's face, but Gwen did. It was nice to know that someone valued her presence. "You are going away, then. It's not because—" He broke off, flushing to his ears.

Gwen felt her cheeks turn an answering red. "No," she said shortly.

Jane was watching them with interest. "Colonel," she said, "you stayed me in the happy act of writing you a note."

"The happy act . . . ?"

Gwen broke in. "The girls have been found."

Chapter 18

No matter how Plumeria and Sir Magnifico pled, Amarantha remained obdurate. The Knight of the Silver Tower held her in his thrall. So intent were they upon their pleas that neither noticed the darkening of the shadows as the dread knight's minions closed in behind them.
—From *The Convent of Orsino* by A Lady

"*L*izzy? You've found Lizzy? And ... and ..." William couldn't remember the other girl's name.

"Agnes," said Miss Wooliston soothingly. "Yes, both of them. They are safe and well and with my cousin."

"All this time?" Relief surged through him, a relief so intense it made him light-headed. "Are you quite sure?"

"Yes," said Miss Wooliston. "I had a letter from my cousin this morning. They have been taking an unauthorized holiday."

William found himself laughing, laughing out loud, the sound echoing off the plaster ceiling, the gilded mirrors. "I'll be damned! Those little imps!" The laugh turned rough around the edges, just short of a sob. He sat down abruptly on a small gilded bench. "Thank the Lord, they've been found."

"Yes," said Gwen, and there was an odd note to her voice. "The mystery is solved."

The Chevalier broke in, his teeth flashing in a smile. "May I have your permission to relay the news to my cousin? She will be overjoyed. She has been blaming herself."

"Please send her our apologies," said Miss Wooliston gently. "It was very wrong of the girls to worry her."

The Chevalier raised his brows. "What is seventeen if not for causing the heads of one's elders to ache?" He paused before saying delicately, "Since we travel in the same direction, I would offer my escort—but one does not like to keep the Prince waiting."

"Oh, no," said Miss Wooliston. "Most certainly not!"

"Especially not in such matters as wall hangings," muttered Gwen. "The last time he was left to his own devices, he built that wretched pavilion."

Miss Wooliston gave her chaperone a quelling look. "You mustn't let us keep you. We shan't leave for at least another day and probably more. There is no hurry—now that we know the girls are safe and well. It will do them good to have to cool their heels."

Wait? William was ready to set out right now. He wanted Lizzy where he could see her, safe and sound, and he'd be damned if he'd leave her in the care of others again.

"But of course," said the Chevalier. "The chaise outside . . . ?"

"For my parents," said Miss Wooliston promptly. "They return to Shropshire. My father does not like to be so long away from his sheep."

"Lucky sheep to be so loved," said the Chevalier. He tipped his hat. "Perhaps we shall see one another in Sussex."

"Perhaps." Miss Wooliston's voice was all sweetness. "Safe travels, sir."

William turned to Gwen. "All this about not leaving for another day—I'd rather have my Lizzy where I can see her."

"Trust me, sir," said Gwen, and he noticed that there was something celebratory missing from her manner, "you are not the only one."

The door closed behind the Chevalier. Miss Wooliston watched through the window as he swung up into his curricle. The Chevalier slapped the reins. Miss Wooliston let the drape drop back into place.

"He goes to Sussex, does he?" said Gwen, looking at Miss Wooliston with narrowed eyes.

Miss Wooliston inclined her head, saying lightly, "I believe he has an interest in gardening and thinks to find the soil in Sussex particularly fertile. In our time together, it became clear that he was well versed in horticulture." Turning to the butler, she said rapidly, "Gudgeon, lash the trunks to the chaise. The special trunk on top. We leave in an hour."

"But—" William looked from one woman to the other. "I'd thought you weren't leaving until tomorrow."

"A change of plans," said Miss Wooliston briskly. The doll-like sweetness was gone. She was all business. "We can give you the direction if you would like to follow along behind, once your business in Bristol is done."

"But then why—" William looked to Gwen for explanation, but she was watching her charge, her brow furrowed, her lips pursed. Ah, he thought. This had to do with the Chevalier. He remembered the scene in the opera last night, Gwen's obvious distress.

"My business in Bristol will wait. I'll come with you," said William, on an impulse. "It shouldn't take me more than half an hour to set my affairs in order."

"There's not enough room in the chaise," Gwen said brusquely.

To William's surprise, it was Miss Wooliston who came to his aid. "It seats three," she said. "There should be plenty of room for us all. If the Colonel doesn't mind being a bit cramped?"

"I can ride if it would be an imposition," he said, sneaking a sideways glance at Gwen. Was it last night? Was that what this was about? He'd tried to make things right with her, but with Gwen, he wasn't entirely sure what right might be. After that last kiss, he had thought—well, it didn't matter what he had thought. "I just need your man to show me the way."

"No imposition," said Miss Wooliston blandly. "If you'll excuse me, I must see to our trunks."

"Wait." William caught up with Gwen before she could do the same. "Do you mind so badly my coming along with you? You look like you could outstorm a storm cloud." His voice softened as he said, "If it's to do with what happened last night—"

Gwen shook her head. "It's nothing to do with you. I swear."

William didn't know whether to be relieved or disappointed. "Your ward, then?" he asked, and knew he had hit home when her lips pressed tightly together. He took a step closer. "Is there anything I might do to help? I'm told I've a good shoulder to cry on."

Now that he knew Lizzy was safe, he felt like he could carry the world on his shoulders.

"I— It's complicated. William—"

A series of emotions passed across her face. For a moment, he thought she meant to confide in him.

"Never mind," she said, and pushed away from the wall, brushing past him. "You'd best hurry. We leave in half an hour, and the coach waits for no one."

Her straight back forbade further discussion.

She hadn't exaggerated. When William returned from the White Hart with his campaign bag beneath his arm, the carriage was already loaded with trunks and the coachman perched on the back of one of the four horses pulling the chaise. The seat was generous for two, narrow for three.

"Would you mind sitting in the middle, Colonel Reid?" Miss Wooliston asked sweetly. "The jostling can be a bit sickmaking if one isn't by the window."

"Certainly," said William.

He climbed in next to Gwen, who pulled her skirts out of his way with more speed than finesse.

"It's sorry I am to force my company upon you," he said

softly, as Miss Wooliston spoke to the coachman outside. "I wouldn't have but for—"

Gwen presented him with her profile. "I know. But for Lizzy."

"No." A smile played around William's lips. "If it hadn't been for Lizzy, I would have dragged you off to Bristol with me. Perhaps not dragged," he said hastily, seeing Gwen's brows begin to draw together. "Let's just say I would have done my best to persuade you to go with me."

Gwen folded her gloved hands neatly in her lap, those same hands that had made such inroads across his body last night, grasping, scratching, stroking.

"You are not entirely unpersuasive," she said primly.

In the past, William had been called charming, eloquent, even glib. But none had pleased him so much as this grudging accolade.

William grinned at her, feeling like he had the world in his palms. "Are you sure you wish to pay me so large a compliment? It might go to my head."

"Your head is quite large enough already," Gwen said repressively. She contemplated a speck of dust on her skirt. "Now that your daughter has been found, I imagine you will wish to take her away with you."

"I'm not letting her go back to that Miss Climpson's; that's for certain. That woman gives new meaning to the word 'ninny.'" He'd thought of renting a cottage somewhere, making a home for his daughters. He smiled at the image of Gwen in the middle of it, keeping both of his daughters in line. "She'd do better with someone like you."

"A sensible spinster of a certain age?" Gwen pronounced the words as though they left a nasty taste on her tongue.

"A pillar of good sense and fine swordsmanship," William corrected her ebulliently. Lowering his voice so Miss Wooliston wouldn't hear them, he said, "You can't blame a man for trying to find an excuse to keep you by."

He could tell she was taken aback, but she recovered herself quickly. "Are you offering to hire me?"

"I wouldn't dare," he said cheerfully. "But I'm looking forward to your meeting my Lizzy."

"There we are!" Miss Wooliston picked her way up into the chaise, seating herself delicately on William's other side. "Do forgive me. I hope I'm not crowding you."

That had felt like a deliberate hip bump, nudging him towards Gwen. William regarded Miss Wooliston's serene face, innocent under a bonnet lined with pale blue silk. No, he must have imagined it.

The carriage lurched forward, the luggage chained to the back rattling.

"How long a trip have we ahead of us?" William asked.

"If we don't run into difficulties, we should be there by to-morrow afternoon," said Gwen, glancing back through the window.

Before William could ask just what kind of difficulties she meant, Miss Wooliston said, "According to my cousin, it took the girls a full three weeks to make their way to the Hall, walking most of the way."

William thought of the cozy room at Miss Climpson's, not luxurious perhaps, but certainly better than sleeping under a hedgerow. "What possessed them to do such a thing?"

"I imagine they didn't think it would take them that long," said Miss Wooliston.

She spoke so matter-of-factly that it took William some time to realize that she hadn't answered the question at all.

Gwen moved restlessly in her seat. "Do you think they also learned of the Chevalier's horticultural activities?" she said, looking pointedly at her charge.

"It might have come to their attention," said Miss Wooliston noncommittally. "As a simple matter of deduction."

William was beginning to suspect that he was missing something. Horticulture was obviously a euphemism. For attempting to seduce the young ladies at the school, perhaps?

"Are you saying the Chevalier was doing a spot of gardening at the school?" he said heartily.

"You might say that," said Gwen, but she was looking at her ward, not at him.

Miss Wooliston said nothing.

The carriage moved briskly through the early morning traffic, away through the outskirts of the city, leaving the shops, the baths, the assembly rooms, behind. The silence in the coach could only be termed frosty. William took matters into his own hands, saying loudly, "And who is this the girls have gone to?"

"My cousin Amy," said Miss Wooliston. "She lives with her husband at Selwick Hall in Sussex. The girls are most attached to her."

She looked through the window, not the casual glance of a lady admiring the scenery, but craning her neck around, watching the road.

"Are you looking for something?" William asked.

"Hmm?" Miss Wooliston looked at him as though she had forgotten he was there. She shook her head. "No. Nothing. Just a—rare plant by the side of the road."

"More like a weed," sniffed Gwen.

Ah, that was it, then. Miss Wooliston must be looking for the Chevalier's coach, also on the road from Bath to Brighton. And Gwen—well, it was clear to see she didn't approve. A weed indeed. She didn't mince her words, his Gwen.

William's lips twitched. He couldn't help it. It wasn't just that he was ridiculously, euphorically happy to know that his daughter had been found. Something about Gwen made him smile. And it wasn't just the memory of last night, although that in itself was certainly enough to bring a reminiscent grin to his lips. No. It was Gwen in all her prickly cantankerousness. She'd fight for the last word on her deathbed and probably win it, too.

She reminded him, in an odd way, of Maria. Not in looks, although, if truth be told, it had been long enough that Maria's image had faded and blurred in his brain, like a watercolor left out too long in the rain. Maria's voice was a soft Welsh burr, so different from Gwen's cut-glass tones, but there was beneath it all a certain similarity of spirit. Maria hadn't stood for any of his nonsense either.

William found himself thinking again of that cottage, but it was Gwen he saw beneath the apple tree in the yard, scribbling furiously away at that notebook of hers, spinning her tales of Plumeria and Sir Magnifico.

It was a far cry from a Sir Magnifico to a weathered old East India Company army officer with a handful of children and only a small competence to his name. He hadn't much to offer her, certainly nothing so elegant as that house on Laura Place, but she didn't strike him as a woman with a need for luxuries. She had dealt with that primitive room in the inn in Bristol like a seasoned soldier, making the best of what they had.

A sudden jolt of the carriage shook William out of his reverie and back to his senses. When had he started thinking about—well, about honorable intentions? It was madness. He'd known her all of three weeks.

Admittedly, in those three weeks, they'd known each other rather better—in every sense of the word—than he had after a full year of courting his Maria in the accepted and acceptable way, teas and walks and chaperoned outings.

William snuck a glance at Gwen's profile, the long line of her nose, the curve of her jaw, the surprisingly long sweep of her lashes, as black as her hair. She was all bundled up again, primly braided and buttoned, but he knew that beneath that stern exterior was a lifetime's worth of adventure for the man brave enough to win her.

If he could talk her to a standstill first. Or kiss her into confusion.

The carriage swerved again, more violently.

Miss Wooliston turned from the window, a frown marring her fine features. "We have company."

William twisted around to look out the tiny back window. Even through the wobbly glass, half-blocked by a trunk jolting up and down, he could make out ten riders behind them, all with hats pulled down low, coming up fast behind them. William didn't like the looks of them.

The carriage speeded up, the horses giving it all they could. The riders followed suit, and the man in the lead drew something from his belt, something dark and metallic that created a little puff of smoke.

A bullet whizzed past the window, past William's shocked eyes.

"They're shooting at us!" he exclaimed.

"Yes, and we're going to shoot right back." Gwen didn't seem the least bit perturbed. If anything, she seemed happier than he'd seen her since the previous night. Her color was high and her eyes sparkled with excitement. "Hold my legs," she commanded.

"What?" Admittedly, her legs had featured rather prominently in his reverie a moment ago, but not in quite this way.

Gwen gave him a frustrated look. "Do you want me to fall out the window? Hold my legs."

And with that, she squirmed out of the window, not just head and shoulders, but all the way to the waist. William hastily clamped his arms down across her legs. The position provided him an excellent view of her rear end, draped in thin purple muslin, which waggled distractingly before William's eyes.

A muffled voice came from the other side of the window. "Hold *tight*!"

William held tight. The carriage hit a bump. There was a ladylike but vehement curse from outside and some scrabbling about the window frame. Another shot thudded into the back of the chaise.

"All right out there?" William yelled.

"As well"—more scrabbling noises, a thud, and a click—"as can be expected."

There was the report of a shot and the echoing sound of a faraway cry. William slid hastily to the side as Gwen scrambled in backwards through the window, landing with a thump in his lap.

William risked a look through the back window. One of their pursuers was clutching his arm, his horse veering erratically.

"Were you aiming for the man or the horse?"

"The man, of course." Gwen gave him a superior look. "I wouldn't shoot the horse. That would be unjust. It's not the horse's fault he's being forced to chase us."

"Right," said William. "Of course." He didn't know why he hadn't thought of that.

"They're still gaining on us," said Miss Wooliston.

"Highwaymen?" guessed William. He hadn't realized they traveled in packs.

"Someone doesn't want us getting to Selwick Hall," said Gwen grimly. She looked over him at Miss Wooliston, her gray eyes glittering. "I'll just open the special trunk, shall I?"

Wiggling her way off William's lap, she jammed herself back through the window. "Legs!" came an imperious voice from outside.

William's arms automatically clamped down on the backs of Gwen's knees. "The—"

"The special trunk," said Miss Wooliston serenely. She was calmly loading another pistol.

They seemed just a little too well prepared. "What in the blazes is going on?" William demanded. "Why would someone want to stop us going to—wherever this place is?"

Before Miss Wooliston could answer, a hail of hard projectiles pounded down the back of the carriage, bouncing off the back of the coach, ricocheting off one another. There were billiard balls, dozens of billiard balls, streaming down from the now open trunk onto the road.

Gwen wiggled her way back into the window, plopping down onto William's thigh. The exertion had loosened her coiffure, which straggled down on the right side of her face. She shoved her hair back behind her ears, saying breathlessly, "That should hold them. For the moment."

Behind them, horses shied and riders cursed. A shot went wide, nearly hitting one of the other riders.

Miss Wooliston turned to William. "Can you ride?"

Was she really asking him that? "I was a cavalry officer," said William. "Over thirty years in the cavalry."

"I'll take that as a yes, then." Miss Wooliston turned back to her chaperone. "I say we take two of the horses, send the chaise off as decoy, and ride to Bunny-on-the-Wold. We can stay the night at Darlington."

They were speaking a foreign language. "Bunny on the what?"

"It's a small town in Hampshire," said Gwen helpfully. Which, to William's mind, explained nothing. "If Dorrington is in residence, we can pick up reinforcements there." She turned back to William. "Are you ready to ride?"

"What I'd like is for someone to tell me what the devil this is all about!"

"Later." A bullet ricocheted off the side of the carriage. "Blast! I knew we should have packed more billiard balls!"

William looked back through the window. "It's only the one man."

"The others will be up and following him soon enough," said Gwen with authority. The coach swerved dangerously as they went around a corner. "I'll see him off and then we'll take to the horses before the others get close enough to follow."

This road was less traveled, rutted and bumpy. However much he liked her legs, William wasn't fond of the idea of her doing her window trick again.

"Let me," said William quickly. He didn't stop to wonder what he was doing. Snatching up one of the pistols, he used the butt to break the glass on the back window, leveled, and shot. He'd been aiming for the man's shoulder, but the erratic nature of both platform and target meant that he hit the man's leg instead, causing the horseman to veer wildly.

"Nicely done," said Gwen.

"Thank you," said William, and decided to pretend that he'd meant it. Deadpan, he said, "I wouldn't hit the horse."

The two of them grinned at each other like fools.

Miss Wooliston leaned forward. "Just around the next corner," she told the coachman. "That copse over here."

The man responded with an alacrity that made William wonder exactly how many times they'd performed this maneuver before. The coachman unharnessed the two leaders. They weren't saddled for riding, but that didn't deter either of the ladies. The coachman gave Gwen a leg up onto the horse's bare back. She bunched her skirts up to the knees, revealing a pair of rather fetching silk stockings embroidered with small purple flowers.

She held out a hand to William. "Well?" she said. "What are you waiting for?"

"Nothing," said William. He snapped his gaze away from her legs. "Nothing at all."

He swung up behind her, wrapping his arms around her waist, and they were off, riding hell-for-leather down a road that was little more than a track, while in the other direction, the chaise rattled away, pulled by two horses now rather than four, a decoy for their pursuers.

Which put William in mind of the one crucial detail he was missing.

"Why doesn't someone want us to reach—wherever it is?" William bellowed in Gwen's ear, above the rush of the wind, the pounding of the hooves, and the crackles of fallen twigs.

But she just shook her head and urged the mount on faster, following Miss Wooliston's horse.

"—not clear of them yet," he heard her say, the words carried away by the wind.

Behind them, pounding down the road, came one of the riders who had escaped the billiard ball ambush. His horse hadn't been winded by pulling a chaise. He was fresh and gaining. William hadn't a pistol of his own. He hadn't thought to come armed.

"May I?" he said, and drew the pistol from Gwen's belt, gripping the horse's back with his legs, wishing he'd spent more time on a horse these past few years and less on a parade ground.

Turning, he aimed and fired, ducking to avoid decapitation by an overhanging branch. The shot went wide, but the report startled the other man's horse. It reared, sending the bandit flying into the brush. Through the dust of their own passage, William could vaguely see a fleeing horse and squirming shrubbery.

As for their own mount, Gwen was pushing him hard, her skirts hiked to the knees as she leaned forwards over the horse's neck.

"You'll lather him if you keep going like this," William shouted in Gwen's ear. "It's too much carrying two. And we've still a ways to go."

Without argument Gwen reined the horse from an all-out gallop to a trot. He felt her chest rise and fall as she breathed in deeply, nearly as winded as the horse. Her hair was spilling down around her shoulders, her cheeks windburned. She squirmed around to look at him, keeping one hand on the reins, the other braced on the horse's neck.

"You're a good man in a fight, William Reid," she said. "When you're not getting yourself stabbed."

"You're not still holding that against me, are you?" he said jokingly, high on the euphoria of battle, the same euphoria that she was feeling. "But there's just one thing you've forgot to mention. *Why* are we in a fight? Who's following you?"

Gwen's lips pressed together. "People," she said.

"I didn't think they were squirrels," said William, but he was speaking to the back of her head.

His amusement faded as their horse plodded on, down untraveled byways. What had begun as a simple trip to Sussex to collect his daughter had turned to a very different kettle of fish indeed.

Like a kettle of fish, it stank to high heaven.

Whatever had occurred on the road today, the two women had been expecting it—there was no denying that, or explaining it away. Constantly looking out the window, checking the road—and who in the blazes traveled with a trunk full of billiard balls?

Who was following them? Why? And why did a respectable lady and her ward travel armed to the teeth? He didn't know England or English mores, but he strongly suspected that this was something out of the ordinary.

"Don't you think you owe me an explanation?" he asked, but Gwen pretended not to hear, and William, recognizing a losing battle when he saw it, settled back on the rump of the horse and tried not to sneeze on Gwen's hair, which, freed from its usual confinement, was doing its best to colonize William's nose.

It was twilight by the time they reached the gates of a great estate, the sun setting in shades of violet and orange. Down a long and winding drive, William could make out the roofs of an estate large enough to house a rajah's retinue, built of a pale stone that gleamed golden in the light of the setting sun. The ornate metal gates were decorated with an entwined *D* and *L*.

"No gatekeeper," grumbled Gwen. "We'll have to get down and shift them ourselves."

"Where are we?" William asked, swinging down from the horse. That was the least of his questions, but it would do for a start. One of the first rules of campaign: always know the field.

"Darlington Court," said Gwen.

"It's the country seat of the Viscounts Loring," provided Miss Wooliston helpfully. She was leading her own tired horse. "The son of the current viscount is my cousin's husband's sister's husband."

William didn't even bother to start to untangle that.

"All right," said William. "We're here. There's no one coming after us with pistols, knives, or small artillery. Would one of you tell me what in the devil is going on?"

"We're stopping for the night," said Gwen loftily. "And there's no need to swear. Help me down?"

As far as William was concerned, there was every need to swear. He reached up to help Gwen from the horse, lifting her by the waist and swinging her down. Once her feet touched the ground, he gave her a little shake.

"Why do you carry a sword in your parasol?" he demanded. "Why were you looking out the window the whole bloody way from Bath? Why are we set upon by brigands every time you leave the house?"

Gwen folded her arms across her chest. "How do you know they weren't setting upon you?"

"Because I wasn't the one who came prepared with billiard balls!" Raking a hand through his hair, William got control of his temper and his voice. In a gentler tone, he said, "Are you in some sort of trouble? Just be honest with me, and I'll help you however I can."

Gwen pressed her lips together, shaking her head. "It's too complicated for that."

William wasn't budging until he got an explanation. "Try me."

Miss Wooliston stepped forward. "Let me."

Gwen made an automatic gesture of negation. "But—"

"No, I think it's time," Miss Wooliston said. Turning to William, she said, in a conversational tone, "Did you know that your son was a French spy?"

Chapter 19

Sussex, 2004

"Have you heard of someone called the Moonflower?" asked Jeremy.

We had gone to the pub for dinner, none of us having felt particularly inspired in the culinary department.

The Heavy Hart was our favorite pub. It was also the only pub, at least in the immediate vicinity. If you drove for a while south and east of Selwick Hall, you came upon the decaying Victorian tackiness of Brighton; several miles west, in the other direction, there was a chichi, upmarket, revitalized village center, with an organic grocer's and one of those make-your-own-pottery places. Colin felt a local's scorn for the resulting gastropub with its London chef, so to the Heavy Hart, with its bangers and mash, we went.

The fact that Jeremy would have preferred the gastropub might also have had something to do with it.

It was a misleadingly cozy scene, the dark wood paneling scarred by generations of tipsy darts players, the battered oak tables sticky with the residue of spilled beer, scattered with round mats celebrating the virtues of various malt concoctions. A television mounted over the bar broadcast yet another game of football (the British kind), which only a handful of diehards appeared to be watching. A poster tacked to the wall above our table featured the blurry muzzle of a dog and, above it, uneven lettering saying, "Have you seen Fuzzy? If so call . . ."

Fortunately, none of the usual gang seemed to be in the pub tonight. Joan Plowden-Plugge, my local nemesis, had stopped attending as soon as she started dating a pretentious museum curator with delusions of stealing my dissertation thesis. They went to the gastropub, which was another reason we didn't. That would be all we needed, to have them after the jewels, too.

On the other hand, they and Jeremy might mutually destruct, which would make the world a better place for everyone.

To be fair, Jeremy had been pretty well behaved so far. We were already on day two of his sojourn at Selwick Hall. As far as I could tell, he had stayed in the spot in the library where I had placed him, reading only the papers that were set before him, although that might have had something to do with my plumping myself two chairs down with the collected oeuvres of Miss Gwen.

He didn't make his bed and he had left his towels on the

floor of the bathroom, but I couldn't really hold that against him, at least not as an act of malice. One had the feeling that in Jeremy's world, little elves took care of that sort of thing. In this case, the little elf was me. It had seemed easier than leaving the towels in a damp heap on the floor.

"Does this Moonflower wear long skirts and smell of patchouli?" Colin asked.

"Not that kind of Moonflower," I said.

I'd come across the Moonflower before, when I was looking into the Pink Carnation's activities in India. Upshot: The Pink Carnation didn't have any activities in India. Which made sense given that the nearest port in India was five months from England, on a good day. What I had discovered was a net of French spies, loosely under the guide of a master spy named the Gardener—loosely because of the distance between India and the Continent. On the ground, these agents had a fair amount of autonomy. There had been a Marigold, who had been trying to stir up an anti-English rebellion among the local rulers.

Then there was the Moonflower. . . .

I said slowly, "He's the one who was supposed to have something to do with the jewels of Berar." Then, just in case it wasn't a good idea to sound too informed, I added, "Unless it was the Marigold."

Jeremy was drinking white wine. He'd made a point of it. He was also wearing an Italian blazer that looked rather ridiculous next to Colin's rumpled polo shirt. I suspected Colin of having smeared extra mud on his shoes, just because.

"Wait, I remember now." I repositioned a beer mat in the

little puddle of condensation that had formed under my G&T. "I thought the deal was that the Moonflower claimed the jewels of Berar had disappeared, that they were only being held out as a lure but didn't actually exist."

That much was actually true. From what I'd been able to discover, last time around, the Marigold had been promising various jewels to local rulers, only to be told by his counterpart, the Moonflower, that both he and they had been hoaxed, that the jewels had been lost, genuinely lost, when Berar fell.

"That's not what the files you gave me say." Jeremy took a swig of his wine. The man looked like he needed it. "How many letters did that woman write?"

"Lots," I said. "Hey, it was before TV."

Jeremy gave me a look but held his peace. "According to that Lady Henrietta—"

"Your ancestress," I pointed out.

Neither of the males at the table appeared pleased by that observation.

"The Moonflower sent the jewels to his sister"—Jeremy consulted his notes—"Libby."

"Lizzy," I corrected him automatically and then remembered that it was the sort of thing I wasn't supposed to know. "Er, Libby wasn't the sort of nickname they used at the time. It would have to be Lizzy."

No need for him to know that I had stayed up half the night reading through those letters before he could. I viewed it as a sort of safety check. If he recounted them correctly, he was to be trusted, at least on a limited basis; if not, we would know he was trying to scam us.

Not that Colin would believe that Jeremy was operating in good faith even if he came with a certificate signed by Mother Teresa, the Archbishop of Canterbury, and assorted local saints.

"In the event," said Jeremy, leaning back in his chair with a studied movement reminiscent of Alistair Cooke announcing *Masterpiece Theatre*, "according to Lady Henrietta, this Lizzy fled to safety at Selwick Hall. Presumably taking the jewels with her."

He looked more than a little bit smug.

Colin balked. "Even if the jewels did come to Selwick Hall, we don't know that they stayed there. It has been——"

He looked to me for help.

"One hundred and ninety-nine years." April of 1805 to July of 2004. I abandoned exact math for convenient generalization. "And a bit."

"Two hundred years," Colin translated. "They could be anywhere by now."

"Speaking of that," said Jeremy, his tone silkier than his socks, "weren't you meant to be searching the tower?"

Colin had. He had come back covered with miscellaneous animal droppings and a nasty scratch on one arm from some- thing unidentified but rusty.

"Nothing in the tower," said Colin tersely.

"Are you sure?" Jeremy was vibrating with suspicion be- neath his Italian wool. "The rhyme did say——"

"I know what the rhyme said," said Colin, setting his pint firmly down on the table. "There's nothing there but stone, mold, and old plows."

"Tetanus on the hoof," I said, but they both ignored me. They were too intent on staring each other down.

They didn't look alike. Jeremy took after his grandfather's side. I had seen the pictures of Robert Alderly, handsome and dissolute, in a Duke of Windsor sort of way, with carefully slicked-back hair and clothes that spoke of the close attention of a valet. Like his grandfather's, Jeremy's skin had been carefully protected from sun and wind, his hair coaxed and nurtured with a variety of designer products, most of which I had wound up having to clear off the side of the bathtub that morning. Colin took after the Selwick side, outdoorsmen, midblond hair streaked with sun, skin darkened to a nondesigner tan. I'd seen pictures of Colin's father, an older, grayer version of Colin.

You would never have guessed that Colin and Jeremy were related. The one thing they had in common was their mutual dislike, and that came through loud and clear, imprinted on both their features.

"There's nothing there," repeated Colin.

Jeremy's face hardened. "How do I know you'd tell me if there was?"

"Because your grandmother would kick his ass."

Wait, had I said that out loud? Well, at least it had broken the tension. Both of the men were staring at me as though I had grown an extra head.

It seemed like the time for a show of girlfriendly solidarity. "Also, Colin doesn't lie."

"Thanks, Eloise," said Colin drily.

It was not exactly a wholehearted endorsement, but then, neither was mine. Yes, Colin was fundamentally a good and honest guy. I would trust him in a room full of scantily clad women, knowing that he'd never so much as think of cheating on me. When it came to Jeremy, however . . . even Colin's probity had its limits.

Before Jeremy could jump in again, Colin turned to me, asking, "How was *Nightmare Abbey*?"

Hmm. If I hadn't seen him come in from the tower, cranky as only the unsuccessful and scratched can be, I might have suspected him of hiding something myself. That change of subject was just a little too pat.

"You mean *The Convent of Orsino*," I corrected him. I sensed many Gothic novel jokes in my future, which seemed a little unfair, considering I was taking one for the team, here. "It's—um—"

"An action-packed thrill ride?" suggested Colin.

"Pretty much, yes." In prose so purple you could use it to paint your house. "So far, they've been cursed by Gypsies, passed out in an enchanted grove, narrowly escaped an orgy—"

"Escaped an orgy?" Colin said incredulously.

I could tell from the looks on both male faces that this concept did not compute. "Avoided an orgy, then. Hey, I didn't write it. I'm just summarizing. Look, can we get away from the orgy?"

A laminated menu hit the floor. The server hastily gathered it up and dropped the menus on the table in front of us.

"I'll just leave those with you, shall I?" she gabbled, and fled back to the bar, where I saw her whispering something into the ear of the bartender, who wiped his hands on his apron and raised a brow in our general direction.

I rounded on my boyfriend. "Why didn't you tell me she was standing behind me?"

Colin was laughing soundlessly into his pint.

"We're never going to be able to come here again, you know," I said darkly.

"I don't know," said Colin. "We might get some interesting invitations."

Or rather, Colin would get some interesting invitations. I wouldn't be here. It was a distinctly sobering thought.

"And by interesting, I think you mean alarming," I said firmly. "I've seen the local talent. And by talent, I mean livestock."

"We're not Dibley," said Colin, referring to the television show.

"No," I agreed. "You don't have Dawn French."

As I was saying it, I realized that Jeremy was watching us or, more precisely, watching Colin, a little confused and a little bit wary. For a moment, we'd fallen back into our usual patterns (read, absurd back-and-forth over nothing). We'd forgotten that Jeremy was there. Colin looked more relaxed than I'd seen him since yesterday morning. And it suddenly hit me that I'd never seen him like this around Jeremy. The minute Jeremy entered the room, Colin started radiating tension, like the nuclear reactor in a Bond film, the sort that came complete with handy self-destruct button.

From the look on Jeremy's face, the same thing had occurred to him. If I didn't know better, I'd say he even looked a little bit wistful.

Which, of course, was utterly absurd. Would Darth Vader be wistful? Hard to tell with that helmet.

Colin followed my gaze and his smile faded, whatever crack he'd been about to make dying on his lips. Instead he said, "Anything else about the book we should know?"

"You mean, other than the orgies?" Colin didn't crack a smile. Apparently, we were back to business. I tucked my hair behind my ears. "Basically, once you get past all the heavy Gothic hoodoo, it turns into your classic vampire novel."

"I thought vampires began with Bram Stoker," said Jeremy, sounding just like his disagreeably smug self. Good. I didn't want to have to feel sorry for him. "Wasn't he later?"

"He was, but he didn't invent the vampire myth; he only built on it. There was a huge vampire scare in Austria in the mid–eighteenth century, and English poets and writers picked up on it at the beginning of the nineteenth. Even Byron wrote a vampire poem."

I could state all this with authority. I'd done some quick source checking once I'd hit the vampires in the plot and had the same reaction as Jeremy. It wasn't entirely idle curiosity. If the work was a late-nineteenth-century piece and not actually by Miss Gwen, then it would be entirely useless to us.

"Miss Gwen was on the early side with the vampire craze,

but she didn't invent it," I said. "There are some interesting twists, though. Her vampire isn't an old guy with a Transylvanian accent. He's young and vaguely French."

"*Vaguely* French?" said Colin.

"Nationalities are never specified as such. The entire book is all set in some mythical kingdom far, far away, in a sort of pseudo–Middle Ages. Anyway"—I stared down the peanut gallery—"the vampire, who is young and vaguely charming, is condemned to preside over an endless party of ghouls in his dark tower until he can find the one maiden who holds the precious jewel that will set him free. Yes, *jewel*."

Jeremy, who looked like he had been about to make some kind of crack, closed his mouth.

Colin looked thoughtful. "And what is this jewel?"

"Unspecified." A collective sigh went around the table. "I'm not at the end yet, though. Hey! It's five volumes long. I've had one day." With a minimum of sleep the night before, what with staying up half the night to preread everything I'd given to Jeremy. "And believe me when I tell you that it reads as if Danielle Steel had a love child with Vincent Price."

Both men shuddered.

"It's rather fascinating, really," I said. "At least from a lit-crit point of view. The real heroine isn't the ingénue; it's Plumeria, who's her preceptress—that's the word they use. Plumeria and the girl's father, Sir Magnifico, battle all sorts of obstacles to get to the Silver Tower, where the girl is being held, only to discover that the girl has fallen in love with her captor, just as Magnifico has formed an attachment for Plumeria. It's all parallels and mirrors. In some ways, it's a little bit like Spenser's *Faerie Queene*. The characters are constantly being tested and forced to question their true natures."

"Fascinating," said Jeremy flatly.

"Whatever this magical jewel is that Amarantha carries, she keeps it in a magic mirror, which only she has the power to unlock." Elbows on the table, chin on my hands, I was in full-blown grad student mode. "I think the mirror is meant to be a metaphor for her virtue or something like that. If the Knight of the Silver Tower smashes it, he gets the jewel and lives, but some unspecified doom will come upon her. If she keeps it intact, he's doomed to spend eternity with his goblin crew. It's her salvation or his."

To my surprise, it was Jeremy who quoted the obvious lines. *"'The mirror crack'd from side to side / "The curse is come upon me," cried the Lady of Shalott.'"*

"It does make you wonder if Tennyson read *The Convent of Orsino*," I said. "They're both set in a pseudo-medieval fantasy-land, although Tennyson's is explicitly Arthurian and Miss Gwen's is set in some unspecified place on the Continent that might be either France or Italy or a mishmash of both."

"What happens?" said Colin. He couldn't resist one-upping his cousin. "Singing her song she dies?"

"I don't know," I said. "I haven't made it to the end yet."

A depressed silence fell.

It was Jeremy who perked up first. He lifted his head, a gleam of cupidity lighting his eyes. "You say the jewel is hidden in a mirror. . . ."

"It's a metaphor," I said quickly. "Like that china vase in the Pope poem."

Colin was more to the point. "I'm not smashing all the mirrors in the house."

"Not all the mirrors," said Jeremy persuasively, and I got a glimpse of the face he must show to his clients. "But if there were one from the right time period . . ."

"*No,*" said Colin.

Jeremy took a delicate sip of his wine. "Afraid of the seven years' bad luck, cousin?"

Colin crackled his knuckles. "Maybe I don't believe in wantonly destroying something that has managed to survive this long."

Okay. We weren't talking about mirrors anymore.

"Just because something is old doesn't mean it's worth deifying," said Jeremy snarkily. "You heard my grandmother. You can't turn the old place into a shrine."

Nothing could have been more calculated to infuriate Colin. "No," he said. "You'd just sell off anything worth a quid and play squire with the rest."

"You've always wanted to keep me out." The gloves were off now and there was no stopping it. "You and your father, treating me like trash."

"He was right, wasn't he? You couldn't even wait until he was dead before—" Colin broke off, his lips pressing tightly together.

"Right," said Jeremy, kicking back in his chair. "That was all my doing. You never bothered to ask your mother for her side of it, did you? Your father never appreciated—"

Colin didn't let him finish. "And you did?"

"Yes." The intensity with which Jeremy said it made me sit up and take notice. "Caroline was wasted on your father."

I'd always assumed, as Colin had said, that Jeremy had gone after Colin's mother to get at Colin's father, just another play in a long-standing feud. But something about the look on Jeremy's face, the absolute conviction of his voice, made me wonder if Jeremy's feelings might not have been at least a little more genuine than we gave him credit for.

Not that he wasn't still slime, but he seemed to be slime who genuinely loved his wife.

Colin had turned an odd shade of gray. "I don't want you in my house," he said.

Jeremy smiled nastily. "That's just the thing, isn't it? It's not your house. It's our house—yours, mine, and Serena's. Just one big, happy family."

"We were until you came along," said Colin in a low voice, although, from everything I'd heard, that was pretty palpably untrue.

"Stop!" I banged my glass down between them.

Unfortunately, it was plastic, so it didn't make quite the ding it might have, but it was still enough to get their attention.

"This is *exactly* what Mrs. Selwick-Alderly was talking about," I said furiously. "You're never going to get anywhere unless you stop rehashing the same old grievances. Both of you."

I knew that I wasn't being tactful, but I didn't care. "You know what? You're stuck with each other. Deal with it."

Not exactly after-school-special stuff, but at least it knocked them out of their endless argument loop. For the moment.

Colin turned to Jeremy. There were two deep lines between his brows. With an effort, he asked, "Is she really sick?"

"I don't know." You could tell that Jeremy hated admitting ignorance just as much as Colin hated asking. He lifted his glass in an ironic excuse, his face twisting. "If she'd tell anyone, it would be you. She always did like you better."

Colin's brows pulled together. "You must be joking. You're her grandson."

Jeremy's smile was bitter. "But I wasn't a Selwick. Not a real one. Not by her lights."

It was like opening a pretty Victorian picture book to find that the center had been eaten out by mold. It all seemed so quaint and charming, Selwick Hall, Mrs. Selwick-Alderly, all their family stories and traditions, but there was a deep well of poison in the middle. I wasn't quite sure how it had started—Mrs. Selwick-Alderly blamed it all, beginning and end, on Colin's mother—but somewhere things had gone terribly wrong.

I pushed back my menu. "I don't know about you, but I'm not really all that hungry. Anyone else up for grilled cheese back at the house?"

"I'll settle our tab," Jeremy said quickly and pushed away from the table.

Colin watched him from under furrowed brows. "He's always been a bastard," he muttered, but it didn't come out quite as confidently as usual.

What a mess.

Wiggling out of my chair, I draped my arms around Colin's shoulders and dropped a kiss on the top of his head. "I adore your aunt," I said, "but, boy, did she do a real job on that guy."

"Mmph," said Colin.

They were both quiet as we drove back to the house, Colin and I in the front, Jeremy in the back. To call it a truce would be overstating matters. It was more that each side had fired the last of his shots and was trying to decide where and how to regroup.

I just didn't want to be in the middle when it happened.

I wondered if finding the jewels would make things better or worse. On the one hand, there would be the shared thrill of accomplishment, of achieving something that no one in their family, for generations back, had managed. On the other, one bone, two dogs. I could just see them snipping and sniping. Either way you looked at it, it was a no-win.

"Didn't we leave the light on?" I asked as the Land Rover pulled into the gravel sweep in front of the house.

Usually we left the front porch light burning when we went out. It got pretty dark out there at night in the country, and my shoes weren't always well suited to picking my way from the car in the dark.

"It might have gone out," said Colin, pulling up in his usual spot and turning off the ignition. "Or we forgot."

He held out a hand to help me down from the car. I took it, giving it a squeeze before letting go again.

The only light came from inside the car, casting a dim circle on the gravel. In the dark verges beyond, I could hear the rus-

330 of small animals scrabbling in the bushes and the mourn-

tling of small animals scrabbling in the bushes and the mournful cry of a bird of prey.

Colin slammed the car door behind me, plunging us into darkness.

"Christ, it's dark," said Jeremy. "Do you have a torch?"

"It's all right," I said, groping my way to the front door with the ease of practice. "I'll just get the door and turn on the—ah!"

"Eloise?" I heard Colin say at the same time as Jeremy's quick, excited, "What is it?"

"I'm okay!" I said hastily, catching myself on the doorjamb just as Colin, behind me, caught me by the shoulders. There was empty space where the door should have been. "It's just— the door's open."

"Open?" said Colin.

Moving me aside, he stepped forward and flicked the switch. The hall light flickered reluctantly on. Faux candles stuck into a central chandelier illuminated a scene of destruction. The vase that usually sat on the hall table lay in pieces on the floor. The hall rug, a threadbare Persian, was bunched up, half in a puddle of water. Fallen flowers from the vase strewed the floor, like a bizarre funeral arrangement.

Behind me, I could hear Jeremy's quick, sharp breath.

Colin stood, one hand on the light switch, staring at the ruin of his beloved front hall.

"Guys?" I said, taking a cautious step forward, around the shards of what once had been a pretty, if not particularly valuable piece of chinoiserie. "I don't like this."

Colin looked at Jeremy. "Neither do I."

Chapter 20

"Did you know the truth of this tower? Of the ancient secret it keeps?"

In the dungeons where they lay, Plumeria twisted her hands and essayed an answer. "There might have been a whisper of it, in my books of ancient lore—but of the whole truth of it I knew not, not whole and entire, not until he bared his fangs and carried Amarantha from us."

"You knew," quoth Sir Magnifico, "and yet you did not tell me."
                              —From *The Convent of Orsino* by A Lady

"My—what?"

"Your son," said Miss Wooliston. "Jack, I believe you call him."

"I know who he is," William said.

Miss Wooliston patted her horse's neck. "According to my sources, your son has operated for several years under the alias of Moonflower, gathering information for the French government." She looked at him shrewdly. "You don't seem surprised."

By the change of subject, yes. By the content of her words, no. "Why would I be? He always did support their cause."

Gwen made a noise of surprise.

William turned on her. "Sure and why wouldn't he? It was the English who wouldn't let him into their army or their diplomatic service. He had an Indian mother, you see. Those laws are an abomination, setting father against son, brother against brother—"

He broke off, shaking his head to clear it. This was all very interesting, but it was getting him no closer to the answer to his questions.

Conversationally, he said, "I've no particular allegiance for the English myself, when it comes to it, but that's all beside the point. What I don't understand is what my Jack has to do with your billiard balls."

"Everything," said Miss Wooliston. "Have you heard of the jewels of Berar?"

"Heard of them? I've seen them." The Rajah liked to deck himself out to impress visiting dignitaries. William had been invited to his durbar a time or two, in his official capacities. An officer in the East India Company's army played many roles, only some of them military. "Some of them, in any event. He had a prodigious number of them. But what—"

"Your son," said Miss Wooliston delicately, "in the course of his duties, managed to make off with the jewels of Berar. There are various parties who want those jewels very much indeed."

"Jack wouldn't—," William began automatically and stopped. He hadn't seen his son, not to speak to, since Jack had stormed out five years before, vowing revenge on his father's people. William had tried to argue that they weren't his people, not really, that a Scoto-American was a far cry from an Englishman, but he had taken the East India Company's coin and eaten their salt and that was enough for Jack.

It was no use to say Jack wouldn't. He would.

"He was in that area, it was true. I kept tabs on him, you see, even when he wasn't writing. I still have friends scattered about, and they would write me, letting me know how he was, if he seemed well, nothing much, just enough to put a father's mind at rest. He'd been close to Scindia, high in his counsel, but he was seconded to the service of the Rajah of Berar, just before—"

"Just before the siege?" Miss Wooliston supplied.

William glanced at Gwen, who stood silent and pale beside the great gates. "I'd never understood why. Why Scindia sent him off to do a journeyman's job in Berar when he might have kept him by his side. I'd thought they might have had a falling out, that Jack had pulled one of his tricks on him. He isn't always the most diplomatic person, Jack."

"No," said Miss Wooliston gently. "I would guess that it wasn't Scindia's choice at all." She pronounced the foreign name without hesitation, mimicking his pronunciation. "Scindia had French aid. It seems likely his French backers requested that the Moonflower—Jack—be sent to Berar for just that purpose. There was just one slight hitch to their plan. Your Jack switched sides."

The news hit him like an electric bolt. "No," he said. "That I won't believe."

On a branch overhead, a bird cawed, launching itself in a flurry of black feathers from branch to post. The muted colors of an English twilight surrounded him, the trees, the gates, the women standing beside him blurred and dim in the half-light, so alien, so unfamiliar, compared to the vivid, sun-drenched country he had for so long called home.

"No," he said again. "Jack's anger ran deep. He wouldn't have helped those who had shunned him."

Or would he? The tree branches shivered in the breeze, the night drew around him like a web, in the half-light, where nothing was what it seemed. Gwen, in her purple traveling dress, blended into the shadows, a blur against a blur. He could feel everything slipping away from him, everything he thought he had known.

Miss Wooliston stood her ground. "It's true, whether you believe it or not. He's been a double agent for some time. I gather that his former masters only found out about it last winter. The news only just made its way back here." Her voice was somber as she said, "They've sworn out a price on his head."

A price. He remembered his little boy, gap-toothed and laughing, sun-browned and healthy, squabbling with his older sister in the zenana quarters of their bungalow in Madras. Kat running to him: *Father, Jack—*

Why did he have to go courting trouble, always? David's lament for Absalom ran through his mind: *My son, my son.*

"Enough!" Gwen stepped out of the shadows, ranging herself beside him. "Can't you see he's heard enough for now? We can continue this in the house."

What else had she known that she hadn't been telling him?

This woman with whom he had, he thought, achieved such an intimacy over the past few weeks, the woman who had patched him up, body and soul—but to what end? Not for pure affection, as he'd thought. Not even for lust. For what?

He tried to look into her face, but the light played tricks on him, blurring her features like smoke.

"No," he said slowly. "We'll continue this now. I want to know what else you haven't told me. I'll have the rest of it. Now. Before we go anywhere else."

Gwen rubbed her hands along her arms as though she'd grown cold.

Miss Wooliston was all business. "The French want the jewels back. They believe your son sent them here to England."

William remembered that visit to Kat. "The boxes," he said at last. "The boxes he sent to Kat. They weren't looking for opium. They were looking for jewels."

"We believe that Mr. Reid sent those boxes to his older sister as a decoy," said Miss Wooliston. William didn't miss the quick, surprised look Gwen sent her. "He also had boxes delivered to several other addresses, many of them empty or abandoned."

"He did?" Gwen broke in. "You never told me that."

William felt a petty satisfaction in that—that she had been kept in the dark as he had. It was short-lived, however. No matter what else she might not have known, she had known enough.

Miss Wooliston regarded her warily. "I have not managed to secure the contents, but I believe that those, too, were intended as a distraction."

William took a deep breath. "All right. I can see where this is leading. So what you're saying is that Jack handed off those jewels to someone. That's why those men came after us in the alley—and again just now. I can't blame them. I've just come from India. Who better for him to give them to than me?"

It was as he was saying it that the full corollary of his own words struck him, with a deep and burning pain.

He turned to Gwen, forcing himself to say the words. "Is there even an Agnes Wooliston? Or was that why you attached yourself to me all along? To find the jewels?"

"I—I didn't attach myself to you!" sputtered Gwen. "If anything, it was the other way around!"

"Colonel," said Miss Wooliston sharply, "I can assure you I do indeed have a younger sister and that sister disappeared with your daughter from Miss Climpson's seminary. I am as eager as you to reclaim them both."

"Then what's all this about these jewels?" The question came out as a howl of frustration. He was tired, he was sore, and above all, he was hurt, the mindless pain of an animal with a thorn in the pad of his paw, incapable of removing it, driving it in deeper and deeper with every movement.

"Did you know that your son has been paying his sister's fees at Miss Climpson's?"

The apparent non sequitur made William's head jerk up. "No. That can't be right. She was on a scholarship."

"They haven't any scholarships. The fees have all been paid for by a Mr. John Reid. It was he who arranged for your daughter's place at the school."

"Jack paid Lizzy's school fees?" The entire world had turned on its head.

Of all his siblings, Jack had always had the softest spot for Lizzy, but this—this was something out of the ordinary, too odd to compass.

"He might have done it out of kindness," Gwen said quickly. "You said he cared for her, as much as he cared for anyone."

"It also helped," said Miss Wooliston evenly, "that his employer's cousin was a member of the faculty."

William's head was swimming. "His employer?" All he could think of was Scindia, and he doubted the Maratha chieftain had much to do with a girls' school in Bath.

"The spymaster known as the Gardener. The Chevalier de la Tour d'Argent." Miss Wooliston was speaking purely to Gwen now. "He was too assiduous in his attempts to aid us. And there was that other incident at the school two years ago. The only way for it all to make sense was for the Gardener to be in some way connected with the school. And so . . ." She spread out her hands.

William had had enough of gardeners and spymasters. "But what about my Lizzy? Where does she come into all this? What would your spymaster"—he choked on the word—"want with my girl?"

Miss Wooliston's well-bred voice replied, measured, inexorable. "Your son sent her a package that arrived not long before her disappearance. Baubles, her teacher called it."

She didn't need to explain further. It was painfully, sickeningly clear. Baubles. From a man who might have made off with the missing jewels of Berar. William felt sick, sick deep in his gut with a horror that made the rest of it, the lies, the revelations, seem as nothing in comparison.

"No," he said. Jack wouldn't have. He wouldn't have put Lizzy in danger like that.

Or would he?

"Certain parties," said Miss Wooliston primly, "believe that your son sent the jewels to your daughter. Hence her precipitate departure from her school and those charming people on the road today."

William paced back and forth, his boots leaving no mark on the hard-packed dirt of the lane. "Even if I were to believe that this was all true, even if Jack had those jewels, even if he were— were what you say he is, why would he send them to Lizzy?"

Gwen shook her head, a blur in the twilight. "It doesn't matter whether he truly has or not. What matters is that someone believes he has."

Someone. A dangerous someone. Someone to whom one girl would be a small price in pursuit of his end.

All this time, all this time they had been going in circles, attending the opera, laughing, flirting, speculating, all this time his Lizzy had been on the run, burdened by jewels for which more than one man had already shed his blood.

William turned sharply on his heel, towards Gwen. "All this time," he said, in a low, harsh voice. "You knew. You knew my Lizzy was in danger."

She took a step back, her voice uncharacteristically hesitant.

"We didn't know for certain until yesterday," she said. "It might have been Agnes they wanted."

That only made William angrier. Images flashed through his mind, of their carriage trip to Bristol, his stripping his soul to her in the opera the other night. And all that while . . .

"Either way, you knew that they hadn't just run away from school. And yet you let me go on believing—"

Gwen's hands balled into fists at her sides. "It wasn't my secret to tell."

How was it not her secret?

"She's my child!" The words echoed in the air between them. "How do you know all this? Why do you know all this?" He turned on Miss Wooliston. "Don't try to tell me it's just the inquiries of a concerned sister—I wasn't born yesterday. Concerned sisters don't come armed."

Gwen looked towards Miss Wooliston, who gave a barely perceptible nod. "You might— Well, you might call us agents." As he stared at her, disbelieving, Gwen raised her head a little higher. "We work for the War Office. Sometimes. We gather information."

"I see," William said, his voice low and flat. And he did. Everything that had passed between them, every confidence, every kiss, had been a lie. A means to an end. "I can see that you're good at what you do. You always get your information in the end, do you? Even if you have to go to bed with the odd man to get it."

Miss Wooliston's eyebrows shot up.

Gwen stumbled back, her mouth opening and closing. "I've never—"

William stalked forward. "Didn't you? What was last night, then?"

Bright patches of crimson appeared on Gwen's cheeks. "That wasn't what last night was about! And if you were any kind of a gentleman, you wouldn't have mentioned it."

Miss Wooliston's eyebrows were charting hitherto undiscovered country beneath her hairline.

"And if you were any kind of lady—" All of William's rage and hurt came pouring out at the woman in front of him, the woman he had cradled to his breast. He had thought her so gallant and fine. Little did he know it was all an act. "I'm sorry I didn't have anything better to tell you. You must have been very disappointed. All that effort for nothing."

"It wasn't an effort," she blurted out.

"What a relief it is to hear that," said William acidly. "I'd hate to think I was an unpleasant assignment."

"Damn you!" Gwen burst out. "If you can stand there and spout such filth—"

"Tell me I'm wrong," he said. "Tell me none of this is true."

"I'll go find someone to open the gates," said Miss Wooliston tactfully, and dissolved into the dusk.

Gwen appeared to be going through some sort of massive internal struggle. She started to hold out a hand to him and thought better of it.

In a low voice, she said, "Don't you think I wanted to tell you?"

"You lie for a living," William said. "You've just told me as much. You've lied to me since I met you."

The words seemed to strike sparks off her. "Not lied, omitted."

He looked at her as he might a bug. "Am I meant to believe there's a difference in that?"

She balled her hands into fists at her sides. "The end was the same. We were both looking for the girls. What good would it have done to tell you? You'd never have believed me, anyway. You'd have thought I was mad."

He hated that there was truth in that, when there was no truth in anything else she had told him.

Gwen seized her advantage. "If it had gone well," she said, taking a step towards him. "That would have been all. You would have had your Lizzy back and there would have been no need for you to know—any of the rest."

"No, no need," he said bitterly, feeling like the worst sort of fool. "No need because you never intended to have anything more to do with me, did you? Not once you'd got what you wanted."

"William—"

The sound of his name on her lips stung like salt on a wound. "That's Colonel Reid to you," he said brutally. And then, just because he was hurting, because he couldn't help himself, "Do you know the worst of it? The most damnable bit was that I actually thought I might be coming to care for you. That just goes to show how good you are—or how gullible I am. Take it as you will."

She looked like a man hit with a mortar, in that moment of sheer shock before the pain sets in and the screaming starts.

Her lips pressed together, her hand was at her throat. "William," she said, and her voice shook as she took a step forward. The words came out jerkily. "I don't want to lose you."

The same words he had said to her once. Before he knew better. "There's the man to open the gates," William said, and turned his back and walked away, leaving Gwen standing there alone in the lane, the horses grazing beside her, her hand at her throat and her heart in her eyes.

What heart? She had no heart. It was an act, a ploy.

His sense of ill use drove him, and it overwhelmed the small voice that protested that there might have been some justice in what she had done. He wanted spirits, strong ones. He wanted to get rousingly drunk, as he hadn't for years, blotting out memory, desire, sense. He wanted to get so drunk he couldn't remember the look on her face as she said, "I don't want to lose you."

Lose him? More likely use him. All the while he'd been mooning about love in a cottage, she'd been plotting—whatever it was that agents plotted. Nothing to do with him. He'd been nothing but a source of information and a quick roll in the scenery.

This had been— Well, whatever it had been, it was over. He just had to make it through the night, collect Lizzy and be off, and he'd never have to see her or hear from her again.

He wouldn't have to wonder just whom else she might be collecting information from or to what lengths she might go to do it, wonder if she might not be looking at someone else with wide, shocked eyes and protesting that what they had meant more than a tumble on a storage room floor.

The house to which the path led him turned out to be an Italianate fantasy, a massive pile of marble plunked on the English countryside, built in a low rectangle and bristling with columns, pilasters, and assorted satyrs.

"It's a bit of an abomination, I know," said his host cheerfully, "but we call it home."

He was a young man just about the age of William's oldest, with floppy blond hair, a rather rumpled cravat, and easy and open manners.

His wife, Lady Henrietta, greeted the ladies in the party with cries of delight and made noises about hot baths and cold suppers.

Their small and ragged party was welcomed as though fugitive guests on horseback without luggage were a perfectly normal occurrence. And perhaps they were. No one here seemed to operate in the logical workaday realm with which William was familiar.

There was no need to avoid Gwen; he couldn't have found her if he'd tried. A liveried servant showed him to a room the size of his bungalow in Madras, with a balcony looking out over acres of formal gardens dotted with follies and statuary. A small brigade of servants poured steaming, scented water into a copper tub, while nameless gnomes left clothing for him on the bed, if not his own size, then a close approximation and finer by far than anything he himself had ever owned.

In his borrowed finery, he went down to supper, which was

served in a long room with crimson walls. Gwen was at the far end of the table, by the left hand of their host. She, too, had found or borrowed a gown. William could only guess that it belonged to their hostess; the white gauze embroidered with flowers wasn't at all in Gwen's usual style, too light, too playful, too décolleté—William hastily averted her eyes before he could betray himself—but she had made up for the youthful dress with the severity of her hairstyle.

It was some small consolation that she looked nearly as unhappy as William felt.

In her case, it translated into a forbidding aspect and a marked imperiousness of tone. William recognized both of these. This was the woman he had met at Miss Climpson's a lifetime ago, cold and rude—and miserably unhappy.

He didn't want to feel sorry for her. He was supposed to be feeling sorry for himself. He was the one who had been used, wasn't he?

But he watched her all the same. He watched her as he made polite conversation with his hostess, as he put food in his mouth with no recollection of what it was that he chewed. It was as though she had retreated into a plaster mold of herself, all the life, all the animation that had so captivated him, buried beneath a cold and brittle shell. That tremendous zest he had seen again and again diverted itself into haughty comments and cutting asides.

And no one, no one in the room, seemed to find anything out of the ordinary in this.

They smiled at one another and rolled their eyes as she

cracked her wit at them, but not one of them noticed the pain beneath it. They all, William noticed, referred to her casually as Miss Gwen, the honorific serving to set her apart from the rest of the group, a stranger even among her own friends.

Instead of separating after supper, the entire party retired to a long room replete with trompe l'oeil alcoves and an excess of statuary "to plan their strategy," as his host enthusiastically put it.

Everyone seemed to take as entirely natural that his daughter should be under siege by French spies.

"Good for her," declared Mr. Dorrington stoutly. "It was most ingenious of her, slipping out from under their noses the way she did."

"I don't understand why she didn't come to us," said Lady Henrietta, sounding slightly piqued. She took a sip of wine from her husband's glass. "We're much closer to Bath than Selwick Hall."

"Yes, but half the time we're *at* Selwick Hall," pointed out her husband. "Um, I say, Hen, wasn't that mine?"

Lady Henrietta considered the former and ignored the latter. "More like a third of the time, really."

"I only go there for the ginger biscuits," said her husband cheerfully. Seeing William's expression, he added, earnestly, "If your daughter had to go anywhere, Selwick Hall is as safe as she could be. They have it battened down like a—"

"Great battened thing?" suggested his wife.

"I wouldn't call it a great battened thing," said Mr. Dorrington. "More of a slightly nice battened thing, but still rather well battened for all that."

William watched them with a certain amount of consternation. He looked, automatically, for Gwen, to see if she could make sense of them, before remembering that she was a deceiver and a despoiler of middle-aged army colonels.

Lady Henrietta leaned forward, taking pity on his distress. "You really mustn't worry, Colonel Reid. We've had a great deal of experience with this sort of thing." In ringing tones, she announced, "My brother was the Purple Gentian."

It sounded like a form of disease. "I am sorry," said William apologetically. "I'm afraid I don't know . . ."

Lady Henrietta's face lit up. "Finally!" she said with satisfaction, lifting her eyes heavenwards. "Someone who hasn't heard of Richard. I shall twit him mercilessly about this. After we rescue the girls, of course," she added.

"Do you really think they'll be needing rescuing?" William asked her husband, who was contentedly munching on a ginger biscuit the size of a small plate.

"After what happened to you on the road?" Mr. Dorrington said thickly, around a mouthful of biscuit. He swallowed, brushing crumbs from his waistcoat. "Most likely. But it's nothing we can't handle. We have had some experience with vicious French spies," he said modestly. "Right, Hen?"

"Don't look at me; I'm just a talented amateur," she said with a wave of her hand. Her expression sobered as she looked at William. "But we do take getting your daughter back very seriously indeed."

William wasn't sure whether he should feel comforted or very, very afraid.

Either way, there was something rather exhausting about their youthful exuberance. After that ride, he felt every one of his fifty-four years. It was more than just the physical aches. They were so young, his host and hostess, so careless in their happiness. He didn't begrudge them that, quite the contrary, but watching them made him feel shopworn, old and scarred.

On the far side of the room, Miss Wooliston studied a map or a plan of some kind. Removed from her, from everyone, Gwen sat, her head bent over her notebook. Charting more of the fictional adventures of Sir Magnifico and Plumeria? Perhaps, but her pen wasn't moving, and her eyes were fixed on the same bit of the page.

William heaved himself painfully out of his chair. "If it's all the same," he said to his host and hostess, "I might go for a bit of a walk before bed."

"Just straight out that way," said Mr. Dorrington, gesturing to a pair of French doors to their left. "You can't get lost as long as you stick to the paths."

There were many things William might have said to that, but none of them particularly cheering, so instead he simply conveyed his thanks and slipped out the French doors into the moonlit gardens.

Chapter 21

Their prison was no dungeon of the ordinary sort. If there were stone walls, they saw them not; the bounds of their prison were the green hedges of the garden, the moon and stars their gaolers. The paths wound and twisted, through verdant ornaments carved in ever more fanciful shapes. And yet, and yet, when Plumeria set her hand against the prickly yew hedge, she could have sworn it felt more like the smooth and damp stone of a dungeon wall.

"I' faith," quoth Sir Magnifico. "What strange enchantment is this?"

"A very strange enchantment," quoth Plumeria, "if it bids thee set aside thy anger and find thy tongue!"

—From *The Convent of Orsino* by A Lady

*T*he gardens of Darlington Court shimmered in front of Gwen in the moonlight like a treacherous sea, the uncertain light hinting at hidden shoals and depths.

Gwen descended the weathered stairs from the balcony

slowly, the train of her unfamiliar gown dragging on the steps behind her, her hand resting heavily on the broad marble bannister. Somewhere out there, among the fantastical beasts and weeping nymphs, the dry fountains and dancing Nereids, was William.

She had seen him leave, seen him make his way out among the garden paths. Now she paused on the final terrace, surveying the seemingly endless miles of carefully engineered botanical illusion, fighting her own desire to turn back around, to march back into the house, plunk firmly down on her chair, settle a pair of pince-nez on her nose, and stick her nose in the air, secure in the knowledge that a mission was a mission and if William Reid couldn't understand the importance of what she was doing, what she had done, then he wasn't worth seeking out and it was his loss anyway.

So there.

She had grown very good at turning up her nose over the years. She snapped and snipped and snarled, keeping the softer emotions at bay, scaring away anyone who might have the temerity to attempt to treat her with affection. But that rogue of a Reid had slipped under her guard, and she couldn't, wouldn't, leave without setting things right.

She cared what he thought of her.

It was a horrifying thing, but there it was. His good opinion mattered to her. The scorn on his face down by the gate had abraded her like a cloak of nettles, scouring her raw.

Gwen took a cautious step down, then another, her boots crunching on gravel. The boots didn't go with the gown, but

Henrietta's slippers were the wrong size for her, too small, so her boots it was, incongruous under the satin and lace, rather like herself, mutton dressed as lamb in a dress more fit for a debutante. She yearned for the armor of a high collar and a well-boned bodice, a fan, even one without an attached stiletto. Anything to form a barrier between herself and the world, and something decidedly more substantial than the flimsy shawl that rode low between her elbows, more ornament than warmth.

A stone lion snarled at her from the one side. On the other, a unicorn lowered its horn to her feet. There were rabbits everywhere, disporting themselves among the carefully clipped yew hedges, frozen forever in marble in the imitation of movement. The gravel beneath her feet glimmered like pearls in the moonlight, marred only by the shadowy shapes of the topiary on either side.

She wove her way past dancing nymphs and leering satyrs. The house, with its lights, its conversation, felt very far away. She had no idea what she would say to William when she found him. She only knew she had come too far to turn back.

She saw him, at last, in a summerhouse posing as a Roman temple, a round structure with a domed top and carefully scaled columns circling all around. It was the sort of summerhouse that demanded a lake, but no one had ever bothered to build one.

There was a small flight of steps leading up, bounded by the bare stalks of rosebushes, pruned down for winter. William stood by the railing, his elbows on the ledge, his shoulders bowed, looking out over the acres of garden.

It was, Gwen realized, a rather pretty inversion, the prince in the tower, the lady clambering up the path below. It was steeper than it looked; the folly stood on its own rise. Stones slid and crunched beneath her half boots.

William turned, sharply. When he saw her, he straightened as if to leave.

"Don't go," she said quickly. "I'll be right up."

Gwen struggled up the final few steps, her gown tangling around her ankles like vines. The ridiculous gossamer shawl straggled from her elbows, catching on a thorn. In the summer, the temple would be banded by bank upon bank of fragrant roses. Now there were only thorns.

"It's more of a climb than it looks," she said tartly, plucking a thorn from her borrowed shawl.

William had stayed—that was true—but only in the most literal sense. His expression was removed, remote. All the liveliness that usually animated it was gone. He looked at her as though she were a not very interesting species of bug on a naturalist's table.

Fighting against a rising sense of panic, Gwen joined him by the curve of the balustrade, resting her elbows on the pitted stone. Up close, it wasn't marble, but a coarser substance, worn down by the English weather.

"There ought to be a lake here," she said. "With swans."

William didn't reply. To be fair, it wasn't necessarily a comment that demanded a response, but she had never before known him to resist the chance to remark on anything, however trivial.

Gwen fidgeted with her borrowed shawl, drawing it closer around her shoulders and letting it drop again. William's continued silence made her twitchy. It would have been easier if he had stormed off down the hill; then she might have stomped down after him, demanding explanations, berating him for turning his back on a lady, whatever came to mind.

It felt very quiet without William talking. She had never realized before how much she had relied upon him to keep their conversations going, to bounce her witticisms back to her and coax her out of her self-indulgent tempers. He had dealt with her sulks, her storms, her snits, but she hadn't the slightest notion of how to respond to his silence.

An animal rustled in the underbrush. Somewhere nearby, a bird squawked, an unlovely, unromantic sound. But William might have been carved from marble.

Gwen slammed the balustrade with the flat of her hand. Her palm stung with it, but her temper stung more. "For the love of God," she cried, "why won't you speak?"

Very slowly, William turned to face her. "What do you want me to say?"

He didn't sound angry, just immensely weary. Anger might have been easier to counter. One could return anger shout for shout.

She wanted—

Oh, blast it all. She didn't know what she wanted. She wanted to go back before yesterday. She wanted him to smile at her again. She wanted him to storm at her so that she could storm back.

There were half a dozen things she might have said, but the one that came out was, "I didn't sleep with you for information."

William raised his brows. "I suppose it was for my handsome face, then," he said.

"No," Gwen shot back. "For your glib tongue, more like."

It was only once the words were out of her mouth that she realized that there were many ways that could be interpreted, none of them good.

"Not like that. I didn't mean it like that." She tried again, lifting her head haughtily. "If I'd wanted information from you, I would have had it."

Somehow, that didn't sound much better.

"I'm very good at what I do, you know," she said shrilly.

William rubbed the side of his hand against his eyes. "Is your name even Gwen Meadows?" he asked wearily. "Or is that just more fustian?"

That inn in Bristol felt a thousand years ago, a tale told by another person, but even that small reference to their shared past felt like encouragement.

"Only the Fustian was fustian," Gwen said eagerly. She leaned towards him, the words pouring out of her like water from a dam, "I was christened Gwendolyn Meadows; I've spent most of my life in Shropshire; I was hired as chaperone for my neighbor's daughter. Ask me anything you want to know and I'll tell you. As long as it's mine to tell."

William's voice was carefully neutral. "There's much that isn't, I imagine."

"I've kept all kinds of secrets." Some of them hardly worth keeping, others a matter of life and death. She tried to catch his eye, to make him understand. "A slip of the tongue and a life might be forfeit for it. I've learned to keep my own counsel. There's no other way."

She remembered Jane, the other night, berating her for treating it all like a game. A game, maybe, but a very dangerous one. She'd grown used to it, the prevarications, the lies. It was all easy to justify when one was in the midst of it.

It was only when one stepped away that one realized the loneliness of it.

She'd thought that shared dangers created shared camaraderie; Jane had shown her the falsehood in that. They were strangers even to each other.

"How long have you been . . . a spy?" William pronounced the word with difficulty.

Gwen seized it as the olive branch it was. "Just over two years now." It seemed vitally important to make him understand, to make him understand she had a reason for doing as she'd done, that it wasn't wanton or careless. "I had a chance to go to France as chaperone to a neighbor's daughter, and it just . . . happened."

William raised his brows. "I hadn't realized you could catch spying like the measles."

That was more like himself again. Gwen took heart. "Not precisely, but the opportunity arose. I would have done anything rather than go back to my brother's house. In Paris, I was *free*." At least, she had felt free, in comparison with Shropshire.

"No relations carping at me, reminding me that I was dependent on them for every mouthful of bread I ate, just waiting for me to—to commit some indiscretion."

"If it was that bad," said William, still in that noncommittal tone, "why not just leave?"

Gwen looked at him, her lips pressing together. It would be easy to make some excuse, to dodge the truth. She'd made a habit of silence, relentlessly protecting her secrets.

But of all the secrets she couldn't tell, this was the only one that was truly hers to share. She owed William that much. However painful it might be.

"I had no money. And I couldn't expect anyone to marry me, not after— I made a terrible mistake a very long time ago. I was disinherited for it." In a rush, before she could think better of it, Gwen said, "I had a child. Out of wedlock. There. Now you can jeer and mock and what you will."

She felt more naked than she had the other night in that storeroom, with her skirts hiked to her knees and her bodice falling from her shoulders. She was stripped bare, all of her weakness exposed.

She raised her head, gathering the shreds of her pride around her, waiting for the inevitable expression of censure.

There was nothing but sympathy on William's face. "Would you truly expect me to condemn you for a child out of wedlock? I've three of my own such." He put out a hand, resting it on the balustrade beside her, not touching her, but there. Just there. "What happened?"

Gwen shook her head wordlessly, her neck bent, staring at

his hand, the fingers relaxed on the stone, strong and steady. It felt almost indecent to air the story of her youthful idiocy; she had kept it decently shrouded for so long. Her throat closed around the words.

"Do you really want to hear the full tale of my folly?" Gwen was embarrassed to hear how her voice shook. She tried to make a joke of it. "I could say I was young and stupid, but I was old enough to have known better. Four and twenty."

Just about Jane's age.

William's voice was soft and musical. "You don't have to tell me if you don't care to—but I'd like to hear it if you do."

Gwen took a deep breath, looking out over the fantastical topiary, the moon-washed paths. "His name was Timothy Fitzgerald."

The name felt strange on her lips. For years, it had been forbidden in her father's and then her brother's house, the silence speaking louder than words. Now, in the vastness of the Darlington gardens, it was reduced to what it was, just a name and not a particularly distinctive one.

Gwen cleared her throat. "He claimed to be the grandson of an Irish earl. Whether he really was or not, I don't know, but whatever he was, he had a way about him." She turned her head to look at the man next to her. "You put me in mind of him when I first met you."

William shifted on his feet, positioning himself more comfortably. "I'm guessing that's not intended as a compliment."

"You don't anymore," she said gruffly. She dared a quick glance at him. "Not now that I know you better."

William didn't say anything, but his hand covered hers and stayed there.

Gwen let the warmth of it seep into her, taking strength from the gesture. "My father told me he'd sooner cut me off without a shilling than see me married to an upstart Irish fortune hunter. I assumed he was bluffing. He had never denied me anything before."

She had been the spoiled darling of an indulgent parent. Her brother was the butt of their jokes, the object of their wit, but she—she could do no wrong. Until Tim. It had never occurred to her that she wouldn't be able to wear him down. She had blithely flouted his wishes, meeting with Tim in barns, in inns, in the disused attics of their own house.

"He wasn't bluffing?" William said gently.

"He was right, on all counts, but I was too stubborn to see it. I told Tim what my father had said. Tim said"—even now, even twenty years on, the memory made her shrivel inside, at her own fatuous credulity—"Tim said he had friends in high places, he just needed some time to muster them on our behalf. He'd be back in two weeks and then we could be married."

She'd gone around the village with her head high, wearing the secret of their engagement like a gaudy cloak.

"He didn't come back, did he?" William's hand tightened around hers. He said, conversationally, "Is it wrong to want to punch a man for something he did twenty years ago?"

"The two weeks passed, then a month, then two." Gwen stared woodenly ahead of her, seeing, not boxwood and marble, but the walls of her old bedroom, the flowered hangings on the windows. "And I found I was with child."

She had been so lonely those long, awful months. So scared. Her brother had just married. She remembered her sister-in-law's titters and sideways glances, her father's rage, her brother's smug delight.

Gwen stared straight ahead, out over the bushes. "Even then I was stupid. My family spirited me away to an elderly cousin on the Isle of Wight. I was to be a young widow, and the baby taken away as soon as it was born."

William's arm curved around her shoulders, offering her the support Tim hadn't. "I can't see you submitting to that."

"No." Her voice broke on the word. "It was easy enough to escape. They hadn't thought I would try. I had more than enough money—my father had never kept me short of coin. I made my way to Tim's old lodgings and was told he could be found at a place called Hadley Hall, in Hereford. It had been," she added, with clinical detachment, "seven months since I had last seen him."

"What happened?" Gwen could feel the flat of his hand on her back, moving in slow, soothing circles.

She was dimly aware that she didn't deserve this sympathy, but she was in the grip of the past. The images, so long denied, rolled over her. She could see it as if it were happening now, the pretty brick house with the white woodwork, an open carriage harnessed and ready before the house, with lap rugs and hot bricks in plenty.

It had been winter. There had been frost on the ground,

nipping her cheeks, making her nose drip, her belly heavy and uncomfortable beneath her shawl. She had climbed the stairs awkwardly, and then, just before she reached the top, the door had opened.

"I arrived just as they were going out for a drive. The maid opened the door, and there they were, the two of them, Tim all smiles, with his arm around her waist. She was wearing figured brocade. Blue."

Not that it mattered now, but the details were engraved on her brain, like a print from a morality tale. Blue, and her blond hair in long curls. Her face was plain, but that didn't matter. The sapphires around her neck more than made up for any defect of countenance.

Gwen looked up at William, all the anguish of memory in her eyes. "It was his wife. They had married three months before." Her hands clenched into fists at her sides, the nails biting into her palms. "Married while I was waiting for him to come and take me away, more fool I."

"What of the child?"

The sympathy in William's eyes nearly undid her. Gwen looked away. "The child came early." With a macabre attempt at humor, she said, "Falling down the steps probably didn't help."

She could still remember the feeling of falling, her foot slipping on the step, her clumsy body bearing her backwards, arms flailing, the world circling past her, and Tim, Tim, just standing there, standing at the top of the steps, making no move to help her. She had landed with a jolt that had jarred her to the bone. Jarred her to the bone and jarred Tim's baby from her womb.

Not at once, of course. The pains had started hours after. She had scarcely felt them. What was physical pain compared to the agony of the soul? She had vowed never to expose herself to such pain again.

William drew her against his side, making a comfortable place for her head against his shoulder. "Did he acknowledge you?"

"Are you mad?" Gwen's laughter had a wild edge to it. "He told her I was a cousin, a poor cousin, on my own in the world. I don't know if she believed him."

His cheek touched her temple. "He must have led her a merry dance."

"I had a lucky escape. I know," she said flatly. She had been told so time and again. "But my pride stung all the same."

She could feel his breath against her hair. "Better your pride than your heart."

"No," said Gwen, and pulled away, nearly bumping him on the nose. "Don't you think I haven't thought that myself? But it's wrong, all wrong."

She had spent all these years atoning. And for what? For nothing. For less than nothing. For a man who hadn't been worth it in the first place. She had confused infatuation with affection and spent twenty years paying the price.

"A broken heart might have been preferable. At least then it would have meant there had been something worth having,"

Gwen said passionately. "Rather than simply having been made a fool."

William threw up his hands. "And haven't we all been? There's no one who hasn't been made a fool for love at some time or another." His expression sobered as he added, "We all have moments in our past of which we're not proud."

"Jack's mother." Gwen's throat felt scratchy and dry. She pulled back, her eyes searching his face. It seemed only right that since she'd bared herself to the bone, his secrets should be forfeit as well. "That was what you said the other night."

"So I did." For a moment, she thought William meant to leave it at that, but with a sigh, he detached himself from her, running a hand through his already rumpled hair. "I'm not proud of my behavior—although I wouldn't give Jack away," he added hastily, "whatever trouble he may have caused."

The exact nature of that trouble lay unspoken between them. That would wait for later, for the intrusion of reality. For now, they were divorced from the world, marooned in the summerhouse with the gardens lying all around them.

William leaned his elbows on the balustrade. "It was just after my Maria died. I was living at the bottom of a bottle, half-soused most days, except in the saddle. My commanding officer sent me off on a diplomatic errand to a petty Rajput warlord who was in the process of signing a treaty with the Company. He meant to do me a kindness."

"I take it that it didn't turn out so?"

"No." William's expression was wry. "We were entertained

lavishly. Quite lavishly." Gwen frowned at the emphasis on those last words. "I stumbled out into the courtyard, looking for a bucket into which to stick my head, I was that drunk. There was a woman there. I thought she must be one of the dancing girls. She certainly gave me that impression."

"But she wasn't."

"No." William's face was grim. "She was the pampered youngest daughter of our host. He'd arranged a match for her with a neighboring landowner, a gentleman of a certain age, and it was that displeased about it, she was. She wanted to get some of her own back. I didn't know that at the time, you ken." He frowned. "It was an odd thing for a gently bred lady to do, but Juli was—" He wrestled for words. "I suppose you could call her volatile. She'd never been refused anything before, and she was mad as fire."

"Not that I've ever known anyone like that," murmured Gwen.

She wondered whether she would have gone to bed with Tim if her father hadn't so vehemently warned her off him. Perhaps. She had certainly been infatuated, and Tim had been persuasive. But it was pique more than passion that had pushed her to make that final leap into his bed.

"Her father caught us together." As Gwen glanced sharply at him, William said hastily, "It wasn't what you think! It was— You might call it an embrace, if you will. A rather enthusiastic one, but clothed, for all that. But it was enough."

Gwen pictured a younger William, drunk and confused, caught, metaphorically at least, with his breeches down. "What did he do to you?"

"He couldn't take it out on me—not officially. I'd have preferred that. A good whipping was what I deserved, but he had his own reasons for wanting to stay on good terms with the Company. So he cast her out. She'd defiled herself, he said. She was dead to him. And I was welcome to take her with me, if I liked. As a gift." William shook his head, incredulous. "His own daughter, and he threw her away like a horse that had cracked a bone."

"So you took her with you." It wasn't a question.

"What else was I to do? She'd been thrown out into the world, and it was all my fault. There was nothing else for it."

Once again, Gwen was struck by the basic decency of the man. He'd had no ties to this girl, nothing but a kiss, and yet he'd taken her home with him, taken her in.

Tim had watched her tumble down the stairs, his child in her belly, and never held out a hand to help her.

She wasn't entirely naïve. She imagined the girl must have been attractive enough. But even so.

William looked at her with eyes like a lost puppy put out on the stoop. "I'd have understood her being unhappy. It can't have been easy, going from being the favorite daughter of a man of property to—well, to being the concubine of a foreign cavalry officer with two motherless children to be cared for. I tried to make it as right with her as I could, but . . ."

"You couldn't have known that one night's overindulgence would land you in such a situation," said Gwen briskly. "It was as much her doing as yours."

William shrugged, uncomfortable with her reassurance. "It

was difficult for Alex and Kat as well. She could be charming, you see, when she was in one of her happy moods. She'd sit them on her lap and tell them stories. But when she was in a rage, she'd call them foreign brats, wouldn't touch them, wouldn't even speak to them. One day she'd be in high spirits, the next day she'd be tearing the canes from the windows and smashing the rods, just to hear them break." William bowed his head, his entire posture an expression of defeat. "She killed herself when Jack was two years old. Took a knife and drove it through her breast."

Reaching out, Gwen rested a hand against his chest. "I'm so sorry."

The words were painfully inadequate.

"So was I." William looked up at her, his face bleak. "The worst of it was that I was glad to be rid of her." He swallowed hard. "I've always wondered, if I'd been more patient, if I'd been kinder—"

"No," said Gwen firmly. "If someone wants to wound himself, he will. Does Jack . . ."

William caught her meaning without her having to say more. "Has he his mother's moods, do you mean? No. If he's angry, no one can say he hasn't had reason for it." He mulled it over. "If anything, he's almost frighteningly self-contained. I imagine it's something to do with his mother. He was just old enough to have the sense that something was wrong with the way she swung up and down."

Watching William's face as he spoke of his son, Gwen felt her chest tighten with an entirely unfamiliar emotion, a fondness so intense that it bordered on pain. This wasn't about lust or passion. She wanted to cradle his head to her chest and stroke his silvered curls. She wanted to soothe away the cares of all those past years, to make comforting noises and press kisses to the top of his head. It was an utterly unaccountable sensation.

It took Gwen a moment to identify it as tenderness. It was just—just that he was so good. She couldn't find the proper words for it. He might play at being devil-may-care, but in the end, when it came down to it, she'd never met anyone who cared so deeply.

The knowledge of it shook her to her very core.

William was looking at her, his eyes the pale blue of a spring sky. "Now you know the worst of me," he said.

"You haven't a very good definition of 'worst,'" Gwen said unsteadily. She felt a little punch-drunk, as if the night air had gone to her head. Tentatively, she reached up and touched his cheek, feeling the faint graze of stubble against her knuckles. "You'll have to work on it."

Gently, he took her hand and lifted it to his lips. He didn't press a kiss to her palm, that rogue's trick. Instead, he brushed a kiss across her knuckles. It was a courtly gesture, and it made Gwen's knees wobble in a decidedly undignified way.

As she stared at him, trying to think of something to say, something witty and cutting, he leaned forward and, very gently, kissed her. It was a kiss for sunlit meadows, for lost innocence, for all the courtships she had never had, delicate and tender.

One would never have imagined that they had rolled on the ground together in pure carnal madness just the night before.

His lips, feather soft on hers, lifted gently away. Gwen slowly opened her eyes to find him looking at her. He still held both of her hands in his, lightly. All it would take would be for her to step away. She knew, without being told, that he would make no move to hold her. It was all up to her.

"There's no fool like an old fool," she said helplessly.

William's eyes crinkled at the corners. He was still holding her hands, and now he tugged her closer. "Is that me you're talking about?"

Gwen looked at him and knew that she was lost. Whatever she had felt for Tim, it was moonlight to sunlight, small beer to brandy. Love, that most inconvenient of emotions, was determined to make a fool of her. Again.

More fool she. "I was referring to myself," Gwen said shakily.

William drew her closer; her borrowed skirts whispered around his legs. "Then shall we be fools together?"

Chapter 22

By morning, the enchantment had faded. The trees and the hedges, the follies and the maze, were again the plain gray walls of their cell. But Sir Magnifico had found the breach in the defenses, and it was he who led the way through the gap in the wall. Down the slope, just ahead of them, lay verdant trees, not an illusion this time, but healthy and true, laden with ripe fruit. They had only to cross the river to reach them, to be free of the dread enchantment that clung like soot to the very air around the doomed tower.

But Amarantha was still inside, and they would neither of them leave her to her fate. It was with a heavy heart that Plumeria set her steps again towards the Tower—although this time, she did so with the assurance of Sir Magnifico's sword by her side as they girded themselves for one great, final battle.

—From *The Convent of Orsino* by A Lady

e with an indefinable sense of content-
kes of which he hadn't experienced for

clothes were warm and soft and faintly scented with lavender, and there was a head pillowed in the curve of his shoulder. As from a dream, snippets of the night before came back to him, less memories than the impression of emotion, hurt and confusion and pity and tenderness, and, in the wake of it all, the wonder of discovering each other, a long, leisurely exploration without hurry or shame.

William remembered, from very long ago, the words of the marriage service, pronounced in a sweltering box of a church in Madras: *With my body I thee worship.* There might not have been a priest to solemnize their arrangements last night, but the words seemed to apply all the same.

In sleep, Gwen's face seemed softer, devoid of the wariness it wore in waking hours. It didn't surprise William that she should be wary, given what he now knew. The thought of the betrayal she had experienced at the hands of that Timothy, that rotter, made his hands itch to form fists.

Too late to track the man down and thrash him now, sadly, at least not without compromising Gwen's reputation further. Still, it seemed unlikely a man like that would confine his attentions to the home. William hoped, devoutly, that this Timothy had contracted a nasty case of the French pox. In India, he'd seen more than one man suffering the effects of sexual incontinence, and the even nastier mercury cure that followed.

The thought cheered William immensely. Yes, a course of mercury applied to a tender spot of the anatomy would serve that Tim just right.

What kind of man denied his own unborn child?

It was worse than repugnant. William glanced down at Gwen's sleeping face. A lucky escape, indeed. That would have been no life for her, yoked to a man like that; she was too intelligent not to have seen eventually what her father had, that the man she thought she loved was a two-bit fortune hunter with no more character than a slug. She would have come to despise him and herself with him.

Not to mention that she wouldn't be in bed with William right now. Odd the twists and turns through which one wandered to come to where one was. Right now, all the reversals, all the disappointments and missteps, felt like nothing but a prelude to this, this moment, this bed, this woman.

The object of William's sentimental musings made a sort of snorting noise and rolled violently over, pulling the covers with her. The tangle of black hair disappeared under the sheets, accompanied by disgruntled murmurings.

William regarded the palpitating sheets with amusement. Not a morning person, was she?

"Good morning," he said cheerfully, and was rewarded with strange wigglings and an exceedingly grumpy mumbling noise from beneath the covers.

After a few minutes of rustles and grumbles, one baleful gray eye emerged from under the corner of the sheet.

"It's almost dawn, isn't it?" she mumbled.

"Regrettably, yes." The sky was turning a pale gray around the edges, the yellow-gray that was the first herald of dawn. "A pity it is that there's no way to turn back the sky as one might a clock. Can't you just see the stars and the moon, all spiraling back into night?"

William could picture it as he said it, the clouds, the stars cartwheeling past, and they still warm and safe in their bed. It couldn't last, of course. Sooner or later, they would have to emerge from their cocoon. There was still Lizzy to fetch and missing jewels to find. But for now, just for now . . .

"Backwards or forwards, the hour is what it is." A tousled Gwen emerged from the covers, fighting her way through the nest of linen. She reached for the candle on the nightstand, lighting it with a quick flick of the flint. A pale golden light diffused itself along her bare arms and shoulders. "Either way, it's only borrowed time."

If their time was borrowed, they might as well make the most of it. Her skin was like honey in the candlelight. William tugged her down to him, the sheet tangling around her waist, her hair falling around them like a veil.

"No regrets?" he said huskily, once his lips were his own again. She was leaning over him, her elbows resting on his chest. It made his just-healed wound ache, but not enough to want her to move.

Gwen shook her head, her hair brushing his chest. "No. No regrets." But her face was troubled. She rolled over off him, back onto her own pillow. "Only . . ."

William propped himself up on one elbow. He could feel

his muscles protesting; this was a form of exercise he hadn't taken in some time. "Only what?"

Gwen stared up at the ceiling, at the ornate plasterwork arrangement of fruit and vines. "Our lives are neither of them uncomplicated." Her expression was wistful. "If we were twenty and unencumbered . . ."

William didn't think she would have liked him much at twenty. He had been an insufferable peacock back then, brash and sure. He wasn't sure why his Maria had put up with him, but for the fact that she was younger still, and no judge of character.

He twined a strand of Gwen's hair around his fingers, dark against his tanned skin. "We would neither of us be who we are," he said. "I wouldn't want to go back to twenty. Would you?"

Her lips pursed together in thought. William knew that expression now, as he did a dozen others. "No. If I'd had the life I wanted at twenty—"

"You wouldn't be here," he finished for her, stretching back against the pillow, his arms up over his head, like a self-satisfied pasha.

"You do think highly of yourself, don't you?" Amusement fading, she propped herself up on one arm, her black hair falling down around her shoulders. "There's no hope in it for us, you know. Perhaps a few more stolen nights, but once we get to Selwick Hall, you'll have your Lizzy back and . . ."

She made an expressive gesture, indicating absolutely nothing.

"I doubt my daughter is that easily scandalized," said William. Not if they kept their bedroom door closed and their voices low.

"Hmph," said Gwen. "Being your daughter, perhaps not."

"As for stolen nights . . ." William grimaced at the words.

There was something repugnant about the image, something hole in the corner that sat ill with him. As for a few nights, he wanted more than that; he wanted months of them, years of them. Just what the corollary of that was, he couldn't quite bring himself to say.

So instead, he said, "We're both of age and free. Where might the barrier be?" A thought struck him. "Is it my family situation? I know I'm not what you might call eligible. I've been an adventurer and a wanderer, with no family name to speak. If that's it—"

"No! That's not it at all." There was something rather reassuring about the haste with which she said it. "If you're an adventurer, then so am I."

He reached up to touch her cheek. "Two rogues together."

For a moment, Gwen leaned into his touch. Just for a moment.

She squirmed to a sitting position, tugging the sheet with her. "It's no good. We only came back to find Agnes. Once Agnes is safe—and the jewels," Gwen added as an afterthought, "Jane will want to go back to France."

William felt a deep sinking feeling in the pit of his stomach. Bath was one thing. Paris felt very far away. "And you with her?"

"She can't stay at her cousin's house without a chaperone. Even in Paris, that might raise eyebrows. If she goes, I go back with her."

"You don't sound altogether delighted by the prospect." William tried not to sound too glad of that.

Gwen shrugged, hitching the sheet higher with a quick, impatient gesture. "It's important work," she said defensively. "I am good at it."

"Of course you are," said William. "I've seen you at it. But is it what you want?"

Her face was troubled. "I thought it was."

"What's changed, then?" William tried to sound as though the answer didn't matter, as though it were purely an abstract inquiry, as if the thought of her going away across the Channel, away from him, wasn't making his stomach twist.

Gwen made a dismissive gesture. "It's foolish."

William captured her hand, twining his fingers through hers. "And wasn't last night proof enough that folly is better than sense? Tell me."

Not that he necessarily thought that he would be the cause, but . . .

Gwen leaned her head back against the carved headboard. "We founded the League together, Jane and I—and her cousin Amy, the one at Selwick Hall. You'll meet her today," she added as an aside.

"Hmm," said William, trying not to look as disappointed as he felt.

"I'd thought we were equal partners, but it seems Jane

doesn't feel quite the same way. She's cut me out, kept information from me. It's her League; she's well within her rights." Gwen's face was bleak. "But I'd believed she thought better of me than that."

William struggled to a sitting position. "Just a moment." Disappointment warred with confusion. "That child is in charge of your operations?"

"That child, as you call her, is one of the foremost spymasters in France."

"Good God." So much of what he'd seen the past few weeks began to make sense, the odd deference shown to the girl, Gwen's concern. She wasn't that young when one thought of it; at twenty-three, he had been leading men. His Jack was just about the same age as this girl, and he'd already run off with the jewels of Berar. "It's genius, it is. Who would ever suspect a slip of a girl like that?"

"That," said Gwen austerely, "is exactly the point. That is what has kept us safe for the past two years. Bonaparte hasn't the highest opinion of women. As for a young and pretty one . . ."

It really was a rather brilliant conceit. "But what about you?" he asked.

He still couldn't quite get his head around the idea of Gwen following the Wooliston girl's orders. Even if he had seen the evidence of it with his own eyes, it was hard for him to imagine his Gwen playing second fiddle to anyone.

The thought caught William up short. When had she become his Gwen? The surge of possessiveness was as strong as it was unexpected. He wanted to wrap his arms around her and defy anyone who tried to take her from him.

Fortunately, Gwen was too caught up in her own thoughts to notice his abstraction. "I'd thought I was indispensible to her."

William squeezed her hands. "Cut you out, has she?" he said sympathetically.

"I was never in." There was a world of pain and confusion beneath Gwen's jaunty facade. He had seen the look before, in soldiers who woke from a drugged sleep to be told they'd lost a limb. "Apparently, I'm too impulsive."

"Charmingly impetuous," William substituted gallantly, repressing the urge to shake the cool and composed Miss Wooliston.

Gwen's lips twisted in something that wasn't quite a smile. "You're not helping."

"You don't have to go back with her," William said. The words were out of his mouth before he could stop them. Once out, there was nothing but to say, "You have a home with me. Should your Paris plans fail," he added quickly.

"You haven't a home for yourself," Gwen protested. "You can't offer what's not there."

William leaned forward eagerly. "That's not entirely true. When I haven't been pursued by ruffians, I've spent a bit of time looking into purchasing a cottage somewhere. I'm not entirely without funds, and—" He broke off, realizing just how foolish it must all sound to her. "A cottage must sound deadly dull after the life you've been living."

"With you in it? Not likely." Realizing what she had said,

she swung her legs over the bed, retreating in a tangle of hair and a flurry of sheets. Leaning over to scoop them off the floor, she tossed William his breeches. "You'd best get back to your own room before anyone comes to wake you. We don't want to shock the younger generation."

William buttoned up his breeches. "I don't know," he said thoughtfully. It might do that Miss Wooliston good to realize that her chaperone wasn't entirely without other options. All of them last night, with the smugness of youth, had treated Gwen as their own personal Methuselah, firmly on the shelf, past the age for human emotions. She might not mind, but he minded on her behalf. "It might do them good. Shake them up a bit."

Gwen ignored him. "There are your shoes, under the bed," she said, kicking them out from under. She peered around the room. "What did you do with your jacket?"

"You mean what did you do with my jacket?" William cocked a brow at her. Her own garments were scattered with betraying abandon across the floor, his shirt intimately tangled with her chemise. "I seem to remember you removing it somewhat impulsively. . . ."

"Shirt," said Gwen, and shoved the aforementioned item at him.

William shrugged into the shirt, tugging it down over his head. "I wasn't suggesting that we pose for them in flagrante," he said innocently. "Just a few rumpled bedclothes, some lingering looks . . ."

"Out!" Gwen said, and punctuated the directive with a wadded-up cravat.

William left, grinning.

He wasn't grinning an hour later when they all assembled in the front hall. The preparations for their departure were, if not military, at least martial. Six hefty footmen, with the look of former pugilists, had been conscripted to come with them.

"Just in case," said Mr. Dorrington airily as they stood in the front of the house, waiting for the horses to be brought around. "Biscuit?"

No one had wanted to stay for breakfast. An air of urgency had infected them all; even Miss Wooliston was tapping her foot against the stair. Pistols bristled from belts, spare ammunition shoved into deep pockets.

This, William realized. This was Gwen's real life. Not their interlude in their borrowed bedchamber, not last night's confessions in the summerhouse, but this world of shadows and dangers, of footmen turned to guards and society ladies who carried pistols with their parasols.

William noticed that Gwen had her trusty parasol, the purple frills incongruous against her starkly tailored traveling dress. He had no doubt that the sword had been cleaned and sharpened.

"How long is it to Selwick Hall?" William asked.

"Four hours," said Gwen. She looked at him and then quickly glanced away again. Four hours and then—what?

"Don't worry," said Mr. Dorrington, mercifully immune to undercurrents. "I know a shortcut. It will take at least an hour off our route."

Lady Henrietta regarded her husband with deep trepidation. Like the other ladies, she was dressed for hard travel, in a well-cut riding habit and sturdy boots. "This isn't going to be like that other shortcut, is it?"

Mr. Dorrington adopted an expression of wounded innocence. "That was a perfectly good shortcut."

"Apart from taking three hours longer than the normal route," pointed out his wife.

William listened to their cheerful bickering with only half an ear. His attention was on Gwen.

He was painfully aware that nothing was resolved between them. From the stiff set of her back, the furtive glances she sent him when she thought he wasn't watching, he knew, without being quite sure why, that she intended to make good her word and go back to France. She wouldn't look at him so otherwise, like a beggar staring at a bakery window, hunger and denial, all in one.

Stay, he wanted to say. *Stay with me.*

But for what? More nights like last night; there was that, at least. The memory of it brought a smile to his lips. Not merely for the obvious reasons, although those were there, sure enough. No, the sweetest memory was falling asleep with her arm across his chest, her head tucked beneath his chin. He wanted to fall asleep with her at night and wake with her in the morning and bicker with her in between.

Not much of an argument, was it? There was no poet had ever won his lady with "Come bicker with me and be my love."

"Do I have something on my nose?" she said, and he realized he had been staring, letting his horse do the work of following the path.

They had fallen a bit behind the others, more by accident than by design. Overhead, the sun glimmered through the leaves, creating a dappled pattern on the dusty surface of the road. It was the sort of day the poets had promised, April in England as April was meant to be, with the sun shining down on them and a breeze rustling the young leaves, a breeze that cooled pleasantly without chilling him through. A lark trilled its courting song, the high, clear notes floating on the breeze.

"Just a bit of dust," William prevaricated.

Come away with me, he wanted to say. Away from these ridiculous young creatures who treated her with mingled tolerance and amusement. Not unkindly, no, but it was there all the same. Surely he could do better than that for her. If love was enough to offer.

He leaned forward, near enough that his leg grazed hers. "Gwen?"

"Yes?" She left off scrubbing the nonexistent dirt from her nose and looked up at him. Her parasol rode by her hip, like the sword of a medieval knight.

The words he had meant to say died in his throat.

Her loyalty, her fierce sense of honor, those were the things he admired about her. How could he ask her to give that up? That might be love too, but it was a craven, selfish kind of love, the sort of love that destroyed the object of its affection.

"Nothing," he said, and mustered a smile that was so palpably fake it made his teeth ache. "Nothing."

Gwen eyed him narrowly, but she didn't question him.

"We're not far from Selwick Hall," she said. "Dorrington's shortcut appears to have worked. Astonishing as that may be."

"I heard that," called back Mr. Dorrington. He looked like he was about to say more in that vein, but something caught his attention. Slowing his mount, he cocked his head, listening. "Was that a shot?"

One by one, they stopped and listened. From the distance, William could hear it, the faint crackle of pistol fire.

Lady Henrietta's face had gone pale beneath her jaunty hat. "It's coming from the Hall," she said.

"Then we'd better get there, hadn't we?" Gwen said tartly, and set her heels to the sides of her horse. The others followed suit, cantering down the road, spurred on by the sound of loud voices, the crackle of broken glass.

The road let out on a slight rise, just above the valley in which the house was set. William drew up his horse sharply, vaguely aware that around him, the others were doing the same.

"This," said Miss Wooliston, "was just what I was afraid might happen." She sounded more annoyed than alarmed.

Selwick Hall would have been a perfectly pleasant house, built of cream-colored stone, with a central block flanked by two smaller wings. There was a pair of tasteful columns on either side of the front door and classical pediments above the windows.

Only one thing marred the classical symmetry of the facade: the mob of roughly garbed men who appeared to be doing their best to fire holes into it. There were a good dozen of them, all of them making a great deal of noise and firing their pistols with a remarkable inaccuracy of aim.

William saw the movement of a curtain and a glint of metal as one of the defenders took a shot through a window, ducking back again against the wall. It was met by an answering burst of fire from the attackers. An arrow whizzed down from an upstairs window, narrowly missing skewering one of the attackers in the nose.

Selwick Hall was under siege.

Chapter 23

The Knight had brought Amarantha to the very highest point of the very highest tower. The mirror lay between them, the sunlight dancing on its gleaming surface, hinting at the mysteries it contained, the mysteries that might crush the one and set the other free—but which?

The Knight of the Silver Tower raised his visor. "It is of no avail," quoth he, and his face was terrible in its beauty. "We are two halves of the same whole. You can no more destroy me than I you."

Plumeria leapt up the final stair. "Perhaps she may not," said Plumeria, and brought she forth her sword, "but I have no such qualms."

—From *The Convent of Orsino* by A Lady

A n arrow whizzed past Gwen's nose.

"Sorry!" shouted a girl from the window, who could only be William's daughter. The features were a feminine mold of her father's, impishness incarnate. "Wind!"

Next to her, a paler version of Jane appeared in the window, hauling what looked to be a bucket of steaming water.

"Gardy-loo!" Agnes called out, rather unnecessarily in Gwen's opinion. She dumped the boiling liquid over the heads of the invaders, one of whom jumped back just in time, as his companion sputtered and ran in circles.

"Enjoy your bath!" yelled Lizzy, ducking as the maddened attacker, shaking water out of his eyes, stooped and lifted a handful of small stones, flinging them in her general direction. Gwen could hear the crack of glass breaking and an indignant squawk from William's daughter, which sounded like something about not being the least bit sporting, and if that was the way they were going to behave . . .

William didn't wait to hear more.

He rose in his stirrups, holding his pistol aloft like a sword. The sun lit his bright hair, hiding the lines on his face, the circles beneath his eyes. His horse lifted on its hind legs, man and mount moving in such concert that it dazzled Gwen's eyes.

"After me!" he cried. His voice was like a bell, calling men to arms.

"Huzzah!" shouted Miles Dorrington, waving his hat in the air, and Gwen realized she was shouting too, her throat raw with it as they pounded down the slope, at the startled mob of motley attackers, who turned and gaped and then broke and ran, every man for himself. One had the nerve to take a potshot at Gwen, but William was between them, leveling and firing before Gwen had even seen the danger. The pistol spiraled out of the man's hand.

"Nice shot!" shouted Gwen.

William grinned at her. "I was aiming for his horse."

Before Gwen had time to point out that the man didn't have a horse, William was cantering away again, riding down a fleeing crew of attackers while his daughter sent arrows flying over their heads, most of which landed in the brush far to the side but added to the general air of excitement and confusion.

The rout was quick and total. The attackers broke and scattered, running for the hills. They didn't even bother to make an attempt to fight back.

Gwen thought that very poor form. It was also more than a little bit suspect. Their crew abandoned the fleeing attackers and pounded down towards the house, boisterous and triumphant, with Agnes and Lizzy cheering them on from the windows.

"The cavalry is here!" shouted Miles, waving his hat to the defenders in the windows.

Lord Richard's head popped out of a window. "You're about half an hour too early," he said enigmatically, and disappeared again.

"Of all the ungrateful—," began Lady Henrietta indignantly, but her husband silenced her by pulling her close and pressing a smacking kiss to her lips.

From inside, Gwen could hear the sound of bolts being drawn and miscellaneous pieces of furniture being hauled away.

The great door opened and the defenders poured out: Amy and Richard; their butler, Stiles, who still appeared to be operating under the delusion that he was the scourge of the high seas; and, just behind them, the two schoolgirls.

William was off his horse in a moment. His expression was rather what Gwen imagined one might see on a medieval visionary having his first divine visitation, dazed and joyful and lit from within.

He held out his arms. "Lizzy!"

There was no mistaking the family resemblance. The girl's hair was a bronzed brown rather than carrot red, her eyes brown rather than blue, but the broad smile was the same. At the sight of her father, the girl's face lit up.

"Father!" She dropped her bow and flung herself into her father's arms. "I thought it was you!"

The exuberant Lizzy was subsumed in her father's embrace, her springy hair crushed under his arm, her face buried in his shoulder.

Despite the imminent risk of paternal asphyxiation, Gwen could hear Lizzy's muffled voice still going at a cracking pace, saying, "When did you get here? Why didn't you tell me you were coming to England? Did they tell you—" as her father made vague and happy mumbling noises, stroking her bright hair and doing his best to get a word in edgewise.

It was quite the touching family reunion.

All around her, happy families reunited, hugging, exclaiming, talking over the events of the day as they all streamed back into the house in joyous, chattering groups. Lord Richard and Miles Dorrington bickered with the comfort of old friendship while their wives enthusiastically rehashed the battle. Colonel

Reid and his daughter were lost in each other, although Agnes stayed close by her old school friend, hovering near, occasionally adding something to the conversation.

Gwen backed away, knowing herself to be superfluous. They would never even notice she was gone. Whatever William might have said, in the aftermath of a rather active night, this was his real life, and no matter how he protested, her place in it was done. She had brought him to his daughter. The quest was ended.

She ought to have been triumphant, but she wasn't. Instead, she felt like a week of wet Wednesdays. Better for all concerned if she slipped away here and now, saving awkward good-byes and protestations that wouldn't be meant. It was the coward's way, she knew—she, who had always prided herself on staring danger in the face. But the muzzle of a pistol was one thing. To look in William's eyes and see nothing but kindness—or, even worse, pity—was quite another matter entirely.

It was his pity she feared the most. She remembered, with an uncomfortable twist of the heart, the story he had told her last night, of Jack's mother. He had taken her with him because he felt responsible, because she had nowhere else to go.

Well, then. It wasn't as though she hadn't anyplace else to go. She would go back to France with Jane, and that was all there was to it.

And if she didn't feel quite as thrilled about it as she should, that was nobody's business but hers.

Selwick Hall wasn't so very far from the coast. With any luck, they could be on a boat in time for the next tide. Gwen twisted around, looking for Jane. Agnes was with the Reids and the Selwicks with the Dorringtons, but Jane was nowhere to be found.

A tingle of unease penetrated Gwen's distracted mind as she threaded her way through the ground-floor rooms, looking for her missing charge. Something felt not quite right. And it wasn't just Jane. The windows in the front had been clumsily barricaded, but the ones on the sides had been left unguarded, even unlatched. If the attackers hadn't concentrated all their energies on the front . . .

And why had they? Selwick Hall wasn't exactly fortified. There were French doors around the back and any manner of welcoming windows on the sides. There were trellises that might be climbed and balconies for the taking. If they had scattered, they could have gained entry to the house in any one of a dozen places, and there would have been nothing the hard-pressed defenders could do to stop them.

As it was, they had conducted their attack in the most idiotic manner imaginable, shooting into the woodwork, flinging stones at windows, and then breaking and running at the first sign of reinforcements, as if . . .

As if they hadn't really been trying to gain entry in the first place.

At least, not that way. With everyone at the front of the house, fighting off the motley mob of attackers, the rear was left undefended. It wouldn't be hard for one man, alone, to sneak in and take whatever it was he wanted.

Gwen's steps quickened. Through the window of the music room, she could see a horse tied hard by the old tower, far from the rest of their mounts. There was a man, running lightly through the garden, vaulting the boxwood hedge. He shoved a small packet into the saddlebag, making haste to unloop the horse's reins from the door of the old tower.

Lifting her skirts, Gwen started to run, making for the long salon that ran along the back of the house, with its door onto the gardens. But someone else had preceded her. The door hung ajar, wafting back and forth in the breeze as Jane hurried down the steps, the trailing skirt of her riding habit looped over one wrist.

Jane paused on the steps that led down to the gardens. "Leaving so soon, Chevalier?"

Her voice rang clear and true across the dry fountains and shrouded statues. From the folds of her skirt she withdrew a pistol, shiny with mother-of-pearl. It sparkled in the sunlight as she leveled it at the man who was hastily swinging onto the back of his mount.

"Or should I say . . . Monsieur le Jardinier?"

When the Chevalier lifted his hand, there was a pistol in it as well, a much larger, deadlier-looking pistol. "As we are in England, a simple 'Gardener' will suffice, Miss Wooliston." He cocked a brow. "Or should I say . . . the Pink Carnation?"

Gwen skidded to a stop behind the French doors, hastily turning over possibilities. She could call for the others, but he was already on horseback; all he had to do was turn and run. By the time she had assembled the others and dragged their weary horses from their happy grazing, he would be long gone. She could try to get behind him, but the same problems applied; if he saw her, he would be off like a shot.

A shot . . .

"I pray you, dear lady." The Chevalier smiled at Jane. With the sun lighting his face, he looked like the gallant from one of Fragonard's *fêtes galantes*, charming and free of care. "Don't insult my intelligence by telling me you have no idea what I mean."

"I wasn't going to," said Jane, her wrist steady. "I was going to tell you to drop those jewels and step away from that horse."

"Ah, but why should I? My pistol, darling flower among flowers, is bigger than yours."

"Size isn't everything," said Jane coolly. "Would you back your aim against mine?"

"I should never make the mistake of underestimating so formidable a lady." The Chevalier's voice was disconcertingly warm, almost tender. As if realizing he had betrayed himself, he added mockingly, "You slay me with your eyes alone."

"Yes," said Jane, "but a bullet is far more effective."

Gwen tended to agree. But how to get a clear shot? Jane was between her and the Chevalier, and none of the windows yielded the proper angle.

Cocking her pistol, Gwen edged closer to the door.

"It seems," said the Chevalier, "we are at a standoff. I am sure I do not need to tell you how very much I wish the circumstances might have been otherwise—Jeanne."

"It's no use to presume intimacies that cannot be," said Jane, sounding far more rueful than Gwen considered seemly. Hadn't the man just admitted to being the Gardener? Jane raised her pistol. "I cannot let you leave. You know that."

"I would happily dwell in your heart forever," said the Chevalier, "but I fear I have a boat to catch. Unless—you care to come with me? Think what a partnership we might have. Bonaparte is generous to those in his service."

This, thought Gwen indignantly, was how the devil swayed souls to his purpose.

"Not," said Jane, "unless you change your politics."

"In that case," said the Chevalier resignedly, "I imagine you'll just have to shoot me." He tucked his own pistol into his belt and gathered up his reins. "Such a pity."

"Give yourself in," said Jane desperately. "I can arrange terms for you." Their eyes locked across the field. "Don't make me do this."

"You won't," said the Chevalier softly. "You can't shoot me any more than I can shoot you."

That, decided Gwen, was quite enough of that.

Kicking the door open, Gwen burst out onto the balcony.

"She might not," said Gwen, brandishing her pistol with a flourish. "But I have no such qualms."

As the others stood frozen in shock, Gwen leveled her pistol and fired.

William breathed in the scent of his daughter's hair, marveling at the fact that she was safe and well, even if she couldn't aim an arrow to save her life.

Hard on the heels of relief followed a blaze of paternal indignation. "What the devil were you doing, running away from school like that?" he demanded. "You had us half scared out of our wits!"

"I didn't know you were coming back," said his daughter cheerfully. "And we really didn't think it would take us this long to get here. Agnes said it was four days—"

"It usually is," said the much-put-upon Agnes defensively. "By coach."

"Yes, but we weren't going by coach," said Lizzy. "We dressed ourselves up as boys—rather convincing ones, really—and took to the side roads."

The great relish with which she related their exploits gave William reason to believe that the experience had not, in fact, been an overly onerous one for her. In fact, she seemed dangerously close to enjoying it.

William gave his offspring a narrow-eyed look. "But why did you run? Do you know the state you had us all in?"

Lizzy wafted that away. "Don't worry," she said, giving him her best look of wide-eyed innocence. "It was all quite necessary. Once Jack sent me that letter—"

William held his daughter out to arm's length. "And what letter might that be?"

"Jack said he'd made some changes in his employment and it might get a bit sticky for me at the school," said Lizzy blithely.

"Sticky?" William repeated. He made a mental note to give his second son the dressing-down of his life. If he could find him. Somehow, he doubted he'd have much success with trying to send him to his room. That hadn't worked with the scamp even before he'd become a master of espionage.

"If someone decided to use me as a hostage for his good behavior," explained Lizzy matter-of-factly.

William gaped at his daughter.

Lizzy appeared completely unaware of the impact she was having. "So we packed up our things and bolted, didn't we, Agnes? We even left a false trail," Lizzy added complacently. "Just in case."

The thought of the two of them, on the road, on their own, made William's blood run cold. "Did you realize what might have happened to you, the two of you alone on the roads?"

"Nothing worse than what might have happened had we stayed," pointed out his daughter.

William shook his finger at her. "You might have been robbed, you might have been raped, you might have been—"

"Sold into a harem?" suggested Lizzy brightly.

"I don't think they have harems in Bath," said Agnes doubtfully.

What on earth had they been teaching them at this school? "You might have been set upon by brigands," said William sternly.

As he had been not so very long ago. He still had the ache of the wound to remind him of it. If it hadn't been for Gwen, it would have gone even more poorly for him. Gwen and her sword parasol. The thought coaxed a reluctant smile to his lips, which his daughter, misreading, took as encouragement, nodding to her friend to signal that it was all right; the lecture was over.

"There's someone I want you to meet," said William, looking around for Gwen.

"The Pink Carnation?" said Lizzy eagerly.

"She's my sister," interjected Agnes.

"No," said William absently. Where in the blazes was Gwen?

A cold trickle of fear began to make its way down William's spine. He hadn't scared her off with his talk of cottages, had he? He could picture her on her horse, parasol aloft, riding into the sunset, like a knight in an old tale, off in search of new adventure. Alone.

William straightened. "I'll just—"

He was interrupted by the loud report of a pistol.

"What the—" William felt his body go cold. "Gwen."

"Who?" said Lizzy, but William was already off, pounding down the hall in the direction of the sound, the others hard on his heels.

"This way," said Lady Henrietta, slipping ahead of him, leading the way through a drawing room and a music room.

A large harp toppled over with a twang.

"Sorry!" called Agnes.

There was a masculine grunt and a sharp discord as Lady Henrietta's husband tripped and went flying, right into the pianoforte.

"Oops," said Agnes.

William didn't look back. Why hadn't they examined the perimeter? But no, he had been too busy exclaiming over Lizzy. And while he was with his daughter, Gwen must have come upon one of the brigands. Either that, or one of the brigands had come upon Gwen. What species of idiot was he? Why hadn't he demanded that they secure the area before engaging in joyous reunions?

A pair of wide French doors stood open, giving onto a balcony that led down to a wilderness garden below. And there, standing in the middle of the balcony, feet planted firmly apart, a smoking pistol in her hand and an expression of extreme disgruntlement on her face, stood Gwen.

"You're all right!" William pounced on her, eliciting a startled squeak. The pistol dropped, but he didn't care. He lifted her, swinging her around in a wide circle, sending her skirts flying. "You're all right. Thank God."

Gwen wiggled in his embrace. "Let me down. That . . . that . . ."

William staggered dizzily to a stop, lowering an impatient Gwen to the ground. He squinted at a man on horseback, trotting blithely away with no apparent feelings of haste. "Is that the—"

"Yes, and I missed him, blast it," said Gwen, scrabbling on the ground for her pistol.

"*You,*" said Lady Henrietta, in tones of deepest loathing.

At the sound of her voice, the man wheeled his horse, raising his hat to her. The wind carried his words over to them. "Always lovely to see you, Lady Henrietta. But as you can see, I haven't time to chat."

An arrow sailed over the garden wall, landing about six feet to his right.

"Farewell, Miss Reid," the Chevalier called. "I recommend archery lessons."

"It was the wind!" shouted Lizzy, but he was already off, leaning low over the neck of his horse, galloping across the fields.

"Quick! Someone! Follow him!" Gwen dropped her empty pistol and started to run. "He's getting away! With the jewels!"

"Miss Gwen! Stop!" It was the dark-haired woman who had been introduced to William as Lord Richard's wife, Amy. She lowered her voice to a carrying whisper. "Those aren't the real jewels."

Gwen skidded to a stop. "What?"

"Not the real jewels?" William echoed.

"Wasn't it a cunning plan?" said Amy Selwick blithely. "We knew someone was after the jewels, so we massed our troops in front and put a decoy bag of jewels in the back—theatrical stuff mostly, but hopefully he won't check it too closely before he goes. We made sure to make it look as though it were hidden. So you see, it's really quite all right. He was meant to get away with them."

"That's why I shot so far to the side," said Lizzy complacently. "Well, that and the wind."

Wrapping his arm around his daughter, William threw back his head and laughed, light-headed with relief. "Nicely done!" he said. "Nicely done!"

"Yes, we thought so," agreed Lord Richard. "He should be halfway to Paris before he realizes what he snatched isn't the real thing."

He and his wife exchanged a grin.

"But what if he comes back?" asked Lady Henrietta.

"He won't," said Lord Richard, and there was an air of determination about him that made William inclined to believe him. "We know who he is now."

"We'll have his likeness plastered to every pub wall in England!" said Amy enthusiastically. "He won't dare show his face."

"I hate the idea of just letting him go like that," muttered Lady Henrietta. "Blast the man."

Gwen's voice rang out above them all. "Has anyone else here recognized the gaping flaw in this so-called cunning plan?"

Agnes started to raise her hand and then timidly put it down again, recognizing it, belatedly, as a rhetorical question.

"If," said Gwen, her hands on her hips, surveying the group on the balcony with impartial ire, "we can identify him, he can also identify Jane."

Jane stepped forward. "You mean he can identify Miss Jane Wooliston," she said quietly.

Gwen waved a hand dismissively. "That's exactly what I said. Now, what are we going to do about it?"

She was a warrior queen, calling her troops to battle, bloodied but unbowed. William felt a deep surge of admiration for her, for her courage, her loyalty, her undaunted spirit.

It was selfish, he knew, to wish she would toss all that aside and throw in her lot with him instead.

"It's not the same." Miss Wooliston regarded the little group on the balcony, looking into each face in turn. "The Chevalier can identify Miss Jane Wooliston, of the Shropshire Woolistons, cousin of Edouard de Balcourt. That will do him no good at all should Miss Jane Wooliston fail to return to France."

There was a shocked silence.

In tones of horror, Amy Selwick said, "You're not retiring, are you? Not when it's all going so well."

Gwen looked the most bewildered of all. "I don't under-stand."

"I'm not retiring." Miss Wooliston's hands were clasped tightly at her waist, the one betraying sign of nerves. "I will be going back into the field. But not as Miss Jane Wooliston."

Everyone's eyes were on Miss Wooliston. Except for William's. He was watching Gwen, who looked as though she had been slapped across the face.

Dropping his arm from Lizzy's shoulders, he moved closer to Gwen, trying to provide her the silent support of his presence. She looked like someone who had been walking confidently on a bridge over a rapid river, only to see the pieces start to come apart at her feet.

"It's too dangerous for everyone to go on as we have," said Miss Wooliston earnestly. "I've put you all in danger—Agnes, my parents. Miss Gwen."

"I put myself in danger," said Gwen gruffly, but William could hear the agitation underlying it. "I chose to be a part of this League. Remember?"

No one paid any attention to her. Their focus was on Miss Wooliston.

"If there's one thing I've learned over this past year," Miss Wooliston said, "it's that we can't play at this by halves. The only way to do this properly is to cut all ties, to subsume oneself into the role."

She looked up at Miss Gwen, apologetic and a little bit defensive. "Wherever I go next, I go alone."

Chapter 24

"The quest is ended," said Plumeria. "The hurly-burly is done. The battle is lost and won. It is time for us to turn our separate ways, along the slow and winding path."

Sir Magnifico bent the knee, his armor creaking as he moved. "Lady," he said, and took her hand. "Did you think I should let you go so easily? You are the true jewel of this quest, and I shall have no other."

—From *The Convent of Orsino* by A Lady

"I expect you won't be needing a chaperone, then," said Gwen in a brittle voice. And then, because she couldn't help herself, "You might have told me."

Two years, gone, just like that. Everything she and Jane had been to each other, tossed away in a moment.

"This . . . precipitated the decision. I'm sorry. I wish we could have left it all as it was." Now that the crisis was over, Jane looked very young and very uncertain. "This is for the best; you'll see."

She sounded as though she were trying to convince herself.

From a very long time ago, Gwen could hear William saying, *You love her.* He had been right. Jane was all the children she had, not the child of her body, perhaps—that child had been lost long, long ago—but the child of her heart. She had fought with her and nurtured her and taken pride in her accomplishments, in their accomplishments.

Was this what her father had felt like when she had turned her back and told him she would have Tim or nothing?

Jane was leaving her not for a man but for an ideal, but it hurt all the same.

In a rusty voice, Gwen said, "It was our League, all three of us, yours, mine, and Amy's. You ought to have spoken to us before taking this decision by . . . by fiat."

She saw Richard and Amy exchange a long look.

"We would be delighted to have you at the school," said Richard with false heartiness. "We should have a new batch of recruits in for training in a few months, and your experience is more current than mine."

"Yes, do!" said Amy brightly.

Then, as if that had settled that, they turned back to Jane, with an ex-spy's interest in the technical details of her plans.

Gwen could feel the walls of Selwick Hall closing in on her. It wasn't her brother's house in Shropshire—that was true; she would have a purpose, a role. But she would still be here on sufferance, dependent on others for her keep. She was sick of being superfluous. Just once, she wanted to belong somewhere, truly belong, to be there because she was wanted, and not just because there was nowhere else for her to go.

She could make good on her previous threats and form her own League, but Jane was right; it was too dangerous with the Chevalier at large. And the truth of it was, she would glean little enjoyment from it on her own. It was the shared project that had been so exhilarating.

All around her, the others were chattering, talking, not seeming to notice her abstraction. Except William.

He was watching her with a concern in his eyes that made her want to weep, a foolish, weak reaction.

"Well?" Gwen said crisply. "You have your daughter back. Shouldn't you be celebrating?"

And then he did something entirely unexpected.

"Marry me," he said.

It came out so quickly that Gwen wasn't entirely sure that she had heard him right. "What?"

"Marry me," William said, more loudly this time.

Around them, other conversations trailed off, people elbowing each other in the ribs, turning to stare.

William took a step forward, his blue eyes intent on Gwen's. "You didn't want to go back to France anyway."

Gwen felt a certain fleeting pleasure at the startled look on Jane's face. But any satisfaction she might have taken was rapidly subsumed in confusion, a confusion so complete and entire that she wondered, briefly, if she were dreaming this. No, she couldn't be dreaming it. There weren't any dancing aardvarks.

"Are you proposing marriage to me?" she demanded, wondering if she might have suffered a blow to the head somewhere along the way.

"That is generally the accepted meaning of the words 'marry me,'" said William. His voice was genial, but his eyes were watchful and his hands were not entirely steady. "I've only used them once before, but I gather that was the accepted usage."

Gwen had stared down whole French platoons. She had swung from ropes, leapt from balconies, blithely exchanged blows with highwaymen and brigands. She had lived for two years as an enemy agent in a hostile country where the people ate snails and called it cuisine. But she had never known true fear until now.

She was deep-down, through-and-through terrified, and she couldn't have said why.

"Why?" asked Gwen hoarsely. "Why now?"

"You'd have bit my nose off if I'd asked you sooner." His voice softening, William said, "I'll not see you someplace you don't want to be. You don't have to teach at their school if you don't want, and I'll not let you go back to that brother of yours. Surely I'm not such a terrible alternative?"

He wasn't. He wasn't at all.

And that was what was so entirely terrifying. It was the fact that she wanted to say yes, wanted it with every bone in her body.

William gestured broadly. "I haven't the manner of excitement to which you're accustomed, but watching Lizzy play with arrows should offer hazard enough."

"It was the wind!" said Lizzy indignantly. "Well, it *was*."

William held out his hands to her. "What do you say, my Gwen?"

"No," said Gwen, wrapping her hands in the fabric of her skirt, twisting the material again and again. It was the only way. Otherwise, she might not be able to stop herself from reaching for him. "No."

The smile faded from William's face.

Gwen swallowed hard, making a desperate bid for dignity. "It's quite all right. You don't need to rescue me. Not this time."

"Who said anything about rescuing?" She loved the sound of his voice, the cadence of it, the deep tone. It was absurd, all of it. Gwen steeled herself against the force of his smile, the way the wrinkles at the corners of his eyes crinkled as he said, "On balance, you've been the one to rescue me, and I've the hole in my chest to prove it."

The man could talk the devil into confusion. But it wouldn't serve. She thought of Jack's mother, who had propositioned him in a garden and turned his life upside down. And yet, the man still blamed himself. But he was like that, she thought in despair. He picked up the wounded and the needy.

Gwen hated that the wounded and the needy in this case was she.

She didn't want him to grudgingly take her home to save her from a fate worse than boredom; she wanted him to want her because he wanted her, desperately, madly, passionately. She wanted him to pine for her the way Sir Magnifico pined for Plumeria.

But that was fiction and this was real and she couldn't let herself get swept away into something that would only prove painful for them both.

"Don't try to talk circles around me!" Gwen's voice came out too harsh and too loud. "I know exactly what you're doing. I won't be another stray you're forced to drag home because you feel in some way responsible."

"Forced?" William said incredulously. "Last time I looked, there was no one holding a pistol to my head—which, with the number of pistols here, is really quite remarkable. I'm offering for you because I want to, and there's nothing in the least bit selfless about it. Or have you entirely forgotten last night?"

By now, everyone on the balcony was staring without the least pretense of restraint.

Agnes looked worriedly at Lizzy. "I don't think we're meant to be hearing this," she whispered.

"Shhh!" hissed Lizzy, flapping her hand at her friend. "We're just getting to the interesting bit."

"That," said Gwen primly, glaring down the two young girls, "is precisely what I mean. I won't have you saddled with me out of an outré sense of duty. You needn't martyr yourself to protect my reputation. I'm not twenty anymore."

"No, and it's a good thing, too," retorted William, "for if you were twenty, you'd be far too young for me, and I'd be feeling like a proper cad for the thoughts I've been thinking."

Gwen's face went pink.

Miles exchanged a horrified look with his wife. "We don't need to hear about those!"

William didn't pay the least bit of attention. He had eyes only for Gwen.

"You wonderful fool," he said feelingly. "What makes you

think I'd be martyred or saddled or any of those other lovely words you chose? I'm asking you to be my wife because I'm terrified at the thought of your getting away from me. When you told me you were going back to Paris—don't you think I wanted to tie you to the bedpost then and there?"

"Definitely didn't need to hear that," muttered Miles.

"I don't want to wake up in the morning without you. If I run into brigands in an alley, I want you to be at my side. I want you to be at my side even if I don't run into brigands in an alley. Do you understand what I'm saying?"

She didn't want to understand it. That way madness lay. It hurt to open oneself up to emotion; she had learned that lesson before.

"That you admire my way with a sword parasol?" she said hoarsely.

"I love you," William said simply. "With or without your parasol. And I'm not saying that out of any sense of obligation or, heaven help us, responsibility. I'm saying it because I mean it."

Gwen's stays were too tight; she couldn't breathe. She struggled for air, at war with herself, trying to think of something, anything, to say that didn't involve either flinging her arms around his neck or running as fast as she could in the opposite direction.

"Mmph?" she said.

"I mean every word of it," William said, framing her face with his hands, effectively blocking her off from the others with his body, giving her time to compose herself. He looked back over his shoulder. "And I'm trusting to everyone here to witness it. Since they won't go away," he added in an undertone intended for Gwen's ears only.

Despite herself, Gwen couldn't help but smile. It was a wobbly smile, but a smile all the same.

William leaned forward so that his forehead touched hers. "Is the idea of marriage to me that dreadful?" he asked, only half-jokingly. "If you can't stand the sight of me, I won't force my suit on you. But I'd the impression you might not find me entirely repugnant."

"I wouldn't say that I find you *entirely* repugnant," said Gwen unevenly. "In fact—"

Snails. Firing squads. French fops. She had dealt with them all. Surely, somehow, she could find the courage to say just three little words. Only one syllable apiece. Why was it so hard?

"In fact?" William prompted.

"Oh, bother it!" said Gwen passionately. She would have thumped her parasol if she had been holding it, but since she wasn't, she had to content herself with stamping her foot instead. "You must know how I feel about you. Haven't I made a fool enough of myself?"

There was some debate about that among the various onlookers, none of which either William or Gwen noticed.

"You're like the plague," she said in frustration. "I've caught you and I can't seem to find a cure."

William gave a great burst of laughter. "It's a good thing you're writing a novel, for no one would ever hire you to write their love poetry. The plague! Good God, Gwen."

She looked up into his laughing face. There was such joy there, such zest for life. Such zest for her. It made her feel humbled and strangely shy. "If it makes you feel better," she offered, "I'm not all that eager to find a cure."

He looked down at her, the laughter fading into tenderness. He touched his finger to her cheek. "I suppose I should be grateful for what I can get."

There was so much warmth in his gaze, so much love.

Gwen felt something hard and cold inside herself dissolve and melt away. William's generosity shamed her. If he had been honest with her in front of a whole gaggle of onlookers, how could she, in good conscience, do less?

Gwen swallowed her pride and her fear and said, "I love you. I do." Then, in case that wasn't clear enough, she added, "And I will marry you—so long as your children don't object."

"We'll take Lizzy as a representative of the whole," said William hastily. "Well, my girl? What do you think?" He clamped an arm around Gwen's waist. "And quickly, before she goes changing her mind."

Lizzy eyed her potential stepmother with an expression that could only be called calculating. "About this sword parasol . . . May I have one?"

"You can have ten of them," said her father happily, "in every color of the rainbow."

"But there are only seven colors—," began Agnes.

Lizzy stepped heavily on Agnes's foot. "Lovely," she said benignly. "Ten will do quite nicely."

Gwen glanced up at her husband-to-be, who was beaming proudly at his daughter. "She's just like you," said Gwen. "A rogue through and through."

William grinned. "Welcome to the family," he said. "And don't say I didn't warn you."

With that, he wrapped his arms around her and kissed her long and thoroughly. Gwen wrapped her arms around his neck and kissed him back. William was quite right, after all. The younger generation did need to be scandalized from time to time. It would do them good.

"This calls for champagne," said Lord Richard, when Gwen detached herself from her happy husband-to-be.

"Or something stronger," suggested Miles.

Jane stepped forward. "May I be the first to wish you happy?" Looking down, she added quietly, "I will miss you."

They had never been demonstrative with each other. From Jane, it was the equivalent of hanging around her neck and weeping.

It was silly to feel guilty when Jane was the one who had left her first, but Gwen did, all the same. "You'll stay for the wedding?" she said gruffly.

Jane nodded. "If you'll have me there."

In an uncharacteristic gesture, Gwen leaned over and kissed her former charge's cheek. "Whatever you do, be careful," she said. "And if you ever need a sword . . ."

"You'll have two at your call," said William, putting an arm firmly around Gwen's waist.

Gwen looked up sideways at her husband-to-be. It was

rather nice to know that she would always have someone at her back. If felt more than nice having him there. It felt right.

How very odd.

William squeezed her waist, as though he understood, and dropped a kiss on the side of her head.

"Before we break out the bubbly," said Miles, "there's just one thing."

Gwen looked at him so fiercely that Miles backed away, keeping a weather eye out for her parasol, which had been known to connect with his shins before.

"I wish you very happy and all that," Miles said hastily. "But you're all forgetting something. If those weren't the real jewels that the Gardener made off with, then where are they?"

Chapter 25

The magic mirror lay where it had fallen, tarnished but unbroken. When Sir Magnifico lifted it, he saw not the Tower behind him, but their faces, his and Plumeria's, hallowed in sunlight. And from the trees, a million birds caroled, "Joy!" The bright blue sky was all the canopy they needed and the fruit on the vine their wedding feast.

—From *The Convent of Orsino* by A Lady

"Don't look at me!" said Lizzy quickly.

"But if you didn't have the jewels, why would the Gardener be following you?" said Lady Henrietta logically.

"It would be enough that he thought she had the jewels," said Gwen, coming to Lizzy's defense.

William remembered something that had been said, a hundred years back, on the day he had arrived at Miss Climpson's academy, a day that would be forever blazoned on his memory as the worst of all possible days at the time, and the luckiest in retrospect. He'd had the fright of his life, but he'd met his Gwen.

"Didn't your schoolmistress say you'd been sent a gift from your brother?"

"Well, yes," said Lizzy, taken aback, "but it was all bazaar stuff, brass bangles, clay beads, that sort of thing. Like this."

She drew a necklace from her pocket, a heavy, unlovely thing of irregularly shaped, garishly painted clay beads.

"You used to like to play with those when you were little," said William fondly. "Mostly, you liked to try to eat them."

Lizzy was less than thrilled by this tender reminiscence. "Jack calls me his magpie, because I like bright things," she said. "That was why he sent them."

"May I?" asked Gwen, holding out her hand.

Unsuspecting, Lizzy handed the beads over. "They're nothing terribly special," she said modestly. "Just— Stop that!"

Gwen took the beads and whapped them, with great force, into the wall. Flecks of paint and bits of broken clay filtered down the previously pristine wallpaper.

Lizzy's "I liked those!" warred with Lord Richard's "Not the new wallpaper!" and Amy's, "Oooh, let me have a go!"

Gwen evaded them all, holding the necklace up high. "There," she said triumphantly. "Look at that."

"We're going to have to repaper that wall," said Lord Richard grimly, fingering a hole in the paper.

"Stop whinging and pay attention. Not that. This." Gwen gave the string a good shake, sending bits of clay flaking down.

In the light from the window, there was a sullen reddish gleam. William leaned closer, squinting. Gwen took the piece between her fingers, flicked some more of the clay away, and held the strand forward for inspection.

William cleared his throat. "Is that—"

"Rubies," said Gwen. "He had them dipped in clay."

Lizzy's eyes were like saucers. Her mouth opened and closed, but no sound came out.

William was rather pleased that Gwen had been able to render his daughter speechless. That boded well for their future relationship. He felt a warm and fuzzy feeling as he looked at his two womenfolk. All that was needed was to bring Kat home and the picture would be complete.

Not that the rubies weren't very nice and all, but the ebony and silver of Gwen's hair and the bronze of Lizzy's were all the treasure William needed.

"Here you are." Gwen handed the string of beads back to Lizzy as nonchalantly as though they had been nothing but clay. "I believe these are yours."

Lizzy made a valiant effort at human speech. "You mean— all this time—"

"You've been carrying around a rajah's ransom in rubies," said William grimly. "And what Jack was thinking, I don't know."

"I have a good guess," said Lord Richard. "He was probably thinking he was safer without those on his person."

"He wouldn't have done it on purpose!" said Lizzy quickly. "Not that way. He must have assumed as long as I didn't know, no one else would guess either. And I wouldn't have guessed," she added, looking at Gwen with a combination of respect and annoyance, "if you hadn't thought to bash them into that wall."

"Thank you," said Gwen regally.

"The wallpaper," said Lord Richard.

"I never liked it anyway," said Amy blithely. She turned back to the others. "But what about the rest of it? Not that the rubies aren't lovely, but one strand doesn't make a rajah's hoard."

"Unless he was a very small rajah," contributed Miles. "Metaphorically," he added quickly. "I didn't mean that he was a midget."

William broke in before anyone could pursue that interesting side angle. "Was there more that Jack sent?" he asked gently. "Or did you leave it behind at the school?"

Agnes and Lizzy exchanged a long look.

"There is more," said Agnes hesitantly. "We bundled it all into our packs, in case we needed to trade something shiny for coin along the way."

A collective groan arose from the others.

"I suppose," said Agnes tentatively, "that it was a good thing I still had something left of my allowance?"

Miles shook his head, one lock of blond hair flopping over his brow. "Can't you just picture it? A rajah's treasure spread out between the carters and innkeepers of Hampshire and Sussex."

"And Wiltshire," pointed out Lizzy. She met her father's eye and said, "Er, we'll just get the rest of it now, shall we? Come along, Agnes."

Agnes followed dutifully.

"I'll go with them," volunteered Amy, who followed along after.

The rest of the group dispersed throughout the long salon. William joined Gwen at one of the windows, placing a hand familiarly on the small of her back.

"I," he said, in an undertone intended for her ears only, "am going to throttle Jack when I find him."

"It sounds like you'll have to get in line," said Gwen, leaning back into his hand. She raised her brows at him. "You have to admit, it was clever of the boy."

Pride warred with irritation. "Oh, he's clever all right. I just wish he would show a bit more—"

"Common sense?"

"Concern for those around him." The idea of Lizzy blithely trotting around the English countryside with a sack full of jewels made his blood run cold. What had the boy been thinking, sending them to her in the first place?

"Well," said Gwen practically. "He's certainly done his best for his little sister. A place in an elite academy and a dowry anyone would envy."

"A dowry that made her the target of the governments of two countries," countered William, a worried line between his brows. It felt good to have someone to confide in, someone to share his worries with. He'd missed this. "Jack had to know that someone would be after those jewels."

Gwen put her head to one side. "On the other hand," she said judiciously, "he did a decent job of disguising the jewels. Your daughter herself didn't realize she had them. And he did go to the trouble of setting a false trail with those other parcels."

"Yes," said William wryly. "By sending them straight to Kat."

"Your Kat," said Gwen firmly, "can handle herself against just about anything. I'd back her against those buffoons the Gardener had following us any day. And I'd imagine your Jack knows it. If he has the sense that God gave a duck."

William looked at her, at her elegant, strong-boned face, at the formidable poise that hid such a warm heart beneath. "You've a good heart, Gwen Meadows," he said, "to advocate so for a boy you've not met yet."

"I'm simply speaking sense," said Gwen, with dignity.

William grinned at her. "It's no use. I've sussed out your secret. You make yourself out to be so severe, but at heart, you're as soft as I am."

"I wouldn't say soft—" Gwen looked so appalled that William felt it incumbent upon himself to kiss her again.

"Ahem!" Lizzy cleared her throat and then cleared it again. Entering the room, she dumped a clumsily wrapped cloth parcel on a rosewood card table. "I have the rest of the baubles Jack sent me. If anyone is still interested," she added pointedly.

"*Twenty* sword parasols," said her father.

"Don't be silly," said Lizzy. "Ten will do quite nicely. And a little pistol?"

"Not after seeing your aim with those arrows," said William.

"I'll practice with you," offered Gwen, and it was all William could do not to kiss her again, right there. "Every woman should know how to use a pistol."

"And a sword parasol," William said fondly.

Lizzy rolled her eyes at Agnes and set about fanning out her loot on the table. Presented as it was, it was an unimpressive sight, the term "bazaar baubles," if anything, doing the cheap trinkets too much honor. There were more of the heavy clay beads, clumsy brass bangles, and garish earrings of colored glass. There was a mirror too, gaudily adorned with all manner of bulbous brass work and chunks of rough colored stones.

Lizzy shook out one last earring. "That's the last of it," she said cheerfully.

Miles Dorrington cleared his throat. "It looks like your brother robbed a very unsuccessful jeweler."

Lady Henrietta rolled up her sleeves. "Shall we?"

"Not against the wallpaper!" said Lord Richard quickly.

Within an hour, the unprepossessing collection of bazaar trash was presenting quite a different aspect. As was the wallpaper, but only in a few spots, when Lord Richard wasn't looking. The clay beads all had gems hidden in their centers: sapphire and emerald, ruby and topaz. The brass bangles, which tinkled so discordantly when shaken, carried a loose cargo of diamonds. The earrings Lizzy had confidently dismissed as colored glass were, in fact, rare yellow sapphires. As for the mirror, the elevated brass work hid the cream of the collection, loose gems too large to conceal in a clay bead, while the stones, once polished, revealed themselves as chunks of lapis lazuli and tourmaline.

They all sat, exhausted, on the settees around the table with its glittering, illicit hoard.

"Good Lord," said William. "The boy's gone and robbed Golconda."

"Not Golconda," said Gwen, busily sorting gemstones into piles, like with like. "The Rajah of Berar." She looked up. "There's something missing."

Lady Henrietta surveyed the haul on the table. "Diamonds, rubies, sapphires, emeralds . . ."

"The Moon of Berar."

"I'd thought that was a myth," said William.

Gwen looked up at him. "Bonaparte doesn't think so. That's why the Gardener was so hot to get his hands on these—and on your son."

Miles raised a hand. "What's the Moon of Berar?"

Gwen answered. "It's a mythical jewel that supposedly has some sort of supernatural powers."

"No one can quite agree on what they are," said William, picking up the tale. "Some say it provides the power of omniscience, others that it has the ability to provide one's heart's desire. In many versions . . ."

His voice trailed off.

"Yes?" prompted Gwen.

William reached out and picked up the mangled brass mirror. It was a sad-looking thing, with all the baubles picked off, the stones pried from their settings. Denuded of its borrowed finery, it was a trumpery piece, made of cheap brass and cheaper glass. Or not even glass. The reflected surface was wavy and dim.

"In some versions," he said, "the Moon is said to be a mirror."

"Not that mirror, surely," said Miles Dorrington. "It looks like someone put it together by having an elephant stomp on a piece of brass and then called it done."

"Sometimes," said William quietly, looking at Gwen, "valuable treasures hide under forbidding exteriors."

Gwen slid her hand into his. "Sometimes," she said, "it just takes a clever man to see it."

William twined his fingers through hers, thanking the Fates that had thrown them together that day at Miss Climpson's. "Not clever, but lucky. Very, very lucky."

"I suppose," said Miles, looking dubiously at the mirror. "I wouldn't want to overestimate my quotient of wisdom, but that still just looks like a mirror to me."

According to the legend, or at least one of the legends, the mirror displayed one's ultimate desire. Looking down into the mirror, William saw both their faces reflected, his and Gwen's. Lizzy, who had come up behind for a closer look, was just visible behind them, all nose and eyes in the mirror's slightly distorted surface.

William felt a welling of joy overtake him, a springtime of the soul that was everything anyone had ever promised him in an English spring. There was all the world before them, a lifetime of wonder and joy still to come.

"I don't know," William said mildly, setting the mirror back down on the table. "I think it got it just about right."

And he knew, from Gwen's quick sideways look, that she knew exactly what he meant.

"Yes," said Lady Henrietta practically, "but what are we to do with it?"

"I could just go put it back in my room . . . ," suggested Lizzy, making for the glittering pile.

"I believe it counts as a spoil of war," said Miles Dorrington. "Like a prize ship."

"In which case," said Lord Richard, turning to William, "it belongs to your son."

"Who gave it to me," said Lizzy quickly.

"I helped carry it!" put in Agnes.

"We'll keep it for Jack," said William, although even as he said it, he wondered how long, if ever, it would be until he saw his second son again.

"Surely just one little necklace . . . ," wheedled Lizzy. "It was my Christmas package, after all."

Gwen lightly squeezed William's hand, and he looked up to find her watching him. She gave a little nod. "He'll be back," she said. "If only to make more trouble."

"We're good at that, we Reids," said William ruefully.

Gwen rose from her seat and held out a hand to him. "Then it's a good thing, isn't it," she said, "that I'm so good at rescuing you?"

Chapter 26

S elwick Hall looked as though it had been besieged.

We stood there, Colin and Jeremy and I, among the shards of china, staring at the wreckage. A small table lay on its side, the flowers that had been so pretty in their vase strewn about the floor like Ophelia's weeds. Behind us, the open front door banged in the wind.

Colin hastily turned to secure it. The sound of the bolt clicking was as loud as a shot.

"You can't blame me for this one," said Jeremy quickly.

Colin's expression was implacable. This was beyond anger. This was his home and it had been violated. "Unless you hired someone."

Jeremy was all outrage. "Do you really think—"

"Tell me what else I'm supposed to think," said Colin, his voice hard.

Whatever Jeremy might have said was cut off by a loud crash from the back of the house, a crash and a bang, as though someone had gleefully tossed an entire tray of china in the air and then dropped the tray after it.

Colin flinched as though he had been struck.

"The bastard's still here," he said.

"Couldn't we just call the police and wait here?" I suggested hopefully.

"He'll be halfway to the next county by then," said Colin with a tight-lipped determination that made me think of old Westerns on Sunday afternoon TV. Only this wasn't a movie and Colin wasn't Clint Eastwood. He was a reasonably mild-mannered former investment banker. Someone could get hurt, most likely Colin. "I'm going after him."

"Wait!" I grabbed up an umbrella from the umbrella stand. It was one of those sturdy British models built to last a thousand rains. More important, it had a sturdy steel tip. It might not be quite Miss Gwen's sword parasol, but it was better than nothing. "Take this. Just in case."

Jeremy grabbed up an umbrella out of the stand. He hadn't looked before he grabbed. It was hot pink with a ruffled edge. "I'm coming, too."

"Checking out your handiwork?" said Colin, edging down the hallway like James Bond on the trail of the villain with the nuclear reactor.

"Screw you," said Jeremy.

Only he didn't say "screw." His knuckles were white on the umbrella handle, and there was sweat on his brow. Guilt, anger, fear, goodness only knew what, had made him lose his cool, and lose it in a big way.

He raised the hot pink umbrella. "I've had enough of your—"

I grabbed Jeremy's arm and squeezed. Hard.

"Save it for later, will you?" I hissed. "Both of you. Villain first. Fighting later."

The glance Jeremy cast me wasn't exactly fond, but he complied, ostentatiously rubbing his arm.

In the darkness, the familiar corridors felt like something out of a horror movie, rendered unfamiliar by the toppled tables and shattered vases, unspeakable dangers lying in wait around corners that didn't seem to curve quite where they should. The doorframes loomed like the menacing portals in one of Poe's dark fantasies, and the familiar creak of the floorboards echoed in my ears, making me hunch my shoulders and glance anxiously behind me.

Not that behind was the problem. Whatever the danger was lay ahead. Colin led the way, his umbrella held aloft, Jeremy next, while I took up the rear, where I could keep an eye on Jeremy.

The trail of destruction led to the back of the house, to the long salon that stretched across the garden front. Despite the depredations of the Victorian improvers who had remodeled much of the house out of recognition, that room had remained pretty much the same since the eighteenth century, aside from the addition of a conservatory on one side that sprouted from the side of the house like a toadstool.

Moonlight played against the long glass windows, making the glass seem to sway and shimmer. Was that someone moving by the French doors? No. Just a curtain, wafting back and forth in one of those strange breezes that came out of nowhere. Colin swore they were just from ill-fitting window frames, not ghosts.

Colin said a lot of things. In the moonlight, in the dark room, our own fear a palpable presence among us, ghosties and ghoulies and things that went bump in the night seemed entirely logical.

"The door is still locked," said Colin in a low voice. "He must be in here somewhere."

Those are words you only want to hear in a movie, with a bowl of popcorn on your lap and an afghan tucked around your knees.

I turned, slowly. Moonlight and shadow played tricks with my eyes. In the corner of the room, something moved.

"Over there," I whispered hoarsely, clutching at Colin's arm and missing by a mile.

Everything happened at once. The villain made a desperate leap for freedom. Jeremy ran forward, swinging his umbrella. Colin flicked on the light.

In the sudden glow, Jeremy batted at empty air with his umbrella. Colin pivoted, saying, "Where did he go? Where did he go?"

And I sat down hard on the floor, shaking with slightly hysterical laughter.

"Boys. Boys!" I had a little trouble getting the words out. I pointed, shakily, at the rosewood card table in front of me, which was rocking lightly back and forth. "I think I've found the culprit."

Cowering under the table was a large black dog, his coat matted with mud and burrs.

Colin and Jeremy stood there, blinking like idiots, still holding their umbrellas, while the source of all our worries hunkered down and rubbed his nose against his paw, letting out a low, unhappy whimper.

I knew just how he felt.

"It's that lost dog," I said unnecessarily. My voice sounded very shrill and very loud. "Didn't you see the posters in the pub? We should call the pub and find out who the owner is."

Colin hunkered down next to me. "Come on," he urged, patting his thigh. To the humans, he said, "We must have left the door unlocked. The catch doesn't always catch."

Jeremy lowered his umbrella. "Not our finest hour."

"No," Colin agreed, and I knew he was thinking of more than the latch. He looked soberly at Jeremy. "I owe you an apology."

I clambered unsteadily to my feet. "I'll go call the pub."

The cousins needed some time alone. I only hoped they wouldn't revert to form and bludgeon each other while I was gone. I took some comfort from the reflection that if Jeremy were to go after Colin, those ruffles on the pink umbrella should cushion the blow.

Skirting the destruction in the hall—that poor dog must

have really been frantic, and who could blame him?—I made my way to the kitchen. The number of the pub was on a frayed piece of paper by the phone, along with such other important numbers as the fire station, the oil company, and the Indian takeaway.

The people at the pub were only too happy to hear that Fuzzy had been found. They promised they would call the owner and let her know. I hung up the phone with mutual expressions of esteem, repressed the urge to call back and ask if they delivered gin and tonics, and spent a few minutes contemplating my own reflection in the kitchen window, trying to make sense of a decidedly tumultuous evening.

We had all been behaving like complete idiots. Unless, of course, Fuzzy was at the center of a gang of international jewel thieves, but somehow I doubted that. Remembering my own suspicions of Jeremy, I felt more than a little bit ashamed. The truth was that Colin spent too much time living in his spy thriller and I in the past. When you put those two together, you wound up with a serious case of overactive imagination.

True, I didn't think I was ever going to actually actively like Jeremy, but there was a bit of a gap between finding someone annoyingly smarmy and suspecting him of hiring a hit man.

I didn't even know how one would go about hiring a hit man.

Hopefully, Jeremy didn't either. Colin thought he did, but that was only because he read too many thrillers.

Deciding to give the men a little more time, just in case they were having some sort of deep familial epiphany, I took down the can of coffee from the cupboard and spooned a generous helping into the machine, sniffing the familiar and comforting scent of the coffee grounds. While the coffee perked, I buttered bread for the promised grilled cheese. Now that the danger was over, I was suddenly ridiculously, ravenously hungry.

I'd give that to blind terror—it certainly burned calories, even if in the end the whole thing had turned out to be more Abbott and Costello than *The Convent of Orsino*.

I dropped the first sandwich into the pan, where it landed with a satisfying sizzle. I still had one more book left to read of that blasted—er, lovely—novel, and I strongly suspected I was wasting my time. The whole thing about the jewel being in the mirror was all very interesting, but I couldn't see where that led us. Unlike Jeremy, I was fairly sure that was a metaphor. But a metaphor for what?

Perhaps there were no jewels; perhaps the whole thing was a metaphor for knowing oneself, or something equally smug and unsatisfying.

No. I flipped a sandwich with a spatter of grease. I'd read those letters, and if Henrietta Dorrington was to be believed, the jewels not only existed; they had come here, to—and possibly through—Selwick Hall.

Mrs. Selwick-Alderly had said something about there being a presentation copy of *The Convent of Orsino* here at Selwick Hall, a big, fancy one.

It had belonged to Colonel Reid's youngest daughter, she had said, who had married Richard's son. I jumped back as the sandwich pan spat hot grease at me. Quickly, I turned off the gas, moving the pan to a cool burner as I stood there with the spatula in one hand, staring blindly into space. That made no sense. I'd seen the Selwick family tree. I didn't remember all the myriad branches, but I did know that Richard and Amy didn't start producing little spies in training until early 1806.

Lizzy Reid had been seventeen in 1805. Unless she was the ultimate Regency cougar, she would have been far too old for Richard and Amy's son.

Miss Gwen was in her forties when she married Colonel Reid, a little old for childbearing, but certainly not impossibly so. I stood there, staring at the cooling sandwiches, as the truth dawned. When Mrs. Selwick-Alderly said Colonel Reid's youngest daughter, she meant Miss Gwen's daughter.

Assuming she was conceived fairly rapidly, this nameless girl child would have been born just about the same time as Richard and Amy's eldest. Given all the ties between the families, there were good odds they'd been raised together, or close to it. A girl with Colonel Reid's charm and Miss Gwen's bullish determination? That poor little Selwick boy never had a chance.

A distressing corollary occurred to me. This meant, among other things, that Colin was descended from Miss Gwen.

I decided I didn't want to think about that bit.

Piling the sandwiches haphazardly on a plate, I started down the hall, absentmindedly taking a bite out of the topmost sandwich. I'd forgotten to halve them, but the men would just have to deal. I was too busy playing with a new and fascinating idea. If Miss Gwen were going to leave a clue to the location of the missing jewels, where better than in the volume she left to her daughter?

Odds were that if there were any jewels, the daughter had long since converted them to cash and used them to re-lead the roof of Selwick Hall (I made a note to self to check the early Victorian Selwick account books to see if there were any large and unaccounted expenditures soon after the Reid-Selwick nuptials), but at least we'd have the satisfaction of knowing that it wasn't all a myth, that the jewels had, in fact, passed through Selwick Hall.

Colin and Jeremy were both in the salon where I'd left them, Colin on the floor with the dog, Jeremy sitting on one of the settees. They weren't exactly hugging, but at least they didn't look quite so ready to pulverize each other.

"Guys?" I said.

"You brought sandwiches!" said Jeremy in the tones of someone who is determined to play nice. "Thank you."

I'd forgotten I was holding them. "Right. You're welcome. But there's something I think you'd better come see."

Colin got hastily to his feet. "Another intruder?"

"No, nothing like that." I set the sandwiches down before I accidentally gesticulated with them. "But I think I have an idea of where we might look for the jewels. . . ."

Two hours later, we had eaten the sandwiches. We had drunk the coffee. And we had handed Fuzzy over to a grateful and slightly hysterical owner. What we hadn't done? Found the presentation copy of *The Convent of Orsino*.

"It's not here," said Jeremy, sitting on the floor in the middle of a pile of tattered early Ian Flemings that we had removed to get to the books behind.

Colin's ancestors, like all avid readers, were book double stackers. Jeremy had removed his blazer, rolling up the sleeves of his shirt. He looked closer to human than I had ever seen him.

"I hate to agree," said Colin, his voice echoing down from his perch on the top of the library ladder, "but I think he's right."

"Your aunt Arabella said it was here," I said stubbornly.

"She's not entirely omniscient," said Colin, clambering down the ladder. "Every now and then—"

He stopped short at the base of the ladder.

"Are you all right?" I asked.

"No," said Colin. "I'm a cretin."

From the expression on his face, I assumed he meant someone of limited mental capacity rather than someone who hailed from the isle of Crete.

Colin shook his head, looking like a man who had been dealt a blow with a ruffled parasol. "We've been looking right past it for the past two hours."

"What do you mean?" asked Jeremy from the floor.

"It's the purloined letter," said Colin. "We didn't notice it because it was right in front of us. There."

On a table in the corner, on stands, stood a miscellany of books.

It would be a misnomer to say that they were on display. It

was more that someone had at one point bunged them down there and no one had bothered to dust them since. There was a large, leather-bound copy of *Robinson Crusoe*, a late Victorian travel memoir by someone I'd never heard of—and *The Convent of Orsino*, fully a foot and a half tall and staring us straight in the face. The cover was a miracle of poor taste, covered with brass carbuncles that were clearly meant to be some sort of decorative feature.

I'm not sure who started laughing first, but we all were, at ourselves, at the night, at everything.

"Not exactly Sherlock Holmes, are we?" I leaned against Colin for balance. Every part of me was stiff after two hours of book hauling. "We fail at detection."

"We get points for perseverance," said Jeremy, wincing as he started to lever himself to his feet.

"And teamwork," said Colin, and held out a hand to his stepfather.

For a moment, Jeremy hesitated, and I wondered if he feared that Colin was going to dump him back on the ground. But their tentative entente held. Jeremy took Colin's hand and let him help him off the floor.

While Jeremy was dusting off his trousers, I went for the book. It was huge, large enough that I staggered as I lifted it off the stand, staggered and sneezed. The cover was grimed with a century of dust. Obviously, it hadn't been high on anyone's reading list for quite some time. The leather cover left streaks of dirt on my fingers.

Balancing it against the edge of the table, I flipped it open as

Colin and Jeremy clustered around, Jeremy keeping his expensive trousers well out of the way. It opened to the frontispiece, a much larger and grander frontispiece than in the cheap multivolume edition Mrs. Selwick-Alderly had loaned me.

On one side, Plumeria and Sir Magnifico sat on their horses by the edge of a grove of trees, Sir Magnifico sporting a rather magnificent plumed cap. On the far side, the Knight of the Silver Tower bore a fainting Amarantha away in his arms, the mirror dangling from one of her limp hands. In the middle, the drunken revelers cavorted, dancing and swirling. Above it all loomed the ominous shape of the Dark Tower.

Underneath, in a sprawling, childish hand, someone had written: *Plumeria Reid. MY book. 1815.*

"This is it," I said hoarsely. "We've found the Tower. Plumeria's Tower."

Jeremy was hovering just over my shoulder, popping up and down like a jack-in-the-box, eager to play but not wanting to get too close to the grime. "Is there"—he gestured at the book—"something in the lining? A hollow space in the middle?" He turned to Colin. "There's certainly room enough."

I flipped through, transferring the dust of one hundred and eighty-nine years from the pages to my fingers. The entire volume appeared to be intact. There were no secret compartments, and certainly not enough room in the lining to hide even a modest haul of gems.

"Nada," I said, closing the heavy book and setting it down with a slap. Dust billowed up from the cover. "Except—oh."

That cover. That absurd, ornate cover.

"Do you have a handkerchief?" I said to Colin.

He looked at me as though I were crazy. "Why would I have a handkerchief?"

"I do," said Jeremy, bringing one out with a flourish. It was a lovely piece of nearly transparent linen, lovingly embroidered with his initials.

"Thank you." I took it and began scrubbing away at the first of the brass carbuncles. "We need something stronger. Water. Solvent . . ."

"No," said Colin, leaning over my shoulder. "You've got it."

The old brown paint was flaking off. Or maybe it had originally been gilt rather than brown; with the grime of ages on it, it was hard to tell. Whatever was beneath the ugly paint wasn't brass or any other base metal.

"Is that—," said Jeremy.

I handed him back his handkerchief. "I believe that is a ruby," I said, feeling slightly light-headed and more than a little slaphappy. "You're welcome to have a go at the rest, but I'm guessing you'll find more of the same."

"So it was here," said Colin bemusedly, "all along."

"Hard by Plumeria's Tower!" I said.

Colin turned to me, his eyes brilliant with excitement. "We did it. We found it."

We. And again we. I nodded vigorously, blinking against sudden, silly tears. "We did."

Colin's arms closed around. I gave a little shriek as he lifted me off the floor, the world rocking around me, my arms locked around his neck.

"We did it," he repeated, and kissed me hard, on the mouth.

I wished I could have shared his triumphal joy, but somehow, the fact that we'd succeeded only made it more real that I was going to be leaving. The quest was over and so was my time with Colin. I looped my arms around his neck and kissed him back, harder, trying to kiss away all the fear and doubt and worry.

Jeremy lifted the empty grilled cheese plate. "I'll just go put this in the kitchen," he said loudly. He couldn't resist adding, "If you trust me not to steal the silver."

"There isn't any," said Colin, keeping one arm looped tightly around my waist. "But you'll find the washing-up liquid next to the sink."

Jeremy gave him a look that told him just what he thought of that idea. He did, however, close the door when he went out. And he didn't take the rubies of Berar with him.

"He's not going to do the dishes, is he?" I said, rubbing my cheek against Colin's shirt. If I could have burrowed in and stayed there, I would have.

"No," said Colin. And then, the words muffled by my hair, "I don't want you to leave."

It was the first time either of us had referred directly to my leaving since I'd told him my decision two months ago. It was certainly the first time he had been quite so direct about his preferences.

My throat closed up on me. "I don't want me to leave either. But I'm stuck."

"I know," he said, and wrapped his arms around me, my

cheek against his chest, his chin resting on the top of my head. It was very quiet in the library, quiet and dim, with the shadows of the trees moving softly through the window.

He wouldn't have been Colin if he had pleaded with me to stay. I wouldn't have respected him if he had. It was one of the things I loved about him, that he never discounted the importance of my obligations, never told me that I should drop it all and stay with him. He was too deeply honorable for that.

If he hadn't been, I wouldn't have loved him so.

If I had had any doubts before, I knew it now. This wasn't infatuation or lust (not that I was discounting that factor) or archive envy. I'd lived with Colin long enough now to know the real thing when I saw it. He was true gold through and through. And I loved him.

I loved him and I had never told him so. There had always been something else in the way—pride, fear, whatever it is that drives us to hide our emotions from those we love. I'd been burned, badly, in relationships before. It was safer, all around, to cling to what a friend of mine liked to call plausible deniability, to play it cool and pretend I could take it or leave it.

Safer, but so wrong.

We had only a month left together. I owed it to Colin, to us, to stop being such a coward. We'd accomplished our quest; now it was time for one final hurdle.

I extracted myself from my cozy nook against his chest. "Colin—," I began.

But he beat me to it. "Before you go," he said quickly, his eyes intent on my face. "There's something I need you to know."

I drew in an unsteady breath. "You have a mad cousin in the attic?"

"No," Colin said immediately. "In the kitchen. But that's not it. What I'm trying to tell you is—I'll miss you when you go. A lot." It was very quiet in the library, all the books still on their shelves. Colin gave up the struggle and looked me straight in the eye. "I love you. For what it's worth."

More than a Rajah's jewels—that was for sure. But the glib words wouldn't come to my lips.

"I love you too," I croaked. "So much."

Fortunately, Colin didn't seem to mind that I sounded like an asthmatic frog. When we could speak again, he said, "I just wanted you to know that your going away doesn't change that. My feelings will remain the same."

There was something charmingly old-fashioned about the way he said it. Rather Mr. Darcy-ish.

"Sir," I said primly, "are you trying to inform me that your intentions are honorable?"

"Not entirely . . . ," Colin said, with a familiar glint in his eye. His expression sobered. "But if you mean do I intend to let you go? Not for all the oceans in the world."

I lifted my hand to his chest. "What's a little bit of long distance?" I said recklessly. I nodded to the lost rubies of Berar, adorning a third-rate novel by a first-rate adventuress. "We've managed to find something that most people thought didn't exist."

Colin framed my face in his hands. "Yes," he said, and he wasn't looking at the rubies. "Yes, we have."

Historical Note

As always, I have shamelessly twisted real events and people to my own purposes. By early 1805, Napoleon was, indeed, anxious to form an alliance with the Ottoman Sultan, Selim III. Franco-Russian diplomatic relations had sputtered to a halt and Russia had entered into an alliance with Britain against France. A Franco-Ottoman entente might have balanced the scales, but Bonaparte's ambassador in Constantinople, Brune, made himself less than popular. He was recalled in the autumn of 1804; Brune's successor, Sebastiani, was appointed in April 1805. Into that diplomatic gap, I've slipped my imaginary opera singer, Aurelia Fiorila, who returns to Paris with a demand for a mythical jewel.

Selim III did have a taste for Western opera, importing the first opera troupe to perform in Constantinople. However, as far as I know, neither Napoleon nor his foreign minister ever took advantage of that operatic inclination to slip in a secret negotiator. Aurelia Fiorila, her child, and her mission to Constantinople are entirely my own invention. (Although one wouldn't put any of it past the notoriously wily Talleyrand.)

Likewise, the legend of the lost jewels of Berar is taken from the historical record, but the specific nature of the jewels and their fate are entirely my own invention. Before the siege of Gawilghur in 1803, rumors spread that a king's ransom in gold, silver, and jewels was being kept within the fortress. A small fortune in silver bowls and copper coins was discovered after the siege, but the jewels were never found. Jac Weller, author of *Wellington in India*, posits, "If the treasure ever had been kept in Gawilghur, and there seems to be little reason to doubt that some at least had been there, the Mahrattas got it out in time. . . . It is also possible that the treasure was hidden and recovered later." In that case, why might the jewels not be recovered and removed by a double agent who knew where they were hidden? I was unable to find any specific descriptions of the jewels, so I invented the apocryphal Moon of Berar, both to provide a sufficient prize for an anxious Sultan and also as a nod to Wilkie Collins's *The Moonstone*, which takes as its base a looted Indian jewel.

Similarly, several of my main characters are partly purloined from the past. My hero, Colonel William Reid, is loosely based on Colonel James Kirkpatrick of the Madras Cavalry, commonly known as "the Handsome Colonel." According to William Dalrymple, "the name was apparently a reference not only to his good looks . . . but also to his rackety love life" and a career "more distinguished for its amorous conquests than its military ones." Colonel Kirkpatrick's parents fled Scotland for South Carolina after the failed 1715 uprising. My hero is a generation younger, so his parents fled Scotland after the '45. Like my Colonel Reid, Colonel Kirkpatrick set off for India, where, in between his military duties, he fathered a brood of both legitimate and illegitimate offspring.

The main difference there? All of Colonel Kirkpatrick's offspring were of European descent, a fact with far-reaching legal implications in India at the time. Under the governor-generalship of Lord Cornwallis in the late eighteenth century, a series of laws designed to keep those of mixed birth out of governmental or military positions were passed. In 1791, anyone without two European parents was banned from civil, military, or naval service in the East India Company. By 1795, children of mixed parentage were barred from serving even as drummers, pipers, or farriers. Those wealthy enough to do so sent their children back to England, where there were no such legal barriers to advancement. Those without such resources apprenticed their sons to tradesmen or sent them out as mercenaries to local rulers. Colonel Reid's legitimate son, Alex, is employed in the East India Company's diplomatic service, but, due to Cornwallis's laws, his two illegitimate sons are barred Company employment.

My inspiration for Jack Reid was James Skinner of Skinner's Horse, a real man caught in a predicament identical to Jack's. Like Jack, Skinner was born to a British army officer and a Rajput lady of high birth, who committed suicide when Skinner was a child. Barred by his birth from following his father into the East India Company's army, Skinner was apprenticed to a printer but ran away, signing on as a mercenary with the army of Scindia, a prominent Maratha chieftain with French sympathies. Eager to have Skinner's talents for the British side, Lord Lake engineered a loophole, commissioning Skinner to raise a troop of irregular cavalry. Skinner's solution is notable as the exception rather than the rule; most half-castes didn't have any way around the legal strictures keeping them from gainful employment in the East India Company's army or diplomatic service. Cornwallis's laws created a powerful impetus for divided loyalties.

Interestingly, while being a half-caste had serious social and legal consequences in India in the early nineteenth century, the same did not necessarily hold true in England. As the child of an Indian mother, Lizzy Reid would be likely to face social censure among the British community in India, but not in England, where—at least at this early date—her Indian heritage would more likely be seen as intriguing and exotic. I based Lizzy Reid on Colonel Kirkpatrick's granddaughter, Kitty Kirkpatrick, the offspring of the marriage of Colonel Kirkpatrick's son and a Hyderabadi lady of quality, Khair-un-Nissa. After her father's death in 1805, Kitty was raised at her grandfather's home in England. The famous writer Thomas Carlyle described Kitty Kirkpatrick as "a strangely complexioned young lady with soft brown eyes and floods of bronze red hair . . . pretty looking, smiling, and amiable," with "a slight merry curl of the upper lip." Kitty was a great hit in London society. I am happy to say that Kitty achieved her own love match, marrying a captain of the Seventh Hussars.

Whether Lizzy will do the same is a question for another novel. . . .

Speaking of novels, I couldn't end this note without a brief word about the antecedents of Miss Gwen's horrid novel. *The Convent of Orsino* is a knockoff of Horace Walpole's *The Castle of Otranto*, "Monk" Lewis's *The Monk*, Ann Radcliffe's *Mysteries of Udolpho*, and the many other works of Gothic fiction so popular at the time. The genre was very effectively spoofed by Jane Austen in her own *Northanger Abbey*.

I have no doubt that Catherine Morland would have been a great fan of *The Convent of Orsino*.

Photo © Sigrid Estrada

The author of nine previous Pink Carnation novels, Lauren Willig received a graduate degree in English history from Harvard University and a JD from Harvard Law School, though she now writes full-time. Willig lives in New York City.

CONNECT ONLINE

www.laurenwillig.com
facebook.com/laurenwillig

The
Passion of the
Purple Plumeria

A PINK CARNATION NOVEL

LAUREN WILLIG

AN INTERVIEW WITH THE AUTHOR OF
THE CONVENT OF ORSINO
OR HOW NOT TO INTERVIEW MISS GWEN

The Convent of Orsino—by A Lady—took London society by storm. After a full fortnight of suitable maidenly modesty, the author came forward, identifying herself as one Mrs. Reid, née Miss Gwendolyn Meadows. Crowds of eager admirers clamored for her to address their learned and not so learned societies. Emboldened, Mrs. Reid's publishers put together an ambitious tour of speaking engagements.

However, after an unfortunate episode involving Mrs. Reid's jumping on the settee at Madame Oprah's salon (in an attempt, apparently, to stamp out very small French spies), Mrs. Reid's publishers hastily canceled the rest of her appearances.

One artifact, however, survives from that short-lived *Convent of Orsino* publicity tour. It appears to be a handwritten transcript of an interview between Mrs. Reid (here referred to, familiarly, as "Miss Gwen") and an LW. Scholars believe this to be the lady's author, Lauren Willig, making a rare intertextual appearance.

Based on the handwriting, the best guess of Pink Carnation scholars is that the scribe in question was Lady Henrietta Dorrington, who has clearly amused herself by indulging in her own observations as to Mrs. Reid's moods and facial expressions.

Without further ado, the transcript:

LW: Miss Gwen, I'd like to thank you so very much for joining us here today, especially since I know how busy you are with your writing schedule and with, um, you know. . . .

Miss Gwen: Stop hemming and hawing, girl! There's no need to stare at my stomach as though you've never seen a woman increasing before. In France, they go about in society right up to the last month. [An expression suspiciously like a smirk appears on her face.] I fully intend to do the same. I have already ordered a number of large gowns. In purple.

LW: A number of large gowns or a large number of gowns? Never mind, don't answer that. I have some questions for you from your most devoted followers.

Miss Gwen (turning up her nose): Well, tell them to stop following me and get on with something interesting. As the Bard said, neither a follower nor a leader be.

LW: Er, wasn't that "neither a borrower nor a lender be"?

Miss Gwen: You can't trust that Shakespeare man to get anything right. He was a poet, you know.

LW: Right. Okay. Getting back on track. . . . Yes, you've had some dealings with "poets," haven't you? Like Augustus Whittlesby.

Miss Gwen: If you can call that poetry.

LW: Of all the men you've worked with during your various exploits, who has most pleasantly surprised you?

Miss Gwen: Not Whittlesby, that's for certain! The man was barely competent—and I don't just mean his verse. Hmph. And the War Office calls that an agent. No wonder they're so reliant on us. [After a moment of looking smug, she stops and considers.] My William was undeniably surprising, and quite pleasantly so. But your readers most certainly do not need to hear about that!

LW: Mmm-hmm, right. Moving onto safer topics . . . I've noticed that you seem to have a penchant for purple. Why that particular color?

Miss Gwen: You do ask the most foolish questions, girl! Haven't you ever heard the phrase "imperial purple"? Why would I settle for a color of lesser rank?

LW (mutters): "Imperial" and "imperious" aren't exactly the same thing.

Miss Gwen (looking forbidding): What was that?

LW: Nothing! Nothing. Er . . . Should Napoleon look to his throne?

Miss Gwen (graciously): Would I like to dethrone the nasty little man? Naturally. Do I wish to take his place? Most certainly not. I would as soon rule the French as I would take a position in a young ladies' academy.

LW (consulting her notes): Did you always want to be a spy?

Miss Gwen (looking down her nose): It is hardly an ambition that a young lady of good family nourishes at her maidenly bosom. However, when the opportunity arose. . . . (A reminiscent expression crosses her face.) I would have resorted to far more drastic measures to rid myself of Shropshire. And those sheep.

LW: Speaking of drastic measures, is it true that you've killed a man with your parasol?

Miss Gwen (sniffing): Shouldn't you ask instead whether I've slain anyone with my wit? I pride myself on my rapier tongue. Any man can wield a length of steel. So few can turn a proper phrase.

LW: Yes, but your sword parasols are rather impressive. Where did you find them?

Miss Gwen (with a rather frightening gleam in her eye): If you think those little trinkets are impressive, you will be blown away by my reticule grenade.

LW: I don't even want to know. . . . In fact, it's probably safer not to know. What was your favorite mission?

A very long story ensues, involving honey, bees, a French courtesan, an Italian portrait painter, and a set of secret files. Sadly, the Official Secrets Act—and a certain modicum of good taste—prevents its dissemination at this time. Who knew that anyone would . . . Well, never mind.

LW: We've covered your professional life—now it's time for the human interest side of the story. Was there anyone in the picture for you between Timothy Fitzgerald and William Reid?

Miss Gwen: Human interest? Most humans are scarcely interesting at all. Besides, a lady never seduces and tells.

LW: I'm going to take that as a no . . . despite those strange rumors about you and Talleyrand. [Miss Gwen glowers, so Lauren moves hastily on.] You're suddenly the mother of five—not counting this new little one. How do you feel about having Penelope Deveraux as a daughter-in-law?

Miss Gwen: Penelope Deveraux? She's no problem at all. It's that Lizzy girl you have to look out for. . . .

LW: Why do you dislike sheep so much?

Miss Gwen (slightly incredulous): Have you ever spent an extended period of time among them?

LW: Fair point. (She consults her list.) Can you recommend a good florist in Paris?

Miss Gwen (looking stern): I truly hope that is a euphemism for the leader of a band of agents, young lady. Otherwise, I despair of you. Now, if you'd asked me about a Gardener . . .

Miss Gwen suddenly breaks off, scenting the air like a bloodhound or some other great sniffing thing.

Miss Gwen: There! There he is, the scoundrel. At my own interview! I'll show him how to garden!

Kicking her trusty parasol out of the way, Miss Gwen grabs up her reticule and sets off in pursuit of a shadowy figure wearing what looks like a very floral waistcoat.

LW (grabbing up the forgotten parasol): Miss Gwen! Miss Gwen! You forgot your—

Before she can reach the door, the room is rocked by a sudden loud explosion from somewhere just down the hallway.

LW (dropping the parasol): —reticule grenade?

Here ends the transcript.

The transcript may end here, but the story of the Pink Carnation continues on in the next installment, temporarily titled Pink XI *(until someone comes up with another flower).*

AN INTERVIEW WITH LAUREN WILLIG OR HOW TO BADGER YOUR AUTHOR

Since I got to interrogate Miss Gwen (did I say interrogate? I meant "interview"), Miss Gwen decided it was only fair if she got to ask me a few questions, too. At parasol point.

Miss Gwen: If you must presume to write my life story, why did it take you so long? You gave Fitzhugh—Fitzhugh!—his own volume a good three books sooner. I do not take well to being superseded by a root vegetable.

Lauren: Superseded? Never! It was more that I needed the time and skill to tackle the delicate task of attempting to untangle the intricate workings of so complex a character as Miss Gwendolyn Meadows.

Although it may sound like I'm just buttering up Miss Gwen here (and, yes, her parasol is pointy), there's more than a modicum of truth in the statement above. The longer a side character has been around in the series, the longer they've had to develop a quirky identity, the harder they are to write. Miss Gwen, in particular, was a tough cookie. I knew that the side she showed to the world—sometimes prim, sometimes brazen, but always delighting in shocking and defying expectations—was part of who she was, but not the sum total of her. Somewhere, underneath there, was the real Gwen, the Gwen without the "Miss," and I needed to figure out how to dig her out.

Originally, the tenth Pink book wasn't going to be Miss Gwen's story. It belonged to Tommy Fluellen (Robert's best friend from *The Temptation of the Night Jasmine*, for my Pink followers) and Kat Reid. Yes, the same Kat Reid you met in this book. But, as I sat down to write the first few chapters, I realized fairly quickly that their book just didn't fit into the right spot in the series. The next book to follow logically was Miss Gwen's.

I fought that realization. Trust me, I fought it. (See "scared to write about Miss Gwen," above.) But there was no backing away from it. Once I acknowledged that Tommy and Kat's book needed to cede place to Miss Gwen's, I set about finding new and creative ways of postponing the inevitable: in this case, writing a whole different, entirely unrelated stand-alone novel set around World War I England and 1920s Kenya. (I confess, I wrote *The Ashford Affair* to avoid Miss Gwen. These things happen.)

Once *The Ashford Affair* was safely handed in to my editor, I had to face the fact that I'd run out of creative ways to procrastinate. I girded my loins—to ward off stray parasol shots—ordered a grande skim caramel macchiato, and set about trying to uncover the mystery that is Miss Gwen. Whether I've succeeded or not, I leave to you—and Miss Gwen—to decide.

Miss Gwen: Naturally, my book—and by my book, I mean the book I wrote, not that *Purple Plumeria* nonsense about me—was a raging success. But why did you have to make me write about vampires?

Lauren: Living in the nineteenth century, as you do, you don't know this, but in the early part of the twenty-first century, the literary scene is going to be eclipsed (sorry, no pun intended) by a scourge of teen novels about vampires. When the *Twilight* craze was sweeping the nation, it made me think about the early Gothic novels of the eighteenth and nineteenth centuries, those same books that Jane Austen mocked in her wonderful social satire, *Northanger Abbey*.

I'd already mentioned way back in Pink I that Miss Gwen was working on a horrid novel on the side, partly because, in classic Miss Gwen fashion, she was convinced that she could pen something far, far better than the tripe currently circulating. Miranda Press? Paugh! If Miss Gwen was going to write popular fiction, why not get ahead—way ahead!—of the bandwagon? Vampire fiction isn't just a twenty-first-century discovery. Byron's *Giaour* caught the public's imagination as early as 1813. I couldn't imagine Miss Gwen allowing Byron to beat her to a trend.

I had some other ulterior motives as well. It seemed important to me, for Miss Gwen, that she become a smashing success in her own right. So much of Miss Gwen's adult life has been shaped by her having been disinherited. With her novels minting money, Miss Gwen is finally financially secure—and it seemed quite appropriate that in her relationship with her new husband, Colonel Reid, she would be the one with power of the purse. I don't see Colonel Reid being the least bit perturbed by that.

I must admit, I also just loved the idea of Miss Gwen mobbed by squealing teenage girls. . . . I do not imagine she will respond well to that.

Miss Gwen: Do not presume simply because I am now, as they say "settled," that you can shuffle me off out of sight!

Lauren: Is it just me, or do Miss Gwen's "questions" sound more like pronouncements?

I can safely say that when it comes to you, Miss Gwen, I would never presume anything. I can't imagine that being married will curtail Miss Gwen's extracurricular espionage. She may not be in cahoots with the Pink Carnation anymore, now that the Carnation has gone rogue (more on that later), but Miss Gwen has badgered and bullied most of the major officials of the War Office and every subagent from Dover to Calais. She knows where the skeletons are buried and she isn't afraid to exhume and shake them around. If anything, I imagine that Colonel Reid will be a rather able partner for her in her adventures. She just has to worry about her new stepdaughter, Lizzy's, desire to "help".... And, of course, her book deadlines.

For updates on the progress of Pink XI, *outtakes, bibliographies, and other extras, visit Lauren at her Web site at www. laurenwillig.com.*

QUESTIONS
FOR DISCUSSION

1. What was your initial opinion of Gwen when she was introduced at the beginning of the novel? Did your feelings about her change as the novel progressed? Did you have any revelations about her that surprised you?

2. What did you think of the relationship between Colonel Reid and Gwen? What about each of them made them perfectly suited for each another?

3. What did you think about Gwen's novel, *The Convent of Orsino*? Is this a book you would be interested in reading? Do you think it would have been well received by readers at that time?

4. What are some of the parallels that can be drawn between the historical and modern-day story lines in *The Passion of*

the Purple Plumeria? Do the modern and historical characters play off one another? What are the similarities between
the couples? What are the differences?

5. Why do you think Eloise and Colin have put off revealing
their true feelings for one another for so long? What do you
think is in store for them? Do you think their relationship
will survive?

6. Before he makes off with the fake jewels of Berar, the
Chevalier tells Jane: "I am sure I do not need to tell you how
very much I wish the circumstances might have been otherwise." Do you think they could have had something romantic together if they did not play for opposite teams?

7. Towards the end of the novel, Jane makes the following
proclamation: "Wherever I go next, I go alone." Do you
think her decision to dissolve the League of the Pink Carnation and work alone is a wise one? Why or why not?

8. What is the significance of the Moon of Berar being a
mirror instead of jewels?

9. Did you think Gwen's more audacious methods made her
an effective spy? Why or why not?

10. Do you think Jeremy is as villainous as he appears to be? Do you think the relationship between Colin and Jeremy will be repaired for the sake of their great-aunt?

11. Did you find Gwen's revelation about her ex-lover and scandalous pregnancy to be surprising? How do you think that experience colored her relationship decisions from that point forward? Do you think she would have lost as much if she had been a man?

12. How is the theme of passion addressed in *The Passion of the Purple Plumeria*?

London, 1806

"They say he's a vampire."

It took a moment for her friend's words to register through the blood pounding in Sally Fitzhugh's ears. She banged through the French doors of the balcony, her precarious grip on her temper only maintained by the immediate necessity of getting away, her flat slippers slapping against the polished parquet of the ballroom floor, the satin of her skirt swishing against her legs like agitated whispers.

The crisp October air hit Sally like a tonic, and, with it, Agnes's words finally reached her brain.

She turned, saying shortly, "What?"

Agnes ducked around the rapidly swinging door. "A bloodsucking creature of the night," she said helpfully as she followed Sally out towards the balustrade, away from the crush in Lord Vaughn's ballroom.

"I know what a vampire is. Everyone knows what they are."

Ever since *The Convent of Orsino* (by a Lady) had taken the town by storm the previous spring, the ladies of the ton had become intimate experts on the topic. The men, just as sickeningly, had taken to powdering their faces pale and affecting red lip rouge. Sally found it distinctly stomach-turning.

But, then, she found it all distinctly stomach-turning: the too strong perfumes, the smug smiles, the whispering voices behind fans, the incredible arrogance of those powdered fops and perspiring ladies. It would serve them right if there were vampires in their midst. Not that such things existed, of course. Any bloodsucking that went on in the ton was purely of the metaphorical variety, although nonetheless draining for that.

Sally gripped the cool stone of the balustrade with both hands, breathing in deeply through her nose. It seemed absurd to remember that two years ago she had been itching to leave the cloistered confines of Miss Climpson's Select Seminary to try her wings in the world, to flirt and laugh and bend beaux to her will. She was the oldest of her friends; her family was, she had believed, socially well-connected. She had gone first, sallying off to London in the firm anticipation of champagne-filled evenings of compliments, in which she would hold court among her devoted and witty admirers.

That, she realized, had been her first mistake. Wit was in short supply among the ton. They made up for its lack with waspishness instead.

At Miss Climpson's, she had been the center of a close-knit circle, the leader of their occasionally ever so slightly illicit activities. At home, she was the petted and privileged younger child, the only daughter, with a brother who doted on her, a sister-in-law she liked tremendously, the most adorable little niece in the world, and parents who might be dim but were really rather sweet for all that. Sally had, she realized, made the mistake of taking her brother at his word when he spoke of all those excellent chaps, those good-hearted, honorable, clever souls. Reggie, as he himself was swift to admit, might not be the swiftest in the brainbox, but he had a knack for seeing the best in everyone. It was his greatest gift and more glaring flaw.

And Sally, knowing this, really ought to have known better. But she hadn't. The pettiness of it all had taken her by surprise.

It wasn't that she minded for herself. So what if Martin Frobisher had called her a gilded beanpole? He was just sore because she made him look like the sniveling little thing he was—and jealous because his family hadn't two guineas to rub together. Proud, they called her. Well, yes, she was proud. She knew her own worth, both in character and in coin. What did it matter that her family had never thrown down a cloak for Elizabeth I or provided a mistress for Charles II? Just because they had never toadied for a title didn't mean that they weren't as good as anyone. They were certainly a sure sight better looking.

But it wasn't the slights about the family lineage—or lack thereof—that made Sally's ears burn and her fingers itch for a rapier. It was the way others treated Reggie, like some inferior sort of particularly bouncy dog, to be kicked or scratched behind the ears as the occasion warranted.

Only she was allowed to treat her brother that way.

It was Lady Vaughn who had made the comment tonight, Lady Vaughn with her watchful eyes and her derisive laugh, turning to her husband with a murmur about fools who had left off their motley.

Reggie wasn't a fool. He was just exceptionally good-hearted. And if that made one a fool in the world ruled by the Vaughns, then Sally wanted no part of it.

Except insomuch as it would enable her to rub their noses in it and make them cry pardon.

Belatedly, Sally pulled her attention back to Agnes. Unlike Sally, Agnes didn't have her rage to keep her warm. Her skin was turning a faint shade of blue that matched the color of her gown.

"A vampire? Hardly." Sally paused to glower in the general direction of the ballroom. "Whatever else I may think of the man, Lord Vaughn looks perfectly corporeal to me. Those waistcoats are just an affectation."

"Not Lord Vaughn," said Agnes patiently. "The Duke of Belliston. In the house across the garden." She gestured in the other direction, away from the crowded ballroom, past long rows of perfectly trimmed parterres.

Even in the waning season of the year, Lord Vaughn's shrubbery didn't have a leaf out of place. The garden was arranged in the French style, all gravel paths and geometric designs, scorning the more natural wilderness gardens coming into vogue. Above the close-clipped hedges and the marble statues glimmering white in the moonlight, Sally could just make out the outline of the great house across the way.

Unlike Lord Vaughn's, that garden had been allowed to run to seed, either by accident or design. Weeping willows trailed ghostly fingers over the dim outline of a pond on which no swans swam, while ivy climbed the walls of the house, dangling from the balconies, obscuring the windows. In the heart of London, the edifice had an eerie air of isolation.

It was the largest house in the square, larger by far than Lord Vaughn's. Sally felt a certain satisfaction at that thought. Lord Vaughn could put on all the airs he liked, but he still wasn't the biggest fish in the square. And by fish, she meant duke. The Duke of Belliston outhoused and outranked Vaughn.

He was also remarkably elusive. In her two Seasons in society, Sally had never met the man. There was some sort of story about him . . . something to do with a curse and his parents.

But vampires? Nonsense.

"Where do you hear such things?" said Sally, both cross and a little jealous. At Miss Climpson's, she had been the center of every web of gossip. Here . . . She didn't like feeling on the fringes of things.

"The ladies' retiring room," said Agnes. "They were all whispering about it."

Of course they were. Sally rolled her eyes at the idiocy of mankind. "Vampires are a myth. And not a particularly interesting one," she added repressively.

"People said the same thing about the Duke of Belliston," pointed out Agnes, "about his being a myth, I mean. But you can't deny there are lights in the windows."

That much was true. Through the ivy and the dust, a faint but distinct light shone. For a moment, Sally and Agnes stood quiet in contemplation, regarding that flickering ray of light. There was no denying that there was someone in residence at Belliston House. Whoever—or whatever—that someone might be.

Sally regarded her closest friend askance. "Next you'll be telling me you saw a bat flying around his belfry."

Agnes cocked her head, considering the urns that lined the roof of the house. "I think it's a crow." Her voice dropped to a hushed whisper. "The collective term for a group of crows is—"

"Oh, no," said Sally.

"—a *murder*," finished Agnes earnestly.

As an academic appellation, it was just a little too atmospheric, especially with the moon silhouetted against the chimney pots, casting strange shadows through the abandoned garden. Sally felt a chill shiver its way down her spine, beneath the thin fabric of her gown and chemise.

Not, of course, that it had anything at all to do with the black bird flapping about the chimney pots. Chills were simply what one got when one stood on a balcony in a scoop-necked ball gown in the middle of October.

Somewhere in the depths of the garden, an owl voiced its mournful cry. Sally yanked her shawl more closely about her shoulders and turned her annoyance on Agnes.

"That"—Sally cast about for a suitably dampening adjective— "is absurd."

"No, truly," said Agnes. "It's a murder of crows and an unkindness of ravens."

That last, at least, was appropriate. Sally cast a glance back over her shoulder at the ballroom. "I'd say it's more an affectation of imbeciles."

She knew she shouldn't let them bother her, but she hated to see them treat Reggie so. It wasn't Reggie who was meant to have squired them tonight at all; technically, they were meant to be under the chaperonage of their friend Lizzy's stepmother, the former Miss Gwen, chaperone extraordinaire. But ever since it had come out that Miss Gwen was the author of *The Covent of Orsino*, she couldn't go anywhere without being mobbed by admirers.

Miss Gwen did not admire her admirers.

Sally wondered if Miss Gwen would consider the loan of her infamous sword parasol. Just for use on a few select cads. She would make sure to clean it thoroughly before she returned it.

Agnes leaned her elbows against the balustrade, her fine light brown hair already losing its curl. "They say he sucks the blood of unwary maidens." Agnes paused and thought about it for a moment. "I imagine they're less trouble than wary ones."

"Utter rubbish," said Sally crisply. Before Agnes could argue with her, she added quickly, "Just because the man scorns society doesn't mean that he's an unholy creature of the night."

In fact, at the moment, she would say it was rather a sign of his good sense.

"No one has seen him for seven years," said Agnes. Her face took on the distant look it acquired when she was parsing out a difficult academic question. "Seven is a mystical number. . . ."

"So is three," said Sally. "Or five hundred and thirty-two." She had no idea about five hundred and thirty-two, but something had to be said. Sally pushed away from the balcony, her net shawl catching on the carved edge of an acanthus leaf. She could feel recklessness pulsing through her, fueled by anger and boredom. "Whatever the Duke of Belliston is, he's just a man. And I'll prove it to you."

Agnes looked at her in alarm. "You don't mean—"

Sally nodded decisively. "To go over there."

She could feel her spine straightening, even as she spoke. It felt good to be taking the lead again, even if that lead was towards a deserted garden on the property of a duke rumored to be more monster than man. Which was nonsense, of course.

"Don't worry," Sally said to Agnes, as she had said a hundred times before, on midnight expeditions at Miss Climpson's Select Seminary. "I shan't do anything foolish. Anything else foolish," she amended. "I'll just peer through the window and report back. That's all."

Before Agnes could protest, Sally pushed her cameo bracelets up on her wrists, gave her shawl a tug, and ran lightly down the path.

Gravel crunched beneath her slippers. The cool October breeze lifted the corners of her shawl and set her golden curls dancing. Dimly, Sally was aware of Agnes behind her, a pale presence leaning over the balustrade, prepared, no doubt, to leap into the fray and fight bloodsucking creatures of the night on Sally's behalf, should the occasion call for it. Sally's heart swelled with affection. She really was terribly fond of Agnes.

The formal parterres had been cleverly arranged to provide the sense of an endless vista, but, as was always the case with the Vaughns, the sense of spaciousness was an illusion; it was a London garden, and Sally was at the end of it in moments.

There was no wall separating Lord Vaughn's property from that of the Duke of Belliston, only a series of Cyprus trees. Their spindly shapes lent a funereal aspect to the scene, but they had one major benefit: there was plenty of space between them for one slender woman.

At the Cyprus border, Sally checked slightly. For all her bravado, there was something more than a little dodgy about willfully trespassing on someone else's property. It had been quite another thing to slip down to Miss Climpson's sitting room in the dead of night; the students did that so often, it was practically an official extracurricular exercise.

On the other hand, despite herself, she was just a little, tiny bit curious. And it really couldn't do any harm just to creep up to the house and back. Admittedly, a white gown wasn't the best attire for creeping, but, if spotted, she could always raise her hands above her head and pretend to be a statue.

Which was, Sally realized, a plan worthy of her brother, Turnip.

With a shrug, she plunged through the Cyprus border. And came up short as a candle flame flared in front of her face.

For a moment, she had only a confused image of a dark form silhouetted against the fronds of a weeping willow. Childhood memories of ghost stories surged through her mind, the horrible tales Nanny used to tell her of faceless ghouls and headless horsemen and phantom monks in their transparent habits.

"Who is it?" she demanded, her voice high with—not fear. Just lack of breath. "Show yourself."

A man swept aside the fronds of a weeping willow tree. Sally saw behind it a cracked marble bench. The bench sat hard by the empty basin of an ornamental pool, surmounted by a particularly impish-looking satyr overgrown with moss and cracked with time. A folly. And a man. Just a man. She felt her breathing begin to return to normal.

"Show myself?" The man's voice was well-bred and distinctly incredulous. "I should ask the same of you."

His hair had been allowed to grow down over his collar, curling slightly at the edges, the darkness of it contrasting with the pallor of his skin. He was even fairer than she was, which Sally took as a personal affront. She was accustomed to being the fairest of them all.

"What are you doing in my garden?" he asked sharply, holding the candle high.

The sudden shock of light made Sally wince. Also, he was holding it on her bad side.

"What are *you* doing—" Sally was stuck. She couldn't very well ask him what he was doing in his own garden. She made a quick recovery. She drew herself up to her full height, letting the moonlight play off the rich gold of the cameo parure that adorned her neck, ears, and brow. "What are you doing, addressing me when we haven't been introduced?"

The Duke of Belliston—or, at least, Sally assumed it must be the Duke of Belliston—lowered his candle. "I would say," he said drily, "that trespass was a good substitute for a formal introduction."

He stepped forward, the moonlight silvering his hair, making him look simultaneously younger and older. Sally had thought, initially, that he was about her own age. Now she wasn't so sure. The moonlight played tricks with her, casting shadows that might have been lines, creating strange contrasts between the pallor of his skin and the dark stuff of his coat.

"I am not trespassing," Sally said haughtily. "I was simply admiring your foliage."

The Duke of Belliston raised one thin brow. "Has anyone warned you that strange plants might have thorns?"

If she had wanted a lesson in horticulture, she would have consulted a gardener. "Has anyone ever told you that it is exceedingly annoying to speak in aphorisms?"